A smart, funny, and surprising novel that shows what can happen when a woman who wants it all—a perfect marriage, child, and career— finds a nanny good enough to make her perfect dreams come apart at the seams.

ZORA ANDERSON IS THIRTY YEARS OLD, African-American, college educated, and looking for a job. As fate would have it, Kate and Brad Carter—a White married couple with a new baby— are looking for a nanny. Zora seems perfect. She's an enthusiastic caretaker, a competent housekeeper, and a great cook. And she wants the job despite the fact that her own well-to-do family members would be mortified at the idea of Zora working as a domestic.

Once Zora starts working, the Carter household becomes the picture of domestic bliss, but it turns out everyone is hiding something: Brad is hiding his desire to change careers from his wife; Kate is hiding her professional ambitions from her husband; and Zora is hiding not only her job from her family, but maybe her motivations for staying on the job from herself.

In this tightly wrought drama, the major players believe that as enlightened and progressive people, navigating the tricky waters of sexual tension, race relations, and modern child rearing will be a breeze— that is, until the nanny truly becomes a substitute in ways they never could have imagined.

Praise for Lori L. Tharps's heartwarming memoir,

Kinky Gazpacho

"Tharps blossoms on every page."

—*Entertainment Weekly*

"Moving . . . *Kinky Gazpacho* is at heart a love story, though not the kind you might expect. Tharps's love for her family, for Spain and—most important—for herself makes this an unforgettable and deeply affecting book."

—*The Washington Post*

"Tharps has written a thought-provoking, answer-seeking consideration of race in the Western world that one can lie back and enjoy. The thoughts and answers will continue to haunt."

—*Publishers Weekly* (starred review)

"Alternately funny and self-effacing and serious and smart."

—*The Boston Globe*

"An interesting, charming, and funny true story harboring an unexpected look at Spanish history."

—*Booklist*

"A vivid memoir . . . full of lively dialogue, description, and energy that is compelling to read."

—*Bitch*

"A beautiful memoir reminiscent of *Eat, Pray, Love.* Tharps unfailingly bares soul and human frailties that expose her."

—*Affaire de Coeur*

"Laugh-out-loud moments . . . told with witty sarcasm."

—*BookPage*

"Joining the ranks of such fine books as Frances Mayes's *Under the Tuscan Sun* and Sarah Turnbull's *Almost French,* Lori Tharps's *Kinky Gazpacho* takes us on an adventure of love, language, and travel. In her capable hands, it's not a small world after all—but rather a big one, with much to discover and a great deal of fun to be had."

—Veronica Chambers, author of
The Joy of Doing Things Badly and *Kickboxing Geishas*

"*Kinky Gazpacho* is not just a journey but a 'trip,' as they say. We encounter Frederick Douglass's hot descendant, Michael Jackson fans in Morocco, racist candies, and the love of a lifetime in a memoir that's sometimes heartbreaking, often hilarious, and always quirky."

—Asali Solomon, author of *Get Down*

This title is also available as an ebook.

Substitute Me

ALSO BY LORI L. THARPS

Kinky Gazpacho: Life, Love & Spain

Hair Story: Untangling the Roots of Black Hair in America
(with Ayana Byrd)

Substitute Me

A Novel

LORI L. THARPS

ATRIA PAPERBACK

NEW YORK LONDON TORONTO SYDNEY

ATRIA PAPERBACK

A Division of Simon & Schuster, Inc.
1230 Avenue of the Americas
New York, NY 10020

First Atria Paperback edition August 2010

ATRIA PAPERBACK and colophon are trademarks of Simon & Schuster, Inc.

For information about special discounts for bulk purchases,
please contact Simon & Schuster Special Sales at
1-866-506-1949 or business@simonandsch uster.com.

The Simon & Schuster Speakers Bureau can bring authors
to your live event. For more information or to book an event,
contact the Simon & Schuster Speakers Bureau at
1-866-248-3049 or visit our website at www.simonspeakers.com.

Designed by Kyoko Watanabe

Manufactured in the United States of America

10   9   8   7   6   5   4   3   2   1

Library of Congress Cataloging-in-Publication Data

Tharps, Lori L.
  Substitute me : a novel / Lori L. Tharps.
    p. cm.
  1. Nannies—Fiction. 2. Brooklyn (New York, N.Y.)—Fiction.
3. Domestic fiction. I. Title.
PS3620S83   2010
813'.6—dc22   2010023346

ISBN 978-1-4391-7110-3
ISBN 978-1-4391-7111-0 (ebook)

To my mom,
who always encouraged me to tell stories

For the hand that rocks the cradle
Is the hand that rules the world.

—WILLIAM ROSS WALLACE

CHAPTER 1

Zora

Summer 1999

On paper Zora Anderson was a statistic. A cliché, really. Single. Age thirty. African-American. College dropout. Failure. But in real life, Zora Anderson had a lot to offer. "I am a good person," she would often remind herself. It was a mantra she used to lift her spirits when she contemplated all of the things she'd meant to do with her life and thus far hadn't gotten around to. It was what she remembered as she walked down a quiet tree-lined street on a warm, sunny day in Park Slope, Brooklyn, and tried to prepare herself for what she was about to do. "I am a good person. I am a good person. I am a good person." The phrase repeated and replayed like a network news ticker across her brain, giving her the courage to go through with her plan. If her parents knew what she was about to do, they would completely disown her, probably change the locks on the doors and spit on all of her photographs. But they wouldn't know, she reminded herself, because she would never tell them. By the time they stopped being angry, she'd have moved on, and this thing, this job, would be over.

Zora had to believe that.

She knew the only reason she was applying for the position was because of Sondra. She promised Sondra that she'd sublet her apartment for a year while Sondra went off to begin her under-graduate education at Smith College in Northampton, Massachusetts. Sondra had been dreaming about going to Smith ever since she found out that the prestigious women's college had a special program for old ladies—basically, anyone over age eighteen. At twenty-eight, Sondra fit the bill and had applied right away. But moving to Massachusetts didn't mean she was willing to give up her tiny studio apartment in Fort Greene, because it was rent-controlled, and the landlord lived in Florida. In New York, that combination of coincidence was the equivalent of winning the lottery and then finding out you didn't have to pay taxes on your loot.

Zora had promised Sondra back in the spring, when Sondra had gotten her acceptance letter from Smith, that she'd take the apartment. Back then she'd just been killing time at her parents' house in Ann Arbor, waiting for something to happen in her life. Sondra's offer was the perfect something: her own place, a big city, and all of the endless opportunities New York City offered a girl still trying to figure out what to do with her life. Or at the very least find a decent job. Even her parents thought it was a good idea for her to go. The problem was, Zora had been in New York for six weeks now, her cash reserves were disappearing fast, and she still hadn't found a job. She owed Sondra, though, both money and immeasurable thanks. She'd practically saved Zora's life back when they'd first met, so Zora wasn't going to let her down now. She was going to convince Kate Carter to hire her, and then she could hand Sondra her first month's rent just in time for her to chase her Ivy League dreams at the end of August.

Zora pulled the crumpled newspaper ad out of her skirt pocket and looked at it again.

It read: **Substitute Me.** *Looking for a nanny who will take care of my six-month-old baby as if he were her own. Five full days a week. No cooking or cleaning required. Must love children and be prepared to show it. References required.*

In the margins Zora had scribbled the address Kate had given her on the phone. Maybe she should call her Ms. Carter, Zora worried. The woman had seemed so formal, even though she didn't sound that old. But you never knew. The women here in New York seemed to have children later and later. Sometimes Zora couldn't tell if it was the mother or the grandmother pushing the stroller down the street. For all she knew, Kate Carter could be well into her forties, Zora thought as she started down Second Street. She was careful not to walk too fast, so she wouldn't work up a sweat in the sticky summer heat. Even though she didn't know her way around this area, it was easy enough to navigate. The layout was pretty basic: The streets ran north-south and the avenues east-west. Sondra claimed Park Slope had turned into a storybook neighborhood practically overnight, a place where the yuppies from Manhattan migrated when they were ready to start a family. The Carters' house was supposed to be on Second Street between Fifth and Sixth avenues, so Zora quickly calculated she had three more blocks to walk while simultaneously trying to retard the perspiration process. That meant she had three more blocks to get her head straight for the interview.

Zora barely registered her surroundings—the imposing brownstone town houses with their perfect miniature gardens, cozy stone churches on almost every other corner, and tiny bodegas nestled between some of the houses—as she repeated her mantra, "I am a good person. I am a good person." She didn't know why she was so nervous. Probably because this Carter woman had sounded so intimidating. She had already grilled Zora over the phone, shooting off questions so quickly, Zora hardly had time to catch her breath between answers. By the time the interrogation was over, her heart was beating furiously and her hands were cold and clammy. She hadn't felt that much performance anxiety since final-exam week in college. Thank God for Paris, she thought. When she mentioned to Kate that she'd been an au pair in France, she could hear relief and what sounded like approval in the woman's voice. Kate had asked for the phone numbers of the families she'd worked for in France, and for a moment Zora had panicked. She couldn't remember the numbers, and she didn't want this woman to think she'd been lying about her experience working abroad. Even though Zora had spent four years in Paris, more and more of her memories were disappearing, along with her perfect French accent.

"Don't worry about it," Kate Carter had assured her. "You can bring the phone numbers with you to the interview." So Zora spent ten of her last hundred dollars on a phone card so she could call Valerie in Paris and beg her to track down the phone numbers of the Larouxs and the Bertrands, the two families she'd worked for. Of course Valerie yelled at her for not calling more often, but she promised to help. Luckily, she'd called back the night before with the numbers and updates about the children Zora used to care for. "Hey, Zora," Valerie had said before hanging up, "if you're just going to be babysitting again, why don't you come back to Paris to do it? Remember, everything—" Before she could finish, Zora interrupted. "I know. Everything sounds better in French. But I just needed to come home," she said. Valerie snorted in response. Valerie had been in France for eight years and refused to come back to the United States until she was finished writing the definitive novel about the Black experience in Paris. She also needed to convince Ahmed, the Moroccan bartender, to fall madly in love with her before her mission would be complete. Zora didn't think either of those things was going to happen anytime soon, but she wished Valerie good luck all the same before she hung up.

And it was true, Zora thought. Being an au pair in Europe had far more cachet than being a nanny in Brooklyn. Even her parents could get behind the idea of their daughter being an au pair in the cultural capital of the world, but they would both hang their heads in shame if they knew Zora was interviewing for a job that her ancestors had sacrificed their lives not to do. In Paris, it was a different game. She was learning a new language, visiting art museums, and traveling all over Europe. She had responsibilities taking care of two young children, so she'd been forced to learn how to be both efficient and resourceful in all things related to child rearing. She could whip up a dozen crepes in ten minutes flat, and she learned how to drive a stick shift in twenty-four hours so she could take the kids on field trips outside the city. Back then she had still been able to claim the title of "college student" on a journey toward finding herself. Back then she was testing her independence, exploring a new culture, and learning about life. Now, at age thirty, applying for the same job, she was an embarrassment and a disappointment to her family.

The numbers on the left side of the street were odd, so Zora crossed over to the right. She walked slowly down the block, tracking the addresses on the houses. The Carters' address was 246 Second Street. Kate had said the house was in the middle of the block, but it actually sat two houses from the corner of Fifth Avenue. Sondra had explained that Fifth Avenue technically marked the border between Park Slope and no-man's-land and that it could get kind of sketchy at night. Maybe Mrs. Carter didn't want to admit that her house teetered on the edge of respectability, Zora thought. But it didn't really matter, as far as Zora was concerned. People could invent their lives any way they wanted.

Standing in front of the Carters' house, Zora tried to discern what type of people lived inside. Like most of the other houses on the block, their brownstone stood four stories high with a shiny black shingled roof. There was a separate entrance for the garden apartment on the lower level, and a tall flight of brown concrete stairs led to the front door, which, to Zora's delight, was painted red. The front garden was smaller than her parents' front porch back home in Michigan, but it was ablaze with colorful blossoms in tidy rows, a splendid pink rosebush taking center stage.

As Zora pushed open the iron gate, she noticed someone watching her from the garden apartment. As soon as she raised her hand to wave, the curtains abruptly shut and the face disappeared. Zora glanced down to see if there was something wrong with the way she was dressed for the interview. She had chosen a navy blue denim skirt that was neither long nor short, a kelly green polo shirt, and simple gold post earrings. She had deliberately chosen an outfit that would downplay her tiny waist and curvy lower half because everybody knew nannies should be asexual and nonthreatening. A single gold bangle bracelet graced her left wrist. The look she'd been going for was neutral and stable, qualities she thought a nanny should have. She hadn't bothered to remove the tiny gold stud in her nose, despite its very nonneutral connotations, because most people didn't notice it until at least the second or third time they met her. Also because it was such a pain to remove.

Zora climbed the twelve steps to the front door, recited her mantra one more time, and rang the bell. She waited only two seconds before the door sprang open and a tall, attractive White woman in khaki pants and a pale yellow button-down oxford stood before her.

"Hello," she said. "You must be Zora."

CHAPTER 2

Kate

WHEN Kate Carter opened the door, the first thing she noticed was hair. Lots of long black ropy dreadlocks that hung past slim shoulders. She saw a young Black woman who looked to be about twenty-two years old. Her smooth skin was chocolaty brown, and she smelled like sweet island spices Kate didn't recognize. When she smiled, Kate noticed a gap between two brilliantly white front teeth.

"Hi," Zora said. "Your garden is really beautiful."

"Thank you," Kate replied. "I can't take any credit for it, though. Our tenant downstairs, Mrs. Rodriguez, is the one responsible. She's lived in that apartment forever and has always taken care of the plants. When we bought the place, we didn't think there was any good reason to tell her to stop." Kate laughed to cover up the fact that she was talking too much. "Come in, come in," she said, opening her door wider and willing herself to remain professional, to command authority. As she led Zora into the house, she remarked, "Zora—that's an interesting name."

"Yeah, my mother named me after the author."

"Which author?" Kate asked, wrinkling her brow, trying to remember the name of an author with the name Zora. With a degree in English literature, she figured she ought to know.

"Zora Neale Hurston," Zora said. "She wrote *Their Eyes Were Watching God* and a bunch of other books."

"I've never heard of her," Kate replied, her eyebrows knitted together in concentration.

"Yeah, a lot of people say that, so you can imagine living with the name." Zora sighed.

Kate gave a noncommittal nod, making a mental note to look up this Zora Hurston when she got a chance.

After she asked Zora to remove her shoes, Kate ushered her into a room that served as both living and dining room, with a couch and a TV artfully arranged to make room for a handsome dining room table. "Have a seat," Kate said, gesturing to the couch.

Zora sat down and crossed her legs in front of her and folded her hands in her lap. Kate noticed Zora's fingernails were painted a pale coral.

"So. You're the first person I'm interviewing," Kate announced as she picked up a clipboard from the coffee table. She realized after she'd said it that she probably shouldn't have. She didn't want Zora to know that this in-home interviewing process was new to her. She glanced at her checklist of questions and the list of bullet points she had drafted the night before. She reminded herself that interviewing a nanny shouldn't be any more problematic than interviewing a new account executive, which she'd done plenty of times. She knew it shouldn't be hard, but finding someone to trust enough to leave your child in her care, in your own home? That was huge. It required an enormous amount of faith in the goodness of mankind. But other women did it every single day, so she knew she could, too. She really had no choice, because she certainly was not going to put Oliver in some germ-infested day-care facility when he was so young. A loving nanny was the best option for her son, and even if it was awkward and painful to find a substitute mommy, Kate knew she would figure out how to manage the situation.

After reviewing her talking points, Kate launched into her speech. "As I said on the phone, I'm going to be heading back to work next month, and I'm looking for someone to watch my son, Oliver, Monday through Friday. I leave the house at eight-fifteen, and my husband, Brad, usually gets home by six. Oliver is almost seven months old, and he's a very good baby." She smiled when she said that last part. But it was true. Oliver was so far proving to be an easy child. He rarely cried, and he could sit for long periods of time in his bouncy seat as long as Kate was nearby.

"Tell me a little bit about yourself," Kate said. "Where are you from originally? I can't quite place your accent."

"Michigan," Zora answered bluntly.

"Oh," Kate said, blushing and feeling really White. She'd assumed Zora was from an island somewhere. Since she and Brad had moved to Brooklyn, all she'd seen and heard on the playgrounds and in the mommy groups were Black nannies with their singsongy Caribbean accents. It was just the way it was. And this Zora did look kind of exotic, with her dark skin and gold bangle bracelet. And that earring in her nose. Not to mention her Bob Marley hairstyle. But Kate couldn't say those things out loud. So she swallowed her embarrassment and moved on to the next question. "So, did you bring your references, as I asked?" Kate said, sounding to herself a little bit too much like her own mother.

"Yes," Zora replied, reaching into an oversize cloth purse to retrieve a carefully folded piece of notebook paper. "I wrote down the names and phone numbers of the families I worked for in France and the number of the Head Start center in Harlem where I volunteered."

"Thank you," Kate said, reaching for the paper. "But I thought you said on the phone you'd just moved to New York."

"I did. Just about six weeks ago," Zora explained. "But I lived here three years ago for about ten months as a City Year volunteer working for Head Start. I was such a tourist, though, and never ventured much past midtown."

"Oh. What did you do for Head Start?" Kate asked.

"Basically, I was like the assistant teacher at a preschool for low-income children. I played games with the kids and read them stories. We planned field trips around the neighborhood. Stuff like that. Oh, and I got really good at making lunch out of government leftovers." Zora laughed nervously at her own joke.

Kate didn't. "So what did you do after Head Start?" she asked pointedly.

"Actually, I have a résumé, if you'd like to see it," Zora offered.

It hadn't occurred to Kate to ask for a résumé. She'd read dozens of articles on the Internet and even spent an afternoon interviewing all of her playground mommy friends about the best way to find and hire a good nanny. Not one person mentioned asking these women for a résumé. Instead, the best idea she'd heard was to create a very thorough questionnaire. "Don't just have a friendly conversation," everyone had warned. "You have to ask serious questions to see if they're just in it for the money or if they take child care seriously." Most important, at least two women had recommended background checks. It was easy enough to do these days, and a person could never be too careful.

Kate accepted Zora's résumé and took a moment to look it over. She quickly scanned to the bottom, where she saw that Zora had only a high school diploma but three years of college at the University of Michigan. She had also earned a certificate from some culinary school in Detroit that Kate had never heard of. Before she could stop herself, she blurted out, "Wait, how old are you?"

"I'm thirty," Zora answered.

"Oh my God, you look so young." Kate laughed. "We're almost the same age, but I thought you were twenty-five at most."

"I get that a lot," Zora said, nodding. "I suppose I'll be really happy when I'm eighty and people tell me I look fifty, right?"

"To be so lucky," Kate murmured.

Zora smiled.

"If you don't mind me asking," Kate said gently, "how come you didn't finish college? According to your résumé, you only had one more year to go."

"Yes, well, I left after my junior year to go to France on an exchange program. But then I got the au pair job, which turned into a four-year gig. And by then I felt it was too late to go back to school."

Kate frowned at this explanation because she couldn't imagine dropping out of school with only a year to go. She said so to Zora.

Zora tried to explain her rationale. "You see, at U of M I was double-majoring in anthropology and French," she began. "The whole time I was abroad, all I was doing was learning French and studying people. I kind of felt like I finished my major in the school of life."

Kate listened to Zora's answer and realized that had she been hiring Zora for a real job, she would have been very skeptical. No college degree and jumping all over the map. Literally from Michigan to France, back to Michigan, and then to New York. But the rules were different now. Zora had been an au pair before, and she had worked with young children at Head Start. And the culinary school thing made Kate wonder if maybe Zora would be the type of nanny to bake chocolate chip cookies or frosted cupcakes while the baby slept. But that was so not the point. Kate scolded herself for getting off track.

"So are you fluent in French?" Kate wanted to know.

"Pretty much," Zora answered.

"Oh, that's fantastic," Kate said, imagining how great it would be if Oliver could become bilingual. That would definitely be a bonus. Kate turned back to her list of questions and, with her pencil, checked items off as she asked Zora about her interest in children, activities she'd do with Oliver, why she wanted to be a nanny. When she came to the bottom of her list, she hesitated and then plowed on. "Umm, I have to ask you if you wouldn't mind going to the local police station and get fingerprinted for a background check."

Zora shook her head. "I don't mind."

"Whew, that's good." Kate laughed self-consciously. To change the subject, she added, "So you know, if we do end up choosing you, we won't expect you to clean or cook or anything. I would just want you to take really good care of Oliver. He would be your one and only priority."

"Okay," Zora said agreeably. "That sounds fine."

"Great," Kate said, standing up and signaling that the interview was over. Then she quickly sat back down. "Whoops. Sorry. Do you have any questions for me?"

"Just one," Zora said. "Can I see the baby?"

Kate smiled. This was a good sign. "Of course," she said. "He's sleeping right now, but come, I'll show you." She led Zora up the gleaming hardwood staircase to a bedroom on the second floor. The walls were painted a cool mint green. OLIVER was spelled out in white wooden block letters that hung over a sturdy maple crib. Zora peeked over the railing and inhaled Oliver's baby smell and caressed his leg, which had escaped from under the blanket. A warm smile spread across her face as she mouthed the words, "He's adorable." Kate nodded and made a mental note about Zora's obvious love of children that she would record on her list when she left.

For a first interview, things had gone quite well, Kate decided.

CHAPTER 3

Zora

ZORA and Sondra were supposed to be celebrating. Zora had gotten the job with the Carters, and Sondra had gotten the scholarship she'd applied for. Her hundred-thousand-dollar Smith education would be completely paid for, thanks to the generosity of some very wealthy southern widows who believed it was their duty to help educate the Negro masses.

"To the Negrotarians," Sondra said, raising her glass of tap water to meet Zora's.

"I can't believe I got the job," Zora repeated to her friend for the millionth time as she sipped from her glass.

"Why not?" Sondra asked, her light brown eyes narrowed in concern. "You're more than qualified to be a nanny."

"Yeah, but the interview was so formal," Zora said. "Did I mention the woman had a clipboard and a questionnaire about two miles long?"

"Yes, you did," Sondra said. "But that doesn't matter. What matters is that you got the job and I got my tuition money, so we are two women to be reckoned with, okay? Ain't no stopping us now."

Sondra held her glass up again. She was so excited about going to college and studying psychology so she could, in her own words, "fix all the fucked-up people running around the world." Her caramel-colored skin practically glowed with enthusiasm, and her eyes sparkled every time she mentioned Smith and leaving her old life behind.

Zora raised her glass to Sondra's and said, "Cheers." She wanted to be happy for her friend, but she didn't feel like she had cause to celebrate. Even though she'd gotten the job, she'd still had to call her brother, Craig, for her first month's rent because Kate Carter wasn't going back to work until the first of September. That meant Zora wouldn't get paid until September 15, and Sondra needed the rent money before she left for college in two days.

Zora had to explain all of this to Craig, which meant she had to admit she was working as a nanny, which meant she had to listen to her "perfect" older brother yell at her for an hour for wasting her life. She knew Craig would give her the money eventually, though, because Zora knew all about her brother's secret life in the city, and she wasn't above threatening to out him to their parents to get what she needed.

Sondra interrupted her thoughts. "Did you hear me?"

"No, I'm sorry, what did you say?" Zora asked, trying to appear cheerful for her friend.

"I said we'd better hurry up and order or that man is going to spit in our food," Sondra said, pointing to a surly-looking waiter who was glaring at them from the other side of the tiny, dark restaurant.

"You are so gross," Zora said, laughing as she picked up her menu.

Even though they were celebrating, both Zora and Sondra were living on limited funds, so hitting Little India on Sixth Street in Manhattan seemed like a good choice. For about $7.50 each, they could pig out on a four-course meal. And as long as they ignored the occasional critter scurrying across the floor, everything seemed quite pleasant at Delhi Delight. The sparkle of multicolored Christmas lights and random shiny baubles hanging from the ceilings and draped across every inch of available space in the restaurant helped set the mood. Zora ordered chicken vindaloo, Sondra the curried lamb.

"So when exactly do you start work?" Sondra asked while nibbling on a complimentary chickpea wafer.

"Next week. Monday," Zora answered. "Mrs. Carter . . . Kate . . . Oh, I don't know what to call her, maybe madam. Anyway, she goes back to work on September first, and she wants me there a week ahead of time to show me around and stuff."

"You're going to love Park Slope," Sondra said as she poured more of the sweet chutney dipping sauce on her plate. "There are tons of shops and restaurants, Prospect Park is right there, and a new bookstore just opened, which is always packed with lazy mothers who let their kids run wild, but it's still a great escape when the weather's bad. You'll have fun," Sondra declared, as if she had the power to make it so. "By the way, try this sauce. It is so good."

"I hope you're right." Zora sighed, dunking her wafer in Sondra's sauce.

"What's the matter, Z?" Sondra asked, turning her attention away from the food.

"Nothing," Zora answered, forcing a halfhearted smile.

"Yeah, my Aunt Fanny, nothing." Sondra replied, crossing her arms over her chest.

Zora pleaded her case. "It's just that my brother made me feel so stupid and pathetic for taking a nanny job in the first place. He made it sound like I was taking the race backward three hundred years for working as a domestic for White people."

Sondra rolled her eyes. "Didn't you tell him it was only temporary?"

"Yeah, but he was like, 'Everything you do is only temporary, Z.'"

"Well, bump him," Sondra shot back with a dismissive wave of her hand. "He's not living your life. You are. And you did what you did to survive. It's a job. You're getting paid a decent salary. And you'll be able to support yourself. Why's he got a problem with that? It's not like you're going to be a nanny forever."

"I know," Zora moaned. "But he doesn't get that. He's just like my parents and expects me to go back to college, get my degree, and start my real life already. Like the last ten years have just been one big dress rehearsal."

The waiter brought the food over, and Zora and Sondra took a break from the conversation to eat.

The chicken was too hot and the lamb was kind of greasy, but they scarfed it down anyway. Zora had to refill her water glass three times before she was halfway through her plate of curry. She liked spicy food, but this was serious. Sondra laughed at the tears streaming down Zora's face as she ate.

"We should go get ice cream after this," Sondra suggested when they were almost finished with their meal.

"Definitely," Zora said, imagining the cooling effect a scoop of passion-fruit sorbet would have on her burning tongue.

When they were done, the two friends each threw down a ten-dollar bill and sauntered out into the streets of the East Village. The weather was cooperating with balmy late-summer temperatures: It was still warm but with no humidity. Zora and Sondra wore colorful sundresses and rubber flip-flops in honor of Mother Nature's kindness. Earlier in the day they'd given each other pedicures, so they had matching hot-pink toenails, too. Stomachs full and wallets empty, they decided to walk down toward Little Italy to find some free entertainment and cheap gelato.

As they walked through the crowded streets, Zora took in the wild scene around her. "I never knew all of this existed," she said, marveling at the eclectic range of funky storefronts, restaurants, and boutiques. Cute little shops that sold vintage handbags were sandwiched between sex-toy emporiums and Italian coffee shops. Not to mention all the colorful young kids with their full-body tattoos, nipple rings, and slick leather ensembles posturing on the corners for maximum effect.

"When I lived up in Harlem, I never realized how much more

the city had to offer," Zora exclaimed, drinking in everything around her. "I seriously thought that below Times Square, there was nothing to see."

"You *were* pretty green." Sondra laughed, obviously remembering how she'd first met Zora, lost underground, trying to figure out how to get from the East Side to the West Side of Manhattan on the subway. "And now look at ya. Living in Brooklyn, got your own apartment—"

"And about to start working as a nanny," Zora interrupted sullenly.

"Look, if it bothers you so much, don't take the job," Sondra said, pulling away from Zora in a huff.

"It's not that it bothers me, I'm just worried about what people will think."

"What people?" Sondra demanded, her voice getting shrill. "Your uptight parents and your sidity big brother? Get over it. This is your life."

"I know," Zora said without a lot of conviction. "But my brother just made me feel like I was wasting my life."

"Oh, so was I wasting my life when I spent the last ten years working in a hotel, cleaning up after other people? No, I wasn't. What I was doing was working hard so I could go to college," Sondra said, punctuating each statement with a finger in the air and a minor tilt of the neck. The movement caused her long braids to swish behind her. "Am I twenty-eight years old? Yes. Is my life over? Hell, no! And yours isn't, either."

"But you *had* to work," Zora blurted out. And then immediately wished she could take it back. The fact that she and Sondra came from two totally different economic worlds was one they chose to ignore in order to maintain their friendship. The rules were: Sondra got to be her savior and guide to life in the city, and Zora played her obedient disciple, despite being two years older. Those were the parameters of their relationship, and they worked just fine. Unless and until Zora's cushy upbringing came into play.

"Well, you gotta work now, too, Miss Thing, seeing as how you have to pay my damn rent for a year!" Sondra huffed.

"Yeah, but I'm not working toward anything. I'm not trying to go back to college," Zora answered, hoping Sondra would drop the hostility. She couldn't handle it when Sondra copped an attitude, which, thankfully, wasn't often.

"So, college isn't for everybody," Sondra said, softening. "What do you *want* to do?"

"I don't know what I want to do. I just want to be happy," Zora claimed.

"What makes you happy?" Sondra prodded.

"I don't know," Zora confessed weakly. The truth was, she loved cooking, she loved traveling, and she liked kids. She liked feeling useful, and she liked being in beautiful spaces. She loved music and dancing and the taste of a foreign language rolling off her tongue. She loved reading literary fiction with multicultural characters and watching spoken-word poetry performances in intimate theaters. All of these things made her happy, but none of them fell under any job description she'd ever seen. For a hot second when she was in college, she considered being a nurse, but the sour smell of sickness and death that clung to the walls of the hospital where she worked as a volunteer for one summer rapidly extinguished that idea.

Sondra stopped walking and turned to face Zora. "Girl, you just need to get a plan. Everybody's gotta have a plan. Every day when I was cleaning up shit, I didn't let it get to me because it was all part of my plan to get to this point."

"I know, I know." Zora sighed. "But somehow I just don't think I'm all that good at planning."

"Bullshit," Sondra said. "You've just never had to do it. Your parents always had your life planned out for you, and when you stopped wanting to do what they said, you ran away. To France. To Harlem. Maybe you can stop running now."

"Maybe it's just not that easy for me," Zora responded, trying hard not to whine. "Just because you knew exactly what you wanted from the day you were born doesn't mean everyone else has that same clarity."

Sondra shook her head. "Nobody said it was supposed to be easy, Suzy Q, but that doesn't mean you don't have to do it."

The two women continued to walk and wrestle with their own thoughts.

Zora broke the silence. "You know, I've lived so far without a plan, and I've been okay. So maybe I can just keep going like this." It wasn't a question, exactly, but she wanted to hear what Sondra would say.

Sondra sucked her teeth before replying. "I'm not hearing that," she declared. "You weren't raised to live like this. You're supposed to be one of those educated Cosby kids who make a difference."

This time Zora stopped walking and forced Sondra to face her. "But what if I'm not?" she cried, feeling a wall of tears pressing against her eyelids. "What if I'm just not cut out to make that difference? What if the genetic code for wild-eyed ambition skipped me? I mean, my thirty-three-year-old brother is a corporate lawyer on the path to making partner before he's forty. My mother is the principal of the most prestigious prep school in Ann Arbor, and my dad is a judge. Of course I'm supposed to be Somebody. But I don't know who that somebody is supposed to be. And news flash: if I haven't figured it out by now, it just might not be in the cards for me." Zora shook her head and swiped at her tears with the back of her hand. She tried to laugh it off. "God, I'm so ridiculously dramatic. Ignore me."

Sondra sucked her teeth again, but this time she wrapped Zora in a tight hug. "Girl, you'll be okay. We all come to things at different times and in different ways. Probably the best thing you did was getting out from under Mommy and Daddy so you could figure this out for yourself. But you do have to figure it out. Our people fought too damn hard for your lazy ass to do nothing with your life."

Zora pouted. "I'm not lazy."

"I know you're not *lazy*," Sondra clarified. "I saw you chasing after those crazy kids in Harlem, and I got tired just watching you. But that's not the lazy I'm talking about."

"What are you talking about?"

"I mean your life has just been too damn easy. You've never had to work for anything, and now that you have to really figure this shit out, you don't want to make the effort. I have half a mind to stay here in New York just to make sure you don't sign up for some traveling-circus troupe in the Bahamas so you can avoid growing up."

"I wouldn't." Zora laughed in spite of herself. "I hate the Bahamas. The food there is truly awful."

Sondra shook her head. "Girl, you'd find some way to rationalize it if it meant postponing dealing with reality."

"Okay. Okay. I deserved that," Zora admitted.

Sondra sighed. "What you deserve is a life that you can be proud of. If you couldn't do anything else except watch other people's kids, then that would be one thing. But you're smart and talented, and you've been given a whole lot of opportunities that most people would die for. So you kind of owe it to yourself and our people to give something back."

"Thank you, Iyanla Vanzant," Zora quipped, but she knew Sondra was serious. "I just don't know what it is I'm supposed to give back. I don't feel called to anything special. I don't want to be a doctor or a lawyer or a marine biologist."

"Damn, Zora," Sondra cried. "Nobody said it had to be so grand."

"But you just said I couldn't be a nanny for life."

Sondra shook her head. "There's a lot of distance between a nanny and a marine biologist. And if you seriously want to be a nanny, then be one. But be a good one, and stop all this moaning and groaning about it."

"Right," Zora said sarcastically. "And who should my role model be? Mary Poppins or Aunt Jemima?"

"Whatever works for you, girl," Sondra said. "Whatever works for you."

CHAPTER 4

Kate

Kᴀᴛᴇ walked to Prospect Park and tried not to cry. It didn't help that today the sky had decided to be a mesmerizing shade of blue, sprinkled with fluffy cotton-candy clouds. Not to mention the leaves on all the trees were beginning to hint at their upcoming transformation from verdant green to brilliant red and vibrant gold. And the temperature was still hovering in the comfortable mid-seventies. Mother Nature was making this really hard. Kate never remembered Brooklyn being this supremely gorgeous. And now that she was noticing, it was almost all over. This would be the last Wednesday morning she'd take Oliver to the park. The last day to sit and talk with other mommies at the playground about the addictive nature of daytime television and the best way to get baby puke off living room upholstery. The last day to live off the clock and away from real-life responsibilities. Six months with a baby passed really fast.

Next week she'd be back at her desk at Jacobs & Zimbalist Communications, writing press releases, planning press tours, and stroking the egos of international drug dealers. That's how Brad described her job. "Face it, Kate, you're the gal who makes the drug dealers feel legitimate." He was joking when he said that, sort of. But Kate didn't mind his ribbing. She knew that what she did made a difference in the world. She worked for a multinational public relations agency that, yes, counted a major candy company and a rather famous manufacturer of breakfast cereals as their most important clients, but Kate was an account supervisor in the health-care practice. Her sole client was KasperKline, and right now promoting their new birth-control pill was her top priority. Getting the word out about an innovative low-estrogen-formula birth-control pill was meaningful work. Keeping up with the research and finding studies to fund and events to sponsor that would make her client look concerned and responsible required a lot of mental energy. The pill was on the verge of being approved for use in the European Union, too, so Kate knew she'd be racking up a lot of frequent-flier miles in the coming months.

Kate loved to travel. Granted, business trips weren't the most romantic way to experience new places, but she always found time to get away and do her own thing. Of course, that was before Oliver. Now traveling would mean leaving her baby behind. Would Brad be able to handle Oliver by himself if she had to go to Amsterdam for the next world-population conference? How many ounces of milk would she have to pump to keep Oliver satisfied for a whole week? Kate shuddered at the thought of hooking herself up to that loud, bulky machine for hours. But she was willing to sacrifice for Oliver. Since the lactation specialist at the hospital, not to mention all of the La Leche League groupies at the park, claimed that a full year of breast-feeding would guarantee that Ollie would be healthier and smarter than a formula-fed baby, Kate would suffer through the pain and hassle of feeding and pumping through her son's first birthday. But then, without a doubt, she was cutting him off.

"Mommy would do anything and everything for her sweetie-deetie, wouldn't she?" Kate crooned to the baby in his stroller. Oliver still sat in his reverse-fitting baby seat so Kate could watch every expression that crossed his cherubic little face. "Oh, Mommy is going to miss you soooo much," she said, stopping to plant kisses on his cheeks and hands and feet. Gathering herself, she forged ahead.

"But don't you worry. Zora is going to come and take very good care of you," she promised her son. "She is a very nice lady, and she is going to love you and take you for walks and play with you every single day. Yes, she is."

As they approached the park, Kate wondered who might be there. On Wednesdays a lot of her mommy friends took their kids to music class. Oliver was just six months old, so she didn't feel it necessary to pay hundreds of dollars so she could sit him on her lap and listen to a frustrated musician sing "Old MacDonald." She and Brad could do that at home. Brad agreed with her. They laughed sometimes at how competitive these New York mommies were with their baby-gym and baby-music and baby-art classes. Kate knew some parents with kids as young as Oliver who were already touring preschools, trying to score a spot on a waiting list for a placement three years down the line.

"You're perfect just the way you are, Oliver," Kate announced. She was rewarded with a gummy smile from her son.

"Kate, over here." Cindy DiNuptis called her over to the tot lot on the Prospect Park West side of the park. It was the playground favored by the under-three set. There were a couple of baby swings, a miniature jungle gym with a slide, and a sandbox Kate steered clear of because she'd heard the local stray cats used it as a litter box.

Cindy was Kate's favorite playground mommy. She was funny and smart and, like Kate, didn't try to turn mothering into a full-time profession. In fact, she was getting ready to head back to work, too. Cindy was a high school history teacher and had somehow convinced her school to grant her a one-year sabbatical on top of her maternity leave. Her daughter, Molly, was now almost one and a half, and her time off was just about over.

"Hey, Cindy," Kate said as she took in Cindy's kelly green track shorts, shapeless tie-dyed T-shirt, and designer flip-flops. Kate felt almost dressed up in her pleated khaki shorts and pale pink polo shirt. Cindy bypassed Kate and stooped down to get a look at Oliver. "Hi, kiddo," Cindy said, peering into Kate's stroller. "Does your mom find you the cutest clothes or what?"

Kate laughed. "I have to get it out of my system now. Pretty soon he's going to protest when I want to put him in all these colorful outfits. And besides, after twelve months, boys' clothes just get boring and ugly."

"I know," Cindy sympathized. "And the girls' clothes are just too freakin' cute. I justify the amount of money I spend on Molly's wardrobe with the fact that I'm still wearing the same clothes I wore in high school."

"Hey, at least you still fit into your high school clothes," Kate pointed out.

Cindy winced. "Only reason I can," she said, "is because I was this fat in the tenth grade, too. Sad but true."

Kate knew Cindy struggled with her weight, and she had to bite her tongue to stop herself from dispensing weight-loss advice. It would probably come out sounding like criticism, especially since she probably weighed at least twenty pounds less than Cindy, and her muscles were all nicely toned thanks to her regimented workout routine. That's what Brad kept telling her, at least whenever she tried offering him advice. "It's not what you say, it's how you say it," he would tell her, bristling. So Kate kept her diet and exercise tips to herself. She didn't want to accidentally offend her friend. Instead, she turned back to the kids. "I hear little girls start demanding control of their wardrobe pretty early, so you should take advantage, too, while you still can."

Cindy chuckled. "I hear ya."

Kate pulled Oliver out of his stroller, unrolled the waterproof picnic blanket, laid it down on top of the padded but dirty playground surface, and plopped Oliver on top. She laid a bunch of his toys out across the mat and sat down on the bench in front of him.

Cindy sat Molly down next to Oliver. Even though Molly

could walk quite well, for the time being she seemed content to sit and play with Oliver's toys.

"So are you going back to work next week?" Cindy asked Kate.

"Yeah, I go back Wednesday." Kate sighed.

"Why Wednesday?" Cindy asked while grabbing an old cigarette butt out of her daughter's hand before she could thrust it in her mouth.

"I figured it would be easier to go back for three days before jumping into a full week. And it works out well because my new nanny starts Monday, so I can be home with her for a few days and show her around."

"You found someone?" Cindy asked with a mixture of envy and skepticism.

"Yeah," Kate said. "Her name is Zora, and she seems really sweet. She was an au pair in France before this." Kate chose to emphasize Zora's European work history instead of her time spent in Harlem.

"How'd you find her?" Cindy probed. She still hadn't figured out what to do about child care.

Kate was only too happy to detail her process. "I put an ad in the paper and on the community Listserv. I did preliminary interviews on the phone, and she passed that part. Then I had her come to the house. I just got a good feeling about her, because *she* asked to see Oliver, and you could just tell she likes kids. Really likes them. And all of her references checked out. The families she worked with in France—thank God they spoke English—couldn't say enough good things about her. I feel lucky we got her." Kate didn't know if she was saying all this to convince herself or Cindy. The truth was, she'd picked Zora because she felt familiar. She didn't feel as foreign and old as some of the other applicants, who had made Kate feel like a fraud with her clipboard and her questions. One woman even stomped out when Kate brought up the fingerprinting.

"Is she legal?" Cindy asked.

"Yes, Your Honor." Kate laughed. "She's an American. She's from Michigan."

Cindy paused in her questioning to wipe some dirt off Molly's mouth and fish through her gigantic purple and green diaper bag for her daughter's snack. She located the sandwich bag of freeze-dried peas and poured some in front of Molly, who started gobbling them up immediately. Without looking up, Cindy ventured, "Don't you feel kind of scared leaving your child with a perfect stranger?"

Kate was ready with her answer. "You know, I did a complete background check, and the girl has never even gotten a parking ticket. But of course I'm freaking out about leaving Oliver. To be honest, I think I'd be just as scared if I were leaving him with Brad. I don't think anyone will be good enough or care enough, but what choice do I have? I have to go back to work."

Cindy didn't say anything for a minute, so Kate got busy arranging Oliver's snack. She put some rice puffs in front of her son, who reached for them delicately and placed them in his mouth one at a time. Kate felt like an innocent man on trial, waiting for the jury's verdict. Would her friend declare her a bad mom? After all, Kate wasn't in Cindy's situation. They weren't desperate for money. Brad probably earned more than twice as much as Cindy's husband, who was also a public school teacher. Not to mention Kate and Brad did have other sources of income. They could evict Mrs. Rodriguez, get a new tenant in the downstairs apartment, and raise the rent to market rate. And Kate knew she could probably find a way to work from home, but she didn't want to alter her life like that. She shouldn't have to, either.

Cindy interrupted her thoughts. "Well, she sounds perfect." She laughed. "Does she have a sister?"

Kate laughed, too, relieved that she hadn't been forced to justify her choices. She liked Cindy and hoped their friendship would last once life went back to normal. "I don't know if she has a sister, but I can certainly ask."

"Please do," Cindy implored. "I don't know what I'm going to do."

"I can give you the names of some of the other women I interviewed. Quite a few people answered my ad," Kate said. "I interviewed this one older woman from Jamaica whose accent was so strong, I could only understand every other word out of her mouth, and most of those words were 'Jesus' and 'The Holy Bible.'"

Cindy laughed. "Sure, pass me the list, but make sure you delete all the Holy Roller crazy types."

"Right, I'll do that," Kate promised.

The conversation was interrupted by Molly's squall. She required movement. Cindy and Kate scooped the kids up and carried them over to the swings. Oliver was just big enough to fit and loved the back-and-forth motion. Sometimes he fell asleep while Kate gently pushed him.

Once the kids were situated, Cindy turned to Kate. "So, did you hear about Marcos and Amelia?" she whispered dramatically, making sure no one was in earshot.

"Noooo," Kate said, also whispering, although she didn't know why. "What happened?"

"Let's just say Marcos and the new preschool teacher at Smiling Faces Montessori have been engaging in some private tutoring."

"You're kidding," Kate uttered, eyes widening in shock.

"No, I'm not," Cindy declared. "Sherry Solomon, who works part-time at the school, told me herself. Apparently there's going to be some big parent meeting next week to discuss if disciplinary action should be taken against the teacher."

"What kind of disciplinary action?" Kate asked.

"I guess they're going to decide if they should fire her home-wrecking ass," Cindy pronounced.

Kate winced. "Cindy."

"No, I'm sorry," Cindy fumed. "How can you say you're there to teach these young children when you're messing around with one of the parents? What lesson is that? How to ruin your life in thirty seconds or less?"

"God, that is terrible. What's Amelia going to do?" Kate asked. She knew Amelia only from the playground. Amelia had a four-month-old, as well as Xavier, who went to the Montessori school.

"I'm not sure, but I hope she dumps Marcos. He's such a free-loading asshole," Cindy raged on. She had a strong opinion about nearly every parent on the playground.

Kate felt the need to say something to balance the conversation a bit, since the parties in question weren't there to defend themselves. "Marcos has always been really nice to me. He even came over once to help us fix our porch steps. He's a great carpenter."

"Yeah, when he feels like it." Cindy snorted. "He's perfectly happy to live off Amelia's money."

"She has money?" Kate asked, surprised by this revelation.

"Yeah, her grandfather invented the shoehorn or some other random widget, died a multimillionaire, and left each of his grandkids a nice chunk of change. That's how come she lives in that big brownstone. She bought that house herself and picked up Marcos when she was living in Greece."

"I never knew that," Kate admitted. "I just always thought they were such a beautiful, glamorous couple. He seems to adore Amelia. And he's always got the kids."

"Wake up, Kate," Cindy said. "Nothing is what it seems. I could tell you things about almost every mommy out here that would make you pee your pants."

Kate raised both eyebrows. "Really? And why do you know so much?"

"Because I ask a lot of questions—and I eavesdrop." Cindy laughed. "Keeps my life interesting."

Kate laughed with her. "I am so innocent."

"Stick with me, kid," Cindy said, wrapping her arm around Kate. "I'll make sure you always stay one step ahead of the game."

Back home, while Ollie snoozed in his stroller in the hallway, Kate thought back to her conversation with Cindy. Maybe she was making a mistake hiring Zora. Maybe she should have gone with one of the older Caribbean women who had been doing this kind of thing for years. Everybody else seemed to think the Caribbean women were something special. Maybe she should have called one more reference. It was so hard to be sure. Feeling desperate, Kate started to seriously consider working from home. Maybe start up her own boutique PR firm.

She groaned out loud. "This is nuts. I'm going to make myself crazy." Before she could travel any further off the deep end, Kate marched into the kitchen and picked up the phone. She knew exactly who to call.

Her mother answered on the second ring. "Chloe Logan, may I help you?"

"Hi, Mom," Kate said, "it's me. Do you have a minute?" She knew late summer was a slow time at the foundation, but she still didn't want to make the assumption that her mother would drop all her work to talk her eldest daughter through a babysitting crisis.

"Always for you, honey. How are you?"

"I'm good," Kate answered, trying her best to sound upbeat.

"But something's up," her mother declared. "I can hear it in your voice."

Kate loved that her mother knew her so well. It made these things so much easier. "I'm just freaking out about this whole nanny thing," she blurted out.

"I thought you'd hired that Zelda girl from Michigan," her mother said.

"I did," Kate said. "And it's Zora. But now I'm wondering if she's the right person. What if I made a mistake?"

"Why do you think you made a mistake?" her mother asked.

"I don't know," Kate admitted. "I've never done this before, and how do I know she's the right person to take care of Ollie? What if she's secretly mean? What if she's a kleptomaniac?"

Her mother sighed, but with a smile underneath. "Katie, don't be ridiculous. If there's one thing I know about you, it's that you are an excellent judge of character, and you never make decisions lightly. I can't tell you if Zora is the right person, but I can tell you that I trust your decision making, and you should, too."

"She did seem nice," Kate admitted. "And the families I spoke to in France couldn't say enough good things about her."

"So what are you really worried about?" her mother asked.

Kate shrugged. "I guess nothing, really."

"Katie," her mother nudged.

Kate hesitated to put her fears into words, but finally, she just spit it out. "Am I a bad mother for leaving my baby with someone I just met last week?"

"Absolutely not," her mother protested. "Women have been hiring nannies for ages and ages, and their kids turned out just fine. There's nothing wrong with needing help."

"You didn't use a nanny," Kate pointed out.

"Because I didn't have a career when you girls were growing up," her mother said. "But if I did, I would have hired someone to take care of you, seeing as how my mother wasn't exactly nanny material."

Kate laughed as she thought about her grandmother, who still wouldn't let Kate or her sister sit on the "good furniture" in the living room for fear they'd "muss it up."

"Kate," her mother continued, "don't let all of this stay-at-home-mom nonsense get to you. You are a smart woman with a thriving career. And let me tell you something. When you kids were growing up, do you know what we called stay-at-home moms? What we called ourselves?"

"No. What?" Kate asked.

"Trapped-at-home moms," her mother answered.

"Mom," Kate cried in surprise. "Were you that miserable?"

"I wasn't miserable," her mother hedged. "We just didn't have choices. But you do. So take advantage. It is a privilege and a right for you to go back to your career and have your son well taken care of. Can you understand that?"

"I guess so," Kate murmured.

"Look," her mother continued, cutting to the chase. "You have hired a girl with a lot of experience and good references to take care of Ollie. And at the end of the day, if it doesn't work out, you can get rid of her and find someone else."

"Jeez, Mom, you make it sound so impersonal."

"Because it is," her mom said knowingly. "You are hiring someone to do a job. Yes, the job is in your house, but it is a job nonetheless. And if this girl doesn't meet your expectations, then you will find someone else who can."

"Just like that?" Kate queried, fidgeting with the magnets on the refrigerator.

"Yes, just like that," her mother answered. "And remember, you don't need this woman to be your friend. She is your employee. You need her to take good care of your child. Nothing else."

"Actually, Mom," Kate started to explain, "I could see us becoming friends. We're practically the same age, she seems really nice—"

Her mother cut her off. "Trust me, Kate. These women work much better when you keep the boundaries of the relationship clear. And I'm not saying you can't be nice; just keep it professional."

"Fine," Kate said, nodding, even though her mother couldn't see her. "I'll keep it professional."

"Exactly," her mother said, relief softening her voice. "Everything will be okay. You'll see. You just need to get your routine set up, get back to work, get the nanny started, and you'll be wondering what you were worried about in the first place."

Kate sighed. "Thanks, Mom. I needed to hear that."

"I know, darling," her mother purred. "It all seems so complicated right now, but you'll see how it works out. Women have been combining work and family life since we lived in caves. You should just be thankful that you get to pick and choose your career *and* how you raise your child. Your generation is really lucky."

"Lucky" wasn't exactly what Kate was feeling at the moment, but she knew her mom was right. She knew she had privileges and advantages that many women would kill for, so she had no right to complain.

Her mother's voice broke through her thoughts. "Katie, are you still there?"

"Yes, I'm still here."

"I just wanted to remind you that you guys are supposed to be coming home for your father's birthday party next week."

Kate smiled at the thought of spending a weekend with her parents, Brad, and Oliver. For now she was going to forget all about Zora and going back to work and being a grown-up and enjoy her son and her family. She'd have plenty of time to worry tomorrow.

"We'll be there, Mom. We wouldn't miss it for the world."

CHAPTER 5

Zora

On her first day of work, Zora wore khaki cargo capris, a hot-pink T-shirt, and her favorite pale pink high-top sneakers. Her long locks were pulled neatly into a ponytail. She felt comfortable and nannylike. Whatever that meant. Kate had asked her to arrive at nine today, even though once Kate went back to work, Zora would have to be at the house by eight A.M. sharp. "Sharp" had been Kate's word, so Zora had checked the bus schedule the night before, twice, to be sure. Sometimes she missed her black Volkswagen Jetta, sitting back home in Ann Arbor, collecting dust in her parents' garage. Depending on public transportation in New York had definitely taken some getting used to. It had become painfully clear that buses followed their own schedule and not the one posted on the signs for the bus-riding public. Zora stamped her foot in annoyance as she realized the bus was already two minutes late.

As she stood and waited, she prayed that the greasy odor of fried fish from Big Daddy's fish shop on the corner wouldn't permeate her clothes and hair. She absentmindedly played with the $1.50 in change she had in her pocket for the ride, and tried her best to ignore the raggedy homeless woman next to her, walking in circles and shouting at an invisible tormentor named Tyrone. Zora also tried very hard not to think about the fact that she was about to take the bus to go play mammy. She must be getting old, because this stuff had never bothered her before. Both families she'd worked for in Paris were White. Why was she playing the race card now? Zora stumbled through her memories, trying to recall a time when she'd ever been more hyperaware of being Black in a White world, and nothing came to mind. Growing up in Ann Arbor, she'd always been one of a handful of Black kids in the neighborhood and at school, but it was never a big deal. Her parents were considered a power couple in the community, and Zora received all the privileges that came with being their daughter. One of those privileges was never feeling less than or inadequate because of the color of her skin. But it wasn't like she was oblivious to racism. There was no such thing as that much privilege. And now, as a thirty-year-old Black woman about to start working as a domestic for a White family, she found it hard not to think about the history of such a position. A thousand slave women were probably rolling in their graves as they watched her get ready to go back to the big house.

The number 69 bus came lumbering up the street and allowed Zora to put her depressing *Gone With the Wind* thoughts on hold. She paid her fare and found a window seat up front. The distance from Fort Greene to Park Slope was only a couple of miles, but to Zora, it felt like she was traveling to a different world. Fort Greene was considered an up-and-coming neighborhood, whereas Park Slope was heralded as a flower in full bloom, with its French pastry shops, designer gardening stores, and ample selection of yoga studios. The other big difference between the two neighborhoods, Zora noticed, was the racial makeup. Fort Greene was populated mostly by Black people, with a smattering of young hipster Asians and White people sprinkled in the mix, and Park Slope was an inverse mix of mostly White, with enough spots of color to make it feel multicultural in a Coca-Cola-commercial kind of way. Park Slope reminded Zora a bit of Ann Arbor but with less grass and more grit.

Off the bus, going at a steady clip, Zora timed her walk to the Carters' house. The whole way over, she tried to prepare herself for the job she was about to take on. She knew what was expected of her. What people wanted from a nanny. Ideally, it was a Caribbean immigrant. Somebody Black without the racial baggage of an angry American Negro. A woman grateful for the chance, who didn't ask questions and made simple sentences sound poetic. Minus the island accent, Zora knew how to play the part. Play down her college education and her upper-middle-class suburban upbringing. Play up her love for children, her homemaking skills, and her ambition to do nothing in the world except care for somebody else's offspring. Zora wondered why she didn't pursue a career in theater, considering how much role-playing she had to incorporate into her life.

"Note to self," Zora said aloud. "Think about taking acting classes if the nanny thing doesn't work out."

Smiling at the crazy way her mind worked, she found herself at the Carters' front gate. Zora stopped and checked her watch. She was ten minutes early. She debated whether she should go back to Seventh Avenue and grab a cup of tea or just go in. Some people were always running late, and they resented it if you caught them before they were ready. She nibbled on her pinkie fingernail while she weighed the pros and cons of an early arrival. With a quick double-finger cross for good luck, she pushed open the gate, ran up the steps, and rang the bell. She hoped she wasn't making her first mistake. Judging by Kate's bright smile as she opened the door, she clearly had made the right decision.

"Hello, Zora," Kate said. "Come on in. We are so happy to see you."

"Thanks," Zora said as she stepped into the front entranceway. The house was cool from the air conditioner in the front window, and it smelled like lemon air freshener. Kate wandered into the living room as Zora slipped off her sneakers, then followed, appraising her surroundings. During the interview, she'd been too nervous to take note. She recognized all of the living room furniture from Pottery Barn and Crate and Barrel—the sage sofa, the brown leather chairs, even the soft chenille throw draped across the back of the couch. The antique dining room table looked like an expensive hand-me-down from somebody's parents. Colorful baby toys filled a straw basket near the fireplace, and picture frames with perfectly posed black-and-white wedding photos of Kate and her husband dotted the built-in bookcases. Harmless, Zora surmised. These were the type of people she'd grown up with. The type of people she was supposed to grow up to be. Married. Successful. Employed. Procreating. Zora gave a half smile at the irony and headed toward the baby.

Oliver was lying on his back on one of those baby-gym things, temporarily mesmerized by the jumble of neon-colored noise-makers and toys hanging above his head. He was wearing a cotton jumpsuit covered in an orange and yellow animal print.

Kate laughed at her son. "I don't know why they call those things baby gyms," she said. "Oliver never moves while he's down there. He just sits and stares. His eyeballs darting back and forth are probably the only part of his body getting a workout."

Zora laughed, too. She couldn't help it. The child did look like his eyes might pop right out of his skull.

"Zora, would you like some coffee?" Kate asked. "My husband, Brad, always makes a pot before he leaves."

"No, thanks," Zora answered. "I don't drink coffee."

"I couldn't survive without coffee. I need that caffeine," Kate admitted.

"I didn't say I don't need caffeine," Zora clarified. "I just can't stand the taste of coffee, but I do drink black tea. Always."

"Oh, okay," Kate answered, making a note on her clipboard. "Unfortunately, I don't have any black tea, but I'll make sure to pick some up at the store. Is there any brand you particularly like?"

"You don't have to buy me tea," Zora protested.

"It's okay," Kate said. "You should have what you like in my house. It's the least I can do."

"Okay, then," Zora agreed. "I like plain old Lipton English Breakfast."

"Okay, great." Kate gathered her lists and pencils. "Now that we have all that taken care of, let's get down to business."

Zora took that as a cue and went to stand next to her new boss by the kitchen table. Because of the pass-through window, they could still keep an eye on the baby.

"So, what I wanted to do today," Kate started, "was basically go over how the house works, then take you around the neighborhood. I have a couple of errands to run this afternoon, so I figured I'd leave you alone with Ollie for a couple of hours. Is that okay with you?"

Zora nodded. "Sure."

Just then the baby let out a pained yelp. Kate dropped her clipboard and ran to her son. Apparently one of the baby-gym toys had hit Oliver on the head, as evidenced by the pink mark marring his milky-white forehead. He seemed fine, but Kate scooped him up and planted reassuring kisses all over him. "Is Mommy's angel okay?" she asked.

Oliver responded by diving for his mother's nose and sucking on the tip. Kate laughed and allowed her son to nurse her nose without protesting. Zora watched and wondered how this woman, who seemed so in love with her child, was going to go back to work full-time. Maybe she wouldn't be able to handle it and would want to quit and stay home. Then Zora would be out of a job. Sondra had mentioned that this could happen. "The more these women see their friends staying home, the more they want to do it, too," Sondra had said. "That's the only reason why I didn't try to get a job as a nanny. It's not secure enough."

"Sondra, you didn't try to get a job as a nanny because you hate kids," Zora reminded her friend.

"All the same," Sondra said and sniffed, "being a nanny could be the perfect short-term gig for you. And babies are the best because they're still cute and cuddly, and the mothers want to be around them all the time. So if you have to up and split, the lady might thank you for giving her the excuse to quit her job. Just make sure it's one of those rich ladies whose husband makes megabucks and she can afford to stop working."

Zora studied mother and child. Would Kate be able to leave her "angel" every day?

"What did you say your husband does?" Zora asked.

"He's basically a stockbroker," Kate answered, jiggling the baby in her arms. "It's a very intense job, but he has decent hours because the market closes at four. That's why he can still go to the gym and be home by six."

"That must be nice," Zora said.

"Yeah, Brad likes the pace and the challenge of his work, but he's secretly one of those bleeding-heart guys who wants to be doing something meaningful, like building windmills in China or running some nonprofit organization that lets him travel to Africa to help save all the poor starving orphans."

Zora bristled at the starving-African-orphans comment, but she kept her mouth shut. She wasn't being paid to educate this woman about the vast economic diversity on the African continent.

"I don't think Oliver has suffered any brain damage," Kate joked. "Let's give Zora a tour of the house, okay, Ollie?"

The house tour lasted over an hour, even though there were only six rooms on two floors to explore. But Kate wanted Zora to know things, like the fact that the window in the upstairs guest room got stuck sometimes, and if it ever rained, you had to tap it with a hammer on the left side to close it. She also wanted to show Zora how to use the washer and dryer, the stove, and the dishwasher. Not that she expected Zora to take on any household chores, but you never knew what might come up, and it was better to be safe than sorry. By the end, Zora wished she'd brought her own notebook to write down all of Kate's instructions, rules, and regulations. "Don't worry, I'm a big list fan. I'll write everything down for you," Kate assured her.

"Thanks," Zora said. She hated having to ask questions about what seemed to be basic information. But she hated getting yelled at for doing something wrong even more.

"Okay," Kate said. "Do you have any questions, Zora?"

Zora shook her head. Her mind was spinning.

"Let's get ready to go to the park, then. Ollie takes his first nap around eleven-thirty, so you guys will have a little time to play."

Zora felt a niggling sense of anxiety. Kate definitely possessed one of those type A personalities, like Zora's brother. And from experience, Zora knew type A people had a very low threshold for incompetence and mistakes.

Kate handed Oliver to Zora. "Here, you take him for a minute, and I'll run and get the diaper bag. You can't leave home without it." She dashed up the stairs.

So, for the first time, Zora held Oliver. He fit snugly in her arms and seemed unfazed by his mother's temporary disappearance. He stared intently at Zora's face, his big green eyes unblinking. Then, with a jerky movement, he reached out to grab one of the dreadlocks that had escaped from her ponytail.

"You like my hair?" Zora asked, keeping her voice soft and soothing.

Oliver responded by thrusting her hair in his mouth, then made a face of surprise when it tickled his tongue. Zora laughed. "I don't think you want to eat my hair." Oliver rewarded her with a big smile.

Kate came back downstairs. "It looks like you two are getting along," she declared. "Come on, Zora, let me show you the wonders of our all-terrain stroller. No joke, it took Brad and me three hours to figure this ridiculous contraption out."

"Coming," Zora said, and she followed Kate out the front door.

CHAPTER 6
Kate

Oɴ her first day back to work, Kate wore the black St. John suit Brad had given her the year before for her thirty-first birthday. She clipped her long brown hair into a sloppy-chic ponytail and at the last minute slipped on her three-inch stilettos—which brought her to an imposing five-ten—for good luck. Maybe a little much, she thought when she critiqued her appearance in the mirror, but she wanted people to know she hadn't gone soft while she was out on maternity leave. Judging from her appearance, most people probably wouldn't believe she'd been pregnant less than a year before. Yes, she was bringing a picture of Oliver to put on her desk, but no, she wouldn't be the one flying out of the office at five if there was still work to be done. People constantly bad-mouthed Maggie Brown behind her back because she had the audacity to pack up and leave every day at precisely 5:01 P.M. so she could make the 5:17 Metro-North train to Croton-on-Hudson and be home in time for dinner with her three kids. Kate wasn't interested in being the new Maggie Brown. She had deliberately stretched her three-month paid maternity leave into a six-month "hold my spot and keep my benefits" leave so she could luxuriate in her time with Oliver and not feel guilty when she went back. She'd had her mommy months, but now it was time to rejoin reality. She was ready to dive back into the mix, and she wanted it known throughout the company that Kate Carter hadn't lost her touch.

When she got to her office on the corner of Madison and

Twenty-eighth Street in Manhattan, she realized she had a case of the butterflies. She laughed at herself. Thankfully, it was early, only eight-thirty. Most people didn't start trickling into the office until after nine, which suited Kate fine, since she wanted to put on her game face in private, to set up and prepare before she had to see her colleagues. Laurie, her assistant, had sent her a package every week with an update on the KasperKline account, so she knew what was going on with the team. She just had to get used to corporate culture again. Panty hose and finicky clients. Conference calls and memos for everything. For the past six months, explosive poop and cures for cracked nipples had been the greatest emergencies in Kate's life, so she knew her brain was going to ache for a minute while she readjusted.

Kate took the elevator up to the twenty-sixth floor and then walked slowly down the empty hall to her office. She flipped on the lights and stood in the doorway for a moment. Everything looked the same. Maroon carpet, fake mahogany bookshelves filled with her collection of literary classics, and an abundance of medical journals she'd probably never manage to read. The single window provided an uninspiring view of the office buildings across the street and enough natural light to keep her from falling victim to claustrophobia and seasonal depression. It wasn't a big office, but everything in it was hers. She knew someone, a random temp or an employee from the D.C. office, perhaps, had been using her space while she was out, but her desk was as impeccably neat and organized as when she left it six months ago. A large vase with fresh-cut flowers perched on the edge of her desk provided the only splash of color in the room. She smiled when she saw the elegant bouquet and walked over to get a closer look. Everyone who came back to work after time off was rewarded with flowers. She plucked out the card and read, "Welcome back. We missed you." It was "signed" by the managing director of the New York office, Roger White. She knew Laurie had probably ordered the flowers and dictated the note, but still, the gesture made her feel her return was being acknowledged.

Kate sat down in her five-hundred-dollar ergonomically correct swivel chair and clicked her computer on. She'd been checking her e-mail from home, but she'd gotten a little lax in the last few days, so she had seventy-six new messages clogging up her in-box. There was a small pile of mail in the basket on her desk, and Laurie had penciled in "Morning meeting at 10:00" on her flip calendar. Kate glanced at her watch. It was 8:50. Ten more minutes until the office came to life, so she decided to start attacking the e-mails.

At 9:05 Kate heard a quiet knock on her door. It was Laurie. She came rushing in, newly red hair escaping from its messy bun, and hugged her boss. "It's so good to see you," she gushed. "My God, you lost all that baby weight, and nice suit, by the way."

"Wow, you colored your hair," Kate said, standing up to greet her young assistant. "You look great. And thank you. Thank you and thank you." Kate laughed. She loved Laurie's exuberance. The girl had a smile on her face 24/7. She was only twenty-four, two years out of college, and for reasons unknown to Kate, loved her job. She didn't seem to mind the endless photocopying, filing, and almost daily orders to the deli across the street for coffee and cookies for client meetings. Kate attributed Laurie's perpetual happiness to the fact that she was from Minnesota. It seemed that everyone from the Midwest had those Rainbow Brite personalities.

"So how does it feel to be back?" Laurie asked, perching herself on one of the two simple black armchairs.

"Well," Kate started, conscious of how Laurie treated everything she said as the Truth, with a capital T. "It feels really great to be back to my old life, but the day's barely started. Ask me in a few hours if I wouldn't prefer to be at home in my sweats, watching *Oprah*."

Laurie's brown eyes widened in concern. "Are you missing Oliver? Do you think you came back too soon?"

Kate gave a dismissive wave. "No. No, no. Not at all. Oliver is in good hands, and honestly, I was ready to get back here and be a grown-up again."

As the words tumbled out of her mouth, Kate wasn't sure where they came from. It was like there was a script in her head and she was just reading the words. She didn't know how she felt. On the one hand, it did feel good getting dressed to go play in the grown-up world again, but on the other hand, she'd been away from home only an hour, and she was craving her son with a desperation she usually felt only for chocolate. She missed his sweet powdery smell, his soft weight in her arms, and those beautiful green eyes smiling up in her face. But she knew from reading all of the articles in *Working Mother* magazine that her feelings were normal, that soon enough she'd get into the working-mother groove and everything would be fine. She just had to keep moving forward.

Satisfied with her boss's answer, Laurie jumped up. "Well, call me selfish, I'm totally happy you're back," she chattered on. "That woman Danyel Green, who's been sitting in your office while you were gone, was driving me insane."

"Who is she?" Kate asked, turning back to her e-mail over-flow.

"Oh, she's the new hire in health care. She came from L.A. They assigned me to her while you were out, and she was a night-mare. Thank God she's getting her own assistant. God help who-ever gets that job."

It was unlike Laurie to complain so much, so Kate took her rant seriously. But she also didn't want to encourage Laurie to talk poorly about her coworkers. Especially her superiors.

"I'm sure she isn't that bad," Kate offered. "Which clients is she working on?"

"You'll get to see for yourself how bad she is, because she's being transferred over to the KasperKline account to work with you. Plus, she's holding on to one of her clients from L.A.," Laurie answered with the hint of a smirk.

"Wait," Kate said, looking up from her computer screen. "What level is she?"

"She's a senior account executive, so you have seniority over her, but she seems like one of those real corporate-ladder-climbing types." Laurie grimaced.

"Oh, okay," Kate said, trying not to let her paranoia get the best of her. But why hadn't she been notified of this hire? Were they already getting ready for her to pull the great mommy disappearing act?

Laurie took Kate's silence and deepening frown as a dismissal and slipped out the door. Kate went back to her computer. "I guess I have my work cut out for me," she said to her empty office. "Welcome back to real life."

CHAPTER 7

Zora

THREE weeks on the job, and already Zora's daily routine was fixed. Eight o'clock, Monday through Friday, she was at the Carters' house. By the time she arrived, Mr. Carter would be long gone, and Kate would be itching to leave. If Zora was one minute late, Kate would have that look on her face that reminded Zora of her mother. It was a look that perfectly expressed disappointment and suppressed rage. So, after one slipup, Zora made it a point to always be on time.

As she promised on that first day, Kate always left a note for Zora that was more like a list of instructions, regarding Oliver's lunch, how many bottles he should take, his nap time, and what *Baby Einstein* video he should or should not watch. Zora didn't take Kate's micromanaging personally; she could tell it was part of her personality. She also didn't adhere to the list word for word. Sometimes she goofed and put in the wrong video or gave him applesauce instead of apple/apricot sauce, but she didn't think it really mattered that much, and Kate never brought up these minor transgressions.

On her own, Zora figured out what kind of pureed fruit Oliver enjoyed the most and what temperature his mother's reheated breast milk had to be. She knew he grew fidgety when he watched *Baby Einstein*, but *Sesame Street ABC* made him giggle and coo. He really was a pretty easy baby, and Kate, despite her lists, was a decent boss. Zora knew she just wanted to believe her baby was being well cared for while she was gone, and Zora could provide that service. It wasn't rocket science. The biggest challenge was to keep Kate under the impression that child care was Zora's greatest ambition in life instead of a pit stop on the way to something better.

As she walked the seven blocks to work from the Union Street bus stop, Zora forced herself to go over her strategy again for "what next?" For these first three weeks, she'd given herself a mental vacation from planning, since she was trying hard to make a good impression. But it was coming up on a month, and Zora didn't want to get stuck again. She knew how it would happen. She'd get comfortable working for the Carters. They'd insist they couldn't live without her. She'd feel needed and important and allow herself to stay put. And then poof, another four years of her life would be gone. Here in Park Slope, she wouldn't be picking up any new languages to add to her résumé or justify the time spent. This time would be different, Zora promised herself as she turned the corner onto Park Slope's main commercial avenue. She was going to prove to herself and to her parents that there was more to Zora Anderson than well-traveled babysitter.

Zora paused her mental pep talk to gaze through the window of her new favorite shoe store. Of course it wasn't open yet, but she always liked to peek. There was a pair of beaded flip-flops with a wedge heel in the window with her name on them. The tag said sixty dollars. Considering she still owed her brother money for her first month's rent, she knew she had no business even thinking about buying those shoes, but it was okay to dream. They were so pretty. And she hadn't done anything nice for herself since she'd been in this crazy, crowded city. Tomorrow she got paid, so maybe.

Zora walked the rest of the way to the Carters' brownstone thinking about those shoes. When she arrived, she skipped up the steps and let herself in with the key Kate had given her on her first day. She said hello to Kate—who was packing her briefcase on the dining room table—kicked off her shoes, threw down her purse, and walked right over to Oliver, who was seated in the kitchen in his high chair. She kissed the baby and then started stacking the few breakfast dishes in the dishwasher.

"You don't have to do that," Kate said absentmindedly.

But Zora did it anyway. She always did.

Kate stopped packing for a second to say thank you; then she was a flurry of movement again. She kissed Oliver on the forehead and scrambled out the door, calling her good-byes to Zora over her shoulder.

Zora finished cleaning the kitchen and wiped the remnants of Oliver's breakfast off his face. She pulled the baby out of his seat and took him upstairs to get him dressed.

One hour later, they were out the door. With the weather still feeling like summer, Zora tried to take advantage of outdoor activities. Today they were going to the park. Designed by the famed architect Frederick Law Olmsted, Prospect Park was heralded as the Central Park of Brooklyn. Considering Olmsted had designed Central Park as well, that was a pretty fair comparison. The park stretched for miles in every direction and boasted a zoo, two ponds, acres of play space for sports fans and canines alike, and several age-appropriate playgrounds sprinkled around the entire area. There was also a band shell for outdoor concerts, and plenty of simple wooden benches for relaxing and watching the world go by.

Generally, Zora steered clear of the playgrounds because she didn't have a group to hang with and she felt like such a reject. It was like middle school all over again. All the mommies figured she was a nanny, so she was socially invisible to them. And most of the nannies clung together in tight little cliques and seemed to smell her lack of authenticity. "You're not one of us," they seemed to say with their sullen stares. Maybe she seemed too young or too happy. Or maybe they didn't like her midwestern accent, which seemed so nasal and harsh compared to their melodious island lilt. So after a couple of unsuccessful attempts at penetrating the playground politics, Zora and Ollie made their own fun, usually heading to the pond to feed the ducks. Today they were going to get some sun and hang out on the great lawn. Spying an open spot between two old women doing tai chi and a husky Hells Angels–looking guy reading the Bible, Zora directed the stroller that way. Having claimed their space, Zora laid Oliver's waterproof mat down on the grass, threw some toys out, and plunked the baby in the middle of it all. Then she took a moment to inhale the sweet scent of early fall, kicking off her sandals and spreading her arms out wide to embrace the day. "Ahhhh," she sighed. "Today is a perfect day."

Ollie was too busy trying to shove his toy keys into his mouth to pay much attention to the weather. Zora didn't mind. She smiled at her little charge and plopped herself down in the grass next to him. For her own enjoyment, she pulled out her copy of this month's *Gourmet* magazine from her purse.

While living in France, Zora had developed a gourmand's appreciation for good food. "It doesn't have to be fancy," Madame Laroux always told her, "it is all about the ingredients." For Madame Laroux and the great majority of the French population, food was worth eating only if it was prepared with fresh ingredients purchased from the market that day. And market didn't refer to some sterile, overstocked supermarket, but rather, an open-air market where fishermen and farmers alike brought their best products to the people.

After a year of accompanying Madame Laroux to the market, Zora was permitted to do some of the shopping herself and sometimes even made a meal for the family. Maybe a crisp roasted chicken for dinner, or the kids' favorite Saturday breakfast, fluffy American pancakes with fresh berries and maple syrup smuggled in her suitcase from her occasional trips home. Once she came home for good, cooking had been Zora's way of maintaining a connection to her life in France. And even though she enrolled only out of a desperate sense of longing for that life, the Institute of Culinary Arts was the only school Zora ever attended where she graduated with high honors and the respect of all of her instructors.

Stretching out on her stomach, Zora flipped through *Gourmet*'s glossy pages and thought back to her final days of cooking school. One of her instructors, Chef Marcus, had recommended her for a job as a private chef to some bigwig automotive executive. The idea did not sound remotely appealing. All she could think of was endless days making midwestern comfort food for big men with big appetites. Meat and potatoes, gooey casseroles, and anything with sausage in it. Ugh! Zora politely declined the offer, telling Chef Marcus that she couldn't imagine a life for herself in Michigan. No way. A shudder of revulsion pulsed through her body when she even thought about putting down roots in her hometown. Zora looked up from her magazine and reminded herself that she was indeed far away from home, in one of the most exciting cities in the world. Gazing around the park, drinking in the reassuring vibe of creative energy, Zora relaxed. And then the idea hit her.

Maybe she could be a private chef here in New York for some famous actor or musician and get paid to travel around the world making fabulous meals. That would be perfect, a dream come true. Maybe her parents wouldn't think it was such a great career choice, but the more she played with the idea, the better it sounded. Cooking great meals, traveling, working in an intimate setting instead of an anonymous restaurant kitchen, and of course, not having to wear a suit to work would be the icing on the cake. Fueled by images of herself making exquisite lemon soufflés in a private château on the French Riviera, Zora plucked the copy of *The Village Voice* out of her bag. She turned right to the back of the paper, to the employment section, sending up a silent prayer that she might get lucky. She scanned pages and pages of ads, hoping to find her future in a little block of text, but she came up with nothing. It seemed the only people hiring in New York City this week were strip clubs, telemarketing agencies, and environmental activists. Zora tossed the paper aside in defeat. "Well, Oliver, today is obviously not the day I find my destiny, but we'll keep trying, right?" Zora sighed.

Oliver responded with a screech and a ribbon of drool that slid past his chin and onto his chest. He was starting to get two bottom teeth, and his daily output of saliva kept Zora constantly standing by with a rag to wipe at his soggy little face. But she didn't mind. She was quickly falling in love with Ollie. It was so easy for her to make him laugh and smile. She took a moment to play peekaboo, which was currently his favorite game.

"You know, while I wait for my big break as a personal chef," Zora mused out loud to Oliver in between peeks, "why don't I practice on your parents?" Again no words sprang forth from her little charge, but Zora took his happy eyes and big grin as a "Yes, I agree."

"Okay, then, baby," she said. For the time being, she'd practice cooking for Brad and Kate Carter, until she found a private chef's position. This would be her training period. "Let's go make some magic," Zora said, scooping up the baby and tucking him back in the stroller. While she collected his things, she thought about what she might want to make for Kate and Brad's first meal. It should be something simple but elegant, she decided. Something they wouldn't make for themselves but that wouldn't feel over the top. Just like she would in France, Zora would go to the markets to see what looked good and fresh before she made a final decision about what to cook.

Heading toward the park exit, Zora felt a twinge of excitement as she thought about cooking for her new employers in practice for her future. "Zora's got a plan," she sang quietly to herself. And it felt good.

Back at the Carters', while Oliver took his nap, Zora got busy in the kitchen. Thus far the only food she'd prepared on the job was instant rice cereal for Oliver and an occasional bagel for herself. She had quickly realized that Kate was not an emotional shopper. The food she kept stocked in her fridge and in the cabinets was all useful, practical, and necessary. Chicken broth. Bags of pasta. Emergency cans of tuna, kidney beans, and pineapple chunks. The refrigerator always held eggs, plain yogurt, skim milk, and wheat bread. Nobody would starve here, but mealtimes were probably pretty tepid. Zora wrinkled her nose in distaste. Like the bright colors she liked to wear on her body, Zora liked to cook with flavorful herbs, pungent spices, and exotic ingredients. Like jicama and Spanish saffron. She studied recipes and devoured cookbooks, but when she was in the kitchen, she cooked from pure inspiration. Usually, an idea for a new dish came to her in a dream, and then she'd work it out in her head until she was ready to try it out in real life.

If Zora cooked without inspiration, the food suffered. Her favorite instructor at cooking school, Chef Diego (he was from Mexico but spent most of his professional years cooking in France, so he spoke a kind of culinary mash-up of Spanish, French, and English) had said Zora was an intuitionist in the kitchen. "You cook *de la corazón* and not from the brain," he pronounced fervently when he sampled the final-project recipe she had created—a crispy duck breast covered in a pomegranate reduction sauce served with a goat-cheese flan and sautéed purple cabbage. "You must be careful, because you put much of yourself in your cuisine," he warned her, then gave her an A-plus for a grade.

For the Carters, Zora decided to try a simple pasta dish that she'd serve with the beautiful veal sausages she'd found at a tiny butcher shop on Fifth Avenue. She chose not to tell Kate it was veal, because she seemed like the type who would feel bad for baby cows. While Zora chopped a small mountain of garlic and shredded the soft, furry sage leaves, she hummed one of her favorite French songs. She danced around the kitchen, finding her rhythm again after so many weeks of eating cereal for dinner. It was no fun cooking for herself, and besides, the kitchen in Sondra's apartment was so small that Zora couldn't even unpack one quarter of her culinary tools and gadgets. But the Carters' kitchen—with its olive-green granite countertops, shiny stainless-steel appliances, and one well-placed skylight—jolted Zora's creative juices out of hibernation.

When Kate and Brad stepped into the house together at six-thirty, they were met with the smoldering scent of sage and nutty browned butter.

"My God, it smells amazing in here," Kate exclaimed from the hallway. "What are you making, Zora?"

"Just pasta." Zora smiled to herself.

"That cannot be just pasta," Kate said. "Doesn't it smell delicious, hon?" She nudged her husband as she pulled off her black pumps and made her way over to the living room to throw herself down on the floor with Oliver.

"Yeah, it smells really good," Brad admitted. "But you didn't have to make us dinner, Zora," he added.

"Don't worry, Mr. Carter," Zora said, trying to read his somber mood. "It was no problem." So far it seemed Brad Carter didn't like the idea of having a nanny. He came home later every day, often arriving when Kate did. He spoke to her only when he had to, and even then he seemed standoffish and unnecessarily formal. Zora couldn't figure out if it was something about her or if he really wanted Kate to stay home with Oliver herself. Or maybe he just didn't like Black people. She worried about it at first, but since she had minimal contact with him on the job, she didn't stress about it anymore. He could think whatever he wanted to.

Kate jumped in. "Of course we'll pay you extra. And let me know how much you paid for the food, Zora, because I know whatever you're making did not come from our refrigerator."

"I left the grocery receipt on the counter," Zora said. "I didn't really need that much, just a few things."

"Fine," Kate said. She picked up Oliver and carried him over to the kitchen to peer into the pots and pans on the stove.

Zora gave quick instructions about the meal. The pasta was finished. The sausage was warming in the oven, and there were sliced heirloom tomatoes drizzled with olive oil in the fridge.

"Thank you so much, Zora," Kate gushed once more.

"No problem," Zora said as she began to gather up her things. "Good night, Mr. Carter," she said as she walked to the door.

"Good night, Zora," he answered.

Zora let herself out and smiled all the way to the bus stop.

CHAPTER 8

Kate

THE clock read 7:59 A.M. when Kate strode into work. As she passed by Danyel Green's empty office, she sighed with relief. "The early bird catches the worm," she said to herself. For the last few weeks, Kate had been forcing herself to get to work by eight A.M. Not only did she need to prove to Roger White that she hadn't lost her touch during her maternity leave, she needed to make sure Danyel Green knew who was in charge on this account. After only a week of working with Danyel, Kate knew she wasn't the type to happily play second fiddle. She wanted to be in control. Of everything! To Kate's face, Danyel played nice, but behind her back, she was always trying to prove she knew more about KasperKline and the contraception industry than Kate did. So Kate knew she had to work harder. She hated to do it, but she'd been forced to ask Zora to come to work a half hour earlier and leave Brad waiting at home until she got there. Thankfully, Zora had agreed right away without any fuss.

Kate sat down at her desk and reviewed the talking points she'd drafted the day before for the CEO of KasperKline. The company's senior administrative team was coming in for media training, and Kate was handling the entire session. She called the mailroom and made sure Warren would have all the training guides copied and bound by ten A.M. The client wasn't due to arrive until eleven, but Kate never waited for the last minute to get anything done. Once Warren assured her that he was on schedule,

Kate found the number for the Happiness deli in Laurie's Rolodex and called to add a sandwich platter for lunch and an additional pitcher of iced tea without sugar. Last night on the subway home, she'd remembered that the VP of sales was a diabetic and always requested unsweetened beverages but no sodas. Once that was taken care of, Kate turned on her computer and started to review her PowerPoint presentation. She was going to do half of the presentation herself, and then she was bringing in an outside trainer to do the on-camera work.

A knock on her office door interrupted her concentration. It was Danyel Green. Kate silenced a groan, forced a smile, and asked her to come in.

"Hi, Kate," Danyel said with syrupy sweetness. As usual, she was dressed to perfection in a black wrap dress that showed off her size 2 frame; her three-inch heels made her already long legs look even longer. Kate felt only mildly guilty for noticing that Danyel's longish face and oversize teeth gave her a horsey look around the mouth. "Good morning," Kate said, turning back to her computer screen. She hoped Danyel would get the hint and make a hasty exit.

"I don't want to interrupt," Danyel said. "I just wanted to let you know that Roger asked me to sit in on your media training today." She paused and glanced around Kate's office as if appraising Kate's worth by her surroundings. Kate got the distinct impression that Danyel was looking for something, anything, to use in her crusade to climb to the top of the KasperKline account. It was clear that Danyel had been born without a moral center.

"And?" Kate prompted with an icy stare.

"And," Danyel continued, "I was wondering if you needed me to take care of anything for you. You seem really busy."

Kate resisted the urge to throw Danyel out of her office with all of her fake concerns. Instead, she smiled politely, thanked her for her offer, and informed Danyel that she had everything under control.

"Okay, then," Danyel said. "I guess I'll just meet you in the conference room at eleven." She paused. "Full disclosure: I sneaked one of your manuals from the mailroom, so I'm all caught up on what you've planned. And it looks good. In L.A. I was kind of considered the media training go-to girl, so that's not just an idle compliment." Danyel smiled again as she casually fluffed up her long dark hair.

"Thanks," Kate said through gritted teeth.

Danyel finally turned to leave. "See you in a bit."

"Can't wait," Kate mumbled under her breath. She stood up and went to close the door behind Danyel. She had to hold herself back from slamming it. That woman made her blood boil. And now she was seriously beginning to think that perhaps her job was in jeopardy. Why would Roger ask Danyel to observe her media training unless he had some doubts about her abilities? Maybe he was sending Danyel in as her backup in case she stumbled along the way. But she'd done this so many times before. She could media-train in her sleep. It didn't make any sense. Kate sat back down at her desk and willed herself to calm down. She needed to spend all of her energy on reviewing her presentation, not on analyzing Danyel's modus operandi.

By the time Kate escorted her clients to their waiting Lincoln Town Cars at three, she could barely hold herself together. She couldn't remember if, before Oliver had been born, she'd worn her emotions so close to the surface. She dragged herself back to her office, closed the door, and cried. She was crying partly from relief that this horrible day was almost over, but mostly she was crying because she knew Danyel Green had sabotaged her training session. First Danyel had slid into the conference room thirty minutes late, and her not-so-subtle entrance had destroyed Kate's concentration. She put herself on pause while Danyel apologized to the KasperKline team, shaking each man's hand individually, then finally took a seat. It took a moment for Kate to find her place in the presentation, and of course this was exactly the moment that Roger White decided to pop in and see how things were going. For the rest of the day, Danyel seemed to take pride in asking ruinous questions. It was as if she'd deliberately studied Kate's presentation to find the weak spots and then pointed them all out in front of the client. The nerve of that woman! But the worst part was that Roger White had witnessed the whole miserable thing. Yes, Kate was feeling sorry for herself, but she couldn't help it. Maybe this was how it was all going to end.

Laurie interrupted Kate's pity party with a soft knock on the door. Kate quickly wiped at her tears, flipped on her computer screen, and tried to look busy as she invited her assistant to enter.

Laurie slipped into Kate's office wearing a worried expression. She plopped down in the chair in front of Kate's desk.

"What's the matter?" Kate asked, ready to put her own issues aside to help Laurie out. Laurie's pale cheeks were flushed pink with emotion, and she had to fidget with the collar on her blouse for a moment. Finally, she cleared her throat and launched into a confession. "First of all, I want you to know I wasn't eavesdropping," she said.

Kate raised a dubious eyebrow in her assistant's direction. "Go on," she said to Laurie.

"I happened to hear Roger and Danyel talking in the conference room while I was cleaning up after lunch, and Roger was saying something to Danyel about picking up your slack or something."

Kate tried not to appear distressed, but her heart skipped a beat. So it *was* true. She was being replaced. It felt like the worst kind of betrayal, and she could feel her insides begin to quake.

But she didn't want Laurie to see her fall apart, so she worked at maintaining a calm exterior. "Laurie, you shouldn't eavesdrop," Kate said weakly.

"I didn't plan on it," Laurie said in her own defense. "I just happened to overhear a conversation that didn't involve me."

Kate made a halfhearted attempt to convince Laurie that she wasn't worried and then made the excuse that she had a lot of work to finish up. Laurie looked like she wanted to say something else, then decided against it. She exited Kate's office without another word.

The gentle click of the closing door behind Laurie was all it took for Kate's body to let loose. The tears welled up in her eyes again, and her hands went cold as her heart started to pound in desperation. Kate checked her watch. It was only four, but she knew she had to get out of the office before she completely lost it. If she was getting fired, what did leaving an hour early matter, anyway? She waited until she heard Laurie leave her desk, and then she slid out the door unnoticed.

Back home, Kate changed into sweats and let Zora go home early. She barely spoke to Zora but couldn't be concerned with social pleasantries when her whole world was falling apart. She told herself she would apologize in the morning. Since Oliver was still sleeping, Kate headed straight to the kitchen to make a giant casserole of macaroni and cheese and a Duncan Hines chocolate cake for dinner. She needed comfort food to dull this kind of pain. She knew she would regret the calories in the morning, but right now a carbohydrate hug was just what the doctor ordered. While she waited for Ollie to wake up, instead of sweating through her Tae Bo tapes, she hunkered down on the couch and watched back-to-back talk-show episodes where women pleaded for the return of their kidnapped children and men admitted to having affairs while their wives suffered from incurable diseases. It was the perfect antidote for her descent into self-pity. At least her life wasn't that bad.

By the time Brad came through the door, at 6:20, Kate was devouring a bag of microwave popcorn and sobbing in front of the television. Oliver was nearby in his bouncy seat, happily gumming his rainbow rubber keys. Brad plopped down next to Kate on the couch, and she collapsed into his arms.

"What's the matter?" Brad asked, easing the remote control out of Kate's hands and turning off the TV.

"Why are you so late?" Kate whimpered.

"I'm not that late," Brad insisted. "What time did you get home?"

"Oh, Brad," Kate wailed, ignoring his question so she could move on to the real matter at hand. "I suck. I'm going to get fired. I've gotten soft. And that witch Danyel Green is waiting like a greedy hyena to see me fall so she can swoop in and take my place." All of this was said with a lot of hand gestures and arm flailing for emphasis.

"Whoa, whoa," Brad said, loosening his tie. "What's going on?"

Kate tried to explain her theory about the great mommy disappearing act and the feeling she had that she was about to get booted out of the top position on the KasperKline account, thanks to Danyel.

Brad didn't look concerned as she poured her heart out. "Is it at all possible that you're making this sound worse than it actually is?" Brad asked tenderly.

"No," she moaned, then relayed what Laurie had overheard.

That got his attention. Brad pulled Kate into his arms and held her close. Then he kissed the top of her head and asked quietly, "If they do get rid of you, would that be so bad?" Kate didn't answer, so Brad went on. "Maybe this is a blessing in disguise. Maybe it's your unasked-for opportunity to try to get a real writing job."

Kate pulled away from Brad. She knew he was going to bring

up her master's degree in journalism from Northwestern University. "I love my job," she snapped before he could even utter the word "journalist." "And even though you don't think what I do is important, it is. And just so you know, my eighty-thousand-dollar salary is double what I'd make at any magazine as an associate editor, which is where I'd probably have to start out, since I never made it past editorial assistant in my former life." Kate's former life had included a dream to be a magazine editor, but after two years making photocopies and minimum wage at a very prestigious women's magazine, she'd made a trade on that dream. If she could still write, work with the media, and make a decent salary, she'd be okay. Brad didn't seem to understand her ability to compromise on this, but she was far more practical than her idealist husband.

Brad threw his hands up in surrender. "Hey, I'm on your side. I just wanted you to see that if you lost this job, there's always another door to go through."

Kate took a deep breath and tried to calm down. "I know," she conceded. "But it's the principle of the thing. I know I took an extra-long maternity leave, but I earned that with all of my overtime. And I didn't ask for any special treatment. And I came back when I said I would. I'm in all five days, and I'm not running home when the clock strikes five."

Brad nodded. "I know."

But Kate was on a roll. "And I could, you know. But I'm not. I'm giving a hundred and ten percent, but I guess that's not good enough when creatures like Danyel Green are slinking around."

"I don't think you should worry about Danyel," Brad tried to interject.

"You don't understand," Kate said, getting agitated all over again. "She's so annoying. Do you know she knows the caloric value of every single piece of food ever invented? And as you're eating it, she'll tell you exactly how many grams of fat you are currently ingesting. I swear, she lives only to make other people's lives miserable."

"Kate, what does that have to do with your reputation at the office?" Brad asked, trying to keep a straight face. "Roger White and all those guys at Jacobs and Zimbalist love you. You're like the company poster child. You get to work early, you never complain, and you always work hard. Not to mention you're really smart, and they know that. One bad day doesn't mean you're getting canned."

Kate snuffled and wiped at her nose. Brad waited for her to say something. "So why do you think Roger White told Danyel she'd have to pick up my slack?" she finally asked.

"I don't know." Brad sighed. "But you shouldn't even be worrying about it, seeing as how the information isn't exactly coming from a reliable source."

"Laurie would never make something like that up," Kate insisted.

"I'm not saying she made it up," Brad explained. "I'm just saying she heard part of a conversation, and we don't know what the other parts entailed."

Kate stopped talking and tried to focus on what Brad was saying. She wanted to believe he was right, that maybe there was another explanation, but everything seemed to point toward her impending ouster.

"Where's my fighter?" Brad asked. "Where's the Katie who never quits?"

Kate looked at Brad and said in a small voice, "What should I do? Just tell me what to do."

Brad took his wife's face in his hands and said gently, "Kate, you're going to do what you always do, which is work your ass off and do your best."

Kate raised an eyebrow. "That's it? That's your best advice?"

Brad settled back into the couch and stretched his long legs out to the coffee table. "Look, you're a rock star over there. You know it, and they know it."

Kate mulled this over. "You're right. I am a rock star," she said with a shadow of a smile. "I am so good at what I do, if they want to replace me with Danyel Green, that will be their worst mistake."

Brad smiled. "That's the attitude you need to have."

"Thank you, honey," Kate said, leaning over to kiss her husband on the cheek. "Really, thank you. I needed to hear that. Sometimes I get so caught up in the gossip and competition in the office."

"Yeah, well, you gotta stop doing that," Brad counseled. "Look what it does to you."

"I know. But that's why you're here to help. You're much better for me than this greasy popcorn."

"I'll take that for you." Brad grinned, prying the nearly empty bag from his wife's hands.

Just then Oliver gave an angry yelp as his keys slid to the floor.

Kate scooped Oliver out of his seat and nestled him between her and Brad on the couch. "I guess it wouldn't be so bad if I lost my job," she mused, caressing Ollie's cheek. "Then I'd get to spend more time with this beautiful creature."

Brad smiled. "Are we all better now?"

"Yes, breakdown is over."

Later that night, with bellies full of mac and cheese, Kate and Brad made love. It was sweet and tender and probably the first time Kate had enjoyed herself in bed since Oliver was born. Brad had gone all out, creating a romantic ambience, putting Sade in the CD player and lighting vanilla tea light candles to cast a warm glow over the pale yellow walls. Kate was still waiting for her sex drive to ramp back up to its pre-pregnancy levels and in the meantime had been engaging in mercy sex for Brad's sake. Tonight, however, they both finished perfectly satisfied.

Afterward, Kate was about to fall into a deep sleep, but Brad flicked on his reading light and reached into his nightstand drawer to pull out what looked like a magazine. "I have to read a little bit," he whispered to Kate. "I'm not quite sleepy yet."

"Okay," Kate purred, barely able to keep her eyes open. "What are you reading?" she managed to ask, snuggling deeper into the cream-colored four-hundred-thread-count cotton sheets. Brad didn't answer.

Kate pulled herself up and peeked at his magazine and couldn't believe what she saw. "Brad Carter, is that a comic book?" she asked.

"Yeah." He chuckled, still reading his comic.

"Why?" Kate queried.

"This guy at work was telling me about this new series, and it sounded really good, so I picked up a copy," Brad said.

"Is it one of those real-life memoir comics I've been hearing about? I think I heard one of the authors on NPR the other day."

"No," Brad said, grinning sheepishly. "It takes place in outer space on some made-up planet, and there's, like, this evil plan by mutant aliens to attack the earth."

"Are you serious?" Kate asked, more awake.

"Yeah," Brad said. "Why?"

"Because you are a grown man, and that sounds like something for a child."

"Kate," Brad explained to his wife patiently, "there is such a thing as doing things for sheer pleasure. I like reading comic books. Everything doesn't have to be for a higher purpose."

Kate pouted. "I know. It just seems like if you have some extra time to read, you might want to read something more, more . . ." She reached for the right word.

"What?" Brad challenged.

"Just something more appropriate for your age group. That's all," Kate said.

"You know they say that thirty-year-old men really have the minds of sixteen-year-olds, so at thirty-three, I'd say I'm right on target." Brad laughed.

"Whatever." Kate shrugged. "If your brain starts shrinking, don't come crying to me."

"I promise I won't," Brad said. "Now go to sleep before I attack that beautiful body of yours again. My sixteen-year-old-boy brain is horny again!"

Kate rolled her eyes, rolled over, and fell asleep.

CHAPTER 9

Zora

Something was missing. On her way to work, Zora stopped by the flower shop on Fulton Avenue to buy a plant for the living room. She chose a mature African violet because the blooming purple flower caught her eye. Even though the Carters' house was decorated nicely in soft, neutral shades, it didn't feel homey, Zora thought. Kate's decorating lacked inspiration. You couldn't find fault in it, but each day when Zora walked through the front door, she couldn't shake the feeling that she was walking into a catalog photograph. "Sterile" wasn't the word she would use to describe it; it would be more like vanilla pudding—sweet but lacking flavor. Thus the plants. Zora decided she'd better bring in only one at a time, so as not to overwhelm Kate's well-ordered sensibilities. She considered buying a plant for her own tiny apartment, but the space was so small and cramped, and she spent so little time in it, that she quashed that idea.

Because of her pit stop at the flower shop, Zora got to work two minutes late. Brad rushed past her out the door, mumbling his good-byes. It was only two minutes, but he acted like he'd been waiting for hours. He always seemed to be in a hurry in the morning and never said much more than hello. Luckily, Kate still left Zora little notes. After two months working for the Carters, Zora could honestly say she'd never had more than a casual conversation with either Kate or Brad, yet she knew many things about them. She knew that Brad Carter needed prescription-strength shampoo to control his dandruff, and that he preferred all-natural deodorant to regular antiperspirant. She knew that Kate used French body powder and that she kept her dirty underwear in a laundry bag under the bed. The two of them had separate bank accounts and a shared subscription to *The New Yorker* magazine. Zora had no use for this information, yet the intimate details of their lives lodged themselves in her consciousness just the same. Zora had realized early on in her nanny career that there was a false sense of intimacy that came with the job. It was worse when you actually lived with the people, like she had in France, but even working in someone else's home every single day meant you had access to their inner lives.

After slipping out of her sneakers, Zora headed straight upstairs to check on Oliver. She knew he'd be asleep for another hour, but she checked all the same. He slept later into the mornings these days, since Kate wanted him to stay up until she got home from work. And there he was, flat on his back, thumb in his mouth, toes pointing out in opposite directions. At nine months, Oliver was still almost entirely bald, which gave him a nebulous baby face. Studying him in his crib, Zora couldn't tell whom he really favored. He had his father's generous lips, but he seemed to get his long slim fingers and pale, milky complexion from Kate. Brad Carter was White, too, but his skin was enhanced with a golden undertone, as if he might have some Italian or Greek ancestors in his genetic makeup. That might also explain his thick and wavy dark brown hair, which he wore much longer than most people who made their living on Wall Street.

Assured that the baby was okay, Zora headed back downstairs. Kate always maintained that she didn't have to do any housework, but Zora usually tidied up a bit anyway. Sometimes, if Oliver's laundry was piling up, she'd do a load of wash. She didn't mind, and she couldn't possibly sit and watch television or read all day long. She'd go crazy. After a while she felt responsible for the house, like she felt responsible for Oliver. It was her work space, after all, and she wanted to keep it clean and organized. If she were working in an office, she wouldn't think twice about keeping her desk clear of clutter, so this was no different, she reasoned. And likewise, she might buy a plant or flowers to beautify her environment, and that was why she'd brought the plant in today.

Before she attacked the dishes in the sink, Zora popped her favorite Les Nubians CD in the stereo and slipped on one of Kate's aprons. If her mother could see her now. Zora tried to stop her mind from going there, but she couldn't. Bare feet. Washing White people's dishes. Waiting for the baby to wake up so she could change his dirty diaper. Her mother would die ten deaths. Zora inhaled sharply, just imagining her mother's outrage. She had always wanted her daughter to be a Special Somebody. A Somebody with an important title or at least a couple of extra initials at the end of her name. Her mother believed that with a college education, all problems would be solved, but Zora knew that even with a degree, she'd still be in the same place. Two more semesters in a classroom, discussing the adolescent rites of passage of the !Kung, were not going to transform her into some kind of ambitious overachiever. Not even close.

As she placed the dishes in the washer, a cloudburst of anxiety exploded in her mind. In response, Zora promised herself that she'd pick up the newspaper on the way home and look for another job. Maybe she'd call her brother to see if he had any friends who might need an assistant. Zora had been a professor's assistant back at U of M. She'd typed for him, entered his students' grades in the computer, and sometimes booked his travel arrangements. There were so many busy people in New York, surely there was somebody in need of a gal Friday. The only problem was that the money she was making at the Carters' was really good. Probably better than anything she'd make running errands or waitressing. And the opportunity to cook for Brad and Kate, using their first-rate appliances and their money to buy quality ingredients, was such a bonus. It was the perfect training ground for her future as a personal chef, and that's what she really wanted to do. She was sure of that now. So it made sense for her to stay exactly where she was until her dream job presented itself. She doubted her parents would see it that way. They'd say she was avoiding reality. They'd probably pooh-pooh the personal-chef idea and consider it another unrealistic fantasy. There was no way they'd condone her current position as a glorified babysitter, no matter how good the pay was, so she was stuck lying to her family with no end date in sight.

Before she could figure out how to rectify her situation, Oliver announced that he was awake with a squawk that she knew would turn into screams if she didn't get him out of his crib fast. She dried her hands on the dish towel and ran upstairs, calling, "Oliver, Z's here. I'm coming."

At four o'clock, Kate called home. "Zora, I'm going to have to work a little late again, and I'm wondering if you could stay until I get home, around seven. And Brad says he can't get home until around seven either."

Zora didn't answer right away because she was trying to figure out if she should be annoyed by Kate's and Brad's increasingly regular need to stay late at the office. She'd never signed up for eleven-hour workdays.

Kate quickly added, "Of course we'll pay you for the extra time."

"Okay," Zora answered, trying to calculate how much money she would make. "Would you like me to make dinner for you guys again?" At least she could get some cooking practice out of this.

"You don't have to," Kate said rather unconvincingly.

"I don't mind," Zora answered.

"In that case," Kate said, "please do."

"Okay, then," Zora responded, about to disconnect, but Kate had one more thing to say.

"Honestly, Zora, I don't know how I got so lucky finding you."

Zora hung up the phone and looked at Oliver. He looked back at her. "Well, kid, I'm staying late again tonight. What do you want to do?"

Oliver responded by throwing his ring of plastic keys in her general direction.

Zora laughed. "How about you help me make dinner?"

Oliver made a gurgling noise.

"Good, I'm glad you agree," Zora said. "I've got a great recipe percolating in my brain."

When Zora got to the Carters' house the next morning, Kate was there instead of Brad. She was waiting on the couch.

"Oh, hi, Kate," Zora said when she saw her boss.

"Hello, Zora," Kate said. "Can you come sit down here with me for a minute?"

Zora kicked off her shoes, hung up her coat, and hurried into the living room. "What's up?" she asked.

"Well," Kate began, "Brad and I have been dreaming of going away for the weekend. Literally, the whole day Saturday and back early Sunday afternoon. We haven't taken a vacation since the baby was born. And we were wondering if you'd be interested in staying with Oliver for the weekend."

Zora considered the proposition. Kate took her silence as doubt and rushed to fill the empty air. "We'll work out a suitable payment for you, and we won't be really far, so if anything happens, we could be back in a heartbeat, but if you feel uncomfortable or anything—"

"Sure I could do it," Zora said. And why couldn't she? It wouldn't be that bad. "Did you mean this weekend?"

"Oh, no." Kate laughed. "We haven't planned it out or anything; we wanted to ask you first, before we got ourselves all excited. We're probably looking at the last week of November. Hopefully, the weather will hold out."

That was three weeks away. "That sounds fine," Zora answered.

"Great," Kate said, rising from the couch and glancing at her watch. "We can talk about the details later. I have to get going." In a flurry of movement, she collected her things, pointed out the day's instructions on the table, and was out the door. "By the way, thanks for dinner last night. It was great, as usual," she called from the front steps.

"You're welcome," Zora said, and closed the door behind her.

"So, Oliver, your parents like my cooking," Zora said to the drooling baby as they walked toward the park later that morning. "I might make them something else today if I get the urge to." Oliver squealed, which Zora took to mean he thought it was a good idea. Even though he got ridiculously dirty, Zora had started taking Ollie to the playground. She'd decided it wasn't fair to keep the baby from enjoying himself just because she didn't dig the social scene. Ollie liked to pull himself up on the baby jungle gym and crawl through the colorful plastic tunnels. He seemed to love it so much, and he always took a great nap afterward. Luckily, the weather had been mild. Even though it was November, the sidewalks and parks were still crowded with children and their caregivers.

Zora parked the stroller near the entrance of the playground and hauled Ollie out. She bypassed the multicolored jungle gym, which was being overrun by a nursery school group, and took Oliver directly to the swings.

"Ready, Ollie?" she asked as she secured the chain-link seat belt. She stood behind the swing and gave him push after push and zoned out to the sound of his delighted squeals.

"How old is he?"

Zora turned her head toward the speaker. It was another Black woman, pushing a little white baby in the neighboring swing. The baby looked to be about Ollie's age, but Zora couldn't tell if it was a boy or a girl under the yellow wool hat. The woman, like Zora, could have been twenty-five or thirty-five.

"He's almost ten months," Zora said. So as not to seem rude, she inquired about the age of the other woman's baby.

"She's a year old," the woman said. "Aren't you, sweets?" The baby girl smiled and kicked her chubby legs in the swing.

"My name's Angel," the woman said with an accent that sounded both familiar and foreign to Zora.

"Zora," Zora said, taking note of Angel's wild, unruly Afro, fuzzy purple coat, and black suede knee-high boots. Standing almost a full head taller than Zora, Angel didn't look like any other nanny she'd seen.

"And this is Skye," Angel said.

Zora introduced Oliver.

"When's his birthday?" Angel wanted to know.

"January twenty-ninth," Zora said.

"Perfect," Angel declared. "We could get them together to play sometimes. Do you guys come to the park a lot?"

"Pretty much, but we don't always come to the playground. We like to sit in the grass by the trees," Zora offered. "Sometimes we feed the ducks."

"Let's exchange numbers and make a date sometime. These guys need social stimulation, and to be honest, I'd like some distraction myself. Love my little Skye, but a girl goes batty talking to an infant all day. You know what I mean?"

Zora smiled knowingly. "How long have you been watching her?"

"Just a couple months," Angel said. "I kind of fell into the job."

"Really? How?"

Angel stopped pushing Skye to give her full attention to Zora. "I'd been living in Italy for the past few years, but I ran out of money and had to come home. I picked up this job because Skye's parents were desperate to find someone when their other nanny got deported or something. A friend of mine told me about the job."

"What were you doing in Italy?"

"Painting," Angel stated with pride. "I'm a painter, but I couldn't afford to eat, pay my rent, and buy canvases after a while. It's so expensive over there, but at least they know how to treat creative people with respect. It's not like here, where you have to work yourself to the bone, locked up in an anonymous office building, to prove you mean something." Angel stopped talking and seemed to fall back into a memory. After a moment she shook herself out of the reverie and laughed. "I can't wait to get back. I miss Italy. As soon as I have my little cash reserves built back up, it's *arrivederci, ragazza.* Angel is out."

"I love Italy," Zora said wistfully.

"You've been?"

"Yeah, when I was an au pair in Paris, the family I worked for had a house near Naples. We'd go in the summers. It was gorgeous."

"So you're one of those professional-nanny types?" Angel asked.

"No, no, no," Zora said. "It's just something I can do, and it lets me travel and stuff."

Before Angel could ask any more questions, Oliver decided he'd had enough swinging and started to whimper.

"Duty calls," Zora apologized as she turned her attention back to the baby and started pulling him out of the swing.

"Hey, take this," Angel said, thrusting an apple-green business card into Zora's hand. "Call me sometime if you want to meet somewhere."

"Thanks," Zora said as she balanced Ollie on her hip so she could tuck Angel's card in her pocket. "I think I need a new friend." Motioning to the whimpering Ollie as an excuse, Zora placed him in his stroller and headed for the exit to the playground. "It was nice meeting you," she called over her shoulder.

"Ciao, chérie," Angel yelled back.

CHAPTER 10

Kate

KATE sat in her office on Friday afternoon and worried. She worried that going away with her husband for even a weekend might jeopardize her position at work. These last few weeks she'd been coming in on Saturdays, researching the latest teen-pregnancy statistics from the CDC to add to her report for the advisory board of KasperKline. It wasn't required, but she wanted to include this extra data to make them realize how much added value they were getting from the agency. Plus, she wanted Roger White to appreciate how important she was to the team. She'd prove herself irreplaceable, so Danyel Green could crawl back to Los Angeles with her tail between her long, skinny legs.

Brad didn't mind watching Oliver on Saturdays, but he was adamant that they go away this weekend. Still, Kate sat there in her office, nibbling on her fingernails, trying to decide if they should cancel the trip to Cold Spring. She just felt so vulnerable. And she knew all it would take was one minor slipup. She pulled a yellow legal pad out of her desk drawer and made two columns and labeled them STAY and GO. Before she could start listing the pros and cons of the mini vacation, the phone rang. It was an interoffice call. "This is Kate," she answered.

"Kate, it's Marjorie. Mr. White would like to know if you can come up to his office."

"Now?" Kate asked, trying to remain calm. Maybe her list wasn't necessary.

"Yes, dear," Marjorie answered.

Kate glanced at the clock on her desk. It was four. "I'll be right up."

"Thank you, dear. I'll tell Mr. White," Marjorie said, and the line went dead.

Kate pulled open her desk drawer, grabbed her barely-there lip gloss, and applied a fresh coat. She slipped on her suit jacket and dragged her fingers through her hair. If she was getting fired, she was going to look good. As a final thought, Kate popped a breath mint in her mouth and headed to the hallway.

Riding in the elevator, Kate frantically replayed the last few weeks in her mind, searching for a reason why she was being summoned. Nothing but hard work, late nights, and 100 percent commitment jumped out at her. Then again, she hadn't exactly been welcoming to Danyel and could be fairly accused of not playing nice. But her infractions with Danyel were limited mostly to criticizing her taste in footwear with Laurie and not doing anything to include her in the lunchtime gossip sessions that often took place at the Chinese restaurant around the corner. Could that be it? she wondered. Would she be reprimanded for not being a team player?

"Mr. White is waiting for you," Marjorie informed Kate as she approached Roger White's office. "Go right on in," she said with her signature poker face. Rumor around the office was that Marjorie had worked for the CIA before she landed her current post as Roger White's right hand.

Kate had been in the managing director's office only once before: the day she was hired. Fitting that her last day would be finalized in there as well.

"Come in, Kate," a voice boomed as she poked her head into her supervisor's massive corner office.

Kate walked in and tried to appear calm, cool, and collected, even if it was a lie.

"Have a seat," he said, pointing to the coffee-brown leather sofa in front of his desk.

Kate sat down, crossing her legs in front of her, and attempted to decipher Roger White's body language as he stood behind his desk with his arms folded. Did he seem like he was in a firing mood? In his dark gray pants, cream-colored turtleneck sweater, and impeccably tailored black wool blazer, he exuded power and confidence. His smile seemed plastered on, though, and didn't reach his eyes. He was impossible to read.

"So, how does it feel to be back after the maternity leave?" he asked her.

"Great," Kate said. "Really great. It took a minute to get back into the swing of things, but I'm back up to speed now, and everything is going well in preparation for the presentation to KasperKline next week. I think they're going to like the new sponsorship program we've developed for them." Did she just say too much?

Roger White flashed a knowing smile, showing off a mouthful of brilliantly capped white teeth. Everyone in the office knew the man worked hard to retard the hands of time. He was pushing sixty but could pass for forty on a good day. "How's the baby? What is she, six months old?"

"Ten. *He's* ten months old," Kate corrected. If he was asking about the baby, things must be bad. Maybe he'd seen her rushing to the bathroom with her breast pump one too many times. He was probably going to tell her that she should be happy she was getting fired so she could spend more time with her precious child. Kate bet that Roger White had never changed a poopy diaper, stayed up all night with a baby who had gas, or worn cold cabbage leaves on his sore, cracked nipples. So she wasn't interested in his family advice. Rumor around the office was that he slept in his Manhattan apartment Monday through Thursday and went home to see his scandalously young trophy wife and their three kids in Connecticut only on the weekends.

"Do you have a good nanny, or is the hubby one of those Mr. Mom types?" Roger asked.

"I have a wonderful woman who takes care of my son," Kate answered with mild trepidation. "But if you don't mind me asking, sir, what is this all about?"

"Well, Kate," Roger White said, leaning against the corner of his desk, "I need you to do something for me, and quite frankly, it's going to take up a lot of your time. I need to make sure that it's something you'd be willing to do and that you have the time to dedicate to the project."

Kate was intrigued and sat forward on the couch. "What is it?"

"You know KP Martin has been handling the big Actors and Artists AIDS gala for the past three years."

"Yes."

"It appears that the executive committee had some issues with Martin's choice of venue last year, and they won't be working together anymore. Can you guess who will be handling the next AAA gala, Kate?"

"Us?" Kate said with a hint of a smile.

"You betcha. And do you know who I want to put in charge of the whole shebang?"

"Me, sir?" Kate answered, holding her breath for the confirmation.

"Absolutely," he answered. "You're the perfect person for the job. You know all of the major players in the health-care community, I trust you'll keep the client happy, and you'll put on a fantastic event."

Kate basked in this praise while he continued to speak.

"It's too bad we won't be bringing in any money from all of this, but we need the work for our corporate philanthropy quota, and we need the exposure in the AIDS drug community. I see it as a win-win situation."

"I'm honored, sir, that you're giving me this opportunity," Kate gushed.

"In a few months you may hate my guts for dropping this in your lap." Roger White laughed. Then he added one more piece of information. "If you feel overwhelmed with any KasperKline work, don't feel bad passing some assignments over to Danyel Green. I've already informed her of the situation and asked her to make some room on her plate."

Kate smiled and made a mental note to dump a tedious load of drug analysis on Danyel's desk for review as soon as possible. "Thank you, sir," she said. Roger White moved toward Kate and offered his hand.

"Congratulations," he said. "I think good things are going to come of this."

"Do you understand what a big deal this is?" Kate was telling Brad that night as they got ready for their trip. "Not only is this one of the city's biggest charity events, but I'm in charge of booking the talent and securing all the free swag for the goody bags. And it's all for a really good cause. This party nets, like, half a million dollars for AIDS research every year."

Brad laughed at his wife, his green eyes sparkling with amusement. "I want to see if you're still this excited three months into it, when the shit's hitting the fan and the tablecloths aren't ready and you still don't have anybody to sing the 'We Are the World' party song to guests who paid a small fortune to come to the shindig."

Kate got serious for a moment. She stopped putting clothes in her suitcase and sat down on the bed next to her husband, who was putting film in his new camera. Brad was the official family photographer. "I know this is going to be a lot of extra work for me, but the gala happens in early June, so it will be over before we know it."

Brad looked up from his camera. "I'm not worried. I just don't want to see you overworked and crazy."

"I can handle it." Kate smiled confidently. "Besides, don't you see that this proves that I'm not on probation anymore?"

"Who said you were on probation?" Brad asked as he shoved his camera equipment in his duffel bag.

"You know what I mean." Kate shrugged. "I felt like the higher-ups at Zimbalist were watching and waiting to see if I was really back for good. So I obviously passed the test."

"If you say so," Brad said.

"Honey, please be happy for me," Kate pleaded, planting herself in front of her husband. "I really am excited to do this."

"That's pretty obvious." Brad chuckled, putting aside his packing for the moment. "I am happy for you. And proud, too. See, I told you you were a rock star." To prove his point, he planted a celebratory kiss on Kate's cheek.

Kate beamed. "Thank you."

"You're welcome," Brad offered, but his attention was back on his duffel bag. Kate turned back to her suitcase, too. She needed to focus on deciding which pajamas to take: the sexy tiger-print negligee from her honeymoon or the two-piece very unsexy flannels, in case it was cold up along the Hudson River. She laid both options on the bed and did a quick eenie-meenie in her head. The flannels won.

"By the way," Kate called out to Brad, who was now in the bathroom, "I'll probably ask Zora to stay a little later, till like seven or seven-thirty, for these next few months, so I don't have to panic if I'm running late. And if you have stuff to do after work, you can still take care of it."

"Fine by me," Brad said.

Kate stood in the doorway of the bathroom. It wasn't a very spacious bathroom—there wasn't enough room for a bathtub, only a shower—but Kate loved not having to share her most private space with other people. It was the reason she had fallen in love with the house: the allure of a master bathroom. "Do you think it's okay if I ask Zora to make dinner a couple of nights, too?" Kate asked. "I mean, she's been kind of doing it these last few weeks anyway, and it helps so much, especially if I'm going to be getting home so late."

"I can make dinner, Kate," Brad said, still rummaging around in the bathroom. "By the way, have you seen my travel razor?"

Kate grimaced. "It's behind the toilet paper in the closet. And no, thank you. Dinner for you is a grilled ham-and-cheese sandwich and chips."

"Nothing wrong with that. When I lived in England, we ate like that all the time for supper."

"Let's just say I prefer Zora's cooking," Kate said. "She's a really good cook, don't you think?"

"Yeah," Brad said without a lot of enthusiasm, emerging from the closet and padding back into the bedroom.

"Hey, you've been gobbling up her dinners like nobody's business," Kate said, following.

"I said I liked her food," Brad admitted. "It's just that we told her she wouldn't be expected to cook and clean and all that, and that's exactly what she's doing now. I've noticed you have her washing Ollie's clothes, too."

"I didn't ask her to do that," Kate hedged. "She just started doing it, and I'm certainly not going to tell her to stop, because quite frankly, it's nice not to have to do all that laundry."

Brad held up his hands. "Hey, I'm not saying you should tell her to stop. I just hope she doesn't feel like we're taking advantage of her."

Kate shook her head. "Look, I know this whole 'Black woman working for the yuppie White couple' doesn't sit well with you, but you of all people, Mr. Business and Finance, should understand that not every person on this earth is destined to be a white-collar worker." Brad didn't say anything, so Kate continued, " 'Class' isn't a dirty word, you know. And there's nothing wrong with hiring help."

Brad turned to face Kate with a smirk and an exaggerated sigh. "You're right, your highness. I guess some of us are more used to having servants in the house than others."

"Don't even go there," Kate said, shaking her finger at Brad, but she wasn't angry. This was their favorite "fight": to determine who'd had the more comfortable upbringing in suburban Philadelphia.

The two of them had grown up only about ten miles apart but had never met in childhood. They had to wait until they both lived in New York City to lay eyes on each other in a karaoke bar in the West Village. As a child living in famously integrated, solidly middle-class Mount Airy, Brad had grown up believing everybody could get along. His dad was a high school history teacher and his mother a nurse. Two train stops and a long bus ride away, Kate had grown up surrounded by wealth and ex-cess in the Beverly Hills of Philadelphia, otherwise known as the Main Line. The Main Line housed the city's social elite in taste-ful stone mansions surrounded by immaculate gardens and iron gates that kept undesirables out. Kate's family couldn't be officially categorized as rich, but they were definitely comfortable in their upper-middle-class status. Her father was a partner at one of the city's oldest law firms, and her mother had started working at the foundation when her children were grown. Kate and her sister, Liz, had attended the well-appointed suburban public schools and vacationed in the Caribbean, and each had been given her own car when she turned sixteen. And yes, they had a maid, Carmelita, who was Puerto Rican, not Black.

Brad, on the other hand, had attended public school until his parents decided to pool their resources and send their only son to one of the city's elite private Quaker high schools. So he, too, had been surrounded by privilege, but it was tempered by the reality of the inner-city neighborhood where the school was situated. So maybe Brad had had more experience with urban America, but he, too, had lived a life of privilege, as far as Kate was concerned. Plus, his parents had doted on him. Given him everything he wanted. So he'd had a car at sixteen, too, played tennis at the Germantown cricket club, and backpacked through Europe as a college graduation present. The way Kate saw it, she and Brad were cut from the same cloth. He just didn't want to admit it.

Brad laughed. "Okay, Miss Main Line, I won't argue with you on this one. By the way, how is Carmelita?"

Kate stuck her tongue out at her husband; she didn't have a good enough comeback, considering Carmelita was still gainfully employed by her parents. "You think you're so funny," she said. "Ha-ha."

Brad came over and embraced his wife in a hearty hug. "I still love you, even if you are a snob," he said. Then he changed the subject. "Is the B and B you booked one of those no-electricity, rustic types, or will there be a TV?"

Kate plopped down on the bed and rummaged through her briefcase. She pulled out the printout from the website of the inn. "No, I wanted luxury. This place calls itself a bed-and-breakfast, but it's a straight-up hotel, with room service, terry-cloth bathrobes, and a hundred and twenty-seven cable stations."

"Oooh, that sounds like just what the doctor ordered." Brad grinned. "Thank you, Dr. Kate."

"Hey, I know what we need. You just gotta trust me," Kate said, hoping her double meaning was clear.

Brad got serious. "I do trust you, Kate."

"Good," she said, and jumped up to finish packing.

CHAPTER 11

Zora

THE cold weather finally arrived, forcing Zora and Ollie to find new indoor activities to fill up their days. Usually, it was a rotation of the library, the Brooklyn Museum of Art, and the new coffee shop on Seventh Avenue that featured a lively story hour once a week, led by a well-dressed drag queen named Lola. Sometimes Zora still bundled Oliver up and took him to the park to watch the joggers and walkers who refused to let the icy cold curtail their exercise regime. That's where they'd gone this morning. Even though the temperatures hovered in the forties, the bright sunshine threw an optimistic glow over the neighborhood, and Zora and Ollie enjoyed their session of people-watching.

At lunchtime, rather than head home, Zora stopped at the cozy Mexican cantina on Seventh Avenue. She ordered her favorite spicy pork burrito with a fizzy limeade and sat at a table by the window. She gave Oliver his Tupperware container full of Cheerios and some tiny pieces of banana to munch on while she savored her feast. As far as she could tell, Oliver wasn't missing his mommy's milk at all. He seemed perfectly content eating finger food and drinking cow's milk. The weaning process had been pretty seamless for both Ollie and Kate. In fact, Kate seemed quite relieved to be done with it all, even though she hadn't quite made it to Ollie's first birthday.

Just as Zora was about to dig into her burrito, Angel, the nanny she'd met at the park, burst into the tiny restaurant pushing Skye in her stroller. As soon as she spied Zora, she called out, "Hey, Zora!" As if they were old friends. "Mind if we join you?"

Zora smiled back and waved Angel over to her table.

"How's it going?" Angel asked as she parked Skye's stroller in front of Oliver's so the two babies could stare at each other and share their cereal.

"Fine," Zora answered with a mouthful of burrito.

"Hey, can you keep an eye on Skye for a sec while I order some food?" Angel asked.

"No problem."

"Cool, be right back." Angel dashed over to the cafeteria-style counter to order. Five minutes later she came back to the table, balancing her lunch on a bright red tray.

"That was quick. What'd you get?" Zora asked as Angel placed her tray on the table and checked on Skye.

"Oh, I come here all the time and always get the same thing," Angel answered as she took off Skye's hat and scarf and loosened her pink wool jacket. "Black-bean tostadas and an orange Jarritos soda. I love the tostadas here."

"Are you a vegetarian?" Zora asked.

"Depends on which country I'm in." Angel laughed a big throaty laugh that made Zora think of bold Black women like Nina Simone and Cleopatra Jones. "I don't eat meat in the States, but in Italy, I eat pretty much anything because they take food so personally." Angel slid into the chair opposite Zora, shrugged off her coat, and started to eat. Zora was already halfway done with her burrito.

"So what's your story?" Angel asked between bites and swigs from her green soda bottle. Zora had never seen anybody handle a tostada with such finesse. Not a single bean fell off the shell.

"I don't really have a story," Zora said, maybe a little bit defensively.

"You said you weren't a full-time nanny, so what's your full-time passion? You already know my deal. Born and raised in boogie-down Bed-Stuy and trying to make enough money so I can go back to Italy and back to my real life."

Zora looked down at her food and considered telling Angel about the personal-chef thing, but since the idea existed only in her mind and she hadn't done anything to make it happen, she decided to keep her mouth closed. "I don't have a 'full-time passion.'"

"What do you mean?" Angel asked, looking genuinely concerned, as if Zora had just admitted to having an incurable disease.

"It means that right now I'm Oliver's nanny, with no immediate plans for a passionate future. That's my story." Zora tried to laugh to make it sound like she was joking, but her effort was painfully halfhearted.

"Wow," Angel marveled.

"Wow, what?" Zora challenged, pushing her plate of unfinished food aside and crossing her arms.

"*Chica*, I can just read your body language and tell that you are processing some very negative thoughts. You need to deal with them because they will transform your karma into very dark energy."

"I'll keep that in mind," Zora said as she willed Oliver to start crying so she might have an excuse to get up and leave. When people started to talk about karma and auras and good energy, Zora felt the urge to get far, far away. She didn't believe in that stuff.

"Everybody has to have a passion," Angel said, oblivious to Zora's discomfort. "Passion is what gives us meaning. You just have to find yours. That's why I went to Italy. I knew I liked to paint, but when I was there, living my art, I knew I'd found my real life. It was wild, you know?"

Zora didn't know, and she wasn't sure she ever would. She didn't want to figure it out now, either. She practiced a redirect. "So," she asked Angel, "what do you paint?"

"People," Angel said, licking salsa off her fingers. "I am fascinated by faces. Every single one of them tells a unique story, and I try to capture that story in my work." Zora nodded to show she was paying attention. "I'll show you my work sometime," Angel continued. "I'm supposed to be having a show in a little gallery here in Park Slope in the spring."

"Really? That's great," Zora said.

"Yeah," Angel said. "It's nothing big, but hey, my work is getting out there, you know."

"That doesn't sound like nothing to me," Zora said. "You should be proud of yourself. When's the show, exactly?"

"I'm not sure yet," Angel answered. "I've still got to talk to the gallery owner. We're working it all out."

"Good luck," Zora said as she checked her watch. It was one-thirty. She considered her options for the afternoon. She could rush home and hope Oliver wouldn't fall asleep on the way and then put him down for his nap. Or she could walk leisurely to the Teahouse and let him sleep in his stroller while she finished reading her novel.

Angel interrupted her thinking. "So where are you off to now?"

"I'm trying to decide," Zora answered. She told Angel her two options.

"I think you should go to the Teahouse and enjoy yourself," Angel suggested.

Zora smiled. "Yeah, me, too."

As they stood up to leave, Angel slapped her palm against her forehead. "Oh, yeah. I forgot to tell you that there's a baby sign language class starting up in Fort Greene in January. You should ask Oliver's mother if she wants to sign him up. Skye and I are going. Sign language is supposed to be really helpful for young babies so they can communicate instead of having to scream all the time. Life can be frustrating when you can't get your point across, right, Skye?"

The baby didn't answer.

"I'll mention it to Kate. It sounds like a great idea," Zora said.

"*Fantástico*," Angel declared.

After bundling themselves up first and then the children, the two women rolled their strollers out the door into the afternoon sun.

CHAPTER 12

Kate

"KATE, Brad is holding for you on line one," Laurie announced through her intercom.

Kate quickly finished her seventeenth conversation of the day with the caterer for the AAA gala and switched over to talk to her husband. "Hey, hon," she said. "To what do I owe this pleasure?" She glanced at her watch and noted that Brad should be getting ready to leave his office.

"Hi, Kate," Brad said. "I was just wondering if the world's most attractive and important drug dealer would like to meet her husband for dinner."

Kate smiled. "That sounds mighty nice, but are you sure you want to be seen with a drug dealer as important and well known as I? It might tarnish your reputation as an all-around good guy."

"I'm willing to take that risk," Brad teased.

"That settles it, then," Kate said. "I guess you've got yourself a date." She did a quick mental survey of the work she had to finish and tried to calculate when she would be done.

"What do you think about trying that new tapas restaurant in Tribeca?" Brad suggested.

"Mmm, sounds delish," Kate answered. "Laurie said it was really good, and you know she goes to every new restaurant before the paint is even dry. But can you call Zora and see if she can stay late?"

"Don't you want to call her?" Brad asked in a tone that came dangerously close to a whine.

"Nooo," Kate said. "What I want is for you to call her, since you're done with work and I still have about two hours ahead of me. Don't you think that makes a teeny bit more sense?"

Brad grunted what could be taken as an assent, or maybe it was just a grunt.

"Thank you," Kate said, pretending she didn't understand his lack of desire to deal with Zora. Brad seemed to think if he pretty much ignored her, he wouldn't have to deal with his misplaced White man's guilt. Kate understood his issues, in theory, but in practice, his reluctance to accept the reality was getting on her nerves. It wasn't like she had gone out looking for a Black baby-sitter.

"You know, if Zora were Irish or one of those Filipina nannies that everybody raves about on the Upper West Side, would you be such a butt about this?" Kate challenged.

"Um, did I say something to deserve that?" Brad responded.

"Forget it." Kate groaned. "I don't have time to get into this with you right now. Could you please just call home and get over your guilt already? We're really lucky to have Zora, and you should appreciate that."

"You know I hate it when you say that—'We're so lucky to have her.' As if Zora is our property or something," Brad seethed.

Kate dragged her fingers through her hair and stifled a groan. "Can we not have this conversation right now? I promise we can talk about it over dinner, but there will be no dinner if I can't finish up here first."

There was silence on the other end of the line.

Kate tried to explain herself. "Look, I am not going to apologize, because I do feel lucky to have Zora in our lives. Not only because she's wonderful help but also because she's a wonderful person. I like her."

"I'm glad you and Zora are such great friends," Brad said.

"I didn't say we were friends," Kate answered quickly, "but it's not like we're not, either. I mean, we could be friends."

"Whatever, Kate."

Kate did not want to fight. She wanted to finish working, leave the building, and go drink sangria. Using her calmest tone, she tried again. "Will you please just call?"

"I said I'd call," Brad snapped. "And I will. I'll ask Zora if she can stay late, till like ten. If she can't, I'll ring you back. If you don't hear from me, meet me at the restaurant at six-thirty."

"Sounds like a plan," Kate said, hoping that Zora wasn't always going to be an issue between them.

"Fine," Brad said, and then he drew in a deep breath, which Kate knew meant he was gearing up to say "I'm sorry." She smiled as she waited to hear how he would word his apology.

"Kate," Brad started.

"Yes, Brad?"

"I still think you're the hottest drug dealer in town."

Kate laughed. "I love you, too, honey."

Kate put the conversation with Brad out of her mind immediately and set herself to finishing the pile of work on her to-do list. She still had to set up a meeting with the AAA Foundation and choose the entertainment for the gala. Right now it was between a pop music group or an upstart street magician who was making a name for himself by performing elaborate acts of escape in public spaces in New York and Los Angeles. She had to whittle down more than a hundred products to twenty-five to include in the goody bags, and the eighty-page report for KasperKline needed to be fact-checked.

Kate looked at her clock again. If she was going to meet Brad in two and a half hours, something had to give. She thought about it for a second before she got up, grabbed a copy of the report, and headed out of her office. "Can you cover my phone?" she asked

Laurie as she passed by her desk. She walked to the other end of
the health-care wing, to Danyel Green's office. She knocked, even
though the door was wide open.

"Kate, come in," Danyel said.

Kate reminded herself that this was for her own good and
forced herself to smile. "Are you super-busy?" she asked.

"No, not so much. I have all of my work under control," Danyel
said. To Kate, it sounded like Danyel was bragging, so it gave her
a lot of pleasure to pose the next question.

"Great. Do you think you could handle the fact-checking on
the KasperKline report? Roger told me I should come to you if
I needed any help, and this is a doozy. There's no way I can get it
done and finish up with the gala stuff tonight."

Danyel's eyes flashed anger, but she quickly recovered with an
arrogant grin. "It's no problem," she purred. "I told Roger that if
you seemed in over your head, he could count on me to handle
things. So sure, why don't you hand over the report, and I'll take
care of it. Don't worry about a thing."

Kate had to remind herself that asking for Danyel's help was
necessary if she wanted to enjoy a nice evening out with her
husband. She was sorely tempted to snatch the report right back
and tell Danyel to stick it somewhere not very pretty. Instead, she
focused on her goal.

"Thank you, Danyel, I appreciate it," Kate said, making her
voice as sweet as possible. She turned to go, but Danyel stopped
her with a question.

"Do you want me to tell Roger that you're overwhelmed? I'd be
more than happy to help you out with the AAA gala, too."

Kate forced a smile and threw Danyel's words back to her.
"Oh, that's okay. I have all my work for the gala under control. But
thanks for the offer."

"Don't hesitate to ask," Danyel yelled as Kate practically
skipped out of her office.

Back at her desk, Kate took a moment to reflect on what had just happened. Should she be worried that Danyel would go running to Roger with stories of her incompetence? "Stop it, Kate," she chided herself aloud. Roger White trusted her and liked her. And it was his idea to ask Danyel for help anyway. If she was good about delegating her work, she would get through this. It might even lead to a promotion. Just the thought brought a smile to Kate's lips. Considering everything that was going on at work, it really was a miracle that she still managed to squeeze in a dinner date with her husband and find time to enjoy her son. She didn't care what Brad said. Kate knew full well that if Zora weren't in the picture, none of this would be possible. So yes, she'd sing it from the mountaintops: They were lucky to have Zora in their lives!

Later, at Café Mayte, over tiny plates of grilled baby octopus and sweet figs wrapped in crispy cured ham, Kate recounted how she had dumped the KasperKline report on Danyel's desk.

"You should have seen her face," she practically sang with glee. "I wish I could have taken a picture."

Brad chuckled at his wife. "I'm glad you've learned the fine art of delegating."

"I have," Kate said with a wicked gleam in her eye. "And I think I'll get even better at it. There's a five-hundred-page clinical-trials report that needs to be turned into a one-page press release that I think I will 'delegate' to Danyel next week."

"Wow, I didn't know your vindictive streak ran that deep," Brad joked.

"Hey, you don't want to cross Kate Carter," Kate said, contorting her face into her best gangster mug.

"I guess not," Brad said, eyes widening in mock horror. "Should I be afraid of you, Ms. Carter?"

Kate reached across the table to caress her husband's cheek, still smooth from his morning shave. "You never have to be afraid of me," she promised. "I'll never use my evil powers against you."

"Thank God." Brad sighed, exaggerating his relief. "You know, you've had me fooled all these years, me thinking you were such a nice girl."

"I am nice," Kate clarified. "Just don't get on my bad side, because I will attack."

"Man, I feel sorry for Danyel Green," Brad said, shaking his head. "She probably has no idea who she's messing with."

Kate and Brad finished their meal, washing everything down with Mayte's sweet pomegranate sangria. The restaurant's romantic Spanish decor and haunting flamenco sound track invaded their senses, so when it was time to head home, they decided to walk to the subway instead of taking a taxi. Even though it was early December, it wasn't too cold to be outside. Neither Kate nor Brad wanted the evening to end. Stepping into the brisk night air, onto New York's pulsating streets, Kate and Brad both wanted to grab hold of the energy.

"I love you, Brad Carter," Kate burst out as she walked hand in hand with her husband. On nights like this, she was reminded just how handsome she found Brad. With his chiseled cheekbones and strong jawline, he resembled a Greek god. At the office, Laurie referred to him as Mr. Hottie. And Kate didn't mind. He *was* hot.

"I love you, too, Kate Carter," Brad responded, squeezing her hand for emphasis.

Kate snuggled closer to her husband, winding her arms around his waist. They walked like that for a while, until Kate had a thought. "Sometimes it seems unreal that you and I have a child waiting for us at home," she murmured.

"I know," Brad confessed. "Sometimes I feel like we're still twenty-five, running around this city without a care in the world."

"Exactly," Kate said. "I don't feel like I'm old enough to be an adult or a mother, or a homeowner or a wife."

"Me, neither." Brad nodded in agreement. And then there was nothing to say as they both contemplated the passing of time.

"Are we old?" Kate asked forlornly.

"No, we're not old," Brad soothed. "But New York can wear you out, because there's always a new crop of kids, with all of their twentysomething rah-rah energy pushing in. It's impossible to keep up with all of that."

"But I'm not done with New York; I'm still full of energy. I *can* keep up," Kate declared defiantly. "I'm still happy here." It wasn't a question, but she was waiting for Brad to confirm that he felt the same way. When they first started dating, he stubbornly maintained that New York was only a pit stop for him. He was there to make a lot of money so he could pay off his business school loans and still have enough left over to create some type of international nonprofit organization. His plans were grand but still unformed. He just knew that he was supposed to make a difference in the world. Kate supported Brad's enthusiasm to be the good guy, but he needed a reality check every once in a while. And that's what she was there for, to help keep his feet firmly planted on the ground. He in turn helped Kate let loose every once in a while. They made a good team, Kate thought.

Just then a sharp wind blew up around them. Brad hugged his wife close to protect her from the fierce breath of winter. He whispered in her ear, "I'm still happy, too."

CHAPTER 13

Zora

ZORA hadn't understood at first what Kate wanted. The party was the following Saturday, so she thought Kate wanted her to babysit for Oliver. "No, I want you at the party," Kate had said. So then Zora thought Kate wanted her to cook for the party, which she wouldn't have minded doing. And it would have made sense. Zora now made dinner for Kate and Brad three times a week. She'd propose a menu for the week, and Kate would leave her extra money for grocery shopping on Monday mornings. Zora loved doing it. She didn't shy away from complicated recipes, either. Just from reading and watching untold hours of reality television, she knew that famous people were picky and wouldn't think twice about asking for a lemon soufflé for breakfast and linguine with fresh-shucked clams for lunch. So she wanted to be ready.

But Kate hadn't wanted her to cook for the party, either. "Look, it's not really a big thing," Kate had explained. "I'm just having some friends and family over to celebrate the holidays, and I'd like you to come." Zora knew Kate's younger sister, Liz, was coming for Christmas and staying for a week. Liz lived in Detroit, and Kate had asked Zora if she was familiar with her neighborhood. Zora had never heard of it, but that didn't mean much, because she'd spent as little time as possible exploring Detroit: The city depressed her. In a moment of candor, Kate admitted she was a little nervous about spending an entire week with her sister. "We're just polar opposites and always have been," Kate explained. "Honestly, I don't know what we'll talk about the whole time she's here." But Kate's twisted family dynamics didn't explain why she wanted Zora at the party, unless it was to bond with her sister over their shared Michigan connection.

Kate had called earlier in the morning to issue the invitation. Sondra answered the phone, annoyed that the shrill ring had woken her up at eight-thirty A.M. Sondra was back in New York, waiting out her four-week break between semesters at Smith. She planned on crashing at her old place for two of those weeks, then spending the remaining time hopscotching between her relatives' homes in the Bronx.

Two hours later, having had time to think about it, Zora brought it up to Sondra as they walked to the Laundromat. Zora carried her dirty clothes in a giant purple sack over her shoulder. Sondra pushed her clothes in a bright red grocery cart.

"Why do you think Kate wants me at her Christmas party?" Zora asked Sondra. "Does that seem weird?"

"Are you sure she doesn't want you there to keep an eye on the baby?" Sondra asked.

"Yeah," Zora answered. "She said she wanted me to come and be part of the gathering. Those were her exact words."

"Oh, I don't know, Z," Sondra said with a dismissive wave. "She probably thinks she's doing something nice by inviting the help to the party. But you wait, you'll probably end up scraping the dishes and changing the baby anyway."

"I told her I wouldn't mind keeping an eye an Oliver, or even cooking for the party, but she kept saying that she could handle everything and that she just wanted me to come and have a good time."

"So what's the problem, then?" Sondra asked as they neared the entrance to the Laundromat.

"There's no problem," Zora said, flipping her bag over to the other shoulder. "I just wanted to know if you thought it was weird that she invited me."

"I don't think it's weird," Sondra said. "I think it sounds pretty typical for Perfect Mrs. Kate Carter. She wants to feel like you're her friend so she doesn't have to feel guilty for asking you to work late every damn day of the week."

Zora felt compelled to defend her employer. "I don't mind working late," she started. "The extra money is great, Oliver is asleep by seven-thirty, and I get to watch all of my favorite shows on cable." She didn't add that she didn't have much else pressing on her time. Or that she felt good being needed.

"So you'll go to the party next week. You'll eat and drink and be merry and report back to work on Monday. Life will go on."

"Why do you say it like that?" Zora asked as she surveyed the machines inside the Happy Clean Laundromat and tried to decide which ones looked the happiest and the cleanest. Just the smell—an unpleasant combination of chlorine bleach and dirty feet—made Zora shudder. Kate had offered the use of her washing machine when Zora had stayed over on the weekends, and she longed for the use of it right now. She hated washing her clothes in a public place.

Sondra apparently didn't have such reservations as she threw her clothes in the first two empty machines she came across. The funky homeless man disrobing alongside her didn't even give her pause. After she placed her coins in the washer, she walked over to Zora and answered her question. "I see you making this job your life, girl. You eat all your meals there, you don't have much of a social life, and when you're *not* there, all you're doing is thinking up what you're going to cook when you go back."

"Hey, you're the one who said I should do what I have to do to survive," Zora said, hurt that Sondra was already disappointed in her.

"I know, and you're doing it, but I also expect you to be thinking about Zora," Sondra said.

"I am. You know I think I've decided to be a personal chef.

All of these recipes I keep trying for Kate and Brad are part of my training." This was the first time she'd told anyone about her idea.

"If you say so." Sondra shrugged. "As long as you've got a plan, that's the key."

"My plan is to find a job as a personal chef here in the city," Zora said. "But so far I haven't found that opportunity, and no one is exactly banging on my door, so I'd better keep the Carters happy so I can keep paying your rent. Don't you think?" Zora knew she sounded defensive, but Sondra was making her feel like she had to prove something. That she wasn't wasting her time.

Sondra didn't say anything for a minute. She let the breath she was holding puff out of her cheeks like a balloon with a slow leak. "Girl, if it makes sense to you, it makes sense to me."

"Well, it makes sense to me," Zora said, turning back to her clothes.

Sondra put her arm out and forced Zora to stop what she was doing and look at her. "Zora, I honestly don't care what you do to earn a living, but I know you, and I know you have a tendency to stay put somewhere 'cause you get comfortable. Make sure you're not repeating the same mistakes and getting nowhere with your life. You're better than that."

"I know," Zora said, promising herself she'd think about Sondra's advice later, when she could process the information. But not here and not now. She gave Sondra a smile before saying, "Now leave me alone so I can sort my clothes."

Unlike Sondra, who was content to wash her clothes in two batches, colored and not colored, Zora separated pure whites from lights and darks. If she had her own machine, she'd create a pile of delicates, but she had neither the money nor the patience to sit in a Laundromat that apparently doubled as a public wash-room for the down-on-their-luck. Zora knew she was a snob in so many ways, but she couldn't help it. She'd always lived in comfort-able homes in the suburbs. No matter how exciting it was, there were things about New York City living that seemed wrong. Like washing your underwear in a machine that thousands of other people had used.

"Excuse me."

Zora turned to find herself looking into the eyes of a man her mother would describe as a hunk. His flawless skin was a tawny brown, and he sported thick brown dreadlocks that fell to his shoulders. He wore khaki cargo pants and a worn orange T-shirt. His deep brown eyes were flecked with shards of green, and his lips, it seemed to Zora, were far too pretty to be on a man's face. Zora guessed he was around thirty.

"Yes?" Zora said, trying hard not to fixate on those lips.

"I know this sounds silly, but do you ride the F train?" he asked.

Zora snorted. "I have in the past but don't make a habit of it. Why?"

"You look familiar, and I thought I recognized you from the train," he said with a sheepish grin.

Zora continued to feed her quarters into the washer as she answered those sexy lips. "It is possible you might have seen me on the F train at one time in history, but honestly, it has been a while."

"You just look really familiar," the guy persisted.

"Do you live around here?" Zora asked, trying to help him solve this great mystery.

"Yeah, I live on Fulton Street," he responded.

"I live around here, too, so you probably recognize my face from the neighborhood." Zora paused. "Probably not from the subway system. I'm pretty much a bus girl." She giggled in spite of herself.

The man smiled, showing a row of perfectly straight white teeth. "My name is Keith, by the way," he said, extending his hand.

"I'm Zora," she said without taking it.

"Like the author?" Keith asked.

"You guessed it," Zora responded.

"So let me ask the obvious question: Are you a writer?"

"No, actually, right now I'm a nanny," Zora said. Remembering her recent conversation with Sondra, she added, "But I'm trying to get a gig as a personal chef. That's my plan."

"Wow, that's cool. Maybe you can cook for me sometime," Keith said, dropping his voice to a seductive timbre.

Zora laughed at his audacity. She squelched an evil comeback. She didn't care how beautiful his damn lips were. "I don't cook for strangers," she said, wondering where Sondra had disappeared to. She scanned the Laundromat and didn't see her.

"Then I guess we'll have to get to know each other," he said with a gleam in his eye.

Because her clothes were in the washing machine and she couldn't be sure that Mr. Hobo Man wouldn't steal them, Zora felt she couldn't walk out of the building and away from Keith and his flirtatious come-ons, but that was exactly what she felt like doing. She wasn't so desperate that she had to go man shopping at the Laundromat.

"I don't think so," Zora replied coolly as she turned on her heel in search of a laundry cart. Keith and his sexy lips didn't follow her.

CHAPTER 14

Kate

Iᴛ was finally beginning to feel like Christmas. Even though Mother Nature refused to drop even a single flake of snow, Kate had turned her home into a winter wonderland. The eight-foot-tall Christmas tree dominated a corner in the living room, decorated with delicate Tiffany ornaments Kate had been collecting since she was a child. Three monogrammed red and white stockings hung on the mantel, and a bushy green garland wrapped its way up the banister, infusing the entire house with the deep piney smell. Kate was determined to make Oliver's first Christmas a memorable one. She wanted it to be as special as all of hers had been, growing up in Philadelphia.

Christmas had always been her favorite holiday, thanks to a mother who had made it her personal mission to ensure that both her girls felt the magic every year. That was why Kate couldn't believe her parents would take off this year, of all years, on a cruise. Wasn't her mom the one who'd refused to let Kate go skiing with her best friend, Annie Baldwin, over Christmas break in high school because she would have missed the annual Christmas Eve party? She claimed it wasn't natural to be away from home during the holidays.

"What a double standard," Kate muttered.

"Honey, are you talking to yourself?" Brad asked. He was supposed to be keeping an eye on Oliver while Kate worked on dinner for the party, but she could tell he was mostly keeping an eye on the football game.

"Yes," Kate shouted over the television. "I am talking to myself. I just can't believe my parents aren't going to be here."

"Hon," Brad said, "would you please stop torturing yourself with this? We've been over it a million times. Your parents have a right to their own life."

"That's easy for you to say." Kate snorted. "You're an only child. You *are* your parents' life. And be honest—you'd be as upset if your parents ditched you on Christmas." Of course this would never happen, because Brad's parents lived and breathed for their son. In fact, Brad's parents would probably be standing at the front door by eight on Christmas morning to make sure they got to see Ollie open his presents.

Brad put the TV on mute and walked over to the kitchen to talk to his wife face-to-face. "Kate," he started, using a voice that most people reserve for small children or dogs, "your parents are not ditching you. They are going on a well-deserved vacation, and you should be happy for them."

"Look," Kate said as she turned away from the goose she was filling with chestnut stuffing, "I'm not saying that they don't deserve a vacation. I'm just annoyed that they chose to destroy everyone else's holiday with their plans."

Brad dropped his head in his hands. "Kate, did you ever stop to think that their plans had nothing to do with us? That perhaps now that their children are grown with children of their own, it might be time to do something for themselves?"

Kate knew she was being unfair, but she couldn't help feeling abandoned. Christmas was supposed to be about family. And without her parents, she and her sister didn't feel like family. In fact, without her parents to act as buffers, she and Liz might feel like strangers.

"I just want everything to be perfect for Ollie's first Christmas," Kate said in her own defense, turning back to the goose.

"Just so you know," Brad said, "he's not going to remember this Christmas when he gets older, so you don't have to stress out so much."

"I'm not stressing out; I love doing Christmas," Kate insisted. "I just want my family all together. Is that so wrong?"

"I'm not saying there's anything wrong with wanting to have your folks all here. Just give 'em a break for wanting to do their own thing for once," Brad said, going back to the game.

Kate knew he was finished with her. She also knew she had to stop complaining about her parents or she'd run the risk of truly ruining everybody's holiday. She was going to have a fabulous party, and she was going to make an extra effort to be nice to her little sister and this boyfriend she was bringing.

By the time the first guest arrived at seven-thirty, Kate and Liz had already had one fight. Kate had simply asked her sister to get changed for the party, and Liz had been insulted because she thought Kate was saying she didn't approve of her outfit. They'd had to argue about it for the better part of fifteen minutes. It never got resolved, and Liz left her jeans and tunic top on. She did make the concession of pulling her hot-pink hair, which she knew Kate despised, into a modest but still very pink bun at the nape of her neck. When she saw Liz, Kate had to admit that she actually looked pretty, considering. Kate couldn't help thinking that everything her sister did—like dyeing her beautiful blond hair pink—was done in an effort to distinguish herself from her older, "perfect" sister. It had always been that way. And now that Liz had shown up with a Black boyfriend, Kate couldn't help but wonder if he, too, had been enlisted for shock appeal. Well, his appearance wouldn't cause that much of a stir in her home, Kate decided, since Zora was going to be here, too. Her party was already integrated.

Brad designated himself and Ollie as the official doormen for the evening. Carl and a very pregnant Sheila arrived first. Carl had been Brad's B-school roommate. They were still best friends and tended to act like unruly frat boys whenever they got together. Now that Sheila was about to give birth, Kate suspected that some of Carl's exuberance for stupid human tricks would subside. At least she hoped it would. She actually loved Carl, but there were times when she wanted to give him a spanking and send him to bed with no dinner. He was, after all, the guy who convinced Brad to fly to Barbados two days before their wedding for a bachelor party in paradise. Just thinking about it brought a sour taste to Kate's mouth.

"Hey, you guys, welcome," Kate called from the kitchen. Brad hugged his friend while Sheila struggled out of her coat and made cooing sounds at Oliver. Brad ushered the couple into the living room, where Liz and her boyfriend, Ronnie, were sitting on the couch. Kate came out of the kitchen and made the introductions and then experienced a moment of panic. She hoped Ronnie wouldn't feel out of place with her friends. She didn't know much about him and had to admit that she'd been surprised that Liz's boyfriend was Black. Not surprised like it was a bad thing. Just straight-out surprised. She thought it would have come up in conversation or something. Of course, since she and Liz barely spoke—they stayed in touch mainly through their mother—why would she have known? Maybe, Kate thought, her mother didn't know, either.

"How ya doin'?" Carl said to Ronnie with a nod.

"Hey." Ronnie nodded back at him.

"Hi," Sheila said to Liz and then looked at Kate with a puzzled expression. "I didn't know you had a sister."

"Yeah, she likes to keep me a secret," Liz quipped. Sheila laughed.

Kate shot her sister a dirty look. She hoped Liz wouldn't be a jerk tonight. She knew Liz was perfectly capable of causing a scene, but she hoped, in the name of holy Christmas, that she wouldn't.

"Do you live here in the city?" Sheila asked Liz as she lowered her cumbersome body into a chair next to the couch. Kate was impressed with Sheila's ability to still look elegant in her black silk wrap dress and patent-leather pumps despite her enormous belly. Her shiny black hair spilling over her shoulders served as the perfect accessory.

"Nope," Liz answered. "I live in Detroit."

"Really?" Sheila said, her eyes widening as if Liz had just said she flew in from Madagascar. Sheila had been born and raised in Manhattan and thought Queens was a foreign country.

"Yes, really. Believe it or not, White people actually live in Detroit."

Sheila laughed again. She sounded amused, not offended. "You know, it's true, I always think of Detroit as being a Black city, with Motown and all, but now that I think about it, the two people I know who live there are White. Jewish, actually."

Kate was straining to hear this conversation back in the kitchen. The shutters on the pass-through window were closed; a good hostess never let her guests see her at work. She still had to get the vegetables in the oven and keep stirring the mashed potatoes. She couldn't run interference if things got dicey with her sister. Thankfully, the doorbell rang again. Kate poked her head out of the kitchen. It was Zora. Brad and Oliver let her in.

"Hello, Mr. Carter," Zora said. Under her camel-colored coat, she was wearing a simple emerald-green knit dress and black thigh-high suede boots. Her usual gold hoop earrings adorned her ears, and she carried a white bakery box in one hand. "Hi, Ollie. How's my favorite little man?" she said.

Oliver squealed in delight when he saw Zora and tried his best to wiggle out of his father's arms and fling himself into Zora's, but

Brad had a tight hold on him. He had to laugh in spite of himself. "I'd say somebody is happy to see you," he said. "Come on in, Zora."

Zora hung up her own coat in the front hall closet and then went into the living room. Rather than make the introductions, Brad called to Kate, "Zora's here."

Kate came running into the living room, apron on over her black tuxedo pants and silk blouse. "Hi, Zora," she said. Then she turned to her guests. "Everyone, this is Zora." She didn't give any further explanations, making it sound like Zora was so important that everyone should know who she was. Kate was cognizant of the fact that her introduction sounded half finished, but she didn't want to belittle Zora and introduce her as the nanny, and she didn't feel justified calling her a friend. So it was Zora. Truth be told, everyone in the room knew exactly who Zora was anyway. Except maybe Ronnie. Kate prayed that she hadn't made a mistake, as Brad insisted, in inviting Zora. Maybe it would be too socially awkward.

But it was too late now. Her friends and family all gave a collective "hi."

Ronnie broke his silence. "So are you named after Zora Neale Hurston?"

Zora smiled, answered her least favorite question, and then escaped, following Kate into the kitchen. She placed the bakery box on the counter.

"Oh, Zora, you didn't have to buy anything," Kate said.

"I didn't. I made toffee bars. I just put them in the box to make it look festive. Did you know there's a shop in Chinatown where you can buy just about every restaurant container ever made?"

"Really?" Kate said. "I'm not surprised. You can find anything in Chinatown. One year I bought all my Christmas presents from a grocery store on Canal Street."

"I think I know which one you're talking about. Do they

have a basement level that's full of ceramics and rice cookers and utensils?"

"Yeah, exactly. And there's Peking duck sold in the front window."

"It has to be the same place," Zora confirmed. She looked around the kitchen, and even though it looked like Kate had everything under control, she asked anyway. "Do you need help with anything?"

"No," Kate answered, perhaps a little too forcefully. To compensate, she added, "Please just go enjoy yourself. I can handle things in here. We're waiting for one more person."

So Zora headed back into the living room. Kate sent another silent prayer up to the party gods that all would go well.

And it did. The food was delicious. The goose turned out juicy and flavorful. Everyone raved about the stuffing, and the roasted vegetables were crisp, not soggy. Brad had selected the wine, a dry white from South Africa that everyone agreed was the perfect complement to a perfect meal. Ronnie hadn't been so impressed because he was a vegetarian and he didn't drink alcohol. But he claimed to be perfectly satisfied with his vegetables and tap water. Kate didn't know why her sister hadn't warned her that her boyfriend was a vegetarian, but it was just like Liz to be inconsiderate. Despite Ronnie's slim pickings, Kate glanced around the table and realized that her gathering, so far, was a hit. People were eating, enjoying themselves, and talking. Weren't those the signs of a successful dinner party?

When everyone seemed to be finished and the last piece of meat had been plucked from the goose's bones, Kate smiled at her guests and announced that dessert would be ready shortly. She stood up to clear and begged everyone else to stay seated and continue talking and relaxing. Zora and Tracy, Kate's friend from college who had just moved to the city, jumped up to help.

"No, sit, sit," Kate admonished the two women. She then turned to her husband and said clearly, "Brad will help me." Oliver was already in bed, so Brad was free to help.

"Yes, Brad, please help your wife *and* show my husband what it means to be useful around the house," Sheila implored.

Brad laughed as he got up from his seat and away from his conversation with Carl. "With pleasure," he said as he started gathering plates.

In the kitchen with Kate, as he scraped food into the garbage can and she handled the dishes, Kate casually asked a question. "What were you and Carl talking about? You seemed all deep into conversation."

"Oh, nothing, really. He was just telling me about some friends of his who are trying to put together this new company and they need funding," Brad said.

"What kind of company?" Kate asked as she quickly rinsed plates and stacked them in the dishwasher. She refused to leave a big mess to clean up later. That was the number one no-no in Party Planning 101.

"I'm not even sure I understand it completely," Brad said. "Something to do with video games, comic books, and a movie theater."

"And they want you to invest?" Kate asked with concern.

"No, no, no," Brad reassured his wife. "They just need some advice on how to attract investors without relinquishing creative control."

"Oh. Okay," Kate said, relieved. She went back to loading the dishwasher.

Brad went back to the table to retrieve more dishes. While he was in the living room, he put the music back on, switching the classic carols CD for his favorite *Holiday Songs from Around the World*.

"You know," he said when he came back to the kitchen, "inviting Zora wasn't such a bad idea. I'm sorry for giving you a hard time about it."

"Thank you," Kate said, feeling slightly smug. "What made you change your mind?"

"Nothing, in particular," Brad started. "She just fit in with everybody, so it was a nonissue. I even talked with her for a little while. Did you know she wants to be a personal chef?"

"Yeah, she's mentioned that," Kate said.

"Well, anyway, I completely apologize. I shouldn't have been such a dick about inviting her."

"Apology accepted," Kate said. It had been important to include Zora. Even though Brad had issues with Zora's presence in their life, Kate didn't. Zora was her son's primary caregiver, and that meant something. Having her here tonight was Kate's way of proving that she respected Zora's role in their family.

"Now, can you please start the coffee while I whip the cream for the pie?" Kate asked her husband while searching for the attachments for her hand mixer. She had conceded her limitations and bought an apple pie from her favorite bakery in Park Slope. Everything in the tiny shop was delicious. The muffins, the scones, even the plain sugar cookies were delightful. When she was pregnant with Oliver, Kate had allowed herself treats from their goody basket almost every morning. Since then she'd restricted herself to special occasions and holidays.

Brad started measuring coffee, and Kate tended to her cream. The pie warmed in the oven, producing a delicious aroma of sweet cinnamon and a hint of nutmeg that swirled throughout the house. Kate lowered the speed of her mixer so she could ask Brad another question. "What do you think of Ronnie?" she asked, keeping her voice low.

Brad whispered his answer back. "Honestly, I don't know what your sister sees in him. I mean, he's nice enough but kind of lacking in the personality department. I tried talking with him a few times and could only get monosyllabic answers out of him. I can't believe he's a kindergarten teacher."

"I know, right?" Kate squealed, trying to imagine Ronnie singing his ABC's to a group of five-year-olds. She paused while she measured two tablespoons of powdered sugar into the partially whipped cream. "At least he seems way better than that hoodlum she was dating before. You know, the guy she met at the tattoo parlor. I swear, if we both didn't call the same woman Mom, I'd question our genetic connection."

"Kate, be nice," Brad said, moving over to stand closer to his wife. He put his arms around her from behind and kissed her on the back of her neck. She relaxed in his embrace. "Remember your Christmas spirit." He kissed her again, pressing his whole body against hers. Kate turned in his arms and kissed him back. He looked so handsome in his chocolate-brown corduroys and the hunter-green raw silk sweater she'd bought him for his birthday. Christmas spirit or just the warm glow from a good meal shared with good friends, Kate felt the heat rising in her body from her toes to her cheeks. She kissed Brad with a passion she hadn't felt in a long time.

"I love you," Brad said.

"I love you, too," Kate answered.

Just then the door to the kitchen flew open. "Kate, do you need any help—" Zora stopped when she saw Kate and Brad in each other's arms and quickly backed out of the room.

Startled by the interruption, Kate and Brad flew apart. They looked at each other and laughed. Kate ran a hand through her hair. Brad went back to the coffeemaker.

"Don't think we're done here," Brad warned.

"Is that a threat, Mr. Carter?" Kate teased.

"You betcha," Brad answered with an exaggerated wink and a silly grin.

CHAPTER 15

Zora

WINTER

IT was just too cold outside. These days the temperatures hovered in the twenties, and there was often some kind of unbearable precipitation falling from the sky, making any trip outdoors feel like a nightmare. Zora felt herself suffering from acute cabin fever, and she thought Oliver might have a mild case of it, too. She'd baked cookies, watched too many hours of Teletubbies videos, and, in a fit of desperation, had tried to teach Ollie how to dance the hokey pokey, even though he still couldn't walk. At least in Ann Arbor, Zora thought, she'd had a car and several shopping malls to while away the winter hours. But here, cramped living spaces and long walks between bus stops made winter almost intolerable. Salvation came from Angel, who called to remind Zora about the sign language classes in Fort Greene. A new session was starting the following week, so Zora made a mental note to propose the idea to Kate right away.

When Kate walked in the door that evening, Zora was finishing up dinner. She was picking the ends off a pound of string beans and cutting them in half. Each bean measured the same length. The importance of presentation had been drilled into Zora at culinary school.

"As usual, it smells delicious," Kate said when she walked in the door. "What are you making?"

Zora described the Ethiopian-inspired stew for Kate.

"God, Zora, you really are amazing. You are going to be a wonderful personal chef, but I have to admit, I won't want to give you up," Kate teased.

"Don't worry, I don't have anyone knocking on my door yet," Zora said.

"Good." Kate laughed.

"Um, Kate," Zora started.

"Yes," Kate said, grabbing her vitamin-enhanced water out of the refrigerator.

"I was wondering how you would feel if I took Oliver to this new sign language class. Supposedly, babies can learn sign language as young as six months, and then they can communicate with you at a much earlier age. Apparently, it gives babies a greater sense of control, and they don't have to cry or throw tantrums when they can't tell you what they want."

Kate sipped her water and announced, "I think it sounds like a great idea. Where's the class?"

"That's the only thing. It's in Fort Greene," Zora explained, "so I'd have to take Ollie on the bus. The class meets on Tuesdays and Thursdays."

Kate took another swig of water before she answered. "Let me talk to Brad about it, and I'll let you know. When do the classes start, and do they have a website or something so I can look them up?"

"Hold on a sec," Zora said, wiping her hands on her apron. She figured Kate would need to see something on paper. She ran to get her purse. Angel had given her a brochure about the class. It was pretty homegrown, Angel had said. They met in a church, and two mommies taught the class. Zora handed the brochure to Kate.

"Wonderful, I'll take a look," Kate said. "And thanks for the suggestion. While we're on the subject, I think it would be great for Ollie to learn French. Do you think you could start speaking to him in French sometimes? I think he's ready for it."

"Sure," Zora said, even though she thought Oliver should concentrate on getting some more intelligible English words under his belt. Oh, well, Oliver wasn't her child. To Kate, she said, "I could use some extra practice myself."

"I hear you." Kate laughed. "You know, I spent a summer in France during college, but I've forgotten practically everything."

"If you're not using it, it just disappears," Zora agreed, feeling a wave of nostalgia for the time in her life when she even dreamed in French.

"Well," Kate said, back to business, "I will definitely talk to Brad about the sign language classes and let you know what we decide. You know, I was thinking about signing Ollie up for a music class as well. He seems to love music. Would you mind taking him to that, too?"

"Sure," Zora said, thinking the more time out of the house, the better.

Kate echoed Zora's thoughts. "I don't want you guys stuck in the house every day. I'm sure it's torture."

"Kind of." Zora nodded in agreement as she finished cutting the last green bean.

"That settles it, then," Kate said, tossing her water bottle into the blue recycling bin. "We'll get Ollie involved in some more outside activities."

"Sounds great," Zora agreed as she moved around the kitchen, leaving everything ready for Kate to heat up in the microwave later.

"Okeydokey. I'm going up," Kate announced, and headed upstairs to change. She liked to work out while Oliver was still sleeping. If she got to it right away, she could get in thirty minutes of exercise and a quick shower before Oliver demanded her attention.

Zora bundled herself up in her coat, thick scarf, hat, and boots. Having grown up in Michigan, she knew how to handle the cold, now that it had finally arrived with a vengeance. It was like Old Man Winter was making up for the ridiculously warm weather they'd had in the fall. All dressed, she used a stage whisper to call upstairs and tell Kate she was leaving.

"Bye, Zora," Kate called back down. "And thanks, as usual."

When she got off the bus back in her neighborhood, Zora decided to treat herself to a hot chocolate with marshmallows. She went into the coffee shop that had just opened up on Myrtle Avenue. This was big news, as Myrtle Avenue was still considered the dividing line between the hood and gentrification. The café owners, two middle-aged Black women who had deserted corporate America to pursue their barista dreams, had been welcomed with open arms by local residents, Zora included. She loved to sit in the mismatched upholstered armchairs and watch folks stroll by. It was a perfect people-watching corner, even in the winter. The two owners, Katrina and Hazel, had spent a lot of time creating a space that would invite people in and keep them coming back. The café was a delight, with its cheerful lemon-yellow walls, the always updated magazine rack, and the world-music sound track pumping in the background.

"Hey, Zora," Katrina called out when she saw Zora.

"Hi, Katrina," Zora said as she stomped her feet for warmth and unraveled her scarf from around her neck.

"What'll it be?" Katrina asked.

"A large hot chocolate, please."

"Extra marshmallows?" Katrina asked with a smile.

"You know it," Zora said, then made a beeline for her favorite chair by the window. She laid her coat across the back of the chair after stuffing her scarf, hat, and mittens in the sleeves. She looked to see what magazines were lying around. She grabbed a *People* that she hadn't yet read and made herself comfortable. Katrina, she knew, would bring the hot chocolate over when it was ready.

"Hey, Zora."

Zora pulled her eyes from her magazine, expecting to see Katrina, but it was Keith and his sexy lips from the Laundromat. Today he was wearing jeans and a big gray wool sweater. His locks were pulled back in a ponytail, and he was wearing sneakers.

Zora hesitated while she tried to decide if she should act like she didn't remember him or just say hi and hope he went away. She opted for a cool but polite response. "Hello," she said. "It's Keith, right?"

"Yeah, we met at the Laundromat a while back. You're the chef who won't cook for strangers." Zora smiled in spite of herself. Keith jumped at the opportunity. "So, mind if I join you?"

"I guess not," Zora said. "I'm having a hot chocolate."

"I ordered a tea," Keith said. "I try to drink a cup of green tea every day."

"Oh, really? Why is that?"

"I've been reading all of these articles saying that green tea retards the aging process, and it has a whole bunch of other healing properties."

"Are you afraid of getting old or something?" Zora asked pointedly.

Keith smiled, and Zora was reminded how delicious she found his lips. "No. No. Not afraid, just not looking forward to it," he answered. "My dad died when he was forty-seven. Massive heart attack, just like that. He wasn't in bad shape, but he never exercised, and he loved him some bacon. And boom, just like that, he was gone. If I can avoid that fate, I'm going to do whatever it takes."

"That's terrible about your dad," Zora said softly. "How old are you now?"

"Thirty-four, almost thirty-five."

"You don't look like you're about to die, if that makes you feel any better," Zora said. Before he had a chance to respond, Katrina came over with Zora's hot chocolate and Keith's tea. She placed the two drinks on the table and headed back to the counter, but not before giving Zora a wink and a thumbs-up sign over Keith's head. She mouthed the words "He's cute," and Zora struggled to keep a straight face.

"You know," Keith started as he stirred honey in his tea with a wooden stick, "I've been coming to this coffee shop since I met you in the Laundromat. I figured with you living in the hood and all, you'd have to come in here sometime."

"You've been stalking me?" Zora asked, not sure if she should be flattered or frightened.

"I wouldn't call it stalking." Keith laughed. "I'd say I was trying to improve my chances of running into you again. And look, it worked."

"Why'd you want to find me so badly?" Zora asked.

Keith stopped stirring his tea and looked Zora right in the eye and said, "Because you are undoubtedly one of the most beautiful women I've seen in this city, and something about you just makes me want to get to know you better. How's that for honesty?"

Zora had to admit that Keith's candor was nice to hear. This was a pleasant new experience for her. Up until now most of Zora's experiences with men could be placed in two categories, bad and worse. She had a habit of falling for the guy with the impressive résumé and the hollow soul or the completely unavailable man whom she had to love from a distance. "Thank you," she said. She took an extra-long sip of her hot chocolate while trying to sneak a glance at her new admirer.

"Where are you from?" Keith asked.

"Michigan," Zora answered. "Ann Arbor, to be exact, born and raised."

"Really?" Keith said. "I grew up in Chicago and went to Madison for undergrad. Did you go to U of M for college?"

"Yeah, for a while," Zora said. "Go Blue!" she added for authenticity's sake. "But I never finished."

"What happened between college and your current circumstances?" Keith asked.

Zora told him the details of her life. From France to Kate and Brad. She didn't try to make herself sound any better or worse than she was. She didn't have anything to lose. Keith asked questions here and there, but mostly, he listened. When she was done talking and Keith had no more questions, Zora turned the tables on him. "What do you do?" she asked.

"Me?" Keith answered, looking a little bit embarrassed by the question. "I am an out-of-work actor who supports himself as a waiter. Sometimes, if money is tight, I dance at a strip club in Times Square. But that's only when things get really bad."

Zora burst out laughing. "Are you serious?" She couldn't believe that this man sitting in front of her, sipping green tea and fearing an early death, donned a G-string and body glitter to dance in front of horny women.

"Yes, I am, woman," Keith answered, feigning seriousness. "Those women that come in the club pay good money for a piece of this Nubian god. I can bring down in one night more than I make in tips in a week at the restaurant."

"I'll get back to the 'taking off your clothes for money' thing in a minute." Zora smirked. "But I want to know what kind of actor you are. TV? Movie? Stage?"

"I don't discriminate," Keith said. "If a director wanted to hire me for a hot-dog commercial, I'd be a hot-dog-commercial actor. But I do have a master's degree from NYU that says I specialize in stage acting."

"So you're a legitimate actor, then," Zora teased.

"Not really," Keith said with a bitter laugh. "The way I see it, if

I had to check the appropriate box, I'd have to mark 'waiter and part-time stripper.' I haven't had a paying acting role in a very long time." He shook his head and sucked in a deep breath. "But I remain forever hopeful." He flashed his perfect teeth in a perfect smile. Zora had the urge to clap after that dramatic speech, but she held her hands still, as she didn't want to offend the guy. Instead, she said, "I'm sure there is a hot-dog commercial in the very near future for you."

"Thanks, Zora," Keith said.

"You're welcome," Zora said. She started to re-dress for the cold, even though her apartment was only two doors down.

"Are you leaving already?" Keith asked.

"Yeah, I promised my roommate I'd make her dinner tonight," Zora said, which of course was a big fat lie, since Sondra had left for school a week ago. She just thought this was a good time to end the conversation.

"Can I get your number or something?" Keith asked her.

"How about you keep stalking me, and we'll surely bump into each other again soon," Zora offered. She secured her fuzzy pink beret on her head, pulled on her mittens, and gave Keith a big smile.

"All right, then, Ms. Zora. We'll play your way," Keith said with a lazy smile.

"See you around," Zora said as she turned to the door. She called out good-bye to Katrina on her way out.

CHAPTER 16

Kate

WHEN Kate told Brad about the sign language classes as they got ready for bed on Wednesday night, he wasn't thrilled. "I thought we weren't signing him up for those types of classes until he turned two," he said. And the bus to Fort Greene made him nervous. Brad was the world's most overprotective mother hen when it came to Oliver. He worried that every little thing could be a potential hazard to the well-being of his only child. Sometimes it was funny—like how he cut Ollie's bananas in perfect two-by-two-centimeter chunks so he wouldn't choke—but other times it was plain annoying. "The bus could crash, or Zora could get mugged in Fort Greene," Brad protested.

Kate had to calm him down. "People get mugged on the Upper West Side, too," she pointed out. "And we still go there for brunch every Sunday, don't we?" She continued, "Even though we might not believe in the necessity of these early baby classes, everybody around us does."

"Oh, so we've got to do this because everyone else is?" Brad grumbled.

"Yes and no," Kate said, refusing to let this turn into an argument. "We're not doing it just to keep up with the Joneses, so to speak, but if everyone else's kids are playing the piano at three and speaking three languages at four, then Oliver won't be competitive with his contemporaries. He can't just spend his days playing at the park and watching *Sesame Street*."

"Kate," Brad reminded his wife, "he's a baby. That's what he's supposed to be doing." He stopped talking so he could brush his teeth. When he was done, he stepped back into the bedroom, crawled into bed next to his wife, and in a calmer voice said, "Don't get all caught up in the elitist super-baby crap. I thought we were together on this."

"Think about it this way," Kate said. "Zora brought it up to me because she and the baby are getting bored stuck in the house. And I can understand that. They both need some outside stimulation, and it can't hurt."

Brad turned over in bed and promised he would think about it. He picked up his comic book and started to read, effectively ending the conversation. Kate loved her husband, but sometimes he could be difficult. Rather than try to force him to discuss their son's future, Kate picked up her copy of *And the Band Played On,* by Randy Shilts. She was reading the weighty tome to try to get a more personal understanding of the AIDS epidemic so she could bring that perspective to the gala. It shouldn't be all high fashion, fun, and good times, she reasoned, considering the fact that almost twenty thousand people died from the disease every year in the United States. And those numbers were much higher in third-world countries. AIDS hadn't given anyone a reason to celebrate as of yet. The almost six-hundred-page book chronicled the genesis of the deadly disease and read like a real-life medical thriller. Shaking her head and gasping aloud at the horrors on every page, Kate vowed to raise as much money as she could with this gala.

The following day, Brad came home and announced to Kate that he was okay with the sign language classes.

"What made you change your mind?" Kate asked.

"I was talking to Carl about it," Brad said, "and he told me Fort Greene is turning around and that there are a lot of kid-friendly classes and restaurants in that neighborhood. He and Sheila are thinking about buying there because they're totally priced out of Park Slope."

"I have Carl to thank for this change of heart, then," Kate said, smiling. "This is new."

"Yeah, well, Carl's a papa now, too. He's calming down and getting wise," Brad said.

Kate couldn't tell if he was kidding or not. "Good," she said, walking over to plant a conciliatory kiss on her husband's cheek. "I'll tell Zora that it's a go. And just so you know, I'm going to sign Ollie up for music lessons, too, on Tuesday mornings. Zora's going to take him to those as well. But don't worry. They're right here in Park Slope, so there's no big bad bus to worry about."

"Okay," Brad said, laughing. "Okay."

On Monday morning, Kate left the filled-out registration form for the sign language class with a check on the dining room table. She gave Brad specific instructions to point it out to Zora when she came in. Then Kate stuffed her feet into her black fur-lined boots, put on her black wool coat, black gloves, and pale pink pashmina scarf, and headed out the door. Outside she found Mrs. Rodriguez sprinkling salt on the icy walkway.

"Mrs. Rodriguez, stop!" Kate called to their tenant. The woman had to be almost eighty years old. "Brad will take care of that."

"Oh, it's no trouble," Mrs. Rodriguez said, trying to catch her breath in the cold air. "I wouldn't want anyone to slip and break a hip out here. Think about the insurance claim."

Kate rolled her eyes. She gently pried the bag of salt out of the old woman's hands and guided her back to her apartment. "I'll call Brad right now on my cell phone and remind him to finish salting the walk," Kate promised. "And please don't trouble yourself. You could get hurt."

"Oh, Mrs. Carter, I'm a lot stronger than I look," Mrs. Rodriguez said. "It may say seventy-eight on my driver's license, but my doctor just told me I have the body of a fifty-year-old. Got all my teeth, don't really need my glasses, and I hear everything. Everything," she repeated, and gave Kate a knowing look.

What that look was supposed to mean, Kate had no idea. Maybe she'd heard them arguing about the sign language classes. Or—Kate gasped—maybe she'd heard them having sex on the living room couch the other night. Kate flushed red at the thought. She'd told Brad that they should have gone upstairs.

Mrs. Rodriguez seemed to read Kate's mind. "It's hard to have secrets in this city. People living right on top of each other like crickets. It's not natural," she said.

Kate couldn't help herself, so she asked, "If you don't like it, why do you stay here?"

"I didn't say I didn't like it," Mrs. Rodriguez clarified. "I said it wasn't natural. Besides, where else would I go? I've lived in Brooklyn my whole life."

Kate checked her watch. She was going to be late if she didn't power walk all the way to the subway. "I have to go, Mrs. Rodriguez," she said, already walking to the gate. "I promise to get Brad to take care of the sidewalk."

"All right, then," Mrs. Rodriguez called out to Kate's disappearing form. "I'll be waiting."

CHAPTER 17

Zora

ZORA and Angel pushed their strollers through the slushy snow, heading back to the bus stop. The two babies were enjoying the ride, oblivious to the herculean efforts their nannies had to make to navigate through the frozen mess covering the sidewalks. Zora was happy to have Angel by her side and realized in a moment of warm, fuzzy clarity that Angel had become a real friend. Even though Zora had been kind of skeptical of Angel's left-of-normal approach to life, she knew Angel always meant well, and most important, she was a welcome breath of fresh air in the cloistered world she had created for herself. With Angel, she didn't have to lie about her job or pretend she knew what was coming next. With Angel, she could be herself.

"So, do you have any plans for Valentine's Day?" Angel asked Zora.

Zora had to catch her breath before she could answer. "Not really," she huffed.

"What does 'not really' mean?" Angel asked.

"It means that Keith—" Zora started to explain.

"You mean Laundromat Keith?" Angel interrupted.

"Yes, Laundromat Keith." Zora sighed.

"You mean Stripper Boy Keith?" Angel chuckled as if she needed clarification.

"Yes, Stripper Boy Keith," Zora said, smiling in spite of herself. "Can I finish?"

"By all means," Angel said, trying to keep a straight face.

"Valentine's Day is on Monday, which is when an open-mike performance thing happens at this bar in Boerum Hill. I told Keith I'd go with him sometime, and he picked this Monday. So it's not like a real Valentine's event."

"*Amore,* on the day of love you are going to be with a man who finds you wildly attractive. That's real. Don't try to pretend it doesn't mean anything," Angel said.

"Look, we're just friends," Zora said.

"My ass," Angel sputtered. "He's not looking at you as a friend."

"Right now we're just friends," Zora repeated.

"Don't be afraid of love when it comes knocking on your door," Angel advised. "Hey, watch out for that branch!"

Zora looked down just in time to avoid tripping over a thick tree branch in the middle of the sidewalk that was partially covered by slush. The streets were strewn with debris, thanks to last night's storm of sleet, snow, and rain. The city was a mess, but this being New York, life continued as usual. The buses were extra late, but they were still running, and baby sign language class started on time. Not everyone showed up, but most of the kids were there. Just like Angel and Zora, the other nannies chose to brave the elements rather than stay cooped up in tiny little apartments all day long with young children.

"I'm not afraid of love," Zora said to Angel. "I just met the guy, though. And I'm not sure if he's really my type."

"What is your type?" Angel asked. "Distinguished businessmen who sleep with you when they're in town and leave as soon as they get their next assignment?"

Zora was sorry she'd told Angel about Alexander. The story had tumbled out one day when they were passing those lazy hours in the park, waiting for it to be time to take the babies home for dinner. Pushing babies in swings invited conversation, and the topics always turned personal. It was inevitable. Angel now probably knew more about Zora than anyone else in her life, friend or family.

Angel saw the look on Zora's face and apologized.

Then they slogged along in silence until they finally reached the bus stop. Luck was on their side because they had to wait only a moment before the bus came lumbering into view.

On the ride back to Park Slope, Angel entertained Skye by reviewing "If You're Happy and You Know It" in sign language. Zora found herself pondering Angel's last comment. Did Zora have a "type" of man? Was she a snob, discriminating against Keith because he took off his clothes for money? Why was she keeping him in the friend category and not allowing him to slide into the boyfriend realm? She'd finally relented and given him her number after two more "chance" meetings at the café. They'd been out a few times, and he really was a nice guy. He was kind and laid-back and could keep Zora in stitches with his strip-club stories. He seemed like a good person. A regular guy with a big heart. He was the anti-Alexander, which was definitely a good thing.

Zora allowed herself to revisit memories of Alexander Dean. She'd fallen for him because he was older and sophisticated and seemed so sure of himself. Plus, he had a smooth European accent that made every sentence spilling out of his mouth sound like poetry poured through melted butter. Officially, he was an American because his father had been born in Boston, but he'd grown up in Holland with his mother and now lived in London. He was in New York for a couple of months on business, and he was so out of her league. In fact, at first she didn't even understand what this forty-year-old European businessman wanted with her. Surely their flirtation was a game to him, a way to make their French classes at the Berlitz language school in midtown pass a little quicker. The class was the one luxury Zora allowed herself while she was working at Head Start up in Harlem. Alex was in the class because he had landed a French client at his firm and needed to be able to schmooze *en français*. The class was an opportunity to practice the fine art of conversation in French, and Alexander had selected Zora right away to be his language partner. He started the flirtation.

When she allowed him to take her out to dinner one night after class, he so thoroughly convinced her of his honest intentions that she shoved all of her doubts aside. For six weeks he made Zora feel like a treasure, and she fell for it. He took her to expensive restaurants and Broadway shows, insisting that she stay with him in his corporate hotel every weekend. He even bought her an expensive turquoise necklace that they picked out together during one of their Saturday-afternoon shopping sprees along Fifth Avenue. Though Zora knew it was excessive, she figured he was old enough and rich enough to spend his money any way he pleased. But when the class was over, Alexander said good-bye to Zora with only the slightest bit of remorse before he headed back to London. She, on the other hand, bawled like a baby.

"You knew it wasn't forever, darling," he'd purred as she watched him pack his suitcase. But she hadn't known. She'd let herself believe that this might be the Great Romance of her life, that she might have found her place by the side of this wonderful man.

She had tried to act sophisticated and brave, but she couldn't pull it off. Not when Alex tried to discard her like the pair of sneakers he'd worn twice and decided to leave behind for the hotel staff. He wanted to treat her like a disposable part of his New York package. Like they hadn't been inseparable for an entire six weeks. Like they hadn't talked about going to France together, to rent a château near Cannes, where they would tour perfume factories and sunbathe on the shores of the Mediterranean. Like they hadn't been sleeping together, he whispering in her ear in the heat of passion that he loved her like no other. No, she hadn't been capable of pretending. His cold indifference felt like a sucker punch in the stomach. Unexpected, shameful, and enormously painful. The worst part was, sometimes Zora still dreamed about Alexander and that house in the south of France.

"Hey, did you hear me?" Angel poked Zora in the arm.

"What? I'm sorry," Zora said, extinguishing the memory of Alexander and making a mental note to consider the possibility of a real relationship with Keith.

Right now though, Angel needed her attention. "I said," she repeated, raising a questioning eyebrow at Zora, "do you want to stop at Cousin John's for hot chocolate?" Angel knew it was Zora's weakness.

Zora smiled. "Sure. This icky weather was made for hot chocolate."

Angel turned back to Skye. "Now, don't tell your mother I've been giving you hot chocolate, little one." To Zora, she complained, "Skye's mother is one of those types who keeps the child on a strict diet of no sugar, low salt, and little flavor. Meanwhile, the parents eat crap out of boxes and bags that was probably grown in a factory. You should see the nonsense they eat in that house. They should hire you to cook for them." This was one of Angel's favorite things to complain about. The food in Skye's house, the food in America in general, and, of course, the inherent superiority of the food in Italy. Zora knew Angel was getting itchy to go back to her life of passion and painting.

"So, how's your savings account?" Zora asked. Apparently, as soon as she had ten thousand dollars saved, Angel was jumping on the first plane back to Italy.

"*Mamma mia,*" Angel said. "I've still got seven thousand to go. I'm thinking about putting up a sign to tutor in Italian."

Zora had pretty much ascertained that even though Angel liked to pepper her speech with colorful Italian phrases, she wasn't exactly fluent in the language. Angel laughed at her doubtful expression. "Hey, if people are willing to pay to teach their non-deaf babies to sing songs in sign language, I think there's probably someone out there who would pay me to teach them enough Italian to get by as a tourist. Valentino always told me I had a very good accent." Valentino was Angel's no-good Italian ex-boyfriend whom she refused to speak to on account of the fact that his mother didn't think a Black American woman deserved her son. But Angel still loved him something awful. Her words. Not Zora's.

"Hey, you never know." Zora shrugged. She knew Angel well enough to know that this was one of her many get-rich-quick schemes. By next week she would have a different one. But one thing was sure, she wouldn't stop until the money was in her pocket.

"You know, I could save a lot faster if I quit buying canvases and paints, but I can't stop working," Angel admitted.

"You shouldn't," Zora counseled. "It's your life."

Angel sighed in frustration.

"Why don't you try to sell some of your work?" Zora asked. She'd seen some of Angel's portraits, and they were stunning.

"Oh, I don't know," Angel said, losing her usual bravado. "I'm not sure I'm ready to do that."

"When's your show going to happen?" Zora asked.

"I still don't know," Angel said. "The owner of the gallery keeps promising this date or that date and then backing off. We have to sit down and hammer out an agreement. I can't push him, because he could tell me to fuck off, and then where would I be?"

Zora didn't have an answer for Angel, so she gave her hand a squeeze and told her to keep the faith.

The bus was approaching their stop, so she retied Oliver's scarf, tightened his blanket around him, and put him back into the stroller. Angel did the same with Skye. When the bus left them off on Prospect Park West, they braced themselves against the frosty cold and covered the babies up. "To Cousin John's?" Angel asked, pulling her own scarf tight around her mouth.

"Let's go." Zora nodded. The two women turned their strollers east and headed down the slushy hill in silence, each absorbed in her own thoughts.

Later that afternoon, while Zora was making dinner for Brad and Kate, and Oliver was sleeping off his hot chocolate and raucous day at sign language class, her cell phone rang. She ran to the living room to grab the phone out of her purse. She didn't bother to check the number; it was going to be either Sondra, Angel, or perhaps Keith, reminding her of their date on Monday.

But it was her brother, Craig. "Hey, sis," he started.

"Hi, Craig," Zora said, heading back into the kitchen.

"Whatcha doing?" Craig asked innocently.

"Nothing, just making dinner," she answered.

"Z, it's only four. Are you having a party or something?" Craig asked.

"No, it's for the Carters," Zora answered, already exasperated with this call.

"Oh, so they have you cooking for them, too, huh?"

Zora rolled her eyes and prayed for patience. "Craig, did you call for a reason besides annoying me?" she asked.

"Can't I call my little sister to check up on her and see how she's doing?"

"Yes, you may call to see how I'm doing, but you may not call me for the sole purpose of being an asshole."

"Hey, I'm trying to look out for you," Craig said. "And I'm expressing concern that A) you are being taken advantage of, and B) you promised me that this was going to be a temporary gig. According to my watch, you've been playing mammy now for six months."

"It's only been five months," Zora corrected her brother.

"Six. Five. What difference does it make? It's still a long time for a short-term assignment. Tell me you have something else lined up, and we can drop this."

"I don't have to tell you anything," Zora fumed. "You're not responsible for me."

"Oh, so who was it you came to begging for funds to pay your rent? I'm not responsible?" Craig reminded her.

"I paid you back," Zora said. "On time," she added. "And for your information, I'm not being taken advantage of."

Craig threw out a derisive laugh. "Exploited labor, that's what you are. Doing everything the lady of the house should be doing herself. Changing her kid's diapers and cooking her husband's dinner."

It was Zora's turn to laugh. "When did you become a Neanderthal?" she asked. "I feel sorry for Mimi if she ever makes the mistake of marrying you."

Mimi was Craig's secret shame. She was the love of his life, but she was Korean, and Zora and Craig's parents had no idea she even existed. Zora had found out about her quite by accident when she was living in Harlem and paid her brother a surprise Sunday-morning visit. He swore Zora to secrecy even though she tried to convince him that he was being silly. Their parents wouldn't have a problem with Mimi, but Craig wasn't willing to take the chance. He knew his parents weren't racist, but Mimi's parents were. As soon as they got to this country, they told their daughter point-blank that if she ever brought a Black man home, she would shame their entire family. So Mimi had invented this elaborate double life that included a P.O. box, two phone lines, and a good friend who allowed her to "borrow" her apartment whenever her parents came to town to visit. They had no idea that their daughter lived with Craig, and for that, Craig believed his parents would disown him. He had so little self-respect and pride that he would allow himself to be erased.

"Leave Mimi out of this," Craig bristled. Even though they'd been living together for almost four years, he still felt the need to diminish Mimi's existence in his life. "We were talking about you."

"No," Zora corrected. "You were lecturing me about my status as an exploited worker."

"Look, Z," Craig began, adjusting the tone of his voice from critical to concerned, "if you were stupid or something, and you honestly couldn't do anything else besides clean up after other people, then I'd be giving you props for finding this job. But you are selling yourself short, and I hate to see that. And Mom and Dad do, too."

"Did you tell them what I was doing?" Zora screeched, getting ready to go off on her brother.

"Calm down," Craig counseled. "I haven't told them anything, but I swear, if you don't get on it and do something with your life, then I will. Mom and Dad didn't raise you to be a maid. Where's your sense of pride? Your dignity? If nothing else, you owe them something for the life they gave us."

"First of all, I'm not a maid," Zora shot back. "And don't talk to me about pride and owing Mom and Dad, Mr. 'I don't exist because I'm dating a racist Korean girl.' "

"Mimi is not a racist. She wouldn't be with me if she were," Craig retorted angrily. "You know what the situation is, and we're working on it. But what are you doing to make something out of your life? You're thirty years old, Z."

"I know how old I am," Zora snapped. She took a moment to calm down and stir the winter vegetable stew she was making.

"Hey, Zora, are you still there?"

"Yeah, I'm here," Zora said, seething.

"So, what are you going to do? Do you need my help? Do you want to go back to school? Get the cooking thing going? I could probably set you up with some clients to cook for at my firm. Maybe you could make up some brochures or something. Get some business cards made. You were always the creative one, Z. Nobody is saying you have to put on some panty hose and sit behind a desk. We know whatever you're going to do, it's going to be different, but being a housekeeper—excuse me, a nanny—that's just not right. You can do more than that. And I can help you, if you want."

"Thanks," Zora mumbled, trying to figure out how to tell her brother that she didn't want his help. If she accepted it, then he would expect her to succeed. And if she didn't, then he would be justified in his anger and disappointment. Zora didn't want to take all that on. She just wanted everyone in her family to stop wanting so much from her. Why couldn't they let her move at her own pace?

"What do you want me to do?" Craig asked.

"Nothing," Zora exploded. "Look, I have to go. I have to finish this stew and make some rice before the baby wakes up. Thanks for calling, and I'll call you later, okay?" She hung up before her brother could say anything else, and then she turned her cell phone off.

Talking to Craig made Zora flash back to the four agonizing days at home over Christmas with her parents. Even though they thought she was making ends meet in New York with office temp work, they, too, had spent the whole holiday lecturing Zora about her future. Of course, they tried to be subtle with their nagging.

"Zora," her mother would say over breakfast, "did you know Angela Turner just moved to Chicago and is working as an interior designer?" Angela Turner used to be Zora's best friend in elementary school. She was supposed to be a lawyer but had dropped out of law school after one year. This was supposed to make Zora feel like they had something in common.

"I didn't know that," Zora answered, hoping the conversation would end there. It didn't.

"You know, she had to take a few months after her law school fiasco to figure out what she wanted to do, but then she rolled up her sleeves and made up her mind that she was going to be an interior decorator. She made some calls, and then faster than you'd believe it, she found a job in Chicago."

"Good for her," Zora said without a whole lot of enthusiasm.

"You know, you could do something like that, too, Zora," her mother offered.

"What, move to Chicago?"

"No, be an interior decorator," her mom practically shouted in exasperation.

"Mom, I don't want to be an interior designer."

"How would you know? You've never tried it," her mother cried.

"You don't just sample professions like ice cream flavors, Mom," Zora said, wishing she didn't have to go through this every time she came home. Arguing with her mother was exhausting. "Besides, I know that's not what I want to do for a living."

"Well, what do you want to do?"

"Actually, I'm thinking about—" Zora started to explain her plans but then changed her mind. If she even put it out there that she was contemplating a future as a personal chef, her parents would take the idea and run with it. Tell all their friends and start sending her every article they came across that mentioned the food industry. Soon the idea wouldn't be hers anymore, and she'd have to abandon it, like the others. So she finished her sentence with a half-truth. "I'm thinking about a lot of things," she told her mother.

Her mother shook her head and gave Zora that look again. The look of perpetual disappointment and maybe even worse— a bit of disbelief that this unaccomplished woman seated at her table could really be her daughter.

• • •

Zora was sitting on the couch folding laundry, trying not to think about her family, and watching *Oprah* when Mr. Carter walked in the front door. She quickly flicked the TV off and tried to look busy when he came into the room.

"Hey, you don't have to turn it off," he said. "I love Oprah. What's she talking about today?"

Zora looked at Brad Carter. He definitely had been less hostile toward her since the Christmas party. He didn't always run out the door as soon as she got to the house in the mornings. And on the nights when he made it home before Kate, he usually said something nice about the meals Zora had made for them.

"Today it's suburban housewives who also happen to be crack-heads," Zora said as she turned the TV back on. She was glad he didn't mind her watching, because it really was a riveting episode. These women's lives were crazy.

"Really?" Brad said, easing himself down in the chair. He was wearing dark blue sweatpants and an orange and blue Brooklyn hoodie, so Zora guessed he'd gone to the gym, but it didn't explain why he was home so early. It was only 4:30.

"Yeah, this one woman would get her kids ready for school, make them lunch, put them on the bus, then spend the rest of the day getting high. But she could still make dinner at night."

"Unbelievable," Brad said.

"I know," Zora agreed. "The only reason she got caught is that she was buying all of her drugs on her husband's credit card."

Brad looked at Zora, and they both started to laugh. It wasn't funny, but what else could you do when you heard something so horrifically absurd?

They watched *Oprah* together while Zora finished folding the laundry. When the show was over, she headed back into the kitchen. "Mr. Carter," she called, "can I show you dinner?"

Brad came into the kitchen. "Zora, I call you Zora, so you can call me Brad, okay?" He seemed kind of perturbed as he said it.

"Sorry. *Brad,*" she corrected herself. "So, you have this winter stew that you can serve over rice. The meat is ground turkey. If you mash it up, Ollie should be able to eat it because I didn't make it spicy at all. And he can definitely eat the rice. He loves rice."

"Thank you, Zora," Brad said, and his tone softened. "You know, we really appreciate your cooking for us. Kate is so tired when she gets home, and quite honestly, we'd probably die if I were in charge of meals. We hardly ever eat out during the week anymore."

"Is that a good thing or a bad thing?" Zora asked.

"Definitely a good thing," Brad admitted. "I think I've lost some weight, and I feel healthier not grabbing takeout all the time."

"Good, then," Zora said, smiling. "I'll keep cooking."

"Please do," Brad said, returning the smile.

With that, Zora gathered her things and said good-bye. She left the house with a feeling of accomplishment, the conversation with her brother already forgotten.

CHAPTER 18

Kate

KATE asked Brad one more time to hurry. She hated to be late for anything, even a birthday party for a two-year-old. Cindy's daughter, Molly, was turning two, and Cindy had rented out a yoga studio for the event. Kate knew Cindy could afford the space for only two hours, so she wanted to make sure they were on time for her friend's sake. Plus, she barely got to see Cindy now that they were both back at work, and Kate was anxious to reconnect with her mommy friends. That life seemed so far away. She didn't exactly miss it, but there was a certain nostalgia she held for those months when Oliver had been her single most important client.

By the time they made it out the door—Brad pushing Oliver in his Maclaren stroller, Kate shouldering the diaper bag and the present—it was 1:50. The party started at two. Kate worried that Oliver would fall asleep in his stroller before they got there. He'd taken only a short nap in the morning and was due for his afternoon snooze any minute. The party was a few blocks away, so Kate figured they'd get there right on time if they walked fast. Maybe that way, Oliver would stay awake. Kate knew the slower the pace, the faster Oliver fell asleep.

With Kate power walking in the lead, the Carter family arrived in record time at three minutes past two. The yoga studio was filled with pastel-colored helium balloons clinging to the ceiling and pink crepe-paper swirls dripping from the walls; a purple and yellow sparkly banner that read HAPPY BIRTHDAY MOLLY covered most of the giant om symbol dominating the back of the room. Except for the lingering scent of sweat and dirty feet, the transformation was practically perfect. The Carters were the first guests to arrive, and Oliver was sound asleep.

"Kate." Cindy ran over to hug her friend. And then she crouched down to peek at Oliver in his stroller. "My goodness, he's getting big," she whispered. "I haven't seen him in so long. I'm so glad you guys could come."

Kate smiled and turned to Brad. "Cindy, this is my husband, Brad. Brad, this is Cindy." She paused and looked around the room. "Where's Molly, the lady of the hour?"

Cindy rolled her eyes and looked a little embarrassed. "She's at home, asleep. We didn't want to wake her till the last moment. She's a monster when we wake her from her naps."

Kate couldn't resist. "Yeah, I was kind of wondering why you scheduled the party for two. It's standard nap time."

"I know," Cindy wailed, "but this was the only time I could get this space, and it's so close to our apartment, and everyone knows where it is, so I just said what the hell."

"I'm sure it will be fine," Brad reassured her and shot Kate one of his "be nice" looks.

Kate ignored him but tried to make her friend feel better. "Yeah, Cindy, don't worry about it. Everything will be fine."

"Oh, I know." Cindy shrugged. "It's just that these New York City parties are a trip. You live in tiny homes where you can't possibly fit a bunch of toddlers and their parents, so you have to spend a small fortune renting a space that will inevitably be filled with sticky fingerprints and spilled milk by the time it's over."

"Where are you from?" Brad asked, chuckling. "You obviously didn't grow up here."

"Thanks for noticing," Cindy said with a grin. "No, I grew up in Ohio. We had a house and a big backyard, which meant birthday parties were always held outside. This is just blowing my mind. But you know Rich, my husband, insisted we give the girl a party this year, since last year we celebrated at home, just the three of us."

Kate always wondered why Cindy and Rich didn't move, since they seemed to struggle so much in New York. Cindy always claimed they were thinking about going back to her hometown, but Kate suspected they would stay right where they were. Between Cindy's raunchy sense of humor and her husband's obsession with gourmet food shops and TV cooking shows, they probably wouldn't fit in so well back in suburban Toledo.

Cindy excused herself as a crowd of people arrived at the door.

"What do we do now?" Brad asked Kate. He was new to the toddler-party scene.

Kate grinned. "Stick with me and I'll show you around."

They walked to the back of the room, toward the mirrors and a group of folding chairs. Kate unwrapped Oliver's blanket and removed his hat, mittens, and scarf. She'd seen Zora take off his entire snowsuit without waking him up, but she didn't dare try that trick herself. She placed his things in the small basket under the stroller. She and Brad laid their own coats over the backs of two chairs in the corner.

"You think we can leave Ollie here?" Kate whispered to Brad.

"Yeah, I doubt anyone here wants to steal an extra child," Brad whispered back.

Kate punched him playfully in the arm. "I just mean do you think he'll be okay," she clarified.

"Yes, honey. I think he'll be okay fifteen feet away from us. Besides, we can see him in the mirror from all the way across the room."

Satisfied, Kate took Brad's hand, and they walked toward the table where the food—divided into kiddie and grown-up sections—was sitting. Kate and Brad both helped themselves to thick slices of garlic sausage, sopressata, and hard cured cheese.

Cindy's husband, who had recently arrived with the birthday girl, came over and demanded they also try the pickled hot peppers. Brad immediately popped one in his mouth and gave a satisfied smile. Kate said no thanks but scooped up a handful of green olives. The three adults stood there munching and making small talk as the other party guests chased their children around the room.

In what seemed like a very short amount of time, the noise level in the yoga studio had elevated to the point where Kate had to yell to be heard. A glance around the room showed the place to be at full capacity. There was no way Cindy would have been able to squeeze this many people into her apartment. Kate estimated that at least thirty adults and as many children were at the party. She knew many of them were Rich's family. His relatives pretty much all lived on Long Island and had no problem making the trek to Brooklyn for family gatherings. Kate remembered Cindy's complaints about some of them. His sisters, for example, had wanted Rich to marry a nice Italian girl, not a half-Jewish mutt from the Midwest. That's what Cindy called herself, a mutt. "I'm a little bit of everything without pedigree," she liked to say. "That's why I can relate to everyone."

Just then someone tapped Kate on the shoulder. She turned to find an attractive woman with a stylish blond pixie haircut, freckles, and gorgeous blue eyes smiling at her. She was wearing a denim miniskirt and black leather riding boots and had a baby girl about Oliver's age in her arms. "Excuse me, are you Kate Carter?" the woman asked.

"Yes," Kate answered, smiling, trying to quickly figure out who this woman was. Should she know her?

"I'm Fiona, Skye's mother," the woman said, juggling the baby to her other slim hip. "Angel told me you'd be at this party."

Kate had heard the names Skye and Angel and knew she recognized them, but her brain wouldn't cooperate and tell her why.

In about one more second, this Fiona woman would know she had no idea who she was.

Sure enough, she caught on to Kate's confusion. "Your Zora and my Angel are friends, and they take the kids to sign language class together," Fiona explained.

"Oh my God, right," Kate said, slapping her palm to her forehead. "Of course. Zora tells me how much Ollie and Skye like to play and how they met at the park." It was all coming back to her now. Zora had said Angel was the person who'd told her about the sign language classes, but the information had traveled to the part of Kate's mind where she stored random trivia.

"So, where is Oliver?" Fiona asked, scanning the room. "I'm dying to meet my daughter's first crush."

Kate turned in the direction where they had left Oliver. Brad was sitting by the stroller, watching him sleep. "He's over there." Kate pointed. "Unfortunately, he's sleeping and missing all the fun."

Fiona smiled wistfully. "I wish Skye would be so accommodating. I swear, the girl will never take a nap for me. But with Angel, it's like every day I come home and she tells me Skye slept for two and a half hours, no problem."

"Oh, I know," Kate said. "Zora has no problem getting Oliver to sleep, whereas sometimes with me at night, he'll stare at me like 'You know I'm not going to bed, right?'"

Fiona laughed.

Kate continued, "Zora can get him to eat anything, too. She gets him to eat pureed vegetables like they're candy."

Fiona leaned in as if to tell Kate a special secret. "Do you think it's some kind of special nanny black magic they use?" she asked. "You know, put a spell on our kids when they're with them, and by the time we get home, it's worn off?"

Kate laughed. "I don't think so. I just think since they're with them all day long, they make it their business to get the kids to be as well behaved as possible. It's in their best interest." She paused to let her words sink in. "I mean, to me it shows that they're really good at what they do."

Fiona stopped to think about this. "I guess you're right. I never really thought about it that way. I just kind of feel guilty, like Angel knows more about my own child than I do." She laughed to take the edge off of what she had admitted.

Kate shook her head. "I know if I were home with Ollie all day, we'd be in sync, too. I stayed home with him for six months, and we were. It kind of hurts to think of your child being with another woman for such a huge part of the day, but in the grand scheme of things, this is such a small part of their lives. And I'm glad I found someone as loving and dedicated as Zora to fill in for me."

"I don't know how dedicated Angel is—she told me when I hired her that she was going to go back to Italy to resume her painting career—but she is truly fantastic with Skye." Fiona shrugged. "And I was kind of desperate at the time."

"What kind of work do you do?" Kate asked Fiona.

"I work at an advertising agency."

"Creative or account management?" Kate queried.

"Creative," Fiona answered. "I'm an art director. I work at a smaller firm. We mostly do ads for nonprofits and universities."

"What's the name of your firm?" Kate asked. "I work in PR at Jacobs and Zimbalist."

"Oh, I've heard of them," Fiona said. "You guys work with KasperKline and the New School. I work for Kelite."

"KasperKline is my main client, actually," Kate said. "But I'm sorry, I've never heard of Kelite."

"Don't be sorry," Fiona said. "We're a small boutique firm, but that's why I get to be art *director*. I get to design ads and logos for people and products I really believe in."

Kate chewed on an olive for a minute. Did she need any more friends? She was trying to decide if she should take the chitchat conversation and turn it into something more, but before she could make that decision, Fiona beat her to the punch. "Hey, we should get together with the babies sometime for a playdate. With Cindy, too."

"Yeah, I'd love to," Kate said. She realized she meant it. The truth was, she and Brad had lost a bunch of their friends once Ollie was born. Moving to Brooklyn, baby on board, they had become social pariahs to their childless Manhattan friends. At least Carl and Sheila were new parents, but they were way too green. They still thought every time their son, Austin, reached a developmental milestone, like turning over onto his stomach by himself, it was time for a major celebration. Kate had been there and done that. Sheila and Carl still needed a cooldown period before they'd be fun to hang with again. But she and Fiona seemed to be right in sync. Fiona got it. Working but loving your child. Living in Brooklyn but commuting to Manhattan. There was so much Kate wouldn't have to explain or make excuses for. As much as she loved Cindy, she didn't know how much they had in common besides their kids.

In the midst of the conversation, Skye wandered off on wobbly legs to explore the party space. Kate and Fiona simultaneously pulled out their Palm Pilots in order to record each other's information. They laughed. "Okay, you first," Fiona instructed. "Give me your phone number. No, wait, tell me your last name first."

When they'd finished swapping personal data, the two women promised to make plans to get together soon. Knowing that their grown-up time had expired, each went off to reclaim her child and join the party.

Later that night, Kate and Brad watched a movie, curled up together on the couch. Oliver slept soundly upstairs, worn out after the party and dinner at his parents' favorite Thai restaurant. Lying there on the sofa, Kate experienced a moment of exquisite satisfaction.

"I like our life," she whispered to Brad when the movie was over and they were lying together in the dark. The streetlight in front of their house cast a milky glow over the room. "I love my child, I love our home, and I love living in New York."

"Ahem. And what about your fabulous husband?" Brad whispered in Kate's ear. "Don't you love him, too?"

"Yeah, you're okay," Kate teased, and kissed her husband lightly on the nose. "You know, I really liked that Fiona woman." She sat slightly and turned to face Brad.

"She seemed cool," Brad said, pulling Kate back down to snuggle.

She didn't resist, but she continued with her thoughts. "It's really perfect because our kids apparently are already friends."

"How did you guys meet, exactly?" Brad asked.

"Just today, at the party," Kate replied. "Turns out Zora and Fiona's nanny, Angel, met at the park a while back. Angel is a painter or something, and she keeps threatening to flee back to Italy, where I guess she used to live."

"Is she Italian?" Brad asked.

"No, I think she's Black, or at least I assumed she was."

"Why did you assume that?" Brad asked.

Kate couldn't tell if he was teasing her or expected a real answer. "I just assumed because she was a nanny—" she started.

Brad gave Kate The Look. It said, "Be careful with what you are about to say." He got the same look whenever she tried to explain to his bleeding-heart-liberal parents why she favored the death penalty for sex offenders and serial killers. So Kate clamped her mouth shut and considered her words carefully, hoping to avoid another lecture from Mr. Politically Correct.

"Brad," she started calmly. "It is a fact around here that most nannies are Black. You can't deny that. So just because I assumed Angel was Black doesn't make me a racist. It makes me observant."

"I never said you were a racist," Brad responded, shaking his head. He kissed Kate on the cheek to prove there were no hard feelings.

"But you keep implying it," Kate said. "It seems like ever since we hired Zora, we have to keep talking about these 'issues.' And you always seem to be intent on making me feel guilty for some crime I'm sure I didn't commit."

"Am I doing that to you, or is that your own conscience talking?" Brad asked gently.

Kate stopped to think. Maybe it wasn't guilt she was feeling, exactly; maybe it was a consciousness of race that she was being forced to grapple with that she'd never had to face in the past. Before Zora, she never thought about these things. She didn't have any Black friends, except Lisa at work, but that didn't count because it was strictly a work relationship.

"Maybe," Kate admitted. "But I still feel like you could stop trying to make me feel bad for hiring Zora and actually be grateful that I did."

Brad exhaled a loud sigh. "I *am* glad you hired Zora. I think she's wonderful, and I think she takes really good care of Ollie, which is the key thing. And I'd be lying if I said I didn't love her cooking. Sorry, honey, but she kicks your ass in the kitchen."

"I know." Kate laughed. She wasn't even going to try to defend herself in that realm. "Everything she makes is soooo good."

"Just promise me that you'll think a little bit before you say some things," Brad said, getting back to the issue at hand. "I'm not saying I'm perfect; I just want you to try to be a little bit more aware, that's all."

"Fine," Kate managed. "I'll try to be more aware." She couldn't help adding, "But I think you may be overreacting a bit with this whole Black-nanny thing. I mean, even Black people use nannies from the Caribbean."

Brad sighed. "I know. I understand the economics of the situation, and maybe I am being too sensitive, but that means we both have something to work on. We should keep talking about these things, because they're not just going to go away."

"Do we have to talk about it all the time?" Kate whined.

"Hey," Brad pointed out, "just because we're White doesn't mean race doesn't affect us. Especially now, with Zora in the picture."

Kate knew when to admit defeat. "I guess you're right." She snuggled back down into Brad's arms.

"That's my Katie," he teased. "Always willing to step on over to the dark side with us crazy liberals and Communists."

"Ha-ha." Kate scowled, but she really didn't mind when Brad tried to get her to change her ways of thinking. She knew he meant well. He believed in all of those "We Are the World," everybody's-equal, civil-rights, Quaker values he grew up with in Mount Airy. Plus, his parents were serious Unitarians. What else could you expect? It was what made Brad special, but that didn't mean she had to completely buy into his peace, love, and harmony new world order. Kate knew life didn't work like that, but for now she didn't need to burst Brad's bubble.

The two of them lay there quietly for a moment, trying to decide who had won the last round.

"I love you," Kate whispered to Brad.

"I love you, too, honey," Brad answered.

"Brad?" Kate whispered.

"Hmmm," Brad mumbled as he nuzzled his wife's left earlobe.

"I think I want another baby," Kate whispered.

Brad stopped nuzzling. He sat up, and his expression shifted from shock to confusion. "Where did that come from? I thought we said we'd wait until Ollie was at least three."

"I know," Kate said, wrapping her arms around Brad's neck and pulling him back down. "But we have Zora now, so things would be totally different. She could definitely handle two kids, she's so good at managing it all, and Ollie would be almost three by the time the baby came . . . I'm just saying we should think about it."

"I don't know," Brad said, the uncertainty still clear in his voice. "Things seem to be getting back to normal now."

"Fine, discussion tabled for the time being," Kate conceded. "Just promise me you'll think about it, okay?"

Brad closed his eyes to his wife's request. "I'll think about it," he finally answered.

CHAPTER 19

Zora

Keith loved going to the movies. Zora calculated that in the last month, she'd been at least five times. And that was fine with her. Especially since Keith always paid, *and* he had great taste in films. He wasn't the typical guy's guy who wanted to watch only testosterone-filled flicks where special effects took the place of a believable plot. No, Keith's idea of a good movie often included subtitles, deeply nuanced characters, and an ambiguous ending. Zora was learning a lot about filmmaking and acting from him. Today they were going to see a French film at a blink-and-you'll-miss-it movie theater in the West Village.

Knowing they'd be trudging through the icy streets to get to the theater, Zora put fashion on the back burner and dressed for comfort and warmth. She could now admit it to herself: they were officially dating. Nothing had been discussed, but Zora had opened her heart and mind and let Keith work his way in, and so far things were good. Keith kept her spirits up and always wanted to help her figure out her future plans. Sometimes he was a little too eager, but she knew it came from wanting to help. After she'd cooked for him one time at his place, he declared her the Black Martha Stewart and wanted to know why she didn't have her own domestic empire already. "Lifestyles by Zora," he'd said, framing his hands around an imaginary sign in lights.

She'd snorted and waved her hands at his ambitious plans. "When I get some Martha Stewart money, I'll get back to you," she'd said. Keith didn't push it, but whenever he wanted her to think big about her life, he'd say it again: "Lifestyles by Zora."

Today there'd be no lifestyles talk, because hopefully, Keith would be talking about his audition for a national commercial. Yes, it was for a car insurance company, but it was one of those companies that paid gobs of money for advertising campaigns. Zora had all of her fingers and toes crossed for him. He desperately needed some good luck.

Zora glanced at the clock and realized she'd better hurry up. She had told Keith she'd meet him down at the coffee shop at one o'clock so they could walk to the subway together. They always met outside because Zora had a rule about letting men inside her home before she was ready. This was based partly on superstition, partly on her mother's warnings against letting a boy into your bedroom, and partly on something she'd read recently about attracting your true mate. She knew she had an issue with rushing into intimacy—meaning she always fell too fast and too hard—so she needed to erect some boundaries. Keith was the first guy she was trying her new rules on, and so far he seemed okay with it.

Surveying herself in the mirror, dressed in jeans and a thick orange turtleneck sweater, Zora decided she looked like she'd tried but not too much. As a finishing touch, she sprayed herself with a hint of citrus scent and wet her lips with shimmery gold lip gloss. Mission accomplished. In one fluid motion, she grabbed her purse, keys, and coat and headed out the door.

Keith was standing inside the coffee shop, talking to Katrina, but his eyes were fixed on the entranceway. When he saw Zora, he smiled. She walked in, said hi to Katrina, and kissed Keith on both cheeks, French-style.

"Mmm, you smell good," Keith purred in her ear.

Zora pulled back with a satisfied smile. "Thank you."

Keith took another moment to admire Zora, then grabbed her hand. "Are you ready?" he asked.

"Yep," Zora answered.

"Then let's hit it," he said, pulling her out into the cold.

As they walked the three blocks to the subway, Zora asked what time the movie started.

"Two-thirty," Keith replied, pulling Zora in closer to his body as they walked.

She checked her watch and realized they had over an hour to get to the theater. But considering it was Saturday, which meant the subways could be running on a slow schedule, it was probably a good idea to have time on their side. It meant more time for window-shopping and people-watching in the West Village. With all the cute little boutiques, gourmet food shops, and bistro-style cafés, the West Village always reminded Zora of Paris. Sometimes it even smelled like Paris. Like coffee, cloves, and cigarettes.

"Do you want to stop at Magnolia Bakery to buy some cupcakes to eat during the movie?" Zora asked with a mischievous grin. She'd discovered Magnolia thanks to Angel, and now she tried to find any and every excuse to go into the city to buy one of their famous chocolate cupcakes with mountains of buttercream frosting. Zora had decided a cupcake from Magnolia Bakery, accompanied by a cold glass of milk, was a sin better than sex.

Keith laughed. "I knew you were going to go there," he said, shaking his head. "I seriously think you have a cupcake addiction. What do you think they put in those cupcakes? Crack? The way people line up for them, they should call them crackcakes."

Zora burst out laughing. "Shut up."

"No, admit it," Keith argued. "You are an addict. A cupcake junkie. Junk-kie!" he repeated.

"I am not." Zora pouted. "I could stop anytime I want. Really, I could." While trying to keep a straight face, she added, "But I don't want to stop. So I'm going to buy a cupcake for the movie. You can eat some stale, greasy popcorn if you want."

Keith threw up his hands, chuckling. "Fine. But don't come crying to me when your crackcake addiction gets out of control and you start stealing and lying and showing up to work with frosting tracks all over yourself."

Zora laughed long and hard. "You are such a nut," she sputtered, and realized at that exact moment that she might really be falling for this man.

As they stood on the platform waiting for the A train, Zora decided to ask about the audition. "So . . ." she started, looking expectantly at Keith.

"So . . . what?" he asked without the slightest indication that he knew what she was getting at.

Zora frowned. "How did the audition go?"

"The audition went great," Keith said with a sardonic smile. "But I didn't get the part. They gave it to a light-skinned Mexican guy."

"I thought you said they were specifically looking for an African-American male," Zora said.

"The company found out through market research that they didn't have to go all the way Black to get the message out there that they sell insurance to colored folk. Jose was ethnic enough to do the trick. So that means my Black ass got bumped again."

"I'm sorry, sweetie," Zora said, squeezing Keith's hand. She watched him try to contain his anger, the veins throbbing in his temple and down his neck giving away how hard he was working to stay under control.

Keith shook his head and uttered through clenched teeth, "Yeah, well, that's show business."

Zora didn't say anything. A cool breeze dragging the scent of stale garbage meant a train was approaching the station. When the giant metal beast screeched to a halt in front of them, Zora and Keith stepped aboard, found two seats, and sat in silence for the entire ride.

• • •

After the movie, Keith and Zora headed back toward the subway in no real hurry, stopping to peer into windows and shops whenever Zora saw something she liked—mostly shoes and kitchen gadgets. While they stood in front of a tiny Japanese tea shop and debated whether or not to go in, Zora's cell phone rang. It was Angel.

"Where are you?" Angel asked before saying hello.

Zora chuckled. "I'm with Keith in the Village. Why?"

"Cool, I'm about to jump on the train at Canal Street. I'll meet you. Where are you, exactly?"

Before Zora could decide if she wanted to share her date, Angel blurted out, "Hurry, I hear the train. Just tell me where you are."

Zora ignored Keith's raised eyebrows and told Angel to meet them at the tea shop. She put her phone back in her purse and informed Keith that Angel would be joining them for tea.

Keith knew who Angel was, but this would be the first time they'd all hung out together. Zora was pretty sure Angel and Keith would get along fine; she just hoped Angel wouldn't mention any of the things she'd told her in confidence about her doubts about Keith, or worse, about her disastrous relationship with Alexander. She didn't think Angel would do that to her, but with Angel, you never knew exactly what was going to pop out of her mouth.

When Angel arrived at the teahouse, she squealed in delight as she saw Zora. "*Ciao, bella,*" she said, walking over to their table and stopping right in front of Keith. Today she'd pulled her hair into two fluffy Afro puffs, and she wore a pair of lavender earmuffs against the cold. She gave Keith the once-over and then pronounced, "You were right, he is a hunk."

Keith burst out laughing, and Zora shook her head, feeling a warm blush spread across her cheeks. Angel was Angel. You were either going to love her or hate her.

"Hello, Angel," Zora said, pulling out the empty chair at their table. "Come on, sit down."

"Thank you," Angel answered, and with a grand flourish she slipped out of her coat and slid into her seat in one fluid motion. She loosened her nubby green crocheted scarf, poured herself a cup of tea from the delicate porcelain pot in the middle of the table, and turned her attention to Keith. "So, you're the man who's been keeping our Zora company." She started warming her hands on her cup.

"Yes," Keith drawled, remaining remarkably cool under Angel's penetrating gaze.

"Well, I've heard a lot about you, Mr. Actor and all that."

Zora prayed Angel wouldn't bring up the stripping thing. Not like it was a secret, but she didn't want Keith to think she was out there putting his business in the streets.

Keith grinned. "I hope it was all good."

"You know, it's all information," Angel said. "So it's all good. But I do have a question for you."

"Shoot," Keith said.

"How much do you make from a night of stripping?"

It was Zora's turn to squeal. "Angel," she admonished her friend.

Angel turned to Zora with an expression of exaggerated innocence. "What? I just want to know because I'm thinking about getting a gig like that myself. The nanny business—between you and me—isn't bringing the cash in fast enough."

"Angel is trying to make enough money to go back to Italy, back to her life as a famous expat artist," Zora explained to Keith.

"Look, I can sympathize," Keith said to Angel, "but honestly, what men make as strippers and what women make are two totally different animals."

"Really?" Angel said, giving Keith her full attention.

"Yeah, you need to talk to another female stripper to get the real deal. To find out what clubs are hot and all that."

"Do you know any chicks who strip?" Angel probed.

Keith grinned. "No, and even if I did, I probably wouldn't admit it in front of my girl, here."

Zora kind of liked the way he referred to her as his girl. But she needed to clear up his erroneous assumption. "Look," she started, "if there's anything I've learned from you, it's that stripping is just another side hustle. So if you've got female friends who are strippers, I'm cool with that. I knew this Canadian girl at Ann Arbor who paid her senior-year tuition by stripping at some of the hottest clubs in Detroit. She might have done more than stripping, too."

Angel interrupted. "Not me. I just want the good old-fashioned 'take my clothes off, shake my ass' type of gig."

Keith laughed again. "I might be able to make a few calls to some of my fellow struggling-actor friends who could hook you up. I'll pass their info along through Zora."

Angel smiled. "Thank you."

Eager to change the subject, Zora jumped in to ask Angel what she was doing in the city. Angel launched into a long saga about trying to find the right color paint for a new portrait of a homeless man she was working on. As evidence, she whipped out two tubes of oil paint and asked them which color looked more appropriate for a gruesome bloody scab.

"Seriously, the guy has this gash on his head that looks like someone whacked him with a meat cleaver. It's disgusting," Angel explained.

"So then why are you painting him?" Keith asked.

Angel looked at Keith as if he'd just asked the stupidest question in the world. "Because that's what life and art are all about. Blood and pain and the shit we all have to deal with. I'm trying to get that mess on my canvas, really capture the details, which is why I have to have just the right color for the scab. *Capisce*?"

Keith nodded while Zora sipped her jasmine tea and nibbled on a red-bean rice cake. She loved listening to Angel talk about her work. Sometimes she wished she had that much passion for something. Then again, Angel's enthusiasm required a lot of energy. So for the time being, Zora was happy being Angel's friend, experiencing passion through association.

Zora looked at the two paint colors, one called brick red and the other called evening crimson, and decided neither one brought to mind a bloody scab. "I think you should mix the crimson with a chocolate brown and maybe add a little purple, and then you'll have the right color," Zora said to Angel.

"Ahh, *bella,* I think you might have it just right." Angel beamed at Zora. To Keith, she said, "I love this girl. She has a gift, you know, with colors and details. I don't know what I would do without her." With that, she leaned over and planted a loud, wet kiss on Zora's cheek.

"I know," Keith said, getting caught up in Angel's enthusiasm. "I keep telling her she needs to leave the nanny business behind and start up her own thing."

Zora rolled her eyes and shook her head. "Don't even go there."

Keith threw up his hands. "Sorry," he said. "I won't say anything else about it. Won't even mention 'Lifestyles by Zora.'"

"Keith," Zora said, frowning. "I mean it."

Keith gave her an apologetic smile, and then he, too, leaned over to plant a kiss on her cheek. "Sorry, baby."

Angel looked at the two of them as if to ask whether everything was okay. Zora ignored her and said, "What do you guys want to do now? Back to Brooklyn or somewhere in the city?"

"I don't know about you two, but my canvas is calling me. Now that you've given me the color combination, I've got to get home and try it," Angel said, standing up and putting her coat back on. She kissed Keith and Zora each on both cheeks and sashayed out of the teahouse.

Keith reached for Zora's hands and smiled. "Wow, she's intense, isn't she?"

"Yeah," Zora admitted.

"But I can see why you like her," Keith continued. "She seems like good people."

"She is," Zora said. "She's my closest friend here in New York. And she's one of those people who always makes time go by a little bit faster. You know what I mean."

"Yeah," Keith said, staring intently at Zora. "I know exactly what you mean."

CHAPTER 20

Kate

Kate checked her phone one more time. No messages. She gave a sigh of relief and then told herself to stop worrying so much. But this was her first business trip since Oliver had been born. Granted, she was only going to be away for three days, but since she had to get on an airplane and fly into a different time zone, it felt like a big deal.

Navigating the hectic crowds at LaGuardia made her focus on her mission to get to the gate on time instead of evaluating her worth as a mother. Really, she wanted to get to the gate before Danyel did. The two of them were flying to Chicago to attend a conference on reproductive health in urban communities at the University of Chicago. KasperKline insisted that everyone working for them had to stay abreast of current trends in birth-control practices and procedures. Kate didn't mind these conferences. In fact, being forced to learn made her feel like there was some intellectual content to her job, and she wasn't just a media whore. The whole trip would just be much more enjoyable if she didn't have Danyel Green as a traveling companion.

At least Danyel didn't balk at taking separate taxis, considering Kate was ready to leave the office at one and Danyel claimed she still had a report to finish. One thing Kate never did was wait until the last minute when it came to flying in and out of LaGuardia. She was always there at least ninety minutes ahead of time. She hated rushing and worrying that she might miss the plane.

Especially today, she had enough to worry about, leaving Ollie home alone with Brad.

Technically, Brad wouldn't be completely alone. Kate had paid Zora extra to come in on the weekend to relieve Brad for a few hours and make a couple of meals. To sweeten the deal for Zora, she offered the use of their washer and dryer. Zora had mentioned in one of their conversations how much she hated communal laundry facilities. "It's just too close for comfort," she'd said, making Kate coo in sympathy. Before she and Brad had gotten the brownstone, when they lived in their "cozy" one-bedroom in Manhattan, she'd bundle up her clothes and carry them all the way home to Philadelphia to wash them at her parents' house rather than go to the Laundromat on the corner. There were certain things she could never get used to, no matter how long she lived in the city.

"Excuse me," a woman shouted as she rolled over Kate's foot with her Tumi suitcase, racing down the hallway with a look of sheer panic. Kate shook her head. "This is not the subway, people," she wanted to exclaim. It was like everyone thought they could jump on an airplane at the last minute and the captain would hold the door for them. Was it so hard to leave your house a few minutes earlier?

She rounded the corner and saw that she was one of the first people to arrive for the flight. She had her pick of seats in the waiting area and was relieved to see the red lights flashing "on time" under the flight information for Chicago. Now, if only Danyel Green would run into horrible midday traffic and miss the plane, everything would be perfect.

"Ah, to be so lucky," Kate said aloud, thinking how nice this little sojourn to Chicago could be sans Danyel. She would go visit her friend Lesley from college, who now worked at the Field Museum, and she might even slip out of the conference early to do a little shopping on the Gold Coast. But with Danyel there, she'd be restricted to all work and no play. It would be disastrous to give Danyel any shred of ammunition. She'd probably run straight to Roger White or the client, claiming she had proof that Kate should be fired immediately.

Kate pushed her evil feelings aside and decided to call home. This would be her last check-in before she took off. She dialed her home phone number and Zora picked up on the second ring. "Hi, Zora," Kate said.

"Hey, Kate," Zora replied. "Aren't you supposed to be on an airplane?"

Kate smiled and slouched in her seat to get comfortable. "Not yet. I still have about thirty minutes until they start boarding. I just wanted to make sure you were okay with everything."

"Everything's fine," Zora said. "Ollie's sleeping right now. It wasn't that cold, so we took a long walk around the park and found some ducks to feed at the pond. Then we met up with Angel and Skye for lunch at that cute new kids' café on Sixth Avenue."

"What café?" Kate asked. "I don't think I've noticed it."

"Oh, it's fantastic," Zora said. "The menu is totally geared toward kids. They have peanut butter sandwiches, grilled cheese, and Ollie's favorite, the finger-food special, which is chunks of fruit and cheese served with crackers and Cheerios."

"That sounds adorable," Kate said.

"Yeah, it is," Zora said. "And you have to ask for a separate mommy menu if you want to see the grown-up selections, which are okay, pretty much sandwiches and a few salads. But it's all the rage with the mommy set."

"I can't believe I haven't heard of it," Kate mused. "How long has it been open?"

"Just a few months," Zora confirmed. "People like it because, besides having kid-friendly food, it has a pretty big play area, so once they're done eating, the kids can play and the mommies can chat."

"I'll definitely have to check it out," Kate said.

"Just remember, they're not open on weekends," Zora informed her.

Kate noticed more and more people coming to the gate and realized Danyel would be showing up any minute, so she changed the direction of the conversation. "Are you sure you're okay with coming by on Saturday and Sunday?"

"It's no problem," Zora said. "I'm going out with Keith on Saturday night, but other than that, I didn't have any plans, so it's fine."

"Thank goodness," Kate said, "because honestly, I know Brad is an excellent dad, but I feel a little bit better knowing that he won't be totally on his own with Ollie. You know men can be totally useless sometimes."

Zora laughed. "I hear you."

"I hope you don't mind, I gave Brad your cell number and told him to call you if he needs anything," Kate admitted.

"That's fine," Zora repeated.

"Good," Kate said with relief. "And I'm sure nothing will happen, but it's always better to have a contingency plan in place."

"Kate," Zora soothed, "don't worry. Brad and Ollie will be just fine. I've already decided to make a lasagna tomorrow, which will probably last all weekend, but I'll whip up something else on Sunday morning so Brad won't have to worry about cooking or grocery shopping. He can focus on taking care of Ollie."

Kate could feel the tension in her shoulders ease, listening to Zora. She knew exactly what to say and do to make Kate relax. She knew she wouldn't have to worry about the baby while she was gone.

But she would have to worry about Danyel, who obviously didn't get stuck in traffic. Kate watched as Danyel came hustling down the hallway, dragging her suitcase and barking at someone on her cell phone and generally looking very annoyed.

Kate sighed. "Well, it looks like I have to go."

"Is your plane boarding?" Zora asked.

"Not quite," Kate said. "I have to deal with something unpleasant that just came up."

"Okay," Zora said. "Well, have a great trip."

"Thanks," Kate said. "It doesn't look like that will be possible, but I'll try."

CHAPTER 21

Zora

ZORA had to walk to the bus stop after sign language class without Angel. Skye was home sick with another ear infection. For a child who was fed only organic food, she sure got sick a lot. Angel told Zora it was because her mother stopped breast-feeding her at eight weeks: Fiona had gone back to work after two months of maternity leave. And after only one week of pumping breast milk at work, Fiona introduced Skye to organic soy-based formula. "It's still formula," Angel said and sneered, as if Fiona had been feeding her daughter grape Kool-Aid.

Zora didn't mind walking alone. After class, she pushed Oliver through Fort Greene Park and wasted almost an entire hour meandering through the neighborhood. Even though she lived in Fort Greene, she spent most of her time in Park Slope, so this was a good time to explore. She loved to look at all of the stately brown-stones on Clinton Avenue. Some of them had fallen into disrepair, with boarded-up windows and graffiti-marked walls marring their facades, but most of them stood graceful and imposing, appearing every bit like the summer homes of New York City's former elite. Even though Fort Greene was considered a Black neighborhood— where "Black" was code for less desirable real estate—Zora thought the houses in Fort Greene were far grander than the average brown-stones and town houses in Park Slope. She related her opinions to Oliver as they strolled, and he peeped and squeaked and clapped his hands in encouragement. When an airplane flew overhead or they passed a flower poking its head through the warming earth, she pointed it out and said the word in French. "*Avion,* Oliver. *Fleur.*" Sometimes he would mimic her. Sometimes he would just smile. Zora wanted Oliver to say at least one or two words in French so Kate would feel like she was getting her money's worth.

As they approached DeKalb Avenue, Zora checked the time on her cell phone. Kate had called while they were in class to say she would be home late again. Not until seven-thirty. Brad wouldn't be home until at least six-thirty. He had another late meeting at work. This had been a recent occurrence in the past few weeks. Zora quickly calculated. It was five-thirty now. There was a bus in five minutes, or she could get a hot chocolate at Tillie's and catch the six-fifteen.

"What do you say, Ollie?" Zora poked her head into the stroller. "How about some hot chocolate?"

Oliver clapped and gurgled his reply. It sounded like "na na." French? She laughed to herself. Kate and Brad should be happy if their son managed to squeak out any intelligible word in English. He liked to say "da da da," but nobody believed he was referring to Brad—except maybe Brad. Clearly, Oliver was not going to be one of those precocious kids speaking in full sentences before age two. Like that incredibly obnoxious eighteen-month-old in their music class who seemed to know all the words to the songs before the teacher even sang them. The girl would have you thinking she was sixteen, with the way she strung sentences together. Her mother was only too proud to show off her daughter's "absolutely amazing" vocabulary. Zora hated it when parents did that. Why not let their babies be babies for just a little while?

Zora turned the corner at DeKalb Avenue, trod a wide circle around the surly-looking bulldog tied to the bike rack, and pushed the stroller right up to the front stoop of Tillie's. Because the door pushed out, Zora had to pop the wheels of the stroller up the step and balance them there while she simultaneously pulled the door toward her. At just the right moment, using the momentum from the pull, Zora gave the stroller a mighty push and got everyone inside before the door slammed on her backside. Once inside, Zora allowed her eyes to adjust to the dim lighting. The sweet, earthy aroma of roasted coffee beans assailed her nostrils as she scanned the room, looking for an empty table where she could park Ollie while she ordered. She had to make sure he'd be within viewing distance of the counter but not too close to anyone who looked deeply entrenched in work and might get annoyed by his baby babble. As she was looking around, she noticed a man who seemed familiar. She squinted to make sure. It was indeed Brad Carter, wearing the same navy blue pin-striped suit she'd seen him in that morning, minus his tie. He was sitting with a beautiful blond woman who was definitely not his wife. She, too, looked like she might have stepped out from work, with her tailored charcoal slacks and a crisp white button-down blouse. They seemed to be talking, but their heads were bent close together, and they appeared to be deeply engrossed in their conversation.

Zora didn't know where the panicky feeling came from, but just like that, the urge to escape before Brad Carter noticed her was overwhelming. Like she had been caught doing something wrong. It was the same feeling she'd had when she was seven years old and had walked in on her parents having sex on a Sunday morning. Even though it wasn't her fault, she felt guilty for catching her parents in an act that seemed very unparent-like. Zora didn't know what Brad was doing with this woman when he was supposed to be at a meeting in his office, and she didn't want to know, either. There was truth in the saying "Ignorance is bliss."

Zora quickly turned on her heel and pushed her way back out the door, but damn it all, she forgot about the step and tripped. "Shit," she yelped, but quickly recovered. Oliver, on the other hand, sensed her desperation and started to whimper. She tried to shush him while she hustled away from the café as fast as she could. She headed down Clinton Avenue, thinking she would take Ollie to her apartment while they waited for the next bus.

But then she heard footsteps. Clearly, she hadn't moved fast enough. "Zora! Wait!" It was Brad running after her. Obviously, he'd seen her, or probably heard her not-so-subtle exit. Zora considered pretending she didn't hear him. She also considered telling him he was mistaken, that he hadn't just seen her inside Tillie's. But with a sigh of resignation, she stopped walking and waited for him to catch up. She didn't turn around, though. She just waited, holding her breath for whatever was about to transpire.

When Brad finally reached her, he was panting. It took him a moment to catch his breath, but he was smiling. "Hey, Zora, why'd you run away like that? Like you'd seen a ghost or something."

"You looked busy, that's all," Zora said, trying to keep the accusation out of her voice.

Realization registered in Brad's eyes. "Ohhh, you think I was . . ." He didn't finish his sentence.

Zora started walking again. What Brad and Kate did in their personal lives was no concern of hers, but she felt a loyalty to Kate that didn't include being a witness to Brad's infidelity.

"Wait, Zora, it's not what you think," he started.

"What *I* think is not really important. I'm not being paid to think. Just to take care of your child while Kate works and you attend to your *meetings*," Zora said, not even bothering to mask her sarcasm.

"Hey, that's enough. I will not have you insult me like that," Brad shot back. Maybe she'd gone too far. He said in a calmer tone of voice, "I would never cheat on Kate. Never. Not that I need to tell you this, but what you just stumbled onto was a business meeting. It happens to be for a project I'm pursuing outside of work."

Zora wasn't ready to back down. "Kate said you were staying late *at work* for a meeting, so you can imagine why this looks suspicious." Zora continued walking, her head held haughtily in the air. She called out her last response: "But again, it's none of my business. You don't have to tell me anything."

Brad chased her again. "I know I don't *have* to tell you anything, but I want to. Can you stop walking, please?" he practically shouted.

Zora stopped moving. She cocked her head and pursed her lips, waiting for what he would say next.

"Look, come with me back to the café, and I'll explain. Please."

Zora took a deep breath and considered her options. If she didn't go and listen, then she'd be tormented with guilt and unease, wondering if he really was cheating on Kate. If she did go, he might be able to convince her to keep quiet about his possible infidelity. Damned if I do, damned if I don't, she thought as she turned Oliver's stroller around and reluctantly followed Brad back to the café.

It turned out Brad wasn't cheating on Kate. But he was lying to her. The after-work meetings were all about the comic book/video game venture Carl had mentioned at the Christmas party. Brad had been asked to get involved as the financial adviser and a potential investor. He hadn't told Kate yet, he explained to Zora over steaming mugs of black tea, because they were still in the exploratory phase of things and there was no reason to worry her about something that might never happen. And she would worry.

"Look, Zora," Brad said while keeping Oliver entertained with his Spider-Man key chain, "I'd really appreciate it if you didn't tell Kate. It's like a hobby for me right now. A hobby that my wife is not too terribly impressed with." He paused, giving Zora a moment to consider his request. To prove his good intentions, he added, "I would never do anything serious with our finances without consulting Kate. You have to know that."

"Then why not just tell her?" Zora countered. "I've never been married, but I happen to know that lying to your wife is not up there on the list of things you're supposed to do to stay married."

"I know," Brad snapped. "My parents have been married for thirty-six years. I know what makes a marriage last. But look, this group of guys I'm working with—"

"You mean 'group of guys and one very attractive blond woman,'" Zora interrupted. She noticed that the woman had disappeared.

"Yes," he conceded, "and one *woman*, who happens to be happily married and three months pregnant, I might add." Zora bit her lip to quash her smart-ass retort that marriage and babies had never stopped folks from cheating. Brad continued, "These are some really creative, talented people going after their dream. And it might work. I know I'm just the money guy. They didn't come to me because of my great knowledge of comics or art or anything. But I feel like I'm part of the creative energy. It's awesome, and I love it. I don't get to be creative as a stockbroker."

Zora understood Brad's feelings, which was why she found it hard to believe that Kate wouldn't understand, too. She said as much to Brad.

"I love Kate," Brad explained. "I love every little type A blood cell in her body, but she doesn't or won't understand why I want to do this. She seriously believes comic books and video games are for children." He took a swig of his tea. "She would say that this was a waste of my time. That I should be using my free time to do something more meaningful."

"Maybe not," Zora tried.

Brad shook his head. "We've had the discussion before, millions of times, whether it was comic books or snowboarding with my friends, and it always ends up with her upset at my adolescent tendencies. So rather than get her more upset, I'm choosing to keep it to myself. Everybody is happy, and nobody gets hurt."

Zora gave Brad her best "Do I look like Boo-Boo the Fool?" look. It was one of her father's signature responses whenever she tried to explain her rationale for not returning to college.

"Look, it's just for the time being," Brad protested. "Right now we're getting together and shooting ideas around. I'm supposed to start writing the business plan for them in a few weeks, and when I get to that point, I'll let Kate know. But she's so busy right now, and so happy, I don't want to have her worry for nothing."

"So you're lying to her for her own good?" Zora summed up.

"God, you make it sound so dirty," Brad said, exasperated. "But yes, if that's how you want to see it, you can. And I would appreciate it if you, too, would lie to keep her happy."

Zora gave a little laugh of derision. "If I don't, you'll fire me, right?"

"Absolutely," Brad said.

For a minute Zora didn't know if he was kidding or not. "I guess I have no choice." She frowned.

"Oh, don't be so dramatic," Brad said. "Of course I wouldn't fire you. Kate would kill me." He looked down at his son, happily gumming a hunk of cranberry biscotti. "I think this little guy would, too. So, no, I wouldn't fire you. I'd just have to come clean to Kate, risk making her really mad, and possibly give up something that hurts no one but makes me incredibly happy."

Zora thought about this. The way Brad explained it, it didn't sound so bad. Nobody was getting hurt. And again, who was she to get involved in the way they managed their marriage? She would just go on doing her job. Knowing that Brad Carter was with a bunch of people talking about comic books in Brooklyn instead of on Wall Street talking about money wouldn't change her life one bit.

"Zora," Brad asked, "haven't you ever told a lie to spare someone's feelings?"

Zora thought about her parents. They still didn't know she was working as a nanny.

"Yeah, I guess so," she admitted. "Okay, Brad, you win. I won't tell." She sighed. "Your secret is safe with me."

CHAPTER 22

Kate

KATE didn't even bother calling home to tell Zora she'd be late. It had pretty much become the routine that she'd make it home sometime after seven these days. She felt a mild sense of guilt because she probably could have been home on time tonight if she hadn't met Fiona for a lunch that had lasted two hours.

But Zora didn't seem to mind. That's what Kate appreciated the most about Zora. She never seemed bothered or acted like she wished she were anyplace else but in their home. She was so steady and stable. Kate found her presence comforting. She knew she'd struck nanny gold with Zora. She'd heard horror stories of nannies who demanded being paid time and a half to stay one minute later than contracted. Even then they grumbled and complained about it. Then there were the ones who had their own families waiting for them back home. They were the worst, because they always had a legitimate excuse as to why they could never, ever stay a little longer or come in on a weekend here and there. Even Fiona admitted that as wonderful as Angel was with Skye, she never knew for sure if Angel would be there the next day, as she was always plotting her return to Italy.

In a burst of inspiration brought on by an overwhelming sense of love for her nanny, Kate decided she should buy Zora a little gift, a token of her appreciation. It was the right thing to do, Kate felt. She wanted Zora to know how much she meant to her peace of mind. Kate wrote a note for herself to ask Zora when her birthday was, and also to ask more about this Keith guy. Zora seemed to mention him more often these days; it sounded like maybe they were a real couple. Zora kept her personal life private, but if she needed more time off, Kate wanted to know. She didn't want to appear insensitive. She knew if Zora was happy outside of work, she'd be happier at work. That was the golden rule of all human resources managers.

About two hours later, as Kate was finishing up at the office, she dialed home and told Zora she was on her way. She heard music playing in the background and Oliver making a ruckus trying to sing along. Kate smiled as she imagined the scene in her living room. It made her want to get home even sooner to partake in the merriment.

Before she hung up, she asked Zora if Brad was home yet. Zora paused before she answered, "No, not yet, but he called and said he'd be home soon. And that was like twenty minutes ago, so I expect him any minute."

"Great," Kate said. "But Zora, can you stick around until I make it home?"

"Of course," Zora agreed.

There weren't any nice stores around Kate's office, so she jumped in a cab and asked to be taken to Macy's in Herald Square. She knew just what she wanted to get Zora. She headed straight for the housewares department and asked the salesgirl where the mixers were. It was ridiculously expensive for a token of appreciation, but at that exact moment Kate was overcome with a sense of gratitude for Zora. She wouldn't be able to enjoy her life without this person who was doing all the things she would be doing if this were fifty years ago in America. Without hesitation, Kate picked up the box with the baby-pink KitchenAid mixer and headed to the counter to pay. The mixer was almost four hundred dollars, but you couldn't put a price tag on Zora's care for Oliver. Zora had even said that she'd like to do more baking but didn't have a good mixer. Kate and Brad had both gotten their bonuses in December, and there was plenty left over, so what was four hundred dollars?

"Can you gift wrap this, please?" Kate asked the young salesgirl behind the counter.

The girl eyed the enormous box, popped her gum, and said, "No." She didn't sound sorry, either.

"I know I've gotten things gift wrapped at Macy's before," Kate pressed.

"Yeah, well, we gift wrap at the holidays but not during regular time," the girl said, pausing between words to pop her gum.

Kate had to suppress the urge to slap the girl. Her rude behavior was ridiculous. Kate wondered when parents stopped teaching their kids manners and when department-store managers stopped caring about service with a smile.

"Do you sell regular gift bags?" Kate tried again.

"Yeah," the girl said, "but we don't have nothing to fit that big ol' box."

"Fine," Kate said, whipping out her credit card. Zora would have to accept her present unwrapped. Hopefully, she was a firm believer that it was the thought that counted and not the presentation.

By the time Kate walked through her own front door, she was questioning her good intentions. The mixer was so heavy. Carrying it on the subway and then the six-block walk home had been torture.

Brad came to the door carrying a freshly scrubbed Oliver, looking adorable in his green froggy pajamas. Brad had already changed into sweats, so he must have been home for a while.

"Hi, hardworking mama," he said, and kissed Kate on the cheek. Oliver reached out for his mother instantly, and she put down the mixer, grabbed him from her husband, and hugged him hard.

"How's Mommy's angel?" she gushed, covering him with kisses.

"Hey, what's in the bag?" Brad asked.

"It's for Zora," she whispered, still engrossed in kissing every part of her son's soap-scented body.

"Is it her birthday or something?" Brad whispered back.

"No," Kate answered. "I just wanted to say thank you to her for being so great."

"Oh," Brad said, shrugging. "That was nice of you."

"Can you please carry it into the living room?" Kate implored. "It's really heavy."

"What is it?" Brad asked.

"You'll see," Kate replied, already walking toward the living room. "Zora," she called out.

"Hey, Kate," Zora answered from the kitchen.

"Can you come out here a second?" Kate called as Oliver squirmed to get down to his basket of toys. She set him down reluctantly.

Zora came into the living room, wiping her wet hands on her apron. Before Kate could launch into her appreciation speech, Zora got down on the floor with Oliver and smiled up at Kate and Brad. "Watch what Ollie can do," she said.

She put one of Ollie's favorite toys, a purple fuzzy monkey with a yellow face, on the couch. Then she pointed to the monkey and said, "Look, Ollie. Go get your monkey." Oliver didn't disappoint. Right away he gave one of his loudest screeches, which Kate had decided sounded not unlike a baby dinosaur, and he was off. He pulled himself up to his knees, then placed his pudgy little hands on the couch cushions and, through sheer will and brute strength, pulled himself up. Once up, he looked at Zora and his mom and dad and gave one more screech of triumph. He grabbed his monkey and waved it overhead.

"Now, come on, Ollie," Zora encouraged, "bring Z the monkey." And he did. Holding on to the couch with only one hand, with the monkey clutched firmly in the other, Oliver walked his way down the entire length of the couch. Another screech of triumph.

"Good job, Ollie!" Kate exclaimed. "He's going to be walking on his own soon."

"When did he start doing that?" Brad asked.

"We've been working on it, haven't we, Ollie?" Zora said.

Oliver responded with what sounded like "Zee Zee Zee."

"Hey, he's saying *Z* for Zora, I think," Brad said.

"Are you saying my name?" Zora asked. Oliver answered by looking right in Zora's eyes and saying it again: "Zee, Zee Zee."

Kate had known this was likely to happen. That Oliver would call for Zora instead of Mommy when it mattered most. Even though she'd expected it didn't mean it hurt any less. But she wasn't angry and she wasn't jealous. She knew Oliver loved her, and she was okay with the fact that he loved Zora, too. They spent the most time together. It made sense that they would be close. That's what she wanted in a caregiver, someone who would fall in love with her child. Oliver was very lucky to have a loving nanny like Zora, Kate reminded herself. This was not a moment to lament, it was an occasion to celebrate, and that made her remember the present.

"Zora, I got you something," Kate said, trying to strike a cheerful tone. "Watching Oliver here tonight, I know that there is no present I could have gotten you that can say thank you enough for everything that you do for Oliver and us. But I thought you might like this."

Zora made all of the protests and claims that gifts were unnecessary, but Kate could tell she was pleased. It was obvious to Kate that Zora appreciated the simple things in life. She could see the happiness that praise gave her. So with renewed feelings of gratitude, Kate lugged the bag over to Zora.

Zora peeked inside and gave a squeal of delight. "A Kitchen-Aid mixer!"

"And it's pink," Kate added, getting caught up in Zora's obvious enthusiasm. "I knew that with your sense of style, you'd want a fashionable color, although I have no idea what color your kitchen is. I hope it doesn't clash."

Zora didn't answer for a minute. She was too busy reading the information on the sides of the box. "This is so fantastic," she said. "There's this marble pound-cake recipe I've been wanting to try, but it's hopeless without a mixer. Thank you so much." In answer to Kate's question, she said, "Don't worry, my kitchen is standard dull rental white. It matches and clashes with everything." She tried lifting the box. "My God, this is heavy," she groaned.

"I know." Kate laughed. "I carried the thing home."

Zora turned toward the kitchen and then looked back at Kate and Brad. "Feel free to say no," she started, "but can I leave the mixer here?"

"You mean and pick it up tomorrow or something?" Kate asked.

"No, I mean leave it here," Zora said.

Kate looked crestfallen. Maybe Zora didn't like the present so much after all. "I can put you in a car and have you driven home if you're worried about schlepping the thing on the bus," she offered.

"No, no, it's not that," Zora hurried to explain. "I was thinking that since I spend more time over here, I would get much more use out of the mixer if it stayed here."

"That seems reasonable," Brad chimed in.

But Kate didn't think it was right. "Zora, I bought that for you. I want you to have it in *your* home, to use for your own pleasure and to cook for your own friends and family."

Zora shook her head knowingly. "If you could see the kitchen in my apartment, you'd understand why I want to leave this here. Honestly, I don't think there's even a plug in my kitchen, much less enough counter space to fit this beautiful piece of equipment."

Kate didn't want to argue. If Zora wanted to leave the mixer in their kitchen, so be it. Zora practically ran the place anyway. And the kitchen had become her domain.

As she was gathering her things to go, Zora promised that tomorrow she'd give the new mixer a test run with the cake recipe she'd mentioned. She walked out the door with a satisfied smile, and Kate watched her hurry up the street. As she tidied up the living room, Kate knew she'd made the right decision with her gift. She hoped Zora now knew how much they appreciated her services.

By the time Brad came downstairs after putting Ollie to bed, Kate was seated on the couch, flipping through TV channels, looking for a show that didn't involve solving a murder in New York City. She wasn't having any luck. When she noticed Brad, she flicked off the TV and threw the remote to the other end of the sofa in disgust. "There is nothing worth watching on television," she complained.

Brad came over and sat down next to Kate and put his feet up on the coffee table.

"Can I ask you something?" she said innocently.

"Yeah," Brad said.

"Do you like Zora? I mean, do you like her as a person?"

"I don't know," Brad replied. "I guess I never really thought about it."

"What do you mean, you never thought about it?"

"I don't know," Brad tried again. "I think she's really good with Oliver, and she seems like a nice person, and she's a damn good cook."

"That's not what I'm asking. I mean, Zora's our age. You could have met her at a bar or a party. And I'm wondering what kind of person you think she is. Don't you ever wonder about her life and why she dropped out of school and all that?"

"Why are you asking me this?" Brad asked a tad defensively.

"I don't know," Kate answered truthfully. "I guess I was just thinking about circumstances and how we get where we are. Zora works for us, but she could just as easily be one of our friends from college or grad school. So I wanted to know what you think about her."

Brad got up from the couch to gaze out the window. "Like I said, I think she's really good with Oliver, but other than that, I don't feel like I know her enough to answer your question."

"How can you not know her enough?" Kate asked. "She's in our house every day. She takes care of our child. Sometimes you see her more than you see me in a day. What else do you need to render a decision?"

"Jeez, Kate, I guess I like her just fine. But it's not like we sit around and chitchat on a regular basis," Brad admitted.

Kate shook her head. "That's disturbing."

"What? Why is that disturbing?" Brad started pacing the living room. "Are you trying to start an argument for no reason?"

"No." Kate threw up her hands in protest. "You're the one who said we needed to talk about this stuff. And I'm saying I think *you* may be the one in need of a little sensitivity training this time."

"What is it you think I'm so guilty of?" Brad challenged.

"Basically, you admitted that you don't even think of Zora as a unique individual. She's just a worker bee who happens to spend over forty hours a week in your home and washes your dirty socks, but you haven't taken the time to get to know her," Kate summed up.

"Oh, and you have?" Brad challenged. "I don't see you and Zora palling around after hours."

"For your information, we talk on the phone almost every day, but that's beside the point. I never said we should all be hanging around together," Kate clarified. "I just asked if you liked her as a person, and you said you never even thought of her as a person, just an employee or something."

Brad laughed. "You are amazing. I didn't say that at all. You're putting words in my mouth."

"I was paraphrasing for you," Kate defended herself. "Why

don't you tell me what you did say or what you meant to say, for clarification?"

Brad sighed and stopped pacing. He stood in front of the fireplace with his back to his wife. Several moments passed. Kate didn't dare say a word. Finally, when he was ready to talk, Brad turned to look at Kate and quietly admitted he was wrong. "You're right," he said in a voice barely above a whisper. "I haven't taken the time to get to know Zora. To be honest, I haven't even thought about it. I guess I was caught up in being outraged that we'd been sucked into the New York City mind-set, where hiring a Black nanny goes with the lifestyle. I kind of shut myself off from trying to get to know her because I was angry at what she represented for us." He flopped down on the couch and added, "So all this time I've been policing your actions, and I'm just as guilty." He raked his fingers through his hair and apologized. "I'm sorry, Kate."

"Finally!" Kate smirked. "I'm not the bad guy tonight." She loved being on the right side of an ethical discussion for once.

Brad ignored Kate's teasing. "But I'm not that person," he pronounced, the anguish dripping from his voice. "I feel like such a sellout or something. How did I get to this place?"

"Hey, you're not a sellout," Kate assured her husband. "You're just a regular guy like the rest of us, caught up in real life. Don't be so hard on yourself." It was no fun beating Brad in an argument. He took losing so seriously, Kate realized.

Brad laid his head in his wife's lap like a wounded puppy. "I just never thought I'd be this guy," he whimpered. "Having a nanny. Being a stockbroker. Getting bonuses that equal the entire GDP of some small underdeveloped nations. *This* isn't supposed to be my life."

"Hey, you're not *that* guy," Kate admonished while she massaged Brad's temples with her fingertips. "This is not cause for a mental breakdown. You've admitted that you haven't taken the time to get to know your nanny. That is not a crime. And how you make your money is not a crime, either. It's what you choose to do with that money that indicates what matters to you. It's not like Zora's going anywhere. You can still get to know her better, too."

"I know. It's just not how I envisioned my future," Brad said. "I never assumed I'd be hiring a stranger to sit in my home and take care of my child."

"I know, Mr. Kumbayah," Kate said, trying to lighten the mood. "If I recall, when we met, your future plans included ditching your MBA program, moving to South America, and living on some farm to bake organic bread. You'd probably have all of your little bambinos strapped to your back while you tended to your wood-burning ovens."

Brad finally smiled. "Yeah, I would keep my kids with me all the time if I could," he said, sitting up to face his wife. "Instead, I chose to become a contributing member of this booming economy and hire someone else to keep my children close."

"Do you regret your choices?" Kate asked, trying to ignore the lump that had unexpectedly lodged itself in her throat.

"Of course not," Brad said. "I know why I chose this path, and I know why I chose you. I love our life right now, and I love Oliver, but I can do better."

"Better how?" Kate queried.

Brad sighed. "I don't know. I'm just going to have to remember what's really important and make sure I don't forget those things."

Kate released her breath and threw herself into Brad's arms. "Brad, you're going to be fine. You haven't sold your soul to the devil, you know."

Brad grinned at his wife and waggled his eyebrows as an idea took shape. "You know, it's not too late to chuck this all in and head down to South America and start that bakery."

"No, thanks," Kate said, laughing. "*No hablo español.*"

Brad laughed in spite of himself. "You're terrible."

"Nope." Kate grinned. "Just honest."

CHAPTER 23

Zora

SPRING

BY the time Zora and Angel exited the side door of the old Presbyterian church on Lafayette Avenue where the sign language classes were held, they had already decided that they would take Oliver and Skye to the playground for a few minutes before they caught the bus. The tantalizing hint of spring was too glorious to ignore after months of hiding from the cold. Even in the waning afternoon hours, the sunshine still felt warm and comforting, and Zora swore she could smell the green shooting out of the earth. Waiting outside the church, however, stood Brad Carter, dressed in sweatpants, sneakers, and a navy blue fleece jacket. He had his camera around his neck.

"Hey, Zora," he said when he saw her. He leaned down and kissed his son on the nose.

"Hi, Mr. Carter—I mean Brad," Zora said, puzzled. She wondered if she was in trouble. Was she being fired? Did she leave the oven on?

The three of them stood there for a moment without saying anything. Even Oliver and Skye seemed to have better things to do than make noise.

Finally, Angel broke the silence. "Hi, there, I'm Angel," she said. "I take care of Skye, here."

"Brad Carter," Brad said, extending his hand to Angel. She shook it and smiled.

"Oh, sorry," Zora said. Finding her voice, she introduced Angel as her friend and Brad Carter as her employer.

Brad explained that his meeting had finished early and he'd decided to come by to see if the class was still in session. When he mentioned his meeting, Zora assumed it was more of the secret situation.

"We were on our way to the park," Angel said, turning Skye's stroller. "Would you like to join us, Mr. Carter, or do you have to go back to work?"

Zora shot Angel an "Are you crazy?" look. Why would her boss want to be hanging around with them at the park? And an even better question: Why would she want to be around her boss while she was working? Clearly, Brad Carter wasn't having the same thoughts, because he readily accepted Angel's invitation.

The three of them strolled down Lafayette Avenue together, Angel leading the way and the conversation. She managed to talk a lot about herself and her plans and how this beautiful spring weather made her long for Florence more than ever. Brad asked about her paintings, and she launched into a happy expla-nation of her process as an artist. Zora was relieved not to have to participate in the conversation because she was still trying to figure out what Brad was doing here. She'd heard about people spying on their nannies when they suspected them of abusing their children or stealing their credit card numbers, but Zora couldn't think of anything she'd done to warrant being checked up on. Kate mentioned that Brad had been nervous at first about Zora's taking Ollie to Fort Greene, but she'd been coming to these classes for weeks. Why start worrying now? It didn't make sense.

"Earth to Zora," Angel interrupted her thoughts.

"Sorry, what did you say?" Zora said, smiling to hide her train of thought.

"Mr. Carter and I were trying to decide which was the better city, New York or Paris? I say Paris, he says New York. We need you to break the tie."

"Better for what?" Zora asked.

"Oh, you know," Angel said. "Just better in terms of people and art and things to do and freedom to be who you are."

"Paris," Zora said without hesitation. In a flash, she remembered sitting in a café overlooking the Seine, sipping rich hot chocolate, nibbling on a buttery croissant, and feeling that everything was right in the world just because she was young, Black, and in Paris. To this day she'd never felt so comfortable in her own skin.

"Why?" Brad asked.

"Because Paris is freedom. Paris doesn't come with rules about how you have to present yourself, and there seems to be a place for everyone," Zora said.

"You could say the very same things about New York," Brad protested.

"Yeah, but Paris does it better. With more style." Zora shrugged. "I don't know how to explain it. Paris is just Paris. She calls you to her with no judgment and offers all of her charms to you. Paris is like a sensuous woman." Zora laughed at what she was about to say. "And New York," she finished, "is a whore."

Brad laughed a big, hearty, honest laugh. "Well said. I'll have to think about that one."

"Here we are, Mr. Carter," Angel announced, pushing open the big green gates to the playground. "It's nothing fancy, but the kids like it a lot, and it's where we come to get all the juicy gossip."

"Oh, really?" Brad feigned surprise.

Angel played along. "Don't worry, this is strictly Fort Greene information flowing over here. Nobody cares about what's going on in your neighborhood. Right, Zora?"

Zora nodded. "Yeah, whatever people are doing in Fort Greene doesn't make it back to Park Slope."

Brad gave her a funny look. Maybe he thought she was making an underhanded reference to his comic-book meetings. She wasn't, but let him think that, Zora thought. Then maybe he'd come clean to Kate.

Angel must have thought Brad needed to talk to Zora about something important, because as soon as she could, she scooted off toward the jungle gym with Skye, mumbling an excuse that she'd seen a friend of hers from back in the day.

Zora started walking toward the swings, thinking Brad would follow her. If he wanted to see her taking care of his child to ensure that she was competent, let him. She made up her mind that she would carry on like normal. Otherwise, she'd make herself crazy trying to guess what Brad Carter was up to.

Brad did follow her, and he watched as she carefully lowered Oliver into a swing and pushed him gently back and forth. Brad stood in front of the swing, making funny faces at his son. He snapped a few pictures and occasionally would ask Zora questions about her day and Oliver's. Innocent questions, like what they'd had for lunch and how long Ollie had slept. Within five minutes, however, Oliver demanded to be stopped, and the interview was effectively over.

Zora grabbed the swing and pulled it to a halt. "You ready to get out, Ollie?" she asked. "He never wants to be in the swings for more than five minutes at a time," she explained to Brad. "I can time it like clockwork." Zora unlocked Oliver's seat belt and hoisted him out of the swing. He was extra-heavy with his big winter coat. She balanced him on her hip and headed over toward the baby slide and tunnels. She called to Brad, "Can you bring the stroller, please?" If he was going to stand around and watch, he might as well be useful, she figured.

Zora plopped Oliver down on the padded playground. If Kate saw her son on the dirty mats, she'd probably have a cow, but since Zora washed his clothes, Kate never saw how filthy he got. Zora guessed Kate would know now, once Brad told her. But it made Oliver happy, romping around down there, and it was a good place to let him practice his walking. He'd grab hold of the stairs to the slide and hold on for dear life as he made it around the entire jungle gym.

Brad acted like Oliver had run a marathon when he witnessed him complete his first lap. "Oh my God, did you see that?" he shouted. "He just walked around the whole thingamajiggy." The other mothers and nannies on the playground gave Zora knowing looks. Dads weren't frequent weekday visitors, and when they did come, they always seemed amazed by the antics of their offspring.

"I know," Zora said. She couldn't help smiling. She, too, had been pretty excited the first time Ollie had done this, but it was an old trick by now. "He's going to be walking by himself pretty soon," she predicted with authority.

"I hope so," Brad admitted. "He's already fourteen months. That's kind of late for walking."

"Look," Zora said, "everybody is different. Every baby has his own time for doing things."

"I know," Brad said, "but you have to admit that fourteen months is kind of late. Look at Skye. She and Ollie are almost the same age, and she's been walking, I hear, since she was nine months old."

"First of all, Skye's a girl, and they tend to do everything sooner than boys," Zora explained. "Second of all, so what? The worst thing you can do to a child is compare him to someone else. Oliver is a wonderful child, developing at his own pace."

"I know my son is wonderful," Brad said. "I just—"

Zora interrupted. "If it makes you feel any better, my brother didn't walk until he was sixteen months old, and today he is a very successful corporate lawyer with degrees from two Ivy League institutions. So no worries."

"Okay, okay." Brad threw his hands up. "I'm not worried. But for the record, I wasn't really worried before. I just said it was kind of late to be walking." He turned away from Zora, scooped up Oliver, and flew him around the playground like an airplane. When he came full circle, standing in front of Zora again, he said, "Does it look like I don't love my son just the way he is?"

Almost an hour later, Brad left Zora and Angel at the bus stop. He said he was going to catch a cab and head to the gym. "I'll be home by seven," he promised Zora.

Once he was out of earshot, Angel asked, "Are you working till seven every night now?"

"Yeah," Zora admitted. "Kate asked me to, but only until she finishes planning this big gala thing she's doing for work. After the first week of June, it'll be back to six, and she even said that for the summer, I may only have to work half-days on Fridays."

"*Bella*," Angel said with concern, "can you even see your-self still doing this into the summer? If I'm not back in Italy by July, please smack me upside the head with a cast-iron skillet. Hard."

"It's not that bad," Zora said in a small voice.

Angel gave her a hard look. "Maybe for you it's not, but for me it's torture every day that I'm taking care of Skye instead of paint-ing. I should be painting every day. And the way it goes right now, I'm only painting on the weekends."

Zora felt like she should be insulted by Angel's words, but she knew they were true. It was different for her. She didn't have Italy calling her name. "How's the bank account going?" she asked so she didn't have to think about her own situation.

"I'm more than halfway there," Angel said, smiling.

"Really?" Zora asked, getting excited for her friend.

"Yeah. If I could just sell some stuff, I'd be gone for sure."

"It's too bad the gallery show didn't work out," Zora said. "I can't believe that guy turned out to be such an asshole."

"Hey, that's the art business," Angel fumed. "Full of artists and assholes. Go figure."

The bus came then, and Angel and Zora got on. Once they were situated, Zora turned to Angel and said, "Why don't you have your own show and stop waiting for some flaky gallery owner to coordinate this for you?"

"I don't know," Angel said, but Zora detected a whisper of hope in her voice.

"No, really, think about it," Zora said, getting excited. "We could find a space in Fort Greene or in Park Slope to rent out. We'll make posters and postcards and put them up in all the cafés."

Angel started nodding as Zora planned the whole event aloud. "Would you really help me?" Angel asked Zora.

"Of course I would, and I will," Zora said. "It was my idea. And I'll even do all the food. You can't have a fancy art opening without exquisite finger food."

"Ooohhh, perfect." Angel clapped in delight. "Now all we have to do is find some amazing place to have this party."

For the rest of the bus ride, Zora and Angel discussed details. When they parted ways on Seventh Avenue, Angel gave Zora a big hug. "You're the best," she said.

Zora smiled. "You're welcome." She started for home.

Angel cried after her, "Zora, wait." Zora stopped and turned around. Angel came toward her. "What did your boss want, anyway?"

"I don't know," Zora said, shrugging. "He claimed he just wanted to hang out with us for a while. Other than that, he never said anything specific."

Angel made a face. "Strange. I'd keep an eye on that one."

Zora nodded. "Yeah, I know, right? The whole thing was kind of odd."

"Anyway," Angel said, dismissing Zora's issues, "start thinking about what you want to serve for the opening night of the Angel Montgomery show." She crinkled her nose and giggled saying it.

Zora laughed with her friend. "You are crazy."

"I am who I am, *bella*," Angel said.

Zora turned again to walk home.

"*Ciao*," Angel called.

"Bye, Angel."

Right before Zora got to the front door of the Carters' house, her cell phone rang. She considered ignoring it but answered it on the third ring. It was Brad.

"Zora," he said. He sounded like he was out of breath, as if he had been running. "One thing I forgot to mention."

Zora didn't say anything, just waited for him to speak.

"Please don't tell Kate that I met you guys today at the park."

More secrets. "Why?" she asked with frustration. Why should Brad have to hide the fact that he'd spent some time with his child at the park?

Brad made a noise that sounded like something between a groan and a sigh. "Because," he said, "if you tell her I stopped by, she'll want to know what I was doing in Fort Greene, and then I'll have to explain the whole comic-book thing. Rather than lying again about why I was in the neighborhood, can we just not say anything?"

"Whatever," Zora said. It wasn't her problem, even though she felt that all of this lying to Kate could quite easily turn into a very serious problem.

CHAPTER 24

Kate

KATE was relieved to hear about Angel's show and that Zora was heavily involved in the planning. It assured Kate that her nanny enjoyed a life outside of the Carter family. Sometimes she felt guilty for taking up so much of Zora's time. That was why she offered to pitch in and help secure a location. It wasn't hard. She called Cindy DiNuptis and asked about the yoga studio where she'd held Molly's party. And that was that. Both Angel and Zora were overjoyed by the suggestion, not to mention grateful that Kate had been able to negotiate the price down so Angel could afford to rent it out for a full four hours. One night the week before, when Angel came to pick Zora up from work, Kate got to hear how thankful she really was.

"Mrs. Carter, you are absolutely the best," Angel had gushed. Then she'd grabbed Kate and suffocated her in a hug that lasted a little too long. With her wild Afro hairstyle and platform boots, she stood a head taller than Kate, who found herself nestled directly into Angel's bosom. Once Angel released her, Kate offered the two women a glass of wine, but they said they were on their way to a movie in SoHo. Clearly, the meeting wasn't long enough to get to know Angel, but based on her kooky fashion sense and her high-energy personality, Kate figured Angel would be a very successful artist, or at least she could play one on TV.

Every day Zora updated Kate on the show's progress. Sitting in her office now, Kate smiled as she thought about it. If

Zora weren't a nanny, she'd probably make a great event planner. Maybe she should tell her that. Brad thought Kate could be patronizing toward Zora, but she was just trying to help. If anything, she thought of herself as a mentor to Zora. She was only two years older, but experience counted for a lot. She could make a few calls and maybe set up an internship for Zora during the summer, when she didn't need her as much. Then again, that wouldn't be such a smart thing to do if Kate was trying to get pregnant. She'd need Zora more than ever if they had another baby.

Just the thought of another baby filled Kate with such feelings of warmth and longing that she laughed at her fickle self. Not so long ago she had been convinced Oliver would be an only child. In an instant he had consumed her entire life, turned everything completely upside down and inside out. She couldn't have imagined adding another element to their family when brushing her teeth twice a day was a challenge. All of that was BZ—before Zora. Now, with Zora, things seemed eminently more manageable. Under control. Limitless. There were possibilities. It was so easy to imagine adding a new baby to the routine. Kate still had to convince Brad that another baby made sense, but she was sure she could pull it off. He was, after all, the one who'd claimed he wanted four children! Kate was up for only two, and the sooner she could have the second one, the better.

She would never admit such a thing out loud, but she wanted to make sure she had her kids while she was still young enough to enjoy them *and* get back in shape. Losing her pregnancy weight after Ollie hadn't been hard, but she knew that the older she got, the trickier it would be to shed those pounds. But more important, she didn't want to be an old mom. That seemed to be the norm these days in New York, where women delayed childbirth to coincide with the arrival of their Social Security checks. That did not look like fun. Deep down, Kate figured, she was pretty traditional at heart. She wanted a life like her mother's, who at fifty-four looked great, enjoyed her career, and, with her kids launched, could travel with her husband and go on adventures whenever she got the urge. It was all about planning, and that was one thing Kate was good at. She knew she could have the life she wanted as long as she had a plan and stuck to it.

Kate's office phone rang, putting an end to her baby dreams. She let Laurie pick it up. With the gala only ten weeks away, she didn't want to waste her time speaking to yet another publicist trying to get his client on the guest list for free. People didn't seem to understand that a fund-raiser was to raise funds. Not to give rich celebrities a chance to look good in front of the public for free. Let them pay for their good deeds like everybody else.

Laurie poked her head into Kate's office. "Um, it's those people from the Plaza Hotel asking if we care whether the servers wear black or gray ties, and I told them we didn't. Do you want to speak to them?" Laurie paused and then made a dramatic show to see if anyone was near enough to hear what she was going to say next. "Or do you want to come out here and watch Danyel Green get fired?"

Kate jumped up from her seat. "What?"

"You heard me," Laurie said in a bad stage whisper. "She's getting canned as we speak. I saw Roger White storming into her office a second ago."

Kate couldn't have held herself back if she'd wanted to. She had to see what was happening. Even though she knew she was being obvious, she headed down the hallway, pretending she needed some new file folders from the supply closet, which just happened to be kitty-corner from Danyel's office.

She didn't have to make it all the way to the end of the hall. She could hear raised voices coming from Danyel's office. Danyel sounded indignant. Roger reminded Kate of an angry bear, all growls and roars. She heard him tell Danyel that her time at Zimbalist was over. Kate couldn't hear all the details of their heated conversation, but as Roger exited Danyel's office, she clearly heard him say, "Pack up your things. A guard will be up here in precisely fifteen minutes to escort you out."

Kate hurried back to her office, trying to figure out what on earth had happened. As she passed Laurie, who was making no effort to be discreet in her snooping, Kate hissed, "Get into my office now!"

Laurie scooted in right after Kate and shut the door. "What happened?" Laurie demanded, her face flushed with excitement. She had never warmed to Danyel Green, out of loyalty to Kate, but also because she said she found her "completely stank and totally fake."

Kate told her assistant what she had witnessed, then asked if she'd heard any news. Kate promised herself that this would be the last time she encouraged Laurie to gossip at the office.

"Well," Laurie started, relishing the information she was about to share, "according to Kelly, Danyel's new assistant, Ms. Danyel Green has been trying to poach Zimbalist clients."

"What! Why?" Kate gasped. "And for who? Is she starting her own firm?"

"Not even." Laurie snorted. "She's defecting to Rothman PR and was supposed to bring a roster of her own clients with her. Kelly saw the letter from Rothman on Danyel's desk."

"Oh, that's bad," Kate whispered. "And so dumb. I can't believe she would do that. She had to know she'd get caught. She must be really desperate. Or stupid. Or both."

Laurie didn't get a chance to respond, because just then Kate's interoffice line rang. It was Roger White, summoning Kate to his office. And he didn't sound happy. She gingerly placed the phone back in its cradle and felt a cold wave of panic wash over her. Was she somehow implicated in Danyel's mess?

"I hope he's not in a firing mood today," Kate said to Laurie, praying her voice didn't give away her true fears. She could think of nothing that would warrant her own dismissal, but you never knew what could happen when something like this occurred. Managers tended to get trigger-happy.

Laurie's brown eyes widened with worry, but she wished Kate luck. "I'm sure it's nothing," she offered.

Kate nodded. "I'm okay." She asked Laurie to give her a moment alone so she could prepare herself to head upstairs. Once Laurie left, she quickly reviewed all of her recent interactions with Danyel, trying to recall anything that seemed suspicious. Maybe Roger White assumed she'd known what Danyel had been up to and wanted to hear her side of things. Kate pinched her cheeks and chided herself for being paranoid. There was no purpose in sitting here trying to second-guess Roger White. She had to go on up there and see what he wanted.

Marjorie sent Kate right into the lion's den. Roger White didn't even make a pretense of small talk. "Have a seat," he barked at Kate.

Easing onto a couch, Kate didn't have a chance to say hello before her boss let loose a torrent of curse words wrapped tightly around Danyel's name. "She tried to steal KasperKline away from us," he yelled. "Can you believe that bullshit?"

"No, sir." Kate cringed, trying not to let her fear show, as fear could easily be mistaken for guilt.

"I don't want to see or hear that woman's name ever again in this office. Is that clear?" he said, pounding his fist on his desk for emphasis. "You know, I never liked her," he added, coming from behind his desk to pace in front of his window.

"Yes, sir," Kate responded, debating whether she should inform her boss that she'd never liked her, either. Given the circumstances, she decided to keep her opinions to herself.

Completing his tirade with a recollection of all of Danyel's transgressions, from sloppy research to poor client communication, Roger White sat back down behind his massive mahogany desk and worked at regaining his composure. He sucked in deep restorative breaths and then gulped down whatever liquid remained in his coffee cup. Kate thought he'd forgotten she was still in the room, but then he turned his attention back to her.

"So, Kate," he started, "can I still count on you to handle both the AAA gala and KasperKline without Danyel?"

"Of course, Mr. White," Kate answered, relief flooding through her. Her reputation was not being called into question by Danyel's stupidity.

"Good." Roger White sighed. "That's probably the only good news I've had all day." As an afterthought, he added, "And don't worry, I'll make it a priority to get someone in here right away to replace Ms. Green. But you're on your own until then."

Rising from the couch, Kate reiterated her commitment. "Don't worry, Mr. White. The gala will be fabulous, and the KasperKline team won't even notice that Danyel is gone."

Roger White gave a grateful smile. "I knew I could count on you, Kate. You never let us down."

Back in her office with Laurie, Kate realized what a huge mistake she'd made. Even with Danyel's help, handling the AAA gala and KasperKline had been a huge job. Now she had to go it alone? She slumped in her chair and dropped her head between her knees, fearing she might start to hyperventilate. What had she done? She should have said she needed someone on the account with her right away. But with Roger White's current mood, she didn't dare go back up there and admit she couldn't handle it. Still, if she didn't get help and something fell through the cracks, she might be next in line to get the boot.

A pitiful cry escaped her mouth. "Ohhhh. What am I going to do?"

Laurie tried to put things into perspective. "Just think, Kate," she said in a soothing voice while she gently patted Kate's back, "the gala will be over in a couple of months, and then you can go back to dealing with KasperKline." Kate moaned in response. "And," Laurie continued with an air of hopefulness, "if you pull it all off, you'll be first in line for a promotion to vice president."

Kate hated to fall apart like this in front of her assistant. For Laurie's sake, she tried to get a handle on her emotions. Laurie was right. This was a golden opportunity to show what she was made of. To prove to Roger White that she was VP material.

"And I'll be around to help," Laurie promised.

Kate pulled herself up and smiled at her assistant. "Thank you, Laurie," she said. "Really, I mean it. I needed to hear that."

Laurie smiled. "Don't mention it."

Kate pulled a quick mental makeover and politely shoved Laurie out of her office. There was work to be done and neither self-doubt nor self-pity belonged at this party. What she needed to do now, more than anything, was talk to her greatest cheerleader for advice and help. She picked up the phone and called her mom.

The next day, as soon as she got to the office, Kate was told that she could use Kelly Richards, Danyel Green's former assistant, for any and all work on KasperKline and the gala. In fairness to her assistant, Kate planned to give Laurie all the senior work and Kelly the grunt assignments. Laurie had proved herself to Kate over and over, and it was time to pay her back for her loyalty. Kate hoped the two women would work well together and not try to fight for her favor. She told them as much over lunch at the funky new Asian-fusion restaurant around the corner from the office. "We really need to work together to get this gala done, and KasperKline can't be neglected," she said to Kelly and Laurie over crispy duck spring rolls and seafood dumplings.

They nodded, both with their legal pads, furiously writing down everything Kate said. She wanted to tell them to relax, but she knew it was better if they were a little bit intimidated or at least in awe of her. Her mother had reminded her of that. "Just keep everyone on their toes," she'd advised. "Be a good motivator and a mentor. And don't let anyone slack off, or it will be more work for you."

Kate spoke earnestly to Laurie and Kelly. "Look, there're going to be long nights ahead of us, but I think we each have a lot to gain if we can show Roger White and the rest of the management team that the loss of Danyel Green means nothing to our clients."

Both women nodded in agreement. Kate couldn't promise them promotions, just like she couldn't guarantee her own, but she would definitely put in a good word for both of them. "If you guys work hard for me," Kate promised them, "I'll work hard at making sure you're both rewarded for your efforts."

"Thank you, Kate," they gushed simultaneously.

Satisfied with her pep talk, she let Laurie and Kelly lead the rest of the conversation while keeping her eye on her watch. She felt better about everything now that she had a plan of attack and a motivated team. If there was one thing she knew, from both work and home, having a good team to support your efforts could make all the difference in the world.

CHAPTER 25

Zora

ZORA realized it had been two weeks since she had set eyes on Kate. Kate had warned her that things had gotten crazy at work and she'd be getting home late, but Zora hadn't expected to stop seeing her altogether. The way it was, Brad was there in the mornings waiting for her to arrive, and she said good-bye to him at the end of the day.

Sometimes Brad would show up at the park after sign language class and hang out with them, and then they would all take the bus back home together, Zora, Brad, Angel, Oliver, and Skye. On those days, Brad would play with Oliver while Zora fixed dinner. She'd leave it ready for the two of them on the table, always putting Kate's portion on a separate plate to be zapped in the microwave. Zora knew Kate appreciated her setting the food aside because she would call from work in the mornings to say thank you. Sometimes, if she was too tired to eat when she got home, Kate would take the food to work for lunch and call Zora to exclaim how delicious it was. "I don't know what I would do without you, Zora," she would say. "Honestly, I think my life would fall to pieces."

Zora wouldn't say anything to this. What could she say? "Damn straight, your life would suck without me!" But she was glad Kate acknowledged her importance to the family. It made her feel like she'd made the right decision to stick around and continue working for them. Even if she wasn't saving the world in a designer suit and panty hose, she was helping somebody who needed help. It made Zora think about something her grandmother used to say.

Nona had lived in Baltimore and cooked and cleaned for the same White family for twenty-five years. She always said she felt sorry for the wife, who had to pay someone else to do the things any able-bodied woman should be able to do on her own. "I carried the keys to that castle," Nona would say. "I kept that house and everyone in it under my thumb."

Nona's words floated through Zora's mind as she started to gather her ingredients for dinner. Did she hold the keys to Kate and Brad's castle? Nona maintained she was in a position of great power but swore she never abused it. "The woman of the house must never believe she's lost control," Nona said. Zora knew if Kate thought things were out of her control, sparks would fly. She was just that way. Obviously, she didn't seem to mind the little things Zora had added to their home, like the ergonomically correct cheese grater and the stainless-steel lemon zester for the kitchen, not to mention the convenient laundry sorter she had purchased for Ollie's room. Just little items that kept things running smoothly. Zora bet Brad hardly noticed. He was a typical male. Although he did notice the sun hat she'd bought for Ollie. It was madras-printed with an extra-wide brim and flaps that covered his ears. With his big head still covered in only the lightest cap of downy blond hair, Zora worried that Ollie would get sunstroke without some protection.

Zora put her grandmother and her old-world wisdom on the back burner. Kate could keep the keys to her own castle, and Zora would keep doing her own thing. Right now that meant making spaghetti. Nothing fancy, but she made the sauce from scratch, and she'd bought fresh sausage from the new Italian market on Sixth Street. She figured if she threw the pasta into the water before she left, Brad could take it out, and he and Ollie could eat together.

But Brad had another idea. "Why don't you stay and eat with

us?" he asked after she'd explained to him how long to leave the noodles cooking.

She paused before answering. "If you're worried that you're going to mess it up, I can stay and finish it up for you."

Brad laughed. "I know I'm not as competent as you in the kitchen, Zora, but I do know how to boil spaghetti. I just wanted to know if you'd like to eat with me and Ollie."

"I don't know," Zora said, hesitating. She'd decided that she liked Brad, despite his insistence that she keep that silly secret from Kate. But still, did she want to eat dinner with him?

"Look," Brad started, looking a little sheepish, "between you and me, if I only have a fourteen-month-old for dinner conversation again, I think I'll start regressing and eating with my hands."

Zora laughed.

"Please," Brad begged. "Kate's coming home late again tonight."

Since Keith had a gig at the strip club, Zora knew the only things waiting for her at home were the television and take-out Thai food from two days ago, so she said yes.

"Great," Brad said, rewarding Zora with a grateful smile. Without discussion, he went back to entertaining Oliver, and Zora went back into the kitchen to finish dinner. When it was ready, she called Oliver and Brad to the table.

"Wow," Brad said when he saw what Zora had created.

"It's just spaghetti." Zora laughed, but she had put some thought into the presentation. She'd put the pasta in a jade-green ceramic serving bowl and the red sauce in a matching pitcher. The sausages were brown and steaming on a simple white plate with parsley garnish. The bread basket was stuffed with slices of warm rustic Italian bread, and a tiny glass bowl sat nearby with olive oil and crushed garlic for dipping. A simple green salad completed the meal.

"Hey, don't forget, I have a certificate from Detroit's most un-known school of culinary arts," Zora said, making a face.

"I don't care what school it was, this looks delicious," Brad said. "Come on, Ollie, let's eat."

"Yeah, tell me how it tastes before you get all excited," Zora said, securing Oliver in his high chair. She went over to the stove and brought back a small pot of rotini pasta for Oliver.

Brad watched her as he piled a generous helping of pasta on his plate. "Can I serve you, Zora?" he asked.

"No, don't worry about it," she said. "I'll get mine as soon as I get Oliver taken care of."

It took her only a minute to cut Oliver's pasta into bite-size pieces. Then she cut even smaller pieces of sausage and added them to his plate. For vegetables, she pulled out a Tupperware container of cooked peas from the refrigerator. "For some reason, he likes his peas cold," she explained to Brad.

"Aha." Brad nodded. "Good to know."

Finally, Zora sat down, and the three of them ate. Brad had to stop every five minutes to exclaim how delicious everything was. "And I grew up in Philly, so I know what Italian is supposed to taste like. Believe me when I say this is awesome."

Zora glowed under his praise. It felt good to cook for people when they truly enjoyed your food. Zora explained this to Brad. That was why she wanted to be a personal chef and not, say, work in a restaurant where the chef stayed closeted up in the kitchen, cut off from his adoring fans.

When dinner was over, Zora offered to stay and clean up before she left, but Brad refused. "You've worked enough for one day. Thanks for keeping me company," he said.

"No problem," Zora said. And she left.

Eating together became a regular occurrence for Zora and Brad over the next two weeks. He'd ask if she was staying, and if she wasn't meeting up with Angel to do something for the show, she'd stay. Keith's agent had just sent him to Los Angeles to audition for a couple of soap operas, so it wasn't like anyone else was clamoring for her attention. And eating with Brad and Ollie was a much better option than eating alone.

One night while they were at the table finishing dinner, Brad asked Zora what her parents thought about her current profession. The question caught Zora by surprise. She narrowed her eyes and responded with a question of her own.

"Why do you want to know?"

Brad shrugged. "I was just curious. You never talk about your family."

Pushing the leftover food around on her plate, Zora said, "I don't talk about them because I really don't talk *to* them all that much. They would die if they knew I was working for you guys."

"So they don't know you're a nanny?" Brad asked, giving Zora his full attention.

"Nope," Zora said, jumping up from the table to start clearing.

"Why not?" Brad asked. "What's so bad about being a nanny?"

Zora couldn't stifle her snort of derision.

"What?" Brad asked, looking genuinely confused and a little bit hurt.

"Okay, you're White, so maybe you won't understand," Zora began. "But try to imagine you're a well-established Black man who worked every day of his life so his children could get the best education, become white-collar professionals, and get their piece of the American pie." Zora sucked in her breath and let it out in a tragic sigh before she continued. "And then your daughter—mind you, your thirty-year-old daughter—calls you up and says, 'Daddy, guess what? I've found my calling. It's a job that's been in our family for generations. They used to call it being a slave, but today the job is called being a nanny.'"

"Zora, that's not fair," Brad said, but he had the decency to look embarrassed.

"No, really," Zora continued, unable to stop. "My parents are going to be so happy to hear that my grandmother and I have the same job, cleaning up after White people and raising their children. I'm sure they'll be incredibly proud of me. They can tell all of their friends that their son is a successful lawyer and their daughter is an equally successful nanny."

"I'm sorry," Brad mumbled.

She felt the tears sliding down her face and suddenly felt ridiculous and embarrassed for revealing herself to Brad Carter of all people. Why was she telling him these things? He wouldn't understand the situation with her parents. He might not even know any Black people besides her and Angel. She turned her attention to the stack of dirty dishes in the sink, wishing she could snatch back everything she'd just said. She prayed Brad would have the good sense to ignore her outburst.

He didn't. He just got up from the table to help put things away, and continued talking. "You know, Zora, obviously, I'm not Black, but I think I can understand every child's fear of disappointing their parents. That has nothing to do with race. And being a father, I understand parents placing all of their hopes and dreams on their children. No matter what, somebody is going to be disappointed."

Zora nodded like she was listening, but with every fiber of her being, she wished the floor would swallow her up. She didn't want to be having this conversation with her boss. But he wouldn't stop talking.

"Look, you're not going to be a nanny forever, but for now this is your thing," he was saying. "You're good at it, and if it makes you happy, it should make your parents happy. But you have to own it. Are you ashamed of what you do?"

"No . . . yes . . . I don't know," Zora said, getting flustered. "I mean, it's the Black thing again." She stole a glance at Brad to see if it was worth explaining all this to him, or was he getting that glazed-over blank look White people tended to adopt whenever race came up in conversation? No, Brad had stopped washing the counters and seemed to be genuinely interested in what she was going to say next.

Drawing in a deep breath, Zora decided to ease her way into her explanation. "First of all, do you have any Black friends?"

Brad raised an eyebrow and looked mildly offended, but he answered the question. "Yes. Would you like to see their pictures? I carry them in my wallet."

Now it was Zora's turn to look incredulous. "You do?"

Brad laughed. "No. I'm just kidding. But yes, I have Black friends, and a couple of Latino ones, too, and I always talk to the Korean guy on my floor at work. Does that make me eligible to understand your dilemma?"

Zora raised her hands in mock surrender. "My apologies. I didn't know I was talking to the head of the rainbow coalition here."

Brad got serious again. "Sorry. Finish what you were going to say."

"Fine," Zora said. "It's just that I was given a lot of opportunities that most people, or at least a lot of Black people, don't get, and I'm doing work that anyone could do. I'm not . . ." She paused, looking for the right words.

Brad filled them in for her. "Saving your people?"

"Exactly," Zora admitted.

"Like your brother is saving your people by working at a corporate law firm? How many Black souls has he saved lately?" Brad challenged.

Zora had to smile at this. He had a point.

"Look, I'm not saying it's easy, but I'm sure your parents love you, and ultimately, if you're happy, they'll be happy."

"You don't know my parents," Zora charged.

"It may take a minute, but if they really love you, they'll come around."

Zora considered Brad's advice. She turned back to the dishwasher while Brad brought her more dishes. Suddenly, a smile pulled at the corners of her lips. Brad noticed. "What?" he asked, smiling back.

"How about," Zora said, a challenge lighting up her eyes, "I tell my parents that I'm working as a nanny if you tell Kate about the comic-book thing. Because after all, if she loves you, and if you're happy, she'll be happy for you, right?"

Brad laughed that big open laugh Zora was beginning to get used to hearing. "Touché, Zora Anderson. Touché."

CHAPTER 26

Kate

Kate couldn't sleep. It was almost two A.M., but her mind was racing, and her limbs were still tingling. She and Brad had made love for the first time in days. "Wild, crazy, rip-your-clothes-right-off sex" was a better description for what had just transpired. But then afterward, instead of falling right to sleep like she usually did, Kate had slipped out of bed to get a drink of water from the refrigerator to try to cool down. She and Brad had gone at it like two people stranded on a desert island, aching to quench a burning need. The intensity was so strong, Kate figured, because they'd hardly seen each other these last few weeks. She'd gotten home relatively early tonight, and after eating Zora's delicious dinner of shrimp risotto and asparagus, they'd watched a movie and barely made it upstairs before clothes were being torn off. She blushed just remembering the lusty way she'd grabbed at her husband, sending shock waves of pleasure through his body and making him call out her name in ecstasy.

By the time she got back to the bedroom after drinking what felt like a gallon of water, Brad was fast asleep. Rather than wake him up and force him to cuddle, Kate tried reading some of her boring KasperKline reports, but that didn't do the trick. She was still too revved up to sleep, so she decided to go check on Oliver. He was sleeping peacefully, but Kate still wanted to watch her child for a few magic moments. She had barely seen Ollie lately, with her crazy work schedule taking all of her time. These days she found herself calling home and asking Zora to put the phone near the baby so she could hear him gurgle and coo and screech. It was funny—while she was at work, busy with everything, she wasn't consumed with thoughts of her son. She didn't pine for him all day long, wishing she were home with him. If she was honest, sometimes she forgot she even had a child when she was in the thick of things at work. It wasn't until she was back home, holding him in her arms, seeing his adorable chubby face, and smelling his delicious baby smell, that she became aware of how many details of his growth and development she was missing. So for now she stood in his bedroom next to his crib, watching his chest rise and fall, his arms and legs splayed out in every direction, with a bubble of spit hanging from his bottom lip. He was perfect, absolutely perfect, Kate decided.

Again Kate's thoughts drifted to baby number two. She was getting kind of obsessed with the idea. Even though she had a million and one things to attend to at work, she always managed to find a minute here or there to daydream about what their second child would be like. Sometimes she even went online to chart her most fertile days of the month. She loved Oliver, but she'd be lying if she didn't admit she wanted a daughter. She wanted a chance to buy all of those adorable little pink dresses and the hair ribbons . . . But more than the superficial stuff, she craved that special mother-daughter relationship, like the one she enjoyed with her own mother. She knew her daughter would be her confidante, someone to share secrets with and someone who would come to her for advice and counsel. With Ollie, the day would come when it would be Brad he would turn to with all of his serious life decisions, and then he would fall in love and follow another woman to the ends of the earth and forget all about Kate. Her daughter would always stay connected, assuming she didn't turn out like Liz, who seemed to take great pleasure in staying as far away from the family as possible.

Kate chided herself for being silly. It was late, and she was heading down a depressing path. Why was she already mourning Oliver's adulthood when they had tomorrow to look forward to?

Since weekends were the only real time she had to be with her family, Kate insisted that they be special. She worked hard during the week, so she'd never be expected to come into the office on a Saturday or a Sunday. Thankfully, Zora was such an efficient nanny, keeping the house neat, cooking, and keeping the fridge well stocked, that Kate didn't have to worry much about housework during the weekends. Her time was free for fun and family. Tomorrow they were going to a children's concert in Prospect Park with Fiona and Skye. Brad was coming, and so was Fiona's husband, Greg. If everything went well and the kids weren't too tuckered out, they'd probably grab dinner after the show. Kate wanted a full day of good food, friends, and fun for her family. When she was plugged into the playground gossip sessions during her maternity leave, Kate had been only too aware that all work and no play was a recipe for disaster for any relationship. "We just grew apart" was one sentence Kate never wanted to utter about her marriage. "It's not going to happen," she whispered as she gazed at her perfect child. After kissing Oliver on his milky, warm cheek, Kate tiptoed back to her own bed, crawled between the covers, snuggled up to Brad's huddled form, and promptly fell into a satisfied sleep.

Listening to a kids' rock band, Kate was surprised to learn, was a lot like listening to a grown-up rock band. Especially since this particular band's lead singer used to be the lead singer of a heavy-metal band in the eighties. Now that the guy had kids of his own, and no more adult fans clamoring to buy his records, he'd transformed himself into a rock star for the milk-and-cookies crowd. According to the article Kate had read about him in *New York* magazine, he was enjoying far more success as a kiddie performer than he'd ever had as a B-list musician.

Kate liked the band because their lyrics were funny without being stupid. Her favorite song thus far was the one about a frustrated mother and her temper tantrums, called "Meltdown Mommy." Even Brad and Greg were enjoying themselves, practicing their air-guitar techniques along with the bass player, who happened to be wearing green corduroys with hot-pink polka dots. Ollie and Skye liked the fact that they could be as loud as they wanted without being reprimanded. Kate beamed as she watched the two children shake their little tushies in time to the music. Everybody was having fun, just like she had wanted. And as she'd hoped, they decided to keep the good times rolling by having dinner together.

Fiona suggested Luigi's restaurant right away. She had recently discovered their pesto-and-fresh-tomato pizza and couldn't wait to go back for more. Fiona and Greg had lived in Park Slope less time than Kate and Brad. They'd moved in after Skye was born and were still renting, trying to decide whether they should take the plunge and buy in this new urban suburbia. For Fiona, Luigi's pizza was tipping the scales toward their staying. Kate loved Luigi's, too, because while the restaurant was seriously child-friendly, with paper tablecloths that came with crayons for doodling, it still maintained a respectable adult vibe, with a dizzying array of pizza offerings and a spectacular rotation of margarita specials.

The four adults sat at a large round table toward the front of the restaurant. Ollie and Skye were in high chairs side by side. Kate was so happy at the way the day was turning out; she couldn't have planned it any better. She had to hold herself back from yelling out "Group hug" and trying to embrace everybody at the table. Before she could embarrass herself with a public declaration of affection for her new friends, though, she saw a familiar face at the door of the restaurant. She kicked Brad under the table and nodded toward the entrance.

Brad gave her a pained look. "What?" he blurted out, oblivious to her request for discretion.

Kate gave a sigh and said in a low voice, "Zora just walked in."

Brad craned his neck around to see. Indeed it was Zora. She was wearing blue jeans, black high-heeled sandals, and a flowing white linen shirt. She was with a Black man with shoulder-length dreadlocks. That must be Keith, Kate thought. Without hesitating, Kate waved and yelled, "Hey, Zora."

"Do you think I should ask them to join us?" Kate asked her tablemates. She wasn't sure about the protocol for running into your nanny in a social situation, but this was Zora.

Brad answered quickly. "Absolutely not."

"Why?" Kate asked, insulted by the edge in his voice. "What are we supposed to do, act like we don't see her?"

"I think it's too late for that," Brad said under his breath, then added, "and she's not working for us right now. Let the woman have a life that doesn't include us."

Fiona and Greg, Kate noticed, seemed more interested in studying their menus than in her nanny situation. She suspected they didn't want to get involved, but she needed a second opinion. "Would you guys mind if I asked Zora and her friend to join us? I think it would be kind of rude not to."

"Well," Fiona started, while handing Skye another breadstick, "I think Brad has a point, in that this is her free time and she might not want to spend it with her employers."

Greg agreed with his wife. "I say let her enjoy her date."

Brad interrupted to say it didn't matter one way or the other. "They just walked out the door."

• • •

On their way home, Kate and Brad walked in silence. Greg and Fiona lived in the opposite direction, so they'd said their good-byes at the restaurant. Ollie fell asleep almost as soon as they started walking. The roar of the passing cars and the animated conversations of the people all around didn't seem to bother him at all.

"Wow, I wish I could sleep like that," Kate mused.

"Like what?" Brad said, still seemingly lost in his own thoughts.

"Like Ollie. He's completely oblivious to all of the commotion going on around him. He can block it all out."

Brad didn't say anything. They continued to walk on. Kate was worried. Ever since Zora had left the restaurant, Brad had seemed annoyed and agitated. She was sure Fiona and Greg couldn't tell, but she knew he wasn't happy. Kate didn't want to spoil what had been a wonderful day, but she also hated when he did this—got mad and shut down all communication. It was so annoying. She wished he could come out and say what was making him so upset.

After two more blocks in silence, Kate couldn't take it any-more. "Are you going to tell me what's the matter or what?" she asked.

Brad didn't even break his stride, nor did he look at her, when he answered, "Nothing."

"Obviously, it's not nothing," Kate said, "or you'd be talking to me. Let's try this again. What's the matter?"

"Kate," Brad said, stopping to look directly at his wife, "noth-ing is the matter. I'm just thinking. Is that okay?"

"Fine," Kate said, trying to keep the hurt out of her voice. She didn't know what had put Brad in such a funky mood, but she'd let it go if that was what he wanted. Just in case, she added, "I'm here if you want to talk about it."

Brad took Kate's hand and squeezed it. "Thanks." And that was that.

Just before they turned down Second Street, Brad told Kate to go home without him. He wanted to check out the new comic-book store that had just opened on Fifth Avenue. He claimed it wasn't far. Based on the fact that he already seemed annoyed with her for something she didn't even understand, Kate decided to keep her lecture about wasting time and money on comic books to herself.

She watched Brad walk swiftly down Sixth Avenue before she turned and headed for home. She took her time getting Ollie ready for bed, luxuriating in the routine that she hardly got to do anymore, since her son was usually in bed by the time she got home. Now, because he was groggy with sleep, he was easy to manage. He was only half awake as she peeled off his clothes, changed his diaper, and slipped on his pajamas. She held him in her arms and gave him a small bottle of warm milk and rocked him back to sleep, singing his favorite lullabies. When she laid him down in his crib, he was fast asleep again. Kate straightened up his room, putting his dirty clothes in the hamper Zora had bought and piling his toys in the basket. She tiptoed out of the room, closing the door behind her.

Back downstairs, she was startled to find Brad lying on the couch, reading a new comic. "Jeez!" she exclaimed. "I didn't even hear you come in."

"I was trying to be quiet so I didn't wake Ollie," Brad said without taking his eyes off his book.

"Oh," Kate said, wondering how to break through Brad's foul mood. "Whatcha reading?" she asked, sliding onto the end of the couch and trying to peer at the cover of the comic book.

Brad stopped reading to peek at his wife. "Do you really want to know?"

Kate grinned. "Not really, but I'll listen if you want to tell me about it."

Brad playfully tapped Kate on the head with the comic book. "Then why'd you ask?"

"Because I want you to talk to me, and if talking about su-perheroes is the only way I'm going to be able to engage you in conversation, I'll do it," Kate answered truthfully.

"Wow, what a sacrifice," Brad taunted.

Kate groaned inwardly. "At least I'm being honest and telling you how I feel."

Brad put down his comic and studied his wife for a moment. He closed his eyes and laid his head back on the arm of the couch. When he opened his eyes, he kept his gaze focused on the ceiling while he talked. "I feel like I don't see you anymore. And I want my wife back," he confessed.

"Brad," Kate responded with care, "you know I hate this work schedule, too, but it's just temporary. The gala is a little more than a month away, and Roger White promised me that finding another account executive for KasperKline was on the top of his list. I believe him."

"I know," Brad said. "I know all of this, and that's why I haven't said anything, but the fact is, I'm still pissed."

"Pissed at what or at whom?" Kate said.

"At you, at the situation, at your stupid job," Brad yelled.

"Can you please keep your voice down?" Kate said. "You'll wake Ollie."

"Sorry," Brad said in an exaggerated whisper. "But you wanted to have the conversation."

"Not if it means getting yelled at by my male-chauvinist hus-band," Kate shot back.

"That's why I didn't say anything in the first place, because I know I'm not allowed to feel this way," Brad admitted, standing up and heading toward the kitchen. "Do you want anything to drink?" he asked. "I'm getting a beer."

"No, thanks," Kate said as she tried to formulate a response to Brad's complaint.

"Look," he said, coming back to sit on the couch. "I know this is temporary, but it still sucks. I don't ever see you. Oliver doesn't see you, and . . ." He stopped and shrugged and took a swig from his beer bottle.

"And what?" Kate prompted.

"And the last time I checked, our sex life seems to have screeched to a grinding halt."

"What about last night?" Kate reminded him.

"Last night was fantastic," Brad said, "but that was the first time we've had sex in a month."

"This is really about sex, then," Kate spat out. She could feel her temperature rise in fury. "You're mad because we're not having sex as often as you'd like."

"No, Kate," Brad said, and he was shouting again. "I'm mad because my wife has deserted her family."

"That's so not fair," Kate fumed. "I am working this hard *for* my family. Do you think I enjoy working these crazy hours? Not seeing you and Ollie?"

"I don't think you mind, really," Brad said calmly. "Admit it. If you did, you would have done something about it."

Kate wanted to rebut that point, but it was kind of true. She hadn't complained at work. She hadn't asked for help. Not because she couldn't have used an extra set of hands but because she didn't want to appear weak or incompetent. That wasn't how she wanted to be seen at the office.

"Okay, I admit it. I haven't gone whining to my bosses to tell them I can't handle my workload," Kate said. "But you know what? I think I'm doing a pretty good job at balancing my personal and professional lives. I took off half a year to be home with Ollie. And even with these last few months—which, I remind you again, is just temporary—I've done a pretty good job keeping a sane schedule."

"Bravo for you, Kate. What do you want, a cookie?"

Kate glared at her husband. "No, but how about some appreciation for the fact that I'm trying my best? How about some understanding that this is hard for me, too, instead of whining that you're not getting enough sex so you have to pout like a little boy?"

"It's not just the sex," Brad tried again. "It's everything. I feed Ollie every night, put him to bed by myself, and clean up. I feel like a single parent sometimes."

"Oh, and I suppose Zora isn't helping with any of that?" Kate reminded him. "That's why I hired her—so when I *do* have to work late, all of this won't fall on you. Do you need me to ask her to stay later?"

"No, Kate." Brad shot her a dirty look. "*I* don't need a nanny. Then again, maybe that's why you hired Zora. Isn't that what you put in your ad? 'Substitute me.' I do seem to spend more time with her these days than with you."

Kate was getting tired of this conversation. It wasn't leading to any resolutions, which meant insults and accusations were being hurled back and forth. It was pointless and stupid. She swallowed the comment about what Brad could do with Zora if he was so inclined, and decided to try to wrap things up, using her greatest skills as a mediator. "Look, Brad," she began, "I'm really sorry you're feeling abandoned. What would you like me to do to fix the situation?"

"I hate it when you do that," Brad said, finishing off his beer and placing the empty bottle on the coffee table.

"What?" Kate asked, even though she knew exactly what he meant. It was The Voice.

"You know what."

Kate dropped The Voice. "Just tell me what you want me to do," she pleaded. "I don't want to fight."

Brad yawned and stretched his arms over his head. "I don't want to fight, either. I'm just sick of this arrangement."

"It's going to be over soon, though, I promise," Kate said, and slid next to Brad on the couch.

"I hope so," Brad said.

"It will. I promise," Kate repeated.

Brad kissed his wife on the cheek. "You know, I *am* proud of you. I just never get a chance to tell you."

"Thank you," Kate said, resting her head on Brad's chest and enjoying the steady rhythm of his heartbeat. After a few minutes, she broke the silence. "Brad?"

"Yes?" he answered.

"Do you want to tell me about superheroes now?"

"Not really. I'd rather take you upstairs, throw you across the bed, and show you some of my own superhuman tricks."

Kate laughed. Then she jumped up and made a dash for the stairs. "You gotta catch me first."

Brad took the challenge and raced up the stairs after his wife.

CHAPTER 27

Zora

Zora knew Brad was going to ask her. Ever since she'd started staying for dinner, he seemed to think there was nothing off-limits in their conversations. The personal, the political, the private . . . it didn't matter. Everything was up for discussion, as far as Brad was concerned. As she walked to work, Zora tried to figure out what she would say when he asked her why she'd walked out of the restaurant on Saturday night. It must have seemed rude, but she wasn't ready to introduce her private life to her professional one. For one thing, Keith might have gotten her fired, since he felt so strongly that she was wasting her talents working for them. She didn't know what he'd say or do if given the chance to "chat" with Brad and Kate. Also, she didn't want her employers observing her on a date. If they saw her kissing Keith, would they still respect her in the morning? She deserved to have some part of her life remain private.

Zora felt a flash of anger. Why should she have to explain herself to Brad? Why was she turning herself inside out, trying to come up with a nice way to tell him that she didn't feel like seeing him or his wife for one day? That wasn't too much to ask, but people felt like they owned you when you worked in their home. Zora tried to hang on to her righteous indignation as she got closer to the house, but with each step, the truth set in. Somewhere in these past few weeks, Brad Carter had crossed a line. He wasn't only her employer anymore; he had become her friend, plain and simple. Eating dinner together, playing with Ollie at the park, she sometimes forgot he was her boss. And technically, he wasn't. Kate was in charge, so her blossoming friendship with Brad didn't feel awkward or wrong. They were just two people who spent a lot of time together. Their conversations flowed easily, whether they were about babies or baseball. He made her laugh all the time. And he liked watching *Oprah* and wasn't afraid to admit it. Zora sighed. She was right back where she'd started—anger dissipated—wondering how she would answer Brad's question.

She couldn't pretend she hadn't seen them, not with Kate hollering across the dining room like that. She considered coming up with an illness for Keith. Zora smiled to herself. If she had to come up with a name for what ailed Keith, she'd call it "severe-hypocrite chicken-shit-itis." He was a piece of work, with his constant reminders of all her wasted potential while his own career was going nowhere fast. Keith spent a lot of time bemoaning the lack of roles for talented Black actors, but he rarely did much more than run his mouth about the problem. He far preferred to focus his attention on Zora's current state of underemployment. She knew he wanted to help her, but talk about the pot calling the kettle black. Seriously, if she wanted someone to nag her about her career, she'd call her mother.

When Angel went out with them, the fun never stopped. Zora's cheeks would hurt at the end of the night from laughing so hard. Angel was relentless, teasing Keith about his secret life as a stripper. But she also knew how to deal with his complaints about the racist system that wouldn't allow a Black man to find a decent role in show business. Angel said she understood his frustrations because every artist of color in America had it hard. She kept trying to convince Keith to go to Europe. "Think about Josephine Baker," she would say. "If she could do it all those years ago, you can, too." Keith always played along like he was considering an escape across the pond, but Zora sensed he lacked the courage to make such a bold move. She knew he was a homebody. He wanted to stay in his comfort zone. Zora recognized this in Keith because it was how she felt most of the time.

Zora was nearing Second Street and still hadn't figured out what she would say to Brad. He probably wouldn't bring it up this morning, because by the time she got to the house, he'd be leaving. She also needed to remind him that he was driving her to the gallery space with the food on Friday night. He'd volunteered to drive her, or rather, Kate had volunteered him to do it. Zora hoped he didn't mind. He said he didn't, but she wasn't so sure. She'd noticed that there seemed to be some sort of tension between Brad and Kate recently. Even though she never saw them together, Brad spoke about Kate in a sarcastic tone whenever she was going to get home really late. And the way Kate called home, asking for updates on Oliver and now Brad, too—Zora understood enough about human relationships to know that this could be the beginning of a rough patch between Brad and Kate. But it didn't have to be catastrophic. Zora knew that a good marriage could withstand trouble, and she thought Brad and Kate had a very solid union. Not to mention Ollie. She might tell him that if they ended up having dinner together. She thought he might need reminding of how lucky he was to have Kate in his life.

Zora did stay for dinner that night. But before she could tell Brad her thoughts about marriage, he asked about Keith and Saturday night at the restaurant.

"We left because I didn't want to listen to Keith give me grief about my life," she said, giving Brad an approximation of the truth.

"What do you mean, grief?" he asked as he helped himself to another pork chop and more coleslaw.

Zora chewed on a piece of meat for an extra-long time, keeping her gaze downcast as she tried to figure out if she could tell this story without being insulting. Finally, she looked up and said to Brad, "Keith is just like my brother. He thinks I'm wasting my skills working as a nanny and that I should be trying to start my own business. You know, not wait for a personal-chef position to open, just start something myself."

Rather than launch into his usual "Keep your head up" speech, Brad jumped up from the table and ran to the front hall. "Hold that thought," he called over his shoulder. When he came back, he was carrying a small unmarked paper bag. He laid the bag in front of Zora.

"I got you something," he said. "I hope it helps you realize that how you choose to live your life is for you to decide and nobody else."

Zora reached into the bag and pulled out a hardcover copy of *Dust Tracks on a Road,* Zora Neale Hurston's autobiography. It looked like a very old edition.

"Open the cover," Brad urged, barely able to contain his enthusiasm.

On the title page was a handwritten note from Zora Neale Hurston herself: "To thine own self be true." It was signed *Zora.* Zora traced the words with her fingers and then looked up at Brad Carter, her mouth shamelessly hanging open in awe. "Thank you so much. This is so amazing."

Brad grinned. "You're welcome."

"Where did you find this?" Zora whispered.

Brad was so excited he could barely get the words out. "I found it in a box of donated books at the Strand bookstore near Union Square. The Strand is the biggest used bookstore in the city. I don't even think they know what kind of treasures they have piled up in there. The kid working there didn't even open it. It's probably worth a lot of money."

"I don't care about the money. I can't believe she signed this,"

Zora said, and then she admitted, "I never knew she wrote an autobiography. I've only heard about her fiction."

"I wanted you to know something about the woman you were named after," Brad said. "Full disclosure: I kind of peeked and read the book first."

"How could you?" Zora teased. More seriously, she asked, "Did you like it?"

"I did," Brad said, returning to his dinner. "And I think you'll like it, too, because Zora Neale Hurston was a woman who wasn't afraid to take risks, and she didn't listen to anyone who tried to tell her how to live her life."

"You think that's me?" Zora asked.

"Not necessarily," Brad answered. "But I think you might be inspired to know the story of a Black woman who refused to apologize for the choices she made, even when they made other people unhappy. Maybe you'll be inspired. You know, she also studied anthropology, so you have that in common, too."

"Cool." Zora nodded, paging through the book.

Brad shrugged. "At the very least, I think you'll realize you were named after one very cool lady."

Zora took a moment to read the text on the jacket cover. Then she gave a mighty sigh and decided to expose her jumbled emotions to Brad. "I don't even know why I'm telling you all this, but I'm starting to think of our dinners as my therapy sessions."

"Just call me Dr. Brad," Brad quipped. "At your service."

Zora smiled and poured her heart out. "It's just that I've been a disappointment to all of the people in my family for so long. I've never achieved enough. My father says I lack ambition. I'm a classic underachiever. But I've been thinking that the reason I don't try to be Ms. Superwoman is because I know there's no way I'll live up to their expectations. I don't want to fail."

"Is that it?" Brad prompted.

"Nooo," Zora continued, fidgeting with the fake ruby ring

on her finger. "I've considered another possibility. Maybe I was switched at birth and I am really part of a family of low-achieving sloths. Maybe I'm not meant to do anything meaningful with my life."

Brad grimaced in frustration. "Zora, you are not an under-achiever unless you compare yourself to someone else. You are an excellent nanny. You take excellent care of Oliver. You are an amazing chef, and you keep our house feeling like a home. There are women all over the world who spend hours studying and training to do what you do. When I lived in London, I met members of Parliament who paid good money to attend the Annual Professional Nanny Conference because it was such a big deal. This is a real profession, Zora, and you are quite good at it."

"It's a real profession for European White girls," Zora corrected him. "It's not the same for Black people. It's just not."

Brad raised his eyes toward heaven. "Does it always have to be about race?"

"As long as I'm Black and we live in America, yes, it does," Zora confirmed.

Brad took a moment to formulate an answer. Finally, he said, "Look, I can't change four hundred years of history, and I can't make racism disappear. And I'm not trying to say that these things don't matter. As a White guy, I probably shouldn't even be allowed to comment, but I'm going to say this anyway. You can live your life trapped inside some asinine racial rule book, or you can do whatever the fuck you want. You have that choice."

"Oh, really?" Zora challenged.

"Yes, really," Brad responded, refusing to back down.

Zora thought Brad was done with his sermon, but he had another question for her. "Can you even admit it?" he asked. "Can you admit that you like being a nanny? I'm not saying that you wouldn't enjoy being a personal chef or that you wouldn't be good at it. But strip away the racial baggage and your parents' expectations. Can you admit that you like what you do right now?"

Zora felt a mixture of shame and relief with that question thrown in her face. She juggled the idea in her mind and tried to forget about mammy and her parents' disappointed faces. Was she happy being a nanny?

While she struggled with the thought, Brad continued talking. "You can't expect your friends and family to be proud of you and respect your choices in life if you're not proud of yourself."

Zora chewed on the inside of her cheek and fiddled with the pages of her new book. She looked up at Brad and said in a very small voice, "I do like my job. I think I'm good at it. And I feel like what I'm doing makes a difference. It's small, but it's important, in a way."

"You are important in a big way," Brad clarified. "Look, we all know around here that we'd be lost without you. It may seem fucked up in a twenty-first-century kind of way that we need to pay someone to take care of us, but that's where we are."

"Thank you. I think," Zora mumbled.

"I mean it," Brad pronounced. "You keep this household working. And it does make a difference. Neither Kate nor I could concentrate on our jobs if we didn't think Oliver was in good hands. Not to mention all of the extra stuff you do. There's no price for the peace of mind you give us."

Brad really did know how to make her feel better about the choices she was making. But she didn't want to talk about it anymore. The things he was saying made sense, but she needed time to process everything. She changed the subject by telling him her plans for Angel's show.

Brad didn't challenge the conversation detour. "By the way," he said, "I saw your notes for the menu, and I hope you leave some leftovers here for us."

"Perhaps you forgot that you're driving me over to the show

on Friday. It seems to me you can taste the food with everybody else," Zora teased.

"Hey, all that attitude, and I might make you take the bus," Brad shot back.

Zora looked up to see if he was kidding. Of course he had a huge grin on his face.

After eating, Zora stood to start clearing the table.

"I have an idea," Brad said, looking up at Zora.

"What?" she asked, collecting all of the food Ollie had thrown around during dinner. He was still sucking on a pork-chop bone in his high chair.

"Why don't you invite your brother to Angel's show?"

"Why?"

"Because it's time you stopped hiding your life from your family members, and this would be a nice way for you to show off your talents a bit."

Zora thought for a moment. More than likely, Craig would say no. He'd known she was living in Brooklyn all this time, and he'd never been out to check on her. The one time Zora had seen her brother this year, they'd met at Rockefeller Center to go ice-skating. Craig had given her a Christmas present then because he and Mimi had gone to Hawaii for Christmas and skipped going home altogether. Of course.

"He probably wouldn't come," Zora told Brad.

"Invite him anyway," Brad insisted.

Zora looked at Brad. He seemed so sure of himself and so sure that this would all have a happy ending. "I'll think about it," she said.

"Good," Brad answered. "You'll see, I'm right."

• • •

On the bus ride home to Fort Greene, Zora realized she'd never mentioned her theory about marriage to Brad. After dinner, she'd made a pretty hasty exit because she'd promised Angel she would send out e-mail reminders to the invite list. She also wanted to watch TV because there was a *Behind the Music* marathon coming on VH1. When she'd gotten an unexpected raise from Kate, she'd treated herself to cable, something she'd never been able to afford.

Right before she fell asleep that night, Zora decided two things. She'd make sure to tell Brad to keep the faith about Kate, and first thing in the morning, she would call her brother and invite him to Angel's show.

CHAPTER 28

Kate

Kate knew it wasn't likely that she would be able to make it to Angel's exhibit. But she wanted to try. She wanted to be supportive of Zora's life outside of her home. She called Fiona and asked if she was going and was surprised to hear that Fiona hadn't even thought about it. Kate suggested that the two of them go together if they could get off work on time. Fiona worked crazy hours, too, and hers weren't temporary. She'd told Kate it was normal for her to leave the office every night between eight-thirty and nine. Meanwhile, Greg made it home by six almost every day.

Kate and Fiona had sneaked out of their respective offices to meet for coffee when Fiona had explained her work schedule. They'd found a cozy table in the back of the café where they could carry on a conversation uninterrupted. Kate had hesitated at first but then decided to ask Fiona if Greg ever got mad at her for working so much and so late.

"Not really," Fiona confessed, "because he likes what my long hours translate into for our income."

"So he doesn't complain and get moody about not having you home every evening?" Kate asked.

Fiona gave Kate a knowing look. "Why? Are you and Brad having problems?"

"No," Kate said, staring into her coffee cup instead of meeting Fiona's eyes. "It's nothing, really. I mean, it's some adjustment problems. We talked about it, and I think everything's okay, but Brad says he wants me home."

"He wants you to quit your job?" Fiona sputtered.

"No, no, no," Kate rushed to clarify. "He just can't stand these hours and being alone all the time."

Fiona's beautiful blue eyes grew wide. "Are you afraid he's having an affair?"

"Of course not," Kate said, insulted by the question. "Brad would never cheat on me. Especially over something so trivial."

"Okay, okay," Fiona said. "Just asking. So what's the problem?"

"There isn't a real problem," Kate explained. "I'm trying to figure out if it's normal that he's acting like a moody jerk because I have to work late so much."

"Sounds like you're angry, too," Fiona said.

"I guess I am," Kate admitted for the first time. "*I'm* angry that *he* feels entitled to be mad because I have a job that I actually enjoy. Why should I feel guilty about that?"

"Do you feel guilty?"

"Yes and no," Kate answered truthfully. "I feel guilty because I know Brad is lonely, and then there's Ollie, but on the other hand, I'm doing my job. Why should I have to feel guilty about that? And we have Zora!"

"You shouldn't feel guilty," Fiona assured her. "You've done nothing wrong and everything right. Men are hardwired to expect their wives to be home when they get home. Dinner in the oven, slippers in hand." They both laughed at this image.

Kate took a big sip of her *caffè americano*. "Brad's not like that, though," she insisted. "His mother is a nurse, and she always worked when he was little. He's more of a feminist than I am."

"They're all cavemen," Fiona said with a dismissive wave. "But you can train them. And the best way to do that is to give them lots of sex."

Kate choked on her last sip of coffee. "Excuse me."

Fiona giggled. "Haven't you realized yet that most men can be easily tamed with a healthy diet of sex, sex, and more sex? If you give it to them regularly, they'll forgive you all things."

"That is so wrong." Kate felt herself blush. She lowered her voice barely above a whisper and asked her friend, "So you're saying I have to prostitute myself to my own husband to get him to act like an adult?" She shook her head in disbelief and disgust at the thought and answered her own question. "Brad should grow up and be able to handle the situation. It's not like it's forever. I'm asking him to be patient and supportive for a few more weeks. Is that too much to ask?"

Fiona sighed. "Sweetie pie, I'm not the one you have to ask."

Kate continued thinking about her conversation with Fiona as she absentmindedly arranged her work into piles on her desk. She had to file three expense reports, draft a press release for KasperKline's new successful test trials of their four-times-a-year birth-control pill, and make a quick run to the hotel to okay tablecloths and centerpieces for the gala. It was time to practice her newfound skill of delegating. She could hand off her expense reports to Laurie, but everything else, she had to do herself. If she hurried, she might be able to make the last hour of Angel's show. Kate poked her head out of the office and asked Laurie to hold all calls unless they were absolute emergencies.

In the car on the way to Brooklyn, Kate had to bite her tongue to keep herself from shouting at the driver to hurry. After flying out of the office, she had rushed to the closest bodega and bought a small but acceptable bouquet of flowers right before the car pulled up to the curb. She knew that these professional drivers took their work very seriously, and suggestions on how to drive or better routes to take were considered heresy. It was best to keep quiet, seeing as how she might already be in a bit of trouble. Kate had bent the rules and ordered a car service from her office because she knew she'd never make it on the subway, and she didn't have enough cash to pay for a cab all the way to Brooklyn. She was allowed to take a car home any night she stayed past nine. Leaving at eight-fifteen wasn't exactly criminal, she decided, and with all the extra hours she'd been putting in, one unauthorized car service seemed her due. Angel's show was over at nine-thirty. If the driver hurried, she could make it a few minutes before nine.

Once they were on the Brooklyn Bridge, Kate started to relax. She didn't know when the show had become such a big deal. In the end, Fiona had said she wasn't going: she and Greg would order in sushi and watch a movie. Kate had called Brad at four-thirty to see if he was on schedule to get Zora to the gallery space on time. He'd grumbled that he was just about to start loading the car. "Are you going to make it or not?" Brad had asked.

"Of course I am," Kate had snapped. "I said I would, and I will."

Replaying that last conversation with Brad, Kate realized that her showing up at the art show was more for him than for Angel or Zora. She had to prove to Brad that she was in control of her time. She had to show him that her whole life didn't revolve around work. So what if she was making it for only the last thirty minutes of the event. She was going to be there and show her support.

The driver pulled up in front of the building. "Here you are, miss," he said as he handed Kate a voucher attached to a clipboard for her to sign. She scrawled her initials on the paper, grabbed her bag and the flowers, and hopped out of the car. "Thanks," she called as she slammed the door.

Kate ran up the steep staircase, every step bringing her closer to the scent of sweet citrus and something like pine. When she stepped into the room, her jaw dropped at the transformation. No longer a toddler's party space, the yoga studio looked like any other swanky art gallery in the city. Angel's paintings hung in every available inch of wall space. Each oversize oil portrait told a different story of joy or sorrow, anger or despair, in deep, passionate colors. The mirrors were draped with gauzy orange material, and white votive candles flickered on every surface. The room had ambient lighting, but there were floodlights shining up on every painting for maximum viewing pleasure. Kate was truly impressed. She scanned the room for Zora but didn't see her at first, so she took the opportunity to walk around and admire Angel's work.

The show wasn't as crowded as Molly's birthday party had been, but Kate estimated there were about thirty people milling about. Most of the people, she realized, were Black or some shade of brown, dressed in funky hipster clothing that made Kate feel out of place. Her eyes gravitated toward an Asian woman in a smart business suit hanging on the arm of a well-dressed Black man. She quickly noticed two other White people in the room and scolded herself for thinking she might not belong.

She spied Angel, resplendent in a long purple tunic dress with gold threads woven through. She wore gold strappy heels and two enormous gold bangles on each wrist. What a character, Kate thought as she took in Angel's regal attire.

"Hi, Kate. You made it!"

It was Zora. She'd come up from behind, carrying a silver tray of tantalizing appetizers.

"Zora, this place looks amazing," Kate said, plucking a stuffed mushroom from the offerings. "You guys did a great job." She popped the mushroom into her mouth and made a great show of how much she enjoyed it.

"Thanks," Zora said, and gave Kate a smile. "I'll be right back. I have to put these on the table."

Kate studied Zora as she walked across the room. Kate thought she could improve her looks if she fixed that gap between her teeth. She had a nice body—very tight muscles and a flat stomach, but her thighs and rear end were kind of thick. That was more typical for Black women, Kate knew. Zora was wearing a simple white A-line dress that showed off her curves and a pair of black flats. She, too, wore two gold bracelets on each arm, and her signature gold stud flashed in her nose. She looked nice, Kate decided. Minus the nose jewelry, of course.

Kate noticed Keith in the group surrounding Angel, and she remembered Zora had told her he was acting as host for the evening. She never got a straight answer out of Zora if Keith was her boyfriend, but she guessed there was something special going on between them. She could tell by the way his eyes followed Zora around the room. He'd been by the house once or twice to pick Zora up, and he seemed like a really nice guy. They made a cute couple with their matching dreadlocks, Kate thought. While she waited for Zora to come back, Kate continued on her tour of the gallery. She knew enough about classical portraiture, but she couldn't tell if Angel was truly a talented artist. The colors were so bold and the subjects so real, Kate wasn't sure if she was supposed to be shocked by the paintings or enraptured. She longed for a catalog explaining Angel's process and the point of these particular paintings.

After her second go-round, having downed a glass of white wine and a few more stuffed mushrooms, Kate felt like she'd done her duty and could go home. Mission accomplished. She suddenly realized how tired she was. She was so happy she had an entire weekend to look forward to. Maybe she could convince Brad to drive up to Cold Spring for a little antiquing and quiet time. As she headed toward the exit, she noticed Zora talking to the Asian woman and her date. She considered going over to say good-bye but decided to follow Brad's advice and leave Zora to her own life.

Despite her exhaustion, Kate chose to walk home. It wasn't that far, and by the time a car service showed up, she could be in bed. The cool spring air felt good on her face. As she walked, she thought about Fiona's advice to give Brad twenty-four-hour sex and he'd be putty in her hands. She decided to try it out tonight, even though all she craved was a good night's sleep. But no, she was going to seduce her husband, get him in a good mood, and then bring up the Cold Spring idea. If it worked, she'd treat Fiona to a pesto pizza at Luigi's. Just thinking about Brad's shock at her initiating sex on a Friday night, when she was usually so tired, put a smile on her face. He'd be thrilled. Men were pretty easy, Kate thought.

But Brad had other plans. As soon as Kate walked in the door, he informed her that he was on his way out to hang with some friends. He didn't specify which friends, saying only that it was some guys from work whom she didn't know.

"We're going to meet in the Heights for a beer, but don't wait up for me," Brad offered as he brushed his lips against her cheek.

"Okay," Kate stammered as she watched Brad grab his keys and head out the door. It wasn't like they never socialized alone, but Kate had been so caught up in her seduction plans that she felt completely rejected, watching Brad leave her behind with only a cloud of his spicy cologne to keep her company. Kate realized she missed her husband. The idea crept up on her like an unexpected visitor. She knew she was working too much, and she couldn't wait for things to come back into balance. For all of their sakes.

Unwilling to allow herself to dwell on the fact that she'd been dissed by her husband, Kate pinched her cheeks to change the course of her thinking. It took her only a moment to go back to her original plans. Tiptoeing up the stairs to make sure she didn't wake Ollie, Kate took an extra-long, extra-hot shower and fell into bed, asleep before her head hit the pillow. She woke up for only a moment when Brad crawled into the bed beside her. The clock on her nightstand read three A.M.

CHAPTER 29

Zora

Zora couldn't wait to tell Brad. He had been so right. Her brother had come to Angel's show, and he'd been really proud of her. His girlfriend, Mimi, had gushed about the food and promised to call her for a small gathering that she wanted Zora to cater. Best of all, Mimi had convinced Craig to buy one of Angel's larger paintings to hang in their apartment.

"I feel like celebrating," Zora told Ollie on their afternoon walk. "Let's make your dad's favorite dinner."

She didn't even have to stop and think. She knew Brad loved her spaghetti and Italian-sausage dinner the best. She shopped for the ingredients in the markets along Seventh Avenue with love and care. "And you know what, Ollie, let's try to make a lemon meringue pie for dessert." Ollie answered with his favorite response, which was to clap and say something that to Zora sounded like "Whoop de woo." Zora laughed at this child who she freely admitted had wiggled his way right into her heart. She knew she was lucky. He was a good sleeper, a good eater, and he didn't have any of the crazy allergies it seemed every other child suffered from in Brooklyn. As a woman who used food to soothe and comfort the ones she loved, she couldn't imagine dealing with a child on a restricted diet. For this, she gave much thanks.

Kate had let it slip recently that she was thinking about having another child. It was a fantasy right now, she had confessed, but Zora knew Kate wanted a daughter. Taking care of two babies would be a challenge, Zora thought, but she knew she could handle it. In France, the first family she worked for had two little kids, and the Bertrands had three, although Jean-Luc was twelve, so he didn't count. She tried to imagine a female version of Ollie, but it was too hard. He was all boy, in Zora's mind. She wondered if Ollie would grow up to be as handsome as his father. Brad was definitely good-looking, Zora had to admit. It was the contrast of his thick dark hair with his warm green eyes that attracted the most attention. She noticed his features more now that they'd become friends—his structured cheekbones and slightly rounded chin, and his lower lip, which was fuller than the top. She hadn't even registered his looks for the first few months, but now she couldn't help it. You spend so much time with a person, how can you not notice?

Zora pushed Brad's face out of her mind and focused on the meal instead. Standing outside Key Food, the largest supermarket in the neighborhood, Zora took inventory of her ingredients. She had everything for the sauce, including fresh basil and organic garlic, so now she needed to purchase the items for the pie. She pushed the stroller into Key Food and headed straight for the dairy case. She had to purchase an entire pound of butter because she was going to make the crust from scratch, and Kate, weight watcher that she was, never kept butter in the house. She preferred the fake half-butter, half-margarine stuff that Zora's culinary instructors considered a product manufactured by the devil himself. The butter, a bag of flour, a dozen eggs, and two pounds of lemons later, Zora was back outside and heading for the Carters' home.

In a moment of inspiration, she dashed into the flower shop and bought a bouquet of orange Israeli daisies for the table. Their exuberant color perfectly reflected her mood. Zora couldn't remember when she'd felt this good about herself and her family and her life. Her own snobby, judgmental brother had complimented her, telling her she looked great and that the show was fantastic. "I'm proud of you, Z," were his exact words, and she could tell he meant it. Zora knew she'd acted like a puppy that had learned a new trick, but she was so hungry for the acknowledgment from a family member that she'd just stood there grinning. Angel was right there heaping on the praise, saying how much Zora had done to organize the show and how she'd planned the menu. Angel had made her sound like some miracle worker rather than a woman who knew how to make a little magic with some candles and well-placed fabric. The only damper on the whole evening was the fight she'd had with Keith.

They were back at her apartment, polishing off the leftover mushrooms and wine. She sat on the couch with her feet tucked into Keith's lap, and he continued to lay on the compliments about what a great job she'd done. "You could have a career as an event planner, Z," he'd said while massaging the tender inner soles of her feet. "You really know how to make a party happen." Zora smiled but didn't say anything. She waited to see what was coming next. And right on cue, he said it: "I can't believe you're still wasting your time working for those people." That was when she lost it.

She jumped up from the couch and roared, "Enough! I don't want to hear this from you anymore!"

Keith looked stunned. "What is wrong with you, Zora? What did I say?"

"You just don't know when to stop," Zora spat out. She'd been holding this in for so long, her anger scared even her a bit.

"Stop what?"

"Stop telling me I should quit my job. Stop telling me I'm wasting my time."

Keith pulled Zora back down on the couch, and she let him. She wanted him to take it back. She wanted him to accept her the way she was and stop pushing.

Keith waited a moment before he opened his mouth. "Zora,"

he began softly, "I'm sorry if you feel like I'm telling you what to do. I just think you have so much potential, and you're wasting it. I know you're probably scared, but I can help you if you'll let me."

Zora snorted in disbelief and stood up again. "That's rich, coming from you, Keith," she said, shaking her head. "Don't you think you should try fixing your own life before you try to fix mine?"

Keith looked at Zora like she'd chopped off one of his balls. All of this time together, and she'd never turned the tables on him and suggested he stop being a chicken-shit and chase his own dreams. Move to Los Angeles. Get a new agent. Try Europe. No, she'd been supportive and a good listener for all of his woes. Patted his back and nursed his shattered ego. Treated him like she wanted to be treated. No more, Zora decided. It wasn't fair.

Keith stood up slowly. He grabbed his jacket off the back of the couch. "You know what, Zora?" he said as he moved toward the door. "I think I'm going to walk away now before I say something I'll regret later." He stopped and turned back to her and said, "I'm sorry I've been such a disappointment."

When the door closed, Zora grabbed a pillow off the couch and screamed into it as loud as she could.

Zora pushed thoughts of Keith out of her mind as she walked briskly down Seventh Avenue. Keith probably needed time to cool off. And maybe to do some self-evaluation and apply to himself some of that advice he was always doling out. She made a mental note to call him tonight.

She looked at her watch. If she made it back to the Carters' by three-thirty, gave Ollie his snack, and got the sauce going right away, dinner should be ready by the time Brad got home. Tonight she was expecting him by six.

Still calculating whether she'd have time to make the pie, Zora didn't notice Mrs. Rodriguez poking her head out of her front window as she turned Ollie's stroller into the yard. She jumped when the old woman called out, "Hello there, Cora."

"Oh, hi, Mrs. Rodriguez," Zora said with her hand on her chest, trying to calm her heart and wondering how many times she'd have to tell the woman that her name was Zora, not Cora. It didn't really matter, since their relationship had yet to progress beyond hello and good-bye as Zora passed in and out of the house. She started to pull the bags of groceries from underneath the stroller and haul them up the front steps. She'd bring Ollie up last.

"Looks like you're making a feast tonight," Mrs. Rodriguez commented, gesturing to the bags with the fresh herbs spilling over the top.

For some reason, Zora felt the need to downplay her efforts. "Nope, it's just going to be spaghetti tonight."

"The Carters are very lucky to have a girl like you cooking for them. Especially Mr. Carter, since his wife is one of those career women."

Zora rolled her eyes and moved faster. She mumbled, "Uh-huh," so as not to appear completely rude, but at the same time trying to indicate that she wasn't interested in having a conversation.

"You know, they always say the way to a man's heart is through his stomach," Mrs. Rodriguez said. "Do you young people still believe that, Cora?"

For some strange reason, Alexander's face flashed into Zora's mind. She'd never cooked for him. And he'd left her. Maybe that was why. She shook her head. She was being ridiculous. She ignored Mrs. Rodriguez's question, got the food, Ollie, and the stroller inside, and called out a good-bye to the old lady before she slammed the door.

• • •

When Brad walked in the door that evening, he came right into the kitchen. He scooped Ollie up out of his walker and announced with a smile, "I smell spaghetti."

"Yep," Zora said as she dropped the hard pasta in the boiling water on the stove. She turned and smiled at Brad. "We're celebrating tonight. I have great news."

"Really?" Brad pouted, and then his mouth broke into a wide grin. "I have great news, too."

"Hurry up and go upstairs and change," Zora commanded. "Dinner will be ready in exactly fifteen minutes."

"Yes, ma'am," Brad said. He kissed his son on both cheeks and then once on the stomach, sending Ollie into fits of giggles. He then set him back in the walker and turned to go upstairs.

Zora suddenly stopped stirring the sauce. She'd had a sobering thought. She was careful to keep her voice completely devoid of emotion. "Is Kate coming home late again tonight?"

Brad didn't turn around. He kept walking, but he answered, "Absofuckinglutely."

Zora knew the relief she felt at that answer wasn't right, but she shoved the thought out of her mind and set the timer for the pasta. Then she turned to setting the table, starting with the flowers as the centerpiece.

When Brad came back downstairs, wearing track pants and a navy blue fitted long-sleeve cotton T-shirt, the table was set and the food was piled high on the serving platters, filling the room with the romantic scents of garlic, basil, and oregano.

"Wow, this looks fantastic, Z," Brad said, inhaling deeply.

Zora tried to remember when Brad had started calling her Z. "Thank you," she said. "Let's eat it, because I didn't make it to stare at."

Brad and Zora sat down. Ollie had already eaten, but Zora

placed small pieces of pasta and sausage on the tray of his walker.

"So what's the good news?" Brad asked after savoring the first few bites in blissful silence.

"First, do you like the food?" Zora had to know. She couldn't focus on anything else until she knew if the food was acceptable.

Brad looked at her like she'd grown a second head. "Are you crazy?" he asked. "This is delicious. It's scrumptious. It's heavenly. It's my favorite meal that you make."

"I know." Zora smiled shyly. "I made it for you on purpose, because I wanted to say thank you."

"For what?" Brad asked.

"For making me call my brother," Zora said. She proceeded to tell Brad how well things had gone at Angel's show.

"Fantastic!" Brad beamed. "I'm so glad things worked out for you. You deserve to be happy, and you should be proud of yourself. I'm glad you can see that now."

"Yeah, well, I guess I am all that." Zora laughed.

"I think so," Brad said.

Zora refused to meet his gaze when he said that. Instead, she changed the subject, telling Brad about Ollie's latest tricks on the playground. They finished eating, talking about their respective day's work and accomplishments. When they were finished, Zora jumped up and started gathering the plates from the table. "By the way, I finished *Dust Tracks on a Road,*" she said as she moved about the kitchen. "It was really good. I never knew Zora Neale Hurston led such an amazing life. Seriously, from the moment she was born, it was like she knew she was destined for great things."

"Didn't I tell you?" Brad said with glee. He pushed himself away from the table and started putting the leftover food in Tupperware.

"I'm really glad I read it," Zora said. "I'm totally looking at my life differently. I mean, even though she was a famous writer and I'm not, I learned some things from her. She never apologized for being Black or being a woman. And she did live her life the way she wanted to. I'm so ashamed I haven't read her work before."

"Why ashamed?" Brad asked with concern.

Zora stopped stacking dishes before she answered. She studied her hands in front of her and replied, "You know, I made it a point to never learn about Zora Neale Hurston just because my mother wanted me to so badly. It was stupid, but it was my form of literary rebellion."

"Wow. Do you hate your mother that much?" Brad asked, stacking the containers in the refrigerator.

"No, I don't hate my mother. Our relationship is just complicated," Zora explained. "She doesn't get me, that's all."

"We've been over this before, but your parents might surprise you if you'd be honest with them." Zora opened her mouth to protest, but Brad put his hands up. "Hey, you just admitted your brother was impressed."

Zora smiled. "Okay, Mr. Fix-it. I'll think about talking to my parents, too."

"Good," Brad said with a satisfied smile. He walked over to the sink and grabbed the dishrag to start wiping the table and the counters.

"In the meantime, I'm making it a point to read everything Zora Neale Hurston ever wrote," Zora said, attacking the greasy pots and pans. Her enthusiasm for the conversation made the task less unpleasant. "I'm already halfway through *Their Eyes Were Watching God*. It's so good. I think it's semiautobiographical. It's about a woman who loves the wrong type of man but refuses to apologize for it."

Brad cleared his throat abruptly before he responded. "I'll have to read it, then, so we can discuss it at our next dinner."

Zora didn't know if he was serious, but she decided not to ask for clarification. Instead, she brought up dessert. "By the way, I made a pie for dessert. Guess what kind it is."

"What will I get if I guess it right on the first try?" Brad asked, leaning against the refrigerator.

"You're not going to guess."

"But what if I do?" Brad insisted.

"If you guess on the first try, I'll give you the first piece of pie. How about that?"

"Fine, it's a deal," Brad said. He put his fingers to his temples, closed his eyes, and made a big show of concentrating really hard. "I'm going to guess lemon meringue," he announced.

"You peeked," Zora shrieked, throwing the dish towel at him from across the room. It missed wildly.

"You're right, I did," Brad said, laughing. "I couldn't help it. I had to put the food away."

Zora stomped her foot in mock anger. "It was supposed to be a surprise."

"It was a surprise when I saw it in there," Brad assured her.

"Oh, whatever," Zora said, pushing Brad aside so she could pull the pie out of the refrigerator. Still chuckling, he sat back down at the table.

"Here's your winning first piece, even though you cheated." Zora placed a healthy wedge of the lemony-sweet confection in front of Brad. She cut another piece for herself and a small chunk for the baby. "Ollie has to have some, too, don't you, Ollie?" she said. She placed a few pieces of crust on Ollie's tray. He grabbed her finger and tried to suck on it. "You silly thing," Zora said. "Eat the pie, not me." Ollie let her finger go and began investigating the crust. He put a little crumb in his mouth and shrieked with delight. "That's right, baby boy, it's good, isn't it?" She chuckled.

"He really loves you, doesn't he?" Brad said, staring intently at Ollie.

Zora couldn't tell if it was a question requiring an answer, so she asked Brad if he liked the pie.

"It's really good," he said, but he seemed to be lost in thought.

"So what's your good news?" Zora asked, hoping to bring him back down from wherever his mind had wandered.

Brad shook his head as if ridding it of cobwebs. Then he smiled at Zora. "We found an investor for the comic-book venture. He's this rich kid, younger than me, who made a grotesque amount of money in the dot-com boom and now invests solely in video games and e-commerce sites. One of our guys reached out to him through a friend of a friend. We all met up on Friday night, and he seems really interested."

"Brad, that's great," Zora gushed, getting caught up in his enthusiasm. "What's the next step?"

"Well," Brad began, "now I can start writing a real business plan targeted for this guy's interests and requests. Because he's young and gets this stuff, we don't have to start at ground zero to explain the synergy of the comics, the Internet, and the movie aspect. He totally gets it, but he doesn't want to be involved in day-to-day operations. He just wants to put up the initial funds and get his profit out. So I have to make the numbers look really appealing."

"Can you do that without lying?" Zora asked.

"Yeah, I think I can," Brad said. "But it's going to take some creative mathematics to come out right."

"I'm sure you can handle it," Zora said. "Just think, here's your big chance to combine your financial expertise with your creative side."

"Ha-ha," Brad said. "Not exactly the way I envisioned it, but you're right. I'm going to love putting my skills to use on this project. And who knows? If everything goes well, there may be a real job for me out of it."

"Really?" Zora asked. "I didn't know that was a possibility."

"You never know," Brad said, shrugging. "I'd like to think it could happen. That this could be a way for me to walk away from Wall Street and do something more creative. But that is so far off in the future."

"Hey, keep the faith," Zora said. "It could totally happen. You guys have gotten this far, right? And in the beginning you didn't think this idea had a chance in hell."

"We'll see," Brad said, but he looked hopeful. "But I can't get caught up in the what-ifs. I have to stay focused on the business plan for now."

"Okay, Mr. Killjoy," Zora teased. "But at least now you can tell Kate what you've been up to. Isn't that what you said? When you started writing the business plan, you'd let her know."

"I said that, didn't I?" Brad said.

"Yes, you did," Zora confirmed.

"I guess I should tell her, then," Brad hedged.

"Yes, you should," Zora said. "Why the hesitation? Isn't it hard keeping this from her?"

"Yes and no," Brad answered, helping himself to more pie.

"Well," Zora said, "a wise man once told me to trust the people who love me enough to tell them the truth. And I can say that I took this wise man's advice, and he was right."

"I know, I know, I know," Brad said. "It's just that right now I don't think Kate and I . . ." He let the sentence drop. Zora said nothing. She finished her pie in silence.

Brad pushed himself away from the table and announced that he was going to take Ollie upstairs for bed. He begged Zora to stay until he came back down. He made her promise not to do the rest of the dishes. She promised, but she crossed her fingers behind her back. What did he think she was going to do, sit in a messy kitchen twiddling her thumbs until he was done?

The dishes were stacked in the dishwasher and the table and countertops were scrubbed clean of pie crumbs by the time Brad dashed back down the stairs. "I told you not to clean up," he lamented.

"Mr. Carter," Zora said, using her best British accent, "I simply cannot sit around idle with rubbish all about. It does not sit well with my constitution."

Brad laughed. "Okay, Zora Poppins. Please sit down, then, while I make it up to you by brewing you a nice cup of tea."

"Fine," Zora said, sitting at the table. "That would be nice."

As Brad puttered around, pulling out tea bags and lemons and honey, Zora decided now would be a good time to share her advice on marriage. "You know, all marriages hit some speed bumps," she began quietly, crossing her legs under the table, making herself comfortable. "This is just a bump. Kate is working late, you're pissed about it, but things will go back to normal. The same thing happens in a million households every day. You have to wait it out. Be patient."

Brad didn't say anything. He seemed engrossed in slicing the lemon and arranging the pieces on a saucer just so. Finally, he spoke with a great deal of weariness and something else. "I know you're right."

Zora smiled. "Of course I'm right."

"But there's something else," Brad said in a voice barely above a whisper.

"Look, you guys will figure it out." Zora stood up to make her point, making sure to keep her voice upbeat and positive. "Kate will stop working these crazy hours soon, then you're going to be busy with your new project, and you'll get it sorted out. You guys can go away again for the weekend. I'll watch Oliver for you—" Zora couldn't finish her sentence because Brad, in two strides, had crossed the kitchen and grabbed her and kissed her with such a depth of passion, she couldn't process what was happening. Her rational mind turned off, and she wrapped her arms around his neck and kissed him back. In the next instant, reality slapped them both in the face, and they pulled apart.

Brad's breathing was pained, ragged. He looked at the floor and wouldn't meet Zora's eyes. She dragged her hand across her lips as if she could erase what had just happened.

"That's why things won't go back to normal," Brad managed.

Zora looked at her feet. At her hands. At the table where they had just sat. Anywhere but at him. "I have to go," she whispered. "I have to go."

She quickly gathered her things and ran out the door. Brad didn't try to stop her.

CHAPTER 30

Brad

Y OU did *what*?”

Brad had to hold the phone away from his ear while Carl used every combination of curse word to exclaim his disbelief. He was really loud. “So was it worth it?” Carl finally asked.

“Worth what? What are you asking me?” Brad cried. “I just kissed her. We didn't sleep together.”

“Okay, okay. Dude, you gotta give me a minute,” Carl said. Brad could imagine him pacing in his tiny living room, probably wearing his favorite at-home ensemble of faded green velour jogging pants and a T-shirt with an X-rated beer slogan.

While Carl collected his thoughts, Brad did his own share of pacing and worrying. For once, he hoped Kate wasn't coming home soon. He needed time to figure out how to handle this.

Carl had another question for him. This one got to the heart of the matter. “Why'd you do it, man? I mean, was she asking for it?”

“No! I totally attacked *her*,” Brad started to explain. “I didn't *attack* her, but I made the first move.”

“What's this all about, then? Are you and Katie on the splits?”

“No,” Brad hissed. “And could you keep your voice down? Is Sheila around?”

“No worries,” Carl soothed his friend. “She's out with her girl-friend Trudy. I'm all alone on diaper duty tonight.”

Brad sighed his relief. “Look, I called you because I need to figure this out. This is not me. I don't cheat. If one of us were going to cheat on his wife, it would be you."

"Hey," Carl said. "Not nice."

"I'm sorry," Brad said, his stomach roiling in distress. "I'm freaking out here."

"Don't freak out. Whatever you do, don't freak out," Carl advised. "If you freak out, then you'll definitely give yourself away. You must remain calm. Take a shower and brush your teeth. Women can smell other women on their men."

Brad shook his head. "Carl, I don't need you to teach me how to avoid getting caught. I need you to help me figure out what I'm supposed to do."

"Fine," Carl said, getting serious. "Start by answering my question. Why'd you do it?"

Brad hesitated as he tried to find the words for what he was feeling. "You know, I can't get her out of my mind. I'm thinking about her all the time, and then I get home and she's here in my house, cooking for me, having dinner with me—"

"Wait, you guys eat dinner together?" Carl interrupted.

"Yeah, sometimes," Brad admitted. "We talk all the time, and sometimes I hang out with them on the playground. I see Zora these days more than Kate."

"Interesting," Carl mused. "Go on."

"I didn't plan on kissing her. The urge to kiss her was so strong I couldn't help myself. Of course I could have stopped, but I didn't want to. And this sounds so wrong, but at the time it didn't feel like a bad thing. It felt really normal for just a second."

"Dude, dude, dude," Carl started, "this is not rocket science. Look, do you want to leave your wife so you can have sex with the nanny?"

"No," Brad snapped. "Of course not. I love Kate."

"It's very simple. You chalk this up to 'Opportunity Knocked, and You Opened the Door.' Now shut the damn door and forget this ever happened."

"That's it?" Brad queried.

"Yeah, that's it," Carl said. "Unless you think Little Miss Zora is going to go running to Kate."

Brad didn't even have to consider. He knew Zora wouldn't want to hurt Kate that way. Of that he was sure. "She won't tell," he said.

"Then you're free and clear. And from now on, stop eating dinner with the nanny and start paying more attention to your wife."

Brad chuckled. Carl was so black and white. That was why Brad had called him. That and because he knew a few things about his friend that made him sure Carl wouldn't blab to Sheila. "Thanks, man," he said.

"Anytime," Carl said. "But don't make it any time soon. You're supposed to be the good guy in the group. If word gets out that you've gone rogue on Katie, all hell is going to break loose. You'll upset our whole world order."

"Right," Brad said, laughing in spite of himself. "I'll do my best to continue to be your role model."

"You better," Carl said. "We're counting on you. Just like we count on hot wings at happy hour."

Brad hung up the phone and felt better for precisely one minute. Then memories of Zora and the kiss came flooding in, and he was back to being scared and confused. He walked over to the bookcase and stared at a picture of him and Kate on their wedding day. His eyes traveled to the latest photo of Ollie on the playground. It was still waiting for a frame, propped up against the books. This was his family, and he wasn't about to throw it all away. Not now, not ever.

Just in case, he headed for the shower before Kate got home.

CHAPTER 31

Kate

KATE was livid. Zora had called in sick. She knew it was unfair for her to be angry at Zora for catching a cold, but the timing was just so bad. There were only two weeks left before the gala, and Zora knew this. She'd called at seven-thirty, right before Kate was about to leave the house. No explanation. She just said she wasn't feeling well and wouldn't be in today. Granted, they'd never discussed sick days, but surely calling someone thirty minutes before work was not considered professional. Even for a nanny.

Thankfully, after Kate threatened to have a nervous breakdown, Brad agreed to take the day off, so Kate was only minimally late to work, but still, every second counted these days. She checked her e-mail and her voice mail as soon as she got settled in. She hated to treat her coordinators like fetch-it girls, but she had to ask Kelly to go to the deli and get her a bagel and coffee. She hadn't had time to eat before she left the house. Laurie assured her that everything was under control and that the only person who had come looking for her was Marjorie, taking Girl Scout cookie orders for her granddaughter.

Today was going to be all about sending press releases to the media about the gala. Laurie and Kelly could handle that. Kate had back-to-back meetings with the AAA folks for media training and a conference call with the chief of operations at the Plaza to go over expectations for the night of the event. At the end of the day, she'd scheduled one more task, and she was taking Laurie and Kelly along for the ride. They had to catalog all of the donations collected for the silent auction. The items were being held at the AAA offices down in Tribeca. That was the fun part of the job, and she wanted the young women to have a chance to enjoy it, too—to get a chance to see the designer gowns donated by their creators, the original paintings by artists both dead and alive, and the random memorabilia thrown out by movie stars and pop stars that some rabid collector would pay three times their worth to own. Laurie and Kelly were still young and unjaded enough to be impressed by these ostentatious displays of wealth. Kate had been like that, too, when she first got to New York. She could still remember the sparks of excitement she'd felt on her first celebrity photo shoot. She was beyond that now, but it made her feel good to be the one to open the door for Kelly and Laurie.

At four, Kate got her first break, and she called home. She figured Ollie would be waking up from his nap. If Zora had been there, she'd be watching *Oprah,* but with Brad home, Kate had no idea what to expect. Brad was a great babysitter, but like a typical male, he was inconsistent with rules and schedules.

He answered on the third ring. He sounded distracted.

"Hey, hon," she said.

"Hey," he said back.

"How's everything going?"

"Fine," he answered. "Ollie's sleeping, and I'm working."

"What are you working on?" Kate asked.

"Actually, it's a project I wanted to talk to you about," Brad said.

"Hmm," Kate said, intrigued. "Can you give me a hint what it's about?"

"I'd rather wait till you get home," Brad answered.

"Okay," Kate said, although she was rather curious. But she could wait. "So what did you and Ollie do today?" she asked.

"Nothing special," Brad said.

Kate couldn't tell if he was angry or just busy. She didn't have time to figure it out. She returned to her professional voice. "Well, I was just checking in. I have a late meeting in Tribeca, so I probably won't get home till around eight-thirty."

"Okay," Brad said. "See you then."

Kate hung up, irritated and confused. Was Brad annoyed that he'd had to take the day off? He could miss any number of days, and nothing horrible would happen. He was allowed to work from home sometimes, so she wasn't going to feel guilty. And what was this mysterious project he was working on? Kate knew that she needed to stay focused on her work, so she used her uncanny ability to compartmentalize issues and pushed thoughts of Brad to the bottom of her Things to Worry About list. She buzzed Kelly and Laurie and told them to be ready to meet her at the elevators in fifteen minutes.

The two girls sat in the back of the cab with Kate and talked about the best sample sales they'd found to buy cheap designer clothes. Kate tuned them out as she stared out the window and tried not to think about Brad. It didn't work. She was a woman who liked to—or rather, needed to—feel in control. She needed the comfort of knowing that things were in place the way she'd left them. That was why she'd been so confident at work, because she knew exactly what Zora was doing, how she was doing it, and when she was doing it. Zora was the perfect nanny, in Kate's opinion, because she understood her boss's need for order and predictability. Zora was always home when Kate called; she could recite exactly what Ollie had eaten and what time he'd fallen asleep. In this way, Kate felt like she knew everything that was going on in her home even when she wasn't there. She could probably fool someone into thinking that she stayed home full-time, what with the details she knew about Ollie's routines. Kate was again reminded what a blessing Zora was, after having Brad home for just one day. It was playing at her nerves, being out of the loop of her son's routine.

She knew she didn't want to lose Zora. Not now, especially. Not for a long time. Even though it was completely selfish, she hoped Zora wouldn't pursue a career as a personal chef. So, Kate calculated, if she wanted to keep Zora happy, she should sit down with her and discuss sick days. Vacation, too. It hadn't been a year yet, but Zora might want to take a vacation. They'd have to coordinate it so Kate could stay home with Ollie that week, but that wasn't a big deal. Kate started to feel better now that she had an action plan in place. Problem solving was something she knew she was good at.

But that brought her back to Brad. She still didn't know what to do about him. Maybe there wasn't anything to do until the gala was over. She could take a day off, maybe a long weekend for just the two of them, and they could talk and get things back on track. She'd ask Zora to stay with Ollie so they could focus on each other. Some alone time was probably all they needed after these months of madness. Dreaming about a weekend with Brad, trolling through the quaint little antique shops in Cold Spring, lounging in the in-room Jacuzzi at the inn, eating decadent calorie-laden food like molten chocolate cake, Kate felt the tension in her shoulders dissipate. Everything would be fine.

She tuned back in to Laurie and Kelly's animated discussion, remembering when a two-hundred-dollar blouse purchased for a mere forty-five had felt like winning the lottery. Kate joined the conversation, telling her rapt audience of two about some of the best boutiques she'd ever found, hidden in the garment district just above Chelsea.

"Kate, you are such a fountain of information," Laurie gushed. "I swear, you know a little bit about everything."

Kate laughed. "That's why they pay me the big bucks. I always know what's going on."

• • •

By the time the three of them had finished logging in the items for the auction, it was seven P.M. Kate was grateful to have both Kelly and Laurie with her, because it was a big job. Each donation had to be recorded with a description, a price, and the donor's name. Back at the office tomorrow, she'd split the list between the two women and have them enter the information into a computerized database.

On the street corner outside the AAA offices, Kate decided to grab a cab to Brooklyn, while Laurie and Kelly debated which subway to take back to the Upper East Side.

"I'm starving," Kelly announced. "You want to grab something to eat?" she asked Laurie.

"I would, but I'm so broke," Laurie whined. "I think I have just enough money to get on the subway."

Kelly laughed. "If you'd stop buying clothes, you'd have enough money to eat."

"I know, I know." Laurie groaned. "But I still have some left-over lasagna at home from yesterday's lunch. I can eat that."

"Gross," Kelly said, wrinkling her lightly freckled nose in distaste.

Kate couldn't pretend she hadn't heard. She was hungry, too. These two deserved a treat. "Hey, ladies," she said, turning back toward them, "how about we have dinner together and charge it to the company? We've earned it, don't you think?"

Laurie and Kelly both tried to act professional as they nodded, but Kate could see the excitement in their eyes. She smiled. To be young and broke in New York, but with access to a corporate credit card. Life didn't get much better.

"Come on," Kate said. "I know a great little Mexican place around the corner."

Kate put the key in the lock of her own front door at precisely 10:01 P.M. She knew Ollie would be asleep, but she wasn't sure about Brad, so she tried to be quiet. She shouldn't have worried, because Brad was on the couch, watching what appeared to be a vintage basketball game on cable. She did a quick survey of the house, and everything seemed to be in place. The kitchen looked clean, the living room was tidy, minus the few magazines and comics splayed out on the cocktail table, so Kate relaxed. Brad had apparently survived his day at home.

"Hi," she said, peeling off her trench coat and kicking off her shoes.

"Hey," Brad said without taking his eyes off the game.

"How's it going?" she asked, making her way over to the comfy chair by the couch. It was calling her name, asking her to collapse in it and possibly stay there forever.

"Do you know it's after ten?" Brad said, still staring at the TV.

"Yes," Kate said. "I am aware of the time. I called you from the restaurant and left you a message to say what time I'd be here."

"I didn't hear the phone," Brad grumbled. "I was giving Ollie a bath."

"Did you check the messages?" Kate challenged.

"No, I didn't check the messages," Brad said. "Because I didn't hear the phone. Why would I check the messages? I basically just sat here and thought maybe you'd gotten lost on the way home."

"You didn't call my cell phone, so you couldn't have been that worried," Kate pointed out.

"As a matter of fact, I did. Twice," Brad said sullenly.

Kate immediately grabbed her phone from her purse. It indicated that she had missed two calls. She cleared her throat and apologized. "The restaurant was really loud. I guess I didn't hear it."

Kate let Brad brood and feel self-righteous for precisely five minutes. And then she stood up, walked over to the television, and defiantly turned it off. "We have to talk," she said.

Surprisingly, Brad sat up, dragged his hands through his hair, and said, "I know."

"Look, we both know you hate this arrangement," Kate said. "My hours are insane. I know that. But I'm working really hard to make it better. I know for a fact that once the gala is over, things will slow down significantly. I was thinking today that I'd ask for a couple days off and we could take a long weekend somewhere. Maybe even fly to Bermuda. It's only a two-hour flight from here. Direct, with no layovers."

Brad smiled. It felt good to see him smile at her. It had been too long. "Come here," he said to her, and patted the seat cushion next to him.

Kate walked slowly over to Brad and gingerly sat down on the couch.

"I love the way your mind works, Kate Carter," Brad said, turning to his wife. "You think you can fix everything with one of your no-fail action plans."

"Is something broken?" Kate asked, searching in his eyes for some clue.

Brad stood up and started to pace, which meant he was trying to figure out the best way to say something difficult. Kate prepared herself for the worst. But what would the worst be?

"I do hate your hours, yes. And I do wish you'd find a way to be home more often, but I have to say that your being gone so much has allowed me to do something behind your back. Something I've been hiding from you for a while."

"What are you talking about?" Kate asked. For some reason, Fiona's question, "Are you afraid he's having an affair?," came hurtling into her mind. She tried to push the thought aside, but it hovered there like a flashing red warning light.

"Remember that project I told you I was working on?" Brad started.

"Yes," Kate said, holding her breath.

"It's not exactly about work."

"So what is it?" Kate asked anxiously, wanting and not wanting to know at the same time.

Brad launched into a long explanation of the comic-book project and the investor and his assignment to write the business plan. Kate was so relieved he wasn't admitting to an affair that she almost laughed when he finished talking.

"That sounds really interesting," she said. To Brad, she probably sounded a little too enthusiastic, but so what.

"It does?" Brad asked, doubt lacing his voice. "You're not mad?"

"Honey," Kate answered, "it sounds like something you'd really like doing, and if it lets you get some of your creative juices out, then I say good for you."

Looking slightly chagrined, Brad admitted, "I thought you'd say I was wasting my time."

It was Kate's turn to be honest. "I don't understand your fascination with comic books. I still think they're juvenile and violent, but we don't have to like the same things. We just have to support each other. Besides, it's a onetime thing, right? Why would I mind if you do this side project? And like you said, it's given you something to take your mind off my not being around so much. Right?"

"Yeah," Brad said, still looking doubtful.

Kate stood up and moved over to where her husband stood. She placed her hands on either side of his face, to reassure him. "I love you, Brad Carter, for who you are. And I want you to be happy. You pursue the things that make you happy, and I'll be happy for you." She kissed him lightly on the nose. They stood there like that for a short while. Then Kate spoke again. "And Brad, I hope you feel the same way about me. I hope you can find a way to be supportive of me in the things I love."

"I do," Brad said, nodding. "I want you to be happy."

"Well, my job makes me very happy," Kate said. "I like the work that I do. I like helping young women move up in the professional world. I like making a difference. And I *am* making a difference. In a lot of ways."

"I know you are," Brad whispered tenderly.

"So are we good?" Kate asked. "Are we okay?"

"Yeah, I think we are," Brad said, engulfing his wife in a suffocating embrace.

"Good," Kate murmured into Brad's chest, enjoying the sound of his steady heartbeat and the comfort of his arms wrapped around her body. Both of them stood there, unwilling to shatter this peaceful truce, until Kate recalled Fiona's advice. She pulled away ever so slightly so she could look Brad in the eye. "Do you want to come upstairs and show me just how okay we are?" she asked in her best imitation of a wanton seductress.

Brad responded with a lazy smile. "Mrs. Carter, are you trying to seduce me?"

"Why, yes, I am." Kate laughed, making sure to keep her chuckles low and sexy. She waited for Brad at the bottom of the stairs while he turned off all the downstairs lights and checked the locks on the front door. She reached for his hand and held it as they started up the steps together.

"Kate," Brad said right before they hit the landing, "I think I want to work from home for the next couple of days so I can finish this project. Why don't you call Zora and give her the rest of the week off?"

CHAPTER 32

Zora

W HEN Zora heard Kate's voice on the other line, she knew she was getting fired. Kissing the boss's husband definitely wasn't in her job description. But Kate was just calling to tell her that Brad wanted to work from home and that she could have the rest of the week off.

"We'll pay you for the days off," Kate announced. She said it was only fair.

Zora mumbled an okay and then fell back down in her bed. She really did feel sick. How could she have let Brad kiss her? How could she have kissed him back like that? She pressed her palms to her face, thinking she could dampen the rising heat in her body that burned like a mixture of shame and desire. For just a moment, standing in that kitchen, it had felt so right. And so good. And so categorically wrong. Wrong like biblical wrong. Wrong like locust-plagues-for-seven-years wrong.

Zora dragged herself out of the bed, where she'd spent the entire day before, trying to forget what she'd done. Today she was going to do better and at least get in the shower. But in the shower, as she washed her body, she couldn't help thinking of Brad's hands caressing her, the contrast his whiteness would have against the deep chocolate of her skin. "Stop it," Zora shouted over the sound of the running water. She would not allow herself to contemplate this possibility. She liked Kate. She loved Ollie. She loved her job and the money she was making and the life she had in New York.

She was not going to give that up to be a bootylicious, jungle-fever fantasy for a man who was lonely for his wife. And she knew that was all this was. He was lonely, and she, Zora Anderson, was a gullible romantic who had a history of getting involved with the wrong men. Besides, it was such a cliché. Nanny crawls in bed with husband. Ugh. Zora scrubbed herself harder, trying to rid her mind of the lurid images of White men raping the Black women servants in their homes.

Out of the shower, Zora decided she'd take herself to a movie. There was a new French film playing at the Film Forum in SoHo. Then she'd walk to Chinatown and treat herself to soup dumplings and bubble tea. A perfect day, she thought. But right before she walked out the door, her phone rang. It was Mimi, Craig's girlfriend, wanting to talk to her about a party she was planning. One hour later, Zora had her first official catering job. It would be a dinner party for six people, but Mimi couldn't cook anything besides some Korean dishes that she said most Americans wouldn't touch with a ten-foot pole. Zora promised she'd come up with some ideas and they would talk in a couple of days. The party was scheduled for the following weekend, so there was plenty of time to plan the menu. Zora was glad for these extra days off, because she could spend hours in the bookstore, stealing recipe ideas from overpriced cookbooks. And she could watch obscene amounts of repetitive programming on the Food Channel without feeling guilty, because, technically, it was research.

By Saturday, Zora had almost convinced herself that the kiss had never happened. Just in case, she forced herself to scour the entire apartment as punishment and reminder. She cleaned like a woman possessed, scrubbing at ancient grease spots on the walls as if they were spots on her tarnished character. If she could get her apartment clean, her soul would be purified, and she would never get close to Brad Carter again. She left the apartment only once, to buy more bleach from the ninety-nine-cent store around the corner. When she came back, there was an envelope shoved under her door. Her name was written across the front, but other than that, there was no return address or other markings. She pulled out a plain piece of paper with neat handwriting and read:

Dear Zora,

I owe you a big apology. Maybe two or three. You were absolutely right in that I have been a big fat hypocrite (my word, not yours) in trying to force you to get your career in order when mine is such a mess. I guess it's just a whole lot easier to focus on someone else's brilliant future instead of your own. Instead of Lifestyles by Zora, I should have put more work into building up Keith the Superstar. (That's a joke, kind of.)

The point is, I am going to take my own advice and live up to my potential. I've sublet my apartment and I'm going to Los Angeles for a minute to see if I can get more work out there. Don't worry, I've already contacted a strip club or two to make sure I can support myself in the meantime. (Don't be mad at me!)

I'd like to hope that I didn't destroy what might be a wonderful relationship. I'd still like to be able to call you my friend. Maybe more? When I get settled in LA I'll give you a ring. And hopefully you'll take my call.

Stay sweet,
Keith Davis

For some reason that letter made her cry. Keith was a good person. He was the person she should be trying to hold on to. He was available and he wanted her in his life. Zora pressed the letter to her chest and willed his goodness to seep into her skin.

By the time Monday came, Zora felt she had a handle on the situation, and her apartment was spotless. She was going to do her job, and she would not allow anything inappropriate to happen. For one thing, she would not be staying for dinner. That was how all these feelings had started, Zora figured. Or maybe it was when Brad started showing up at the park. Zora shook her head. It didn't matter. Nothing was going to happen. Besides, she was pretty sure Brad had come to his senses, too. The fact that he didn't want to see her was pretty obvious, since he'd decided to work from home. Zora knew what that was about, and she was happy. Kate and Brad were a good couple. She didn't want to see them break up. Brad just needed to move past his moment of weakness and get his groove back on with his wife. Maybe they'd done just that. Maybe they'd fucked like bunnies all weekend long, rejoicing in their holy matrimony.

With those thoughts in mind, Zora let herself into the Carters' house. Brad was standing in the entranceway, looking like he'd been waiting for her.

"I'm sorry, Zora," he said, launching into what sounded like a prepared speech. "What I did to you was despicable and wrong. I hope you know how sorry I am—"

Zora didn't want to hear any more. She just wanted to forget anything had ever happened and move on. "What you did wasn't despicable," she said. "It was wrong. It was wrong because of Kate, so let's leave it alone. Okay?" And then, because she couldn't resist, "Don't worry, I won't sue you for sexual harassment."

Brad looked at her long and hard, like he wanted to make sure she was being honest and not putting up some brave face. Then he let out a breath that he had apparently been holding and said, "Okay."

He grabbed his briefcase and headed out the door.

Zora sighed, relieved that the awkward situation was over, and headed to the kitchen to straighten up.

When Brad came home, Zora was on the couch with her jean jacket on. She gave him quick instructions about how to heat up dinner, kissed Ollie on his warm forehead, and left. It didn't feel right, leaving so abruptly, but she knew after a little more time, things would feel normal again. That was how she'd gotten over Alexander. Time would help them go back to the way they used to be. And soon enough, Kate would be home in the evenings, and Zora would be seeing Brad only in the mornings. Life would go on. One day this would be just another story she told her girl-friends, and they'd laugh and say, "No you didn't," and she'd blush and say she did.

The next few days passed like Monday had. Zora kept her interactions with Brad to a minimum, and he seemed to do the same. But on Thursday afternoon, he was outside the church when Zora and Angel came out of sign language class. Zora had to remind herself that she wasn't supposed to feel happy to see him. Walking to the park, Zora tried hard to let Angel and Brad do all the talking. But she sensed both of them looking at her, try-ing to figure out what was the matter.

At the park, the routine was the same. Zora and Brad took Ollie to the swings. When he was sick of swinging, now that he could walk, he toddled over to the slide and the tunnels, where Brad and Zora took turns following him around, making sure he didn't hurt himself. At one point Zora took Ollie up on the slide, and Brad waited to catch him at the bottom. "Ready to go to Daddy, Ollie?" Zora asked as she sat him on the slippery surface and positioned him to swoosh to his father.

"You better go with him," Brad cautioned. "He might fall."

So Zora wrapped her legs around Ollie and slid down with

him, laughing at the sheer pleasure of sliding, and found herself in Brad's arms at the bottom. He quickly released her, and she ran Ollie around to the other jungle gym, where Angel and Skye were playing. Brad, thankfully, didn't follow her.

"What's wrong with you?" Angel asked her.

"What do you mean?" Zora asked.

"You're acting all jumpy, like a crackhead or something," Angel responded.

Zora knew it wouldn't take Angel long to put two and two together and figure that something about Brad was bothering her. She couldn't allow that to happen. Once somebody else knew, it was impossible to make a secret fade away. So she quickly made something up.

"I thought I saw the playground pervert, that's all," Zora said, praying that Angel would believe her. "He was over there by the rose garden." She pointed.

Angel looked. "I don't see anybody over there."

"He must have just left, because I swear he was over there, and he was looking at my chest."

Angel shook her head and sucked her teeth in disgust. "If I ever see that motherfucker in a dark alley, I'll kick his mother-fucking ass. I don't know why the cops can't pick his nasty ass up. Pardon my French, but he's going to expose himself to some little kid one day, and it's going to be all over."

Luckily, Angel was so agitated by thoughts of the playground pervert that she completely forgot about Zora's jumpiness. And Brad had the good sense to come get Oliver and take him back to the swings to play for a while.

At five-thirty Angel said she had to go. "We'll all go," Zora said. "Like always."

"Actually, I'm jumping on the subway," Angel said. "I have to take Skye to her grandparents' house. Her parents are taking a long-weekend trip to Miami."

"Really?" Zora said.

"Yeah, they don't even want to come and say good-bye to their kid. They're just having me dump her, and they'll pick her up, I guess, on Sunday night." Angel shook her head at the thought.

Brad came over. "You guys packing up to go home?" he asked.

"Yeah," Zora said. "Angel has to take Skye uptown to her grandparents' apartment."

"Are you ready to go, too?" Brad asked Zora.

"Yeah, I guess so," she said, hoping that he would come up with a reason not to ride home with her on the bus. Or maybe he'd be nice and offer to take Ollie home and Zora wouldn't have to go all the way back to Park Slope. But then she remembered she'd left her bag at the house, and she needed her notebook with recipes in it, because she was talking to Mimi tonight about the menu for her party. Zora chided herself for being so dramatic. They were going to ride together on a crowded bus, and she'd run into the house and get her things and call it a day. She'd leave no time for distractions.

That was exactly what happened. She left Brad with his son, dinner in the oven, and not even enough time to say good-bye.

The next day, Friday, Zora knew she would have to break her silence with Brad. She needed him. Mimi loved her menu plan: Chilean sea bass with mango salsa, served with a cold Italian rice salad. But she needed to practice once to make sure the fish would come out right. Fish was easy to prepare but just as easy to mess up. She needed one dress rehearsal before the main event, and the Carters' kitchen was the perfect practice space. Using her own money, she bought everything she needed to re-create the entire meal for Kate and Brad, but she needed Brad's immediate feedback to know what she'd gotten right and what needed tweaking. The party was on Saturday night, so she didn't have any time to waste.

For the first time that week, when Brad came home, Zora wasn't on the couch waiting to leave. She was in the kitchen. Brad came in sniffing. "I smell something incredible," he said.

Zora cut to the chase. "I need your help," she said, and explained the situation.

"You got your first catering job" was the first thing out of Brad's mouth. "I'm so proud of you, Z, that's great. Congratulations."

"Thank you," Zora said, blushing. "It's not like I did anything special to make it happen. Mimi's practically family. But hey, she's paying me to cater her party, so I guess that counts."

"Hell, yeah, it counts," Brad confirmed. "And you did do something to get this. You made Angel's reception a fabulous event. That's something right there, because Mimi obviously liked what she saw. If she wanted to do you a favor, she could have called you a long time ago."

Zora shrugged. "I guess so."

"I know so. And whatever you need me to do or taste to help you get ready, I'm here," Brad said.

"Thanks." Zora smiled and had to hold herself back from giving Brad a hug; she wanted to show him how much his encouragement meant to her. But of course, she didn't. She wasn't trying to add fuel to that fire. Instead, she turned back to the stove, and Brad took the opportunity to go check on Ollie, who was in the living room playing with his toys. "Let me know when you need me," he called from the other room.

Like that, routine was restored. Zora finished dinner, and Brad went upstairs to change. When he came back down, the table was set, but only for one.

"Ollie ate already," Zora explained. "And I can't eat. I'm too nervous. I need you to tell me exactly how everything tastes and if it all works together."

"Don't you want to taste it, too?" Brad asked. "I mean, shouldn't you?"

"I've been tasting it all along," Zora explained. "That's why I need a fresh palate. So please eat and be perfectly honest about what you think, okay?"

Brad nodded. "I can do that."

Zora began the parade of courses meant to tantalize the senses. She began with mini crab cakes with a sour-cream herb sauce. Brad moaned after every succulent bite. She then placed a salad with fresh greens, poached pears, goat cheese, and candied walnuts in front of him.

"I love this," Brad said, munching away. "The contrast in flavors and textures is amazing."

Zora beamed. "Perfect! That's what I was trying to achieve with that salad. Contrast and harmony."

Finally, she served the fish with its accompanying mango salsa and rice salad. Brad claimed to be in ecstasy. He took his time eating, savoring every mouthful. When he was done, he pushed his chair back from the table and rubbed his stomach.

"Zora, you should have your own restaurant. Hands down, that was the most exquisite meal I've ever tasted."

"Oh, stop," Zora admonished. "Just be honest. The fish wasn't overdone? The rice wasn't mushy?"

"No, no, no." Brad got serious. "Everything was absolutely divine. Mimi and her guests will be licking their plates at the end of the meal."

Zora finally allowed herself to relax. "Whew." She exhaled as she collapsed into a kitchen chair. "I just want everything to be perfect."

"If you re-create tomorrow what you did here, it will be," Brad said.

"Thank you," Zora said. And she meant it. She needed the reassurance that someone else approved of her culinary creations. She was never sure whether other people would appreciate her eclectic flavor combinations and choices.

Brad stood up to clear the table, and Zora didn't try to stop him. She was completely beat.

"What are you going to serve for dessert?" he asked as he gathered up the dishes.

"That's easy," Zora said. "I'm going to do lemon sorbet with Danish sugar cookies. I made the cookie dough yesterday, so I can bake them over at Mimi's."

"Sounds good," Brad said, surveying the stack of pots and pans in the sink.

"Sorry about the mess," Zora apologized. "Usually I'm much neater, but I was so preoccupied with the cooking, I kind of—"

Brad interrupted her. "No explanations necessary. Seriously, after that meal, you could ask me to clean the dishes with my tongue, and I'd do it."

Silence hung between them while Brad scrubbed. Before either could say or do something they might regret, Zora jumped up and announced that she would put Ollie to bed. She didn't wait for a response from Brad before she dashed out of the kitchen.

When she came back downstairs, the kitchen was clean and the teapot was on. "Tea?" Brad asked.

"No, I really should get going," Zora said.

"Okay," Brad said. "But—"

"But what?" Zora asked.

"Nothing," Brad started. "I just wanted to tell you that I told Kate."

"You told Kate what?" Zora asked, horrified. "About us? I mean, about the kiss?"

Brad had the decency to blush. "No, I told her about the comic-book project and what I was doing, and she was okay with it."

Zora released the breath she'd been holding, relieved. "See, I told you." She reminded herself that there was no "us" between her and Brad. She gave him what she hoped was an encouraging smile. "I'm happy for you." With that, she turned to leave.

She headed to the front hallway to get her coat and bag, feeling a combination of grief and pride overtake her. She knew she was doing the right thing and that it would get better.

Just as she was about to walk out the door, Brad called her name. She went back to the kitchen.

"You forgot your notebook," he said, pointing to her bible of recipes and notes.

"Oh my God, thank you," Zora said, walking over to grab it off the table. "I need to have that for tomorrow."

"Yeah, I figured," Brad said.

"Wish me luck, then."

"You don't need it," Brad declared. "Just do what you did here tonight."

Zora smiled. "Right. I'll do that," she promised. She turned to go again.

"Zora," Brad repeated, but there was urgency in his voice. A plea.

This time she didn't turn around. But she didn't move forward, either. Brad came and stood behind her.

"Zora," he said, and turned her to face him. "I can't do this."

"Can't do what?" Zora whispered, even though she knew.

"I can't be in this room with you and pretend that I don't want to do this." For the second time in seven days, Brad kissed her. He kissed her lips and tasted her mouth as if she were the final course of her scrumptious feast.

Zora melted in his arms. But it was she who pushed him away. "Brad," she cried. "You love your wife. You love Kate." She willed him to remember that. She willed herself to consider it.

Brad drew a ragged breath. He closed his eyes as he tried to gather his thoughts. "I know it's wrong," he said in a voice filled with anguish. "But I . . . I . . . This just feels right." He held Zora's face in his hands and looked straight into her eyes. He failed to come up with anything more illuminating than "I can't explain it,

Zora, but it doesn't feel wrong. It feels like the most natural thing in the world to be with you."

"I know," Zora whispered, and stopped trying to think of reasons why she should tell him to stop. She let Brad kiss her again. This time the kiss was deep and long. He picked her up and gently sat her on the counter so they'd be the same height. He leaned in to her, and she raised her head to receive the thrusts of his tongue and responded with sighs of pleasure. She gripped the counter because she was afraid if she wrapped her arms around him, she'd never let him go. Brad planted little kisses on her eyelids and her nose, then made a trail down her neck. Zora felt a tingle start at the tips of her toes and shimmy its way up to the top of her head. Somewhere inside she knew she should stop, but not a single muscle in her body moved in that direction.

The phone ringing made them stop. Brad pulled away from Zora, pointed a finger at her, and said, "Please don't move."

Zora found herself only able to nod.

Brad grabbed the phone. She could tell it was Kate. One minute later, he came back to her. "That was Kate," he said. "She was calling to tell me she wouldn't be home for at least another two hours."

Zora suddenly found the whole situation hilarious, and a slightly deranged giggle escaped from her mouth. Clearly, it had to be a setup. Was she supposed to rip off her clothes, fuck Brad on the kitchen table, and be gone before Kate got back? No way. She was going to go home and forget about Brad Carter.

"Why are you laughing?" Brad dared to ask.

"Because we are such a cliché. We're worse than a B movie. Kate calls to say she's going to be late, so we have just enough time to do something we'll regret for the rest of our lives? No, thank you. I'll pass."

Brad snorted, then laughed a bit himself. "You know, we aren't very original, are we?" he said.

"No," Zora confirmed.

"And this is really very wrong, isn't it," he said, serious again.

"Yes," Zora answered.

"And this will never happen again," Brad said.

"Never," Zora whispered.

And then he kissed her once more. But then Zora pulled away. She didn't say anything, she just stopped. Brad let his hands fall to his sides. Without a word, Zora jumped down from the counter, collected her things, and headed to the door. This time she said good-bye.

CHAPTER 33

Kate

KATE was happy. She was feeling that familiar rush of everything coming together, synchronized and under her complete control. She was juggling a million tasks, but she was keeping all of her balls high up in the air. And she was proud of herself because she hadn't had to ask for extra help; she hadn't buckled under the pressure. Roger White had even sent her an interoffice memo, thanking her for her hard work. So he'd noticed. Kate could almost taste the promotion on the other side of all this.

Even though she should have been going over the seating charts for the AAA staff, Kate decided to call her mother at work. They hadn't spoken in over a week, which was a long time for the two of them. She dialed her mother's number and sat back down in her chair.

"Hi, Mom," Kate said when her mother answered.

"Hi, Kate," her mother said, sounding genuinely pleased to hear from her eldest daughter.

"Sorry I haven't called for a while," Kate began, absentmindedly rearranging piles of paper on her desk. "There's just so much to do for the gala." Of course her mother knew all about the AAA gala. Kate had been keeping her posted since she got the assignment. And she understood what it took to pull it off, because she chaired the planning committee for her company's annual fundraiser extravaganza.

"Do you have a handle on everything?" Kate's mom queried. "Is everything ready to go?"

"Yeah, Mom, it is," Kate said, and she launched into a detailed description of everything she'd arranged to make the gala happen. She knew she sounded like a kid bragging about her report card, but if she couldn't tell her mother, who could she tell?

Her mother laughed when Kate finally finished. "It sounds like you've put together the party of the year, honey."

"I hope so," Kate said, beaming. "And Mom, I think I'm going to be up for a promotion after this. I'd be really surprised if they're not ordering my new business cards already."

"That's great, Katie." Her mother laughed at her daughter's naked ambition.

Kate told her mom about the memo from Roger White. "He knows I've been putting in sixty-hour weeks these last couple of months."

Kate's mother immediately switched from cheerleader to mommy. "Katie, that's a crazy schedule. I hope you're taking care of yourself."

"Of course I am, Mom," Kate promised.

"You know, with Ollie and the house and everything, you can't run yourself ragged at work and then have nothing left to give at home. It's not the same as when it was just you and Brad."

"I know, Mom," Kate said.

"Is Zora being helpful? It's okay to ask her to do a little more around the house to help you pick up the slack. With the amount you guys are paying her, she could be doing some light cleaning, too."

"Mom, Zora is a godsend. She already keeps the house immaculate, and Ollie is in really good hands."

Kate's mother softened. "How is my one and only grandchild?"

"He's wonderful. Zora's been taking him to sign language classes, and he already uses the signs for 'mommy' and 'daddy' and 'milk,'" Kate bragged. "And he can say 'airplane' in French."

"That's nice," her mother said. "But what can he say in English?"

"Mother," Kate groaned.

"What?" her mother protested. "I'm just saying I think he should be speaking more. With his mouth. Not his hands. You and your sister both had a very large vocabulary at his age."

"Mom, Ollie is perfect. He communicates just fine. He can tell Zora everything he wants."

"I can't understand anything he says when I call, honey," her mother confided.

"I'm not worried, Mom," Kate said, chuckling.

Her mother changed the subject. "How's Brad?" she cooed. Her mother loved Brad to death.

"He's fine," Kate said. Inwardly, she debated whether she should tell her mom about their "issues."

"Is something the matter?" her mother asked.

Since everything was resolved, Kate gave her mother an abbreviated explanation of what had transpired. Her mother sighed. Kate could imagine her taking off her glasses and rubbing her temples.

"Are you saying everything is okay, then?" Her mother wanted verification.

"It is," Kate assured her. "It really is. Brad and I had a good talk. He's happily ensconced in his little comic-book project, and he understands what my work means to me."

"You're sure, Katie?" her mother asked. "Because deep down inside, every man just wants to be taken care of."

"You are the second person to tell me that," Kate said. "It's like everyone wants to say men cannot evolve beyond their caveman nature."

"They may want to, honey," her mother said, "but I don't think it's possible."

"Well, Brad's making the effort," Kate said. She recounted their weekend activities to prove to her mother that everything was okay. "We spent the whole weekend together. I cooked dinner twice, and we went shopping to buy Brad some new shoes. We were very much the happy family. And I think I played Suzy Homemaker very well."

"Good for you," her mother said, and Kate could hear the smile in her voice. "Sometimes you have to do that to make men feel safe and secure. They need to feel waited on and catered to, or else it upsets their whole worldview."

"God," Kate said, rolling her eyes. "Who knew men got so threatened by women working. I thought we got over those issues in the seventies."

"I think men just got better at hiding their needs," her mother corrected her.

Kate laughed. She knew she had to end the conversation, though, because work was waiting. She started to say good-bye, but her mother had one more piece of advice. "You should ask Zora to keep Oliver in the evenings every once in a while so you and Brad can have a moment to yourselves. Men can sometimes feel jealous even of their own kids."

"Okay, Mom," Kate said, but she was already transitioning away from the conversation.

"I can tell we're done," her mother said.

"Yeah, I gotta go," Kate said.

"Bye, sweetheart," her mother said. "And you take care of yourself. Don't overdo it."

Kate came back to her mother for a moment. "I'll be okay, Mom, don't worry."

"Okay, hon. You knock 'em dead."

"Thanks, Mom." Kate smiled. She hung up the phone.

Right on cue, Laurie knocked on the door and poked her head into the office. "Kate, the AAA folks are downstairs in the conference room."

It was time to get back to work.

Kate got home at eleven that night. She had only enough energy to check on Oliver and then fall into bed next to her sleeping husband. She knew she could handle it, but she couldn't wait for the whole gala to be over. She really was tired.

The next few days passed in a blur. Kate would wake up with Ollie at six A.M., spend precious minutes changing his diaper and giving him a bottle of warm chamomile tea. (Zora swore it was the best thing for a baby first thing in the morning. She claimed it cleaned out his system.) Then Kate would reluctantly put him back in his crib with a few toys and race to the shower. After, she'd retrieve him and bring him downstairs. While she ate her English muffin, he'd play with his toys. Brad would be downstairs by seven-thirty, ready to take over when she left.

Thankfully, since their talk and the reconciliation weekend, Brad seemed to be in much better spirits. He didn't complain about her late nights. He didn't scowl or pout when she said she was too tired to do anything but sleep when she got home at night, and he made an effort to ask her how things were going at work. In turn, she tried to remember to ask about his comic books. This was the partnership she'd envisioned when she married Brad, and contrary to what everyone wanted her to believe, Brad was capable of being supportive of a professional wife.

On Wednesday morning, while Kate was getting dressed and Brad was drying off after his shower, she mentioned her plan to spend the night in the city on Thursday, the night before the gala.

"What?" Brad responded when he heard her idea. "Why?"

"Because," Kate explained, "I have to run through a dress rehearsal of the program, count a million pieces of silverware, and supervise the placing of a gazillion name tags on tables. I'm going to be up till two, so instead of coming home, I'll sleep at one of the corporate apartments in midtown. Roger White kind of suggested it, so I think I have to. But I totally don't mind. It *will* make things easier."

"Kate, we live in Brooklyn. It's not that serious a commute," Brad pointed out.

"Are you worried you won't be able to handle Ollie? Because I was going to ask Zora to sleep over. I'm sure she won't mind."

Brad didn't say anything.

"Did you hear me?" Kate said. "Do you want me to ask Zora to stay over? She can get Ollie up and everything, and then you don't have to change your schedule."

Kate couldn't tell what she heard in Brad's voice when he said okay. But he didn't sound happy.

"Brad, honey," Kate said, walking over to assure him face-to-face, "it's just one night. And then this whole thing will be over."

CHAPTER 34

Zora

Zora knew it was going to happen. She'd been fooling herself into believing that as long as she didn't sleep with Brad Carter, everything could go back to normal. But then Kate called and asked her to sleep over. When she said yes to Kate, Zora knew that yes meant many things.

Why didn't Kate notice what was happening in her own home? Why was she so blind to her husband's wandering affections? Zora tried to muster up some righteous anger toward Kate for allowing this to happen, but she knew it was nobody's fault but her own and Brad's.

When she got to the Carters' on Thursday morning, Zora was surprised to find Brad gone and Kate calmly waiting for her.

"Hey, Zora," she called as soon as Zora stepped in the door. She was sitting on the floor playing with Ollie. Even though she was wearing her work clothes, she didn't seem to be worried about getting messy.

"Hi, Kate," Zora said. "What are you still doing here?"

"I figured since I'm about to put in a twenty-four-hour day, I have the right to go in a tiny bit late." She looked at her son. "Right, Ollie?" Ollie toddled around his mother, picking up toys and dropping them in her lap.

Zora was overwhelmed with guilt, watching mother and child. She thought she might be sick, so she headed straight for the kitchen.

Kate didn't seem to notice her distress. "Thank you so much for staying over tonight," she called out. "It will put my mind at ease knowing you're here for Ollie. And Brad. He needs taking care of, too, sometimes." She laughed.

"No problem," Zora responded. "I don't mind."

"I put fresh sheets on the bed in the guest room, so you can sleep in there," Kate said. "And you can use the bathroom down here."

"Okay, thanks," Zora said. She had to refrain from throwing herself at Kate's feet and pleading for forgiveness. As an alternative, she plunged her hands in the scalding water she was using to wash the dishes and focused on the prickles of pain searing her fingers.

"I should get going," Kate finally announced.

"Do you need help with anything?" Zora asked, coming out of the kitchen. She desperately wanted to do something to help Kate and perhaps assuage her own guilty conscience.

"No, I think I'm all set. I packed last night. My dress is being delivered to the apartment tomorrow morning, and everything else is at work."

"Okay," Zora said. "Good luck with everything, Kate. I'm sure the gala will be fabulous."

"Thank you, Zora."

"You're welcome," Zora said.

"No, I mean thank you for everything you've done for this family."

Zora clenched her teeth and felt her eyes start to prickle with the pressure of unshed tears. She didn't trust herself to speak, so she just nodded.

Kate picked up her bag and called Ollie to her. She planted big kisses on both of his cheeks, and she was out the door.

"God," Zora prayed out loud, something she hadn't done in a long time, "please help me."

• • •

By the time Brad came home that night, God had yet to strike her down with some horrible affliction, so she knew she was on her own. She could tell Brad was in agony as well. He came in as usual and played with Ollie, but he barely spoke to her. She concentrated on making dinner and wondered how she would make it through the next twenty-four hours. The weight of their shared guilt and mutual desire seemed to suck all the air out of the room.

Finally, Brad broke the silence. "Let's get out of here," he announced.

"Good idea!" she practically yelled with relief, wiping her hands on her apron. She turned the stove off, put the milk and butter back in the refrigerator, and turned off the lights in the kitchen. "Are you going to change?" she asked him, knowing he was always more at ease in his sweats rather than his suit.

"No, I'm fine," he said, clearly anxious to get out of the house.

"Do you want to take the stroller or carry Ollie in the sling?" she asked.

Brad hesitated. "Let's take the stroller," he decided. "He's getting too heavy for me to carry him in the sling for very long."

"I know," Zora commiserated. "He's getting thick and heavy."

"It's all that good food you've been feeding him," Brad said.

"Hey, babies are supposed to be chunky," Zora countered.

"Yeah, but what about their fathers? I don't do chunky," Brad said, patting his flat stomach.

"You are not chunky," Zora said. "Not even close."

It was the wrong thing to say.

"Let's go," Brad said, tearing his eyes away from Zora.

Without discussion, they headed toward Prospect Park. Brad pushed Ollie in the stroller. Zora thrust her hands in her jacket pockets and kept the stroller between her and Brad. The warm temperature and the promise of summer meant the streets were filled with people. In some part of her mind, Zora recognized that the three of them blended in with all of the other happy families walking home from work and school. Nobody would know that what they were witnessing in Brad and Zora was the destruction of a family.

"What are we doing, Brad?" Zora finally dared to ask. Neither one of them stopped walking or slowed their brisk pace.

"I don't know, Z," Brad answered. "None of it makes sense to me. I love Kate. I never in a million years would want to hurt her like this. Just the thought makes me sick."

"So I make you sick?" Zora asked.

"No, Zora. Not at all." Brad stopped. "You know that's not true."

Zora didn't want to stop moving. She kept walking, eyes downcast, hoping that something would start to make sense, because this was all so crazy. Brad resumed his pace, pushing the stroller alongside her.

"I don't know what I know," Zora uttered in defeat. "Except that Kate loves you. You love Kate. You have this beautiful child together, and no matter how you look at it, I'm the problem."

Brad tried for humor. "It's true this is definitely a tangled web we've woven here."

Zora tried for logic. "Let's be real. Most people would say this is just chemistry. That what we're experiencing is plain old animal attraction. Instinct, pure and simple. You're a man. I'm a woman. We're around each other all the time. Of course we're going to be attracted to each other. But that doesn't mean we can't get ahold of ourselves and ignore these 'instincts.'"

Brad listened. "Maybe. But . . ."

"But what?" Zora demanded, praying that he would take the free pass she was offering to walk away.

Brad cleared his throat before he answered, but his voice trembled with emotion when he spoke. "How do you explain that I dream about running away with you? How do I ignore that?"

Now Zora stopped walking. "You want to run away with me?" she asked, her eyes widening in disbelief.

Brad grabbed both of her hands and looked straight into her eyes. "Zora, I think about you every morning, afternoon, and night. I dream about you. I think about you all the time."

Zora heard the words come out of Brad's mouth, but her mind went blank, and her heart started pounding a frantic rhythm of hope, fear, and illogical joy. "But why?" she demanded. "Why me?"

Brad pushed the stroller at a slower pace. Now that he'd admitted his true feelings, his urge to run was gone. "I don't know, Zora," he confessed. "And please don't take this the wrong way, but I don't want to feel like this. It would be so much easier to stop if it were just physical attraction. But it's not, for me." He refused to look Zora in the eyes, and he spoke so softly that she had to strain to hear him. "All I can say is that I love coming home to you every night."

Neither of them spoke. They continued walking, Brad exposed, Zora trying to wrap her mind around his words. Rather than throwing herself into his arms and professing her love, Zora tried one more time to offer this man a way out. "You don't really mean that," she joked. "You're just under a spell. I've been putting a magic potion in your food every night." She hummed the tune from *Close Encounters* for effect.

"Oh, really?" Brad smiled. "So how do I get out from under your spell?"

"Easy," Zora said. "Stop eating my food."

They walked without talking until they reached the park. Ollie had fallen asleep. Then Brad turned the stroller onto one of the covered footpaths that wound through the park. They were in complete silence. There were probably thousands of other people in the park at that very moment, but right then and there, Zora felt like the three of them were the only ones sharing the space with the ancient trees and blooming flowers dotting the park with bits of vibrant color. When they reached a clearing that over-looked the vastness of Prospect Park, Brad stopped. They stood there for a moment and admired the view. There was green as far as the eye could see. It was the perfect place for a beginning and an end. Brad turned to Zora and said in a very clear voice, "I think I'm falling in love with you, Zora. Is that wrong?"

Zora looked up at Brad. She could hear Angel's voice in her mind and repeated her favorite phrase: "Love is never wrong." And then he kissed her. And she kissed him back.

"Zora," Brad said, pulling away from her, "I've poured my guts out here. But I don't know how you feel. Am I pushing you? This is all too fast. Am I crazy? Because this is all crazy, isn't it? I know it is."

Zora looked down at Brad's hands holding hers and tried hard to separate her feelings for Brad from her overwhelming sense of guilt and grief. But if love was never wrong, then she knew how to answer the question. "Yes, Brad, this is crazy, and horrible, and too fast to make any kind of sense." She choked, on the verge of tears. "It's probably the stupidest thing I've ever done in my life, but yes, I feel the same—" Before she could get the last words out of her mouth, Brad was planting kisses all over her face, laughing and crying at the same time. His tears mingled with hers.

When they returned home, Zora went back to the kitchen to finish dinner. Brad took Ollie up to get his pajamas on. They de-cided to feed him first and put him to bed so they could eat alone. Zora set Ollie's food out and Brad fed him, making helicopters, airplanes, and farm animals out of each bite of pasta and chicken. Ollie was in stitches. When he was done eating, Zora went up with Brad to put him to bed. He fell asleep almost instantly.

Zora and Brad tiptoed back downstairs. Once they were alone, Brad didn't even try to restrain himself. He put his arm around Zora as they walked to the kitchen. As she reheated the gravy for the roast, he kissed the back of her neck. It was a seduction, pure and simple, and Zora didn't mind one bit. She luxuriated in it and refused to think about what would come next. After dinner, Brad and Zora cleaned the kitchen together. She loaded the dishwasher while he washed the pots. Then they settled down on the couch and watched TV. While she was trying to figure out who the real bad guy was on *Law & Order,* Brad was trying to figure out how to get her bra off through her shirt. She brushed his hand away and made him behave. When the show was over, Brad turned off the TV and the lights and completely ignored Zora's cries of protest.

"Excuse me, I wanted to see the preview of next week's episode," she said, trying to sound offended.

"It's going to be a rerun," Brad answered as he scooped Zora off the couch and carried her to the stairs. "I've been wanting to do this for a very long time, and I can't wait anymore."

And with that, Brad took Zora upstairs to the guest bedroom and made love to her as if his life depended on it.

Afterward, Zora lay naked on top of Brad. She lifted her head from his chest and smiled at him. Her long locks made a curtain around the two of them. Brad kissed her delicately on the nose and played with her hair, twisting and twirling individual locks around his fingers.

"You look happy," Zora teased.

"At this very moment, I am incredibly happy." Brad smiled.

"Can I ask you something?"

"Anything," Brad replied.

"Have you ever been with a Black woman?" Zora asked, not

sure whether she wanted to hear yes or no. Either answer had potential problems.

"Actually, yes," Brad answered, folding his arms behind his head. "My first real girlfriend was Black. In high school. Maia Jefferson. But we never slept together."

"Really? Why?"

"Because we didn't feel like we were ready," Brad answered. "I've always been a very good boy."

"Until now, right?" Zora teased.

"That's right." Brad laughed, rolling over and pulling Zora under him. "You've turned me into a wicked, wicked boy."

Knowing that Brad had been with another Black woman gave Zora a sense of peace that this wasn't simply a game of curiosity about life on the other side. For some reason, that silly refrain ran through her head: "Once you go Black, you can never go back."

"Have you ever been with a White guy?" Brad asked Zora.

Alexander immediately flashed through her mind. "Yes," she answered.

"Good experience or bad experience?" he wanted to know.

"Bad. Definitely bad," Zora said.

"Please let me try to make it up to you on behalf of evil White people everywhere," Brad said. "Perhaps I should start right now."

The next morning Zora and Brad got up and showered together. In some part of her mind, Zora marveled at the fact that she felt so comfortable with Brad that she could shower with him as if they'd been together for years. There were no awkward moments or pregnant pauses. Afterward, she threw on her clothes and ran downstairs to make Brad a quick breakfast before Ollie woke up.

By the time Brad came downstairs, she'd made him a fruit smoothie with soy milk and strawberries, scrambled eggs, and toast. He wolfed it down like he was starving. When he was done, he pulled Zora onto his lap. "You are an amazing woman," he said. "No matter what happens today or tomorrow or the next day, remember that, okay?"

She touched her forehead to his. "I will," she said, not sure exactly what she was agreeing to.

He kissed her longingly and caressed her breast through her T-shirt. She felt her nipple go hard. Right there at the table, he lifted her shirt and put her right breast in his mouth and teased and sucked. Zora felt herself get wet, and she squirmed on his lap.

"Stop," she moaned. Brad apparently didn't hear her, because he moved to her other breast and did the same thing. Then he lifted her up, stood her against the counter, and caressed her thighs, moving his hands higher and higher under her skirt. Zora couldn't think straight; he was driving her mad. But she didn't try to resist. She braced herself against the counter and heard Brad's pants drop to the floor. He was inside her in a second, and she gasped at the pleasure it brought. When they were done, Brad stood leaning against her, panting. She could barely catch her own breath.

"Sorry," Brad said. "I couldn't help myself."

He didn't seem very sorry. Zora smiled at him over her shoulder. "Go to work," she said.

He kissed her tenderly on the nose. "See you after work," he said. "Kate won't be home until two or three in the morning, so . . ." He didn't have to finish the sentence.

"Bye," Zora said.

Before he turned to go, he held her in a long embrace. "Goodbye," he said. And then he was gone.

Again Zora turned to prayer. "Lord, what am I going to do?"

CHAPTER 35

Kate

AFTER the gala, Kate took three days off. She knew she'd put on a fantastic event. Roger White had beamed the whole night long. The AAA board couldn't praise her enough over the menu, the entertainment, and the stellar silent-auction items, which brought in at least forty thousand dollars, from Kate's estimated calculations. Everybody was happy, but Kate was exhausted. If she never heard the words "gala," "AIDS," or "party dress" again, she'd be perfectly happy. She told Brad she didn't even have enough energy to take a vacation. She just wanted to chill out at home with her family and try to catch up on the countless hours of sleep she'd missed in the last few weeks.

Kate called Zora and gave her the next three days off, again promising to pay her for the lost time. Zora tried to tell her she didn't have to, but Kate knew it was the right thing to do. Zora hadn't asked for the time off, so it wasn't fair to dock her pay. God only knew how much she needed the money. Kate never discussed finances with Zora, but she assumed that she couldn't easily live without half a week's pay.

On Monday, her first official day off, Kate slept late, took Ollie to the park, and took a nap when he did. She went to the bodega and bought eggs and deli ham for dinner. On the second day, she suggested they go out for pizza and rented a silly chick flick for after-dinner entertainment. She told Brad that she was so worn out that her brain couldn't process any higher-level functioning.

He laughed and treated her like a delicate patient, bringing home her favorite flavor of ice cream, rubbing her feet, and insisting she go to bed early. By the third day, Kate was starting to feel like herself again. Before Brad left for work, she asked if he wanted to go out for dinner. She offered to meet him in the city. "I'll call Zora and see if she's up for sitting for Ollie tonight," she said.

Brad hesitated for just a second before he said sure.

"Great," Kate said, smiling. "I'll call and let you know what Zora says, and I'll look into restaurant ideas."

She waited until what she considered a decent hour before she called Zora. She didn't want to wake her up. When she asked if Zora could babysit that night, however, Zora said no. It was the first time she'd ever said no to Kate, who couldn't mask her surprise.

"Why not?" Kate demanded. Then she realized how it must have sounded. "You don't have to tell me, Zora. I'm sorry. It is so last-minute. I just thought—"

"It's okay," Zora said, cutting her off. "I just have other plans. Otherwise, I'd be happy to watch Ollie."

"That's okay," Kate assured her. "I have a couple of other people I can try." Which was a lie. Kate didn't have a backup babysitter, because Zora had always seemed available. She made a mental note to get busy finding another babysitter. She said good-bye to Zora and then called Brad at work. "Bad news," she announced when he answered the phone.

"What?" he asked.

"Zora can't sit tonight. So how about we order Thai food and put Ollie to bed early?"

"Actually," Brad said, "it's not so bad Zora can't babysit. I just found out that the guys on the comic-book venture have called an emergency meeting because our primary investor is getting cold feet. So we have to wine and dine him tonight to convince him not to give up on us."

"When did this happen?" Kate whined, trying to remember that she'd been getting home late for the last two months, so she had no right to be angry at this snafu.

"I just got the call this morning," he said. "So it looks like I'll be home pretty late."

"Fine," Kate pouted. "I guess it's just me and Ollie tonight."

"You'll be fine," Brad assured her. "You guys need some bonding time anyway."

Kate knew this was true, but the fact of the matter was, she was officially getting bored. She couldn't remember how she had stayed home for six months with Ollie. She was dying for some adult conversation and one of Zora's exquisite meals. She didn't say any of this to Brad, though. She wished him good luck at his meeting and promised she and Ollie would make it a great day.

After hanging up the phone, Kate looked around the house, searching for a project that needed attending. But she came up with nothing. Zora kept the laundry baskets empty and the refrigerator full, and not a speck of dust marred a single surface. So housework was out.

"Hey, I've got an idea," Kate said to Ollie, who was busy throwing his toys into the fireplace. "Let's go to the Children's Museum."

Ollie didn't stop, but Kate assumed he'd be okay with her plan. She dragged him away from the fireplace, wiped the soot off his toys, and headed upstairs to change clothes.

Later, coming home from the museum, Kate was happy she wasn't going anywhere else that night. She was exhausted, and Ollie was tired and cranky. They'd ridden the subway all the way up to the Children's Museum on the Upper West Side, spent two hours playing mailman and pushing buttons on a plastic cash register (Kate wondered why this was considered museum-worthy, but Ollie seemed to enjoy it), and then shared an apple juice and Cheerios at the museum cafeteria. On the train ride back, Oliver cried for thirty minutes of the forty-five-minute ride because he'd dropped his pacifier on the platform and Kate had absolutely refused to retrieve it for him. When she turned in to her yard, she had only two things on her mind: a glass of wine for her and an early bedtime for Ollie. But she had to deal with her neighbor first. Mrs. Rodriguez was outside tending to her flowers and seemed like she was waiting for someone to talk to. "Hello, Mrs. Rodriguez," Kate said in a voice that she hoped didn't invite conversation.

"Hello, sweetheart," Mrs. Rodriguez purred. "You're home awfully early, aren't you? And with the baby, too. I hardly ever see the two of you together anymore."

Kate knew Mrs. Rodriguez watched all their comings and goings through her window, so she wasn't surprised that she knew her routines, but it still made her hackles rise in defense. Didn't the woman have something better to do than track all of their exits and entrances?

"Yeah, well, I took the day off," Kate said, reminding herself it wasn't nice to be rude to old people. She tried to hustle herself inside, but getting the stroller up the front steps took time.

"Did you give that nanny the day off, too? I see her all the time. She seems really friendly," Mrs. Rodriguez said as Kate huffed and puffed up the stairs.

"Yes, we love Zora," Kate said. She made it to the top and quickly got her key in the door. "Good night, Mrs. Rodriguez," she called over her shoulder.

"Good night, sweetheart. And Mrs. Carter?"

Kate sighed, turned around, and forced a smile onto her face. "Yes, Mrs. Rodriguez?"

"You know, before I met Mr. Rodriguez, I had quite a few suitors asking after me."

"That's nice," Kate said, clenching her jaw to keep from screaming out loud at this woman, who clearly had no ability to recognize a frazzled mother when she saw one.

"It did have certain advantages," Mrs. Rodriguez acknowledged. "I learned a lot about men. They're all the same, you know. And do you know why?"

Kate felt compelled to respond. "No, why?"

"Because they are all faithful to the hand that feeds them."

Kate gave Mrs. Rodriguez a look and nodded as if she understood. Rather than asking for a more detailed explanation, she muttered a quick "thank you" before she slipped inside and shut the door. That woman was a real nutcase!

Once Ollie was fed and in bed, Kate poured herself that glass of wine, a full glass. She had rented a movie and was about to pop it into the DVD player when the phone rang. It was Fiona. Kate was so happy to hear another grown-up voice that she actually hugged the phone.

"Hey, where've you been?" Fiona asked. "I've called your office every day for the last two days."

Kate explained her three mental-health days, and then she confessed her boredom. "Am I a terrible mother or what? Here I have three days to spend with my child, and I'm already complaining," she moaned.

"You're not terrible," Fiona counseled. "It's not normal for a woman of your intelligence and energy level to be content playing with a baby all day. It doesn't make any kind of sense."

Kate had never thought about it that way. But it was true. It was like telling a rocket scientist to spend the day scooping ice cream and then asking him if he felt fulfilled. It was ludicrous.

"But Zora does it every day," Kate noted. "And she seems to like it."

"Hello, you're paying her," Fiona pointed out. "You might not be so miserable if you were making a buck or two on these days."

"No, I truly believe Zora likes watching children and keeping house," Kate said. "She practically told me that herself."

"Look, you can call me racist and elitist and every other name in the book," Fiona began, "but I'm going to say this because I think it's true. I think Black women are naturally better caretakers than White women. They have something in them that makes them good at it. Let's call it the domestic arts so it doesn't sound so bad."

Kate was relieved to hear Fiona's assessment. The same thought had crossed her mind, but she'd never dared to say it aloud, especially to Brad, since he believed he was so in touch with Black people and their struggle.

Kate and Fiona continued to talk. The discussion turned from child care to the gala to their respective plans for the weekend. Kate wanted the two families to get together again. Fiona said she and Greg were game. Before they hung up, she asked Kate if she and Brad were "back on track."

"Yeah, everything is fine," Kate said. "And I didn't have to use sex to get him to behave."

"Oh, no?" Fiona laughed. "What did you use, pray tell, a gun?"

Now it was Kate who laughed. "No, we just talked and worked it out."

"And no bodily fluids had to be exchanged," Fiona joked.

Kate felt herself blush. When she thought about it, she and Brad hadn't had sex in at least two or three weeks. Maybe a month. She didn't mention this to Fiona, though. Instead—and she didn't know where the question came from—she asked, "Do you think Zora is pretty?"

"Zora your nanny?"

"Yes."

"Why are you asking?" Fiona wanted to know.

"No reason," Kate said. "I guess I was just thinking about something my crazy tenant downstairs said to me earlier."

"What did she say?" Fiona asked, sounding intrigued.

"She said something about men being faithful to the hand that feeds them." Kate tried to laugh it off.

Fiona wasn't fooled. "What, now you think Zora's trying to make a play for your husband with her culinary skills?"

"No," Kate protested. "Besides the fact that she'd never do something like that, she's so not Brad's type."

"Why do you say that?" Fiona asked. "She's a hot little thing, and you know there's something else all Black women are good at."

"You think she's hot?" Kate blurted out before she could stop herself.

"She's got that hot-to-trot Black-girl thing going on. You know what I mean. And she's not ugly. You know the number one rule of picking a nanny is making sure she's completely un-attractive."

Kate shook her head, unable to process all of Fiona's warnings and advice. "Stop it," she cried, feeling equal parts offended (for Zora's sake) and worried (for her own). "Zora is really a good person, and Brad . . ." She stopped herself from even imagining it.

"What?" Fiona demanded. "Brad what?"

"No, it's just her hair and her teeth and . . ." Kate shuddered at the thought of Brad with Zora and shut down the idea before it could fully form.

"You never know," Fiona mused.

Kate was quick to cut her off. "Brad wouldn't even look at Zora that way. He practically told me himself that he only thought of her as the nanny. And if you must know, he's always been at-tracted to leggy blondes. I barely made the cut."

Fiona didn't say anything for a moment. "Well, keep me posted on that one. I'll try to see if Angel knows anything. She and Zora are good friends, aren't they?"

"Fiona, promise me you will do no such thing," Kate pleaded. "This is nothing, and I don't want to put ideas in anyone's head."

"Okay." Fiona dropped her line of questioning. "Call me this weekend and let's see if we can get together."

"Fine," Kate said, grateful for the change of subject. "Thanks for calling, Fiona. Let's sneak out for coffee later this week, okay?"

The next day at work, Kate almost scared herself with the feeling of satisfaction she got from being back at her desk. She loved her child, but she loved this, too. She threw herself into getting back up to speed on KasperKline, since she'd practically ignored them for the last couple of weeks. She tried not to fantasize about the call from Roger White, telling her she was being promoted. Wanting something too badly always led to disappointment. She knew that.

At around three, Kate called home. Zora picked up the phone. Kate found herself listening to Zora's voice to see if anything sounded different. But it didn't. Zora gave her usual detailed update on all of Oliver's meals, poops, playmates, and new words. She said she'd found a baby gymnastics class Kate might want to enroll him in over the summer, and she mentioned that she was making a roast chicken for dinner. Kate hung up the phone, temporarily satisfied that everything was as it should be. But for some reason, the image of Brad and Zora that had lodged itself in her brain after her conversation with Fiona came hurtling into her consciousness again. And then she couldn't get it out of her mind. It kept flashing in and out of her thoughts like a scratched record replaying the same few lines. She tried to get on with her work, but no matter how many times she read the latest sales figures from KasperKline, all she could think about was what might be happening in her house at that very moment. At one point she jabbed herself in the hand with a thumbtack to clear her mind of these ridiculous thoughts. She knew they were ridiculous, which was why she was so mad at herself for not being able to get past them. She didn't believe what Fiona had said about all Black women being sex fiends, and certainly not Zora. More important, Brad would never do something so vile and disrespectful. She hated to say it, but she could imagine Carl cheating on his wife in a heartbeat—after all, he'd done it at B-school—but not Brad. He was too good a person to cheat. That was one of the reasons she admired Brad so much. It was why she'd married him with no reservations. He was fiercely loyal, and he treasured his family. If it came down to it, Kate figured Brad would quit his job and sign up for the Peace Corps in Africa without telling her before he'd ever cheat on her.

With that thought, Kate found a few moments of peace from her overactive imagination. But by four-thirty, even though she could have stayed longer, Kate knew she had to go home at that exact moment to put her mind at rest once and for all.

She left her desk unorganized, grabbed her blazer, and rushed out the door. On the street, the warm air startled her, since she'd spent the entire day in her air-conditioned office, but she didn't stop to enjoy the comfortable temperature. She held up her hand and hailed the first cab she saw. She couldn't stand the thought of sitting on the subway and possibly getting stuck on a train underground. She needed to get home right away.

As the cab wove its way downtown toward the Manhattan Bridge, Kate's unwarranted fears started to escalate, and she tried to use rational thoughts to calm down. She was being silly, she told herself. Mrs. Rodriguez was crazy. Fiona had a flair for the dramatic. Brad would never cheat on her. Especially with Zora. Just the thought made bile rise in the back of her throat. Kate's emotions raced from fear at what she was going to find in the house to shame for thinking such horrible thoughts about two people who didn't deserve her mistrust.

She replayed the last few weeks in her head, searching for

clues that there might be something going on with Brad and Zora, but nothing came to mind. Maybe, if he was cheating, it was with someone from work. Maybe the comic-book venture was a ruse for seeing another woman. If he were going to cheat on her, it would probably be with some long-legged numbers wonk from his office. Not Zora. Kate pinched herself. She was letting her mind run wild. This was so unlike her. Why was she doubting Brad? And herself? It didn't make any sense. By the time the cabbie pulled up in front of the house, Kate could hear her own heart pumping in her ears. Her body was drenched in a cold, clammy sweat, but she forced herself out of the car and up the steps. Before she let herself in the door, she peeked into the window, preparing herself for the worst. What she saw, however, was Brad on the floor playing with Oliver. Zora was in the kitchen making dinner. It was the picture of a perfect family.

CHAPTER 36

Zora

K<small>ATE</small>'s key in the door startled Zora. She had planned to be gone before she got home. Long gone. She didn't know if she'd be able to stand in a room with both Kate and Brad at the same time and not crumble to pieces. Brad looked surprised, too. But he quickly cleared his face of emotion before Kate walked in the house.

"Hey, I'm home," Kate announced.

Brad jumped up and brought Oliver over to his mother. "Look, Mommy's home early," he said in a silly voice, and made Ollie wave a pudgy little hand at Kate.

Zora willed her voice to remain calm and tried not to focus on the fact that if Kate had walked in the door fifteen minutes earlier, she would have found her husband making love to the nanny on the kitchen floor. It had been five days since Zora had seen Brad, and they hadn't been able to keep their hands off each other. They'd put *Baby Mozart* on for Ollie upstairs and fallen into each other's arms. Now Zora had to act like what had just happened hadn't happened. So she called out, "Hey, Kate, you're home early."

"Yeah, I wanted to get out of the office," Kate said, strolling into the kitchen, peering into pots. "That chicken smells good."

"Thanks," Zora said. "I'm using a recipe from cooking school. It's one of my favorites, and it's really easy. Just throw some herbs, dried fruit, and wine in with the chicken and let it roast. Anybody could do it." She felt like she was babbling, so she abruptly stopped talking.

Kate said she was going up to change. Halfway up the stairs, she paused. "Hey, Zora," she called out casually. "I think Brad and I can handle the rest of dinner. You can leave now. Right, Brad?"

"Sure," Brad said, and he sent Zora a look of pained apology across the room.

"Okay," Zora said, relieved at the chance to escape. "Thanks, Kate. See you guys later." She quickly collected her things and raced out the door. She cried on the bus all the way home.

Zora was still sniffling when she called Angel and begged her to come over to her apartment. She didn't say why, but Angel could obviously tell she was upset. As soon as Angel arrived with a look of concern, Zora collapsed into a messy heap right in the middle of the floor. Vast amounts of grief, confusion, and pain heaved through her body in rolling waves.

"What in the world is wrong with you?" Angel wailed, trying to pull Zora up from the floor and onto the couch. Curled up in the fetal position, her head in Angel's lap, Zora sobbed for what felt like an eternity while Angel rubbed her back and cooed to her in a soft mix of English and Italian. When her tears were finally spent and she trusted her voice, Zora told Angel everything, from the first kiss to tonight's near miss with Kate.

"What have I done?" Zora moaned. "What is wrong with me? I am the stupidest, most evil home wrecker in the world. I'm going to hell, aren't I?"

Angel shook her head. "And they say Italians are passionate people." She got up from the couch and asked Zora if she had any wine. "I need alcohol running through my veins to process this one. You look like you could use a glass, too." Zora pointed to the kitchen cabinet and told Angel she'd find a bottle of expensive French red wine that she'd been saving for a special occasion. This wasn't what she'd had in mind, but it could definitely go down as a special time in her life.

When Angel came back to the couch, Zora was waiting with a question and a look of desperation. "I should just leave, shouldn't I? I should go home. Or maybe back to Paris?"

"Hold up, Miss Thing," Angel said, "don't think you're going to solve all of your problems by running away. It's time to get some cojones and handle your business. You're a grown-ass woman with grown-woman problems that need solving."

Zora moaned into a throw pillow in response.

"Okay, so let me get this straight," Angel began, wineglass in hand, walking back and forth in front of Zora. "Something real and meaningful is going on between you and your boss."

Zora nodded. "Yes." And even though it was a minor point, she had to add, "Technically, he's not my boss. Kate was the one who hired me."

Angel rolled her eyes. "I'm going to ignore that for the time being. But we can dial back to it if you'd like."

"Fine," Zora peeped.

Angel resumed her questioning. "You're sure you're no black-berry booty call for Brad?"

"No." Zora shook her head, needing to reassure herself as much as she needed to convince Angel. "It's not like that. I know it sounds stupid and naive of me, but he really understands me and likes me for who I am and not for what I should be. We like being together. We can talk about anything. He makes me laugh, and I make him happy. It's that simple and that complicated," she summed up, then groaned. "God, *if only* it was just about the sex."

"Okay. Tell me this. Were you guys using protection?"

"Yes," Zora said. "I'm stupid, but I'm not dumb."

"Okay, okay," Angel said. "Just trying to get the facts. So, what are you two going to do?"

Zora pressed her hands against her burning eyes. "That's why you're here, remember? I'm the one crying because I don't know what I'm going to do. You're supposed to have the answers."

"Right," Angel said. She sipped her wine and didn't say anything for a minute. "You know," she started, "these White women are pretty stupid. They ask us to come into their homes, take care of their children, clean their houses, and feed their husbands, and then they expect their men not to fall in love or at least into bed with us? We clean better, take care of their kids better, and fuck their husbands a whole lot better. It's like, 'Hello, what did you expect?'"

Zora stared at her friend. "What you just said is so racist and fucked up. You make it sound like every White woman should be afraid that some Black hussy is going to seduce her husband. That's not what happened with Brad and me."

"Really?" Angel raised an eyebrow in Zora's direction.

"I didn't try to seduce Brad," Zora insisted.

"But you did all the same," Angel informed her friend. "Men are seduced by women who take care of them. That's what they really want. That's why Picasso left his wife for his housekeeper. And that's what you represent for Brad."

"So you're saying he's not interested in me as a person, he just appreciates the fact that I clean his house and cook for him. Basically, I've reverted to mammy in the master's house."

Angel shook her head in frustration. "No, darling, that's not what I'm saying. You represent a real woman to Brad, because at the end of the day, you're what every man honestly wants—not a woman who goes out to work."

"That's it, huh?" Zora asked, feeling defensive and a little bit scared. What if she was reading this all wrong with her rose-colored romance glasses? Once again she'd be left behind, and Brad would go back to his wife and child, where he belonged.

"Look," Angel said, trying to clarify her point, "love means different things to different people. Brad may be attracted to your giving spirit. You might be into him because he's happy to receive your care. I don't know. Every couple is different."

"Again, all you're saying is that Brad is only interested in me because I take care of him?" Zora said with a frustrated pout.

"Well, that and your hot little body and adorable 'please take care of me' face," Angel deadpanned. "But don't worry about what I think. I'm not involved."

Clutching the throw pillow to her chest, Zora tried to explain her position. "I didn't want this to happen," she insisted.

"Really. What did you want to happen?"

"Nothing," Zora protested. "Why would I want to fall in love with a married man? Why would I want to become attached to someone who already has the perfect life? And why would I think that a man who has Kate Carter for a wife would find me even remotely attractive? I am the anti-Kate."

"Not really." Angel shrugged. "Both of you are hardworking perfectionists who love their jobs. It just so happens that you loved the wrong part of your job." Angel laughed at her own joke.

Zora threw the pillow at her friend for being corny. Both women fell silent.

Zora struggled with her next question. She hardly dared to ask it. "Angel, do you think Brad really could fall in love with me, or am I a colossal idiot? Am I making the Alexander mistake again, putting my faith in a stupid fantasy that only exists in my head?"

"*Bella*," Angel said, "I've hung out with Brad enough to know that he seems like a good man who knows his own mind and heart. If he tells you he loves you, then I'd believe him."

Even though she knew she didn't deserve to, Zora smiled. "So can you tell me what I should do about this horrible situation I've put myself in?" she asked.

"Zora, girl, I have no fucking clue." Angel laughed ruefully. "But let me tell you something. If this is really love that you two have, don't let anyone make you feel ashamed about it. Real love is a gift. Passion is a gift. If you find it, fight for it."

"But it's wrong," Zora protested.

"The love is not wrong," Angel counseled. "Not the love."

"Oh God," Zora cried as the tears started filling her eyes again. "What am I going to do?"

"I think you two lovebirds should run away to Italy together and forget this life ever existed."

"What about the baby?" Zora asked.

"Oh my God, are you pregnant? I thought you said you were using protection!"

"Jeez, Angel!" Zora threw her hands up. "I'm talking about Oliver."

"Oh, right. Leave the baby with his mother, where he should be," Angel answered without a moment's hesitation.

"But Brad loves Ollie, too," Zora protested.

"A baby needs his mother more than his father," Angel said. "That's a fact of life. And they can always reconnect when Ollie's older."

"I don't think so," Zora said, wanting to believe in Angel's laws of right and wrong but knowing she would never ask Brad to give up his son.

"Here's a question for you," Angel asked, draining her glass. "What do *you* want?" Zora opened her mouth to answer, but Angel stopped her. "Stop thinking about Kate and the baby and even Brad for a second. What does Zora want?"

Zora closed her eyes to think. After a while she let out a long sigh and opened her eyes. She turned to her friend. "I just want everybody to be happy."

Angel laughed a wicked laugh. "Too late for that, *carissima*. It's way too late for that."

• • •

Two days later Zora was still thinking about Angel's question as she rode the subway up through the Bronx. This was the farthest she'd ever taken the A train. She wouldn't get off until she hit 190th Street, and then after that, she had to hop on a bus that would drag her even farther north. It was Saturday, and she was meeting Brad at The Cloisters in Fort Tryon Park, a destination chosen for its discreet location in the highest part of the city. It had been Brad's idea. After their kitchen-floor escapade, he'd told her he wanted to spend the day with her alone. Of course she'd said yes, excited by the possibility. But now that she was alone on the subway with her thoughts, a suffocating guilt snuffed out any feelings of excitement. The brilliant sunshine, clear blue sky, and warm weather did nothing to lessen her burdens. In fact, the perfect weather served as a reminder of how disgraceful an act she was about to commit. She was destroying somebody else's sunshine.

Somehow, when she was with Brad at home, with Ollie, what they were doing felt manageable. It was contained in the four walls of that house. But now they were breathing life into this forbidden relationship by sneaking out to be together. Brad had lied to Kate about having to go to New Jersey for the comic-book project, and Zora hadn't even told Angel where she was going, in case her friend tried to convince her not to go. She had officially crossed the line into skanky Other Woman territory. But she was still doing it. She had to. She saw it as some sort of test. She needed to know if Angel was right. Maybe outside of playing house together, maybe without having Ollie as the connection between them, they wouldn't have anything to say. Maybe in the real world, their attraction would prove to be a mirage. Invented and ephemeral. They would realize it had been a horrible mistake, and they could try to put everything back in its rightful place. Brad with Kate, and Zora . . . well, she didn't know where her next place would be. That part wasn't clear.

All of these questions and more burned through Zora's mind

as she got off the train and walked the block to the bus stop, still tormented by her thoughts. During the fifteen-minute bus ride, she considered turning around and going home. She wondered if Brad was considering the same thing. After all, he had far more to lose than she did. Maybe he wouldn't show up. And then what? Zora closed her eyes and tried to center herself. Tried to remember who she was. "I am a good person" raced across her brain. She had to laugh at the irony. "No, you're not," she said aloud. "You are definitely not a good person, Zora Anderson."

The bus let her off only a few feet from the museum. If not for the sign in front, she'd never have known that this gorgeous building, which looked like an exquisite mansion in the south of France, was actually a branch of the Metropolitan Museum of Art. She saw Brad before he saw her. His back was to her as he stood examining a stone sculpture in the front gardens. Zora felt a wave of nausea and fear come over her, and she considered turning around and running back to the subway, but she knew that wouldn't make this all better. Just then Brad caught sight of her and offered up a hesitant smile and a wave. He, too, looked uneasy, which for some reason gave her courage. She walked toward him, trying to keep her thoughts positive. "Hi," she said when she stood in front of him.

"Hi," he answered, almost shyly.

Then they stood in silence, staring at each other. Zora wondered if she'd worn the right thing; she'd chosen an ankle-length linen skirt the color of ripe raspberries and a lemon-yellow peasant top. Her toes, peeking out of a pair of leather sandals, were painted a matching bright yellow, and she had swept her long locks up into a ponytail. Gold hoop earrings and her gold bangle bracelets finished the look.

"You are beautiful," Brad whispered, causing Zora to feel something like a ball of pain tangled with pleasure lodge itself in her throat.

"Thank you, kind sir," Zora said while bending in a exaggerated curtsy, trying to infuse some levity into the air between them. "So, are you going to show me around these ancient grounds?"

"Absolutely," Brad answered, dropping his somber attitude. "But it's not really that ancient. They just created it to resemble medieval European architecture. I think this place was built in like the thirties or forties."

"Hmm, interesting," Zora said, spinning around slowly to take in the scenery.

"It is all very fascinating," Brad answered, grabbing her hand. "And if you follow me, my dear lady, I'll give you a grand tour of the entire property. My parents used to bring me up here every time we visited the city. I love this place."

"Let's go, then." Zora smiled. Brad led the way. He paid their admissions, and they spent the next two hours admiring the Unicorn Tapestries, the medieval art and architecture, and the expansive flower gardens with their intricate carved stone water fountains. Zora tried to teach Brad how to pronounce the names of the French artists, but his talent for languages, he claimed, was in Spanish and Italian. They shared stories of their travels across Europe and discovered they'd eaten at the same Turkish bistro in Brussels five years apart. For two hours they pretended that their lives had a past and a future, but they took pains to avoid speaking of the present.

But the fantasy couldn't last. Eventually, Brad pulled Zora over to the edge of the far garden, where they could look out over the Hudson River. They stood gazing at the water in silence. After a time, Zora sat down on the stone wall and stared at her feet, hovering just above the grass. Without looking up, she uttered a simple but loaded question: "Now what?"

Brad dragged his hands through his hair, then shoved both hands into his jeans pockets and let out a ragged breath. "I don't know, Zora. Never in my life did I see myself in this position, so I don't know how to proceed."

"Great. You have two degrees from Ivy League institutions, and nobody ever told you how to deal with a situation like this," Zora quipped.

"I know, I should ask for my money back, right?" Brad answered with a halfhearted laugh.

"I think so," Zora said.

Brad pulled Zora up to a standing position and enveloped her in a hug. He rested his chin on top of her head and held her there. "You feel good," he murmured.

"Thank you," Zora answered, tilting her head up to look him in the eye. Brad took advantage of her position to kiss her lightly. His lips were soft and warm, and Zora couldn't resist nibbling on the lower one a bit. Brad responded with a deeper kiss that left her breathless and a little bit weak in the knees.

She pushed him away with both hands on his chest. "You had better stop, or else that German couple over there might call security."

Brad lifted his head and noticed an older couple with Bermuda shorts, Birkenstocks, and dark socks staring at them intently. "Oops," Brad said, but didn't sound like he really cared. He pulled Zora close to him, and the two of them didn't speak for a moment.

"Zora, I don't want to hurt anybody," Brad finally said.

She pulled away to get a better view of his face. "I don't, either. But what we're doing is going to hurt a lot of people."

"I know," Brad said, shaking his head. "I know."

Zora took a deep breath and tried to control the quiver in her voice. "Here's the thing," she said. "You never promised not to hurt me. You don't owe me anything. You owe Kate, and you owe Ollie."

"I know that," Brad said with a hint of anger in his voice. "Of course I know that. And I know this is wrong, but I can't convince myself that being with you isn't right. Being with you is the easiest thing I've ever experienced with a woman."

Zora wrinkled her brow in concern. "If it's so easy to be with me now, maybe in a little while, you'll be bored with me."

"I didn't mean it like that," Brad tried to explain. "I just mean that I love talking to you, and I love being with you. I feel at peace when I'm with you. And I'd be lying if I didn't mention that I think you are so absolutely beautiful that I . . ." Suddenly, he stopped talking.

"What's the matter?" Zora demanded.

"I can't do this," Brad announced, as if he'd had a revelation.

"Do what?" Zora asked.

"I can't be with two women. I just have to admit that I don't love Kate the same—"

"Stop," Zora interrupted before he could go on. This was too much. She didn't want to be the reason for the end of a marriage. This marriage. She didn't want that responsibility. "I have to go, Brad," she announced with frantic urgency.

"Now?" Brad asked, confusion etched on his face.

"Yes, now!"

"Why?" he asked.

"I just do," Zora cried as the tears started to cascade down her face.

Brad grabbed her hand and pulled her close. He held her there and shushed her like a baby until she could stop crying. "It's going to be okay," he said.

"It's not going to be okay," Zora insisted without lifting her head from Brad's chest. "You have a wife and a child who love you."

"I didn't say it was going to be easy, but we can figure this out," Brad promised.

Zora pulled away then and stood on her tiptoes to plant a kiss on his cheek. "I don't want to be a part of this decision for you," she said, shaking her head. "I don't want to be the Other Woman. I want to be with you so badly, but not like this."

"Z," Brad called after her as she headed toward the exit.

She stopped and turned. "What?"

"Never mind," he said forlornly.

And she kept walking.

The sound of her cell phone at five on Monday morning woke Zora up.

It was Brad.

"I told her, Z. I had to tell her," he said.

"What happened?" Zora asked, instantly awake. "What did you say? Where are you? Are you okay?"

"I'm sitting outside of our house while Kate packs. She says she can't stay in this house knowing that we've 'defiled' it."

Zora listened to his words and tried to hear what he was feeling. He sounded remarkably emotionless. "Where is she going?" she asked. "Is she taking Ollie?"

"She's going home to Philadelphia, and no, she's not taking Ollie. She's leaving him here with me. She says she can't deal right now. She says she needs a couple of days alone. And I have to give them to her. I hurt her so badly, Z. I destroyed her." Brad's voice broke. He started to cry, and Zora ached to wrap her arms around him.

"Are you okay?" she asked him again.

"I don't know," Brad sobbed into the phone.

There was silence on the line, but Zora heard a passing car and a barking dog in the background, so she knew they were still connected.

Brad started talking again. "Z," he said, "I know I shouldn't ask you this, but Kate's leaving in a few minutes. Can you still come to work today? To take care of Ollie, I mean?"

"Of course," Zora said.

"Thanks," Brad said.

Before he could hang up, Zora had to ask. "Why did you tell her, Brad?"

He didn't answer right away. She couldn't tell if he was crying, or thinking, or both.

"I told her because she deserved to know the truth," Brad said. "And remember, you said you couldn't or wouldn't be *that* woman?"

"Yes," Zora breathed.

"I can't be *that* man, either."

Zora didn't say anything. She wanted to say "good for you" and at the same time wished he could take it all back so none of them would have to travel the painful path that was in front of them. Waiting.

"I gotta go," Brad broke into her thoughts. "I'll see you in a couple of hours."

When she got to the house on Second Street, Zora gingerly put her key in the lock and let herself in. It could be any other day, except it wasn't. Kate wouldn't be home later. Zora dropped her bag in the front closet and left her shoes in the hallway.

"Hi, Ollie," she said as she spied the baby in his walker. *Sesame Street* was on TV. Brad was most likely upstairs. At least Ollie seemed happy to see her. She picked him up and carried him to the kitchen. "Have you eaten, sweet baby?" she asked him as she felt the tears well up in her eyes. "I've ruined your family, and I'm so, so sorry," she whispered into his ear.

CHAPTER 37

Kate

CATATONIC. That was how Kate described the state she was in. She'd been lying in her childhood bed for over twenty-four hours and wasn't planning on moving ever again. If she moved, she'd have to think, and if she thought, she'd have to remember, and if memories of that night came flooding back into her head, she didn't know what she would do except maybe break into a million little pieces. For the first time in her life, she didn't have a plan. She'd told Brad she'd be gone for a couple days because all she knew was that she had to leave. Get out. Escape from the house that was no longer her home. But now that she'd reached the safety of her parents' home, she didn't know what would come next.

Her parents were respecting her desire to be left alone. She'd told her mother the facts over the phone, but she'd left out the sordid details. When her train had pulled into Philadelphia's Thirtieth Street Station, her mother had been on the platform so Kate could collapse in her arms, a sobbing, broken mess. At home, she'd swallowed the food her mother placed in front of her, and then she'd sat in the bathtub until her fingers wrinkled like prunes. She'd been in bed ever since. And that was where she would stay. Her father could continue to leave trays of food outside her door, her mother could continue to sit next to her and try to coax her to talk, and Kate would finish her life like this.

But on the third day of life in bed, Kate's mother came into the room early, meaning before noon. Kate could tell that her mother's patience had run out. She lifted the shades, and the brilliant sunshine blinded Kate so that she had to throw up her arms to shield her eyes. She couldn't remember why she'd ever wanted to paint the walls of her room yellow. The warm, cheery tone only served to mock her current circumstances.

"Kate," her mother said, standing at the foot of the twin bed, "your rat-bastard husband cheated on you, but he didn't kill you. You are not dead. You have a child in New York who needs you and is being cared for by that hussy you hired, so I suggest you get up and start figuring out what you're going to do." As an aside, she added, "Your sister called and sends her condolences."

Kate's throat felt scratchy, and her voice sounded gravelly from lack of use. "How do you know Zora's watching Oliver?" For some reason she'd expected Brad to stay home with Oliver. Alone. Suffering. Forcing him to explain at work that his wife had left him and he had to stay home with his child. Or at least something like that. She never dreamed that he'd have Zora come back into the house. The nerve of him!

"Because I called Brad's mother, that's why." Kate's mother sniffed. "Because I wanted to check on my grandson."

"What did she say?" Kate asked.

"Well," her mother began, perching herself carefully on the edge of the bed, "after apologizing for her son's horrid behavior and carrying on like she'd been the one wronged, she told me not to worry, that Brad was having Zora take care of Ollie as usual."

Some part of Kate was happy that Ollie's routine wasn't being disrupted by all of this, but a bigger part of her was pissed that Brad seemed to be living his regular life despite what he'd done. It wasn't fair. And then that scene of Brad and Zora playing house, with her child in the middle of their despicable little fantasy, flashed through her mind. She pulled the covers over her head to try to blot out the lurid images that continued to haunt her, day and night. Images of Brad making love to Zora. She let out an agonized groan. This was more torturous than any physical pain she'd ever experienced. Worse than seventeen hours of childbirth. Worse than having all four of her wisdom teeth extracted at the same time. Anger, pain, sorrow, and gobs of humiliation sat like a sloppy ten-ton weight on her chest, making it difficult to draw in a breath.

Her mother gingerly tugged the covers back down. "Katie, I wouldn't wish this situation on anyone. There is no easy way out, but you're young and intelligent and beautiful and brave. You will get through it. And whatever you decide to do, your father and I will support you a hundred percent."

Kate started to cry all over again. This was too much for her to handle.

"Oh, don't cry, honey," her mother pleaded, reaching out to smooth Kate's hair.

"Mom," Kate said between sobs, "I honestly don't know *what* to do. I really, really don't know what to do."

Her mother let her cry for a moment longer and then stood up to grab the box of tissues in the window seat. She brought them over to Kate and waited until her daughter got her tears under control. While she waited, she absentmindedly neatened Kate's collection of antique dolls on the shelf above her desk and wiped at some imaginary dust.

"So tell me what to do," Kate finally squeaked.

"The first thing you need to do is talk to your husband," her mother answered, coming back to Kate's bedside. "Do you think you can work things out? Was this just some onetime deal? It all sickens me, but I've seen couples get therapy after someone cheats. It takes time, but it can work out."

"That's just it. It wasn't a onetime thing, Mom," Kate replied. "I think he's in love with her, or at least he thinks he is. My husband fell for the nanny while I was off working. Isn't that the sleaziest, most Hollywood, *Gone With the Wind* bullshit you've ever heard?" Kate tried to laugh, but it came out as hacking sobs.

"Oh, Katie," her mother soothed. "Did he try to say it was your fault that he started sneaking around with the nanny?"

"No, he didn't *say* that," Kate answered. "But he might as well have. I guess that's what I get for trying to 'have it all.' "

"Nonsense," her mother insisted. "I will not have you blame yourself. You should be able to leave your husband in a roomful of Miss America candidates and trust that he'll keep his pants on."

"I never in a million years thought Brad would do this to me," Kate said. "And what makes it so awful is that he fell for . . . this Black girl who's not even attractive, no college degree, whose greatest accomplishment is that she cooks well. How does he go from me to her? What is that about? Why did I work so hard to maintain this body? Have a career? Plan a future . . ." Kate's voice broke. She had to take a deep breath before she could finish her sentence. ". . . if all he wanted was a maid and a cook?"

"I say he was just thinking with his you-know-what," her mother said, pursing her lips as if she'd swallowed something sour. "Those colored girls are quick to jump into bed with any-one."

"So I've been told," Kate mumbled.

"You know you can stay here as long as you like, Katie, but you need to go sort this out with Brad and get back to your child," her mother said as she rose from the bed and went to see if she could raise the shades even more. "Why don't you try getting out of bed today and taking a walk? Take it one step at a time."

"I'll try," Kate promised quietly. "But just not right now." And then she turned away from her mother and the bright sunlight and prayed for sleep to take her away from the nightmare her life had become.

• • •

Two days later, Kate stood in front of her house in Brooklyn. She knew Zora would be there, and she wanted to catch her unawares. Brad wasn't expecting her home until this evening, but she'd taken an earlier train because she wanted this confrontation with Zora. Craved it like hard candy. She had to look Zora in the face and try to see what Brad saw in her, because she still didn't get it. It didn't make sense that he'd give her up for Zora.

Kate let herself in and listened for voices. She heard Zora singing to Oliver upstairs. Just looking around her house, at her furniture, her pictures, brought stinging tears to her eyes. She spied the gleaming KitchenAid mixer and the thriving plants and a new basket by the fireplace and wondered when this had stopped being her house. Then the anger came rushing back. She had the urge to take a baseball bat to that mixer. This wasn't supposed to be happening to her. Nothing bad like this had ever happened to her. Maybe they could work it out. Maybe . . . Zora's footsteps coming down the stairs halted Kate's train of thought. When Zora saw her, she jumped and let out a yelp. "Kate, oh my God, I didn't hear you come in," she said.

"Well, here I am," Kate practically snarled. "Surprise." Zora didn't say anything. Kate supposed she was waiting for her to initiate the conversation. "Is Ollie sleeping?" she asked, aching to run upstairs and grab her child and hold him.

"Not yet," Zora said. "I just put him down for his nap."

Kate didn't have a speech planned and now felt at a loss for words. She'd just imagined Zora cowering in front of her, begging for forgiveness. But now she was face-to-face with Zora, and all words escaped her. All she could think of in the moment was that this bitch, in her pink T-shirt and tight jeans, had stolen her husband right out from under her nose. Zora was probably laughing at her every day.

Zora finally spoke. "Since you're home, I'll leave," she said in a voice barely above a whisper.

"That's it?" Kate yelled. A million words rushed to the tip of her tongue. "I was so nice to you. I cared about you. I mean really cared about you. And you seduced my husband and ruined my life, and that's all you have to say? You fucking bitch!" In all of her life, Kate had never ever called anybody a name like that, but the filthy words flew out of her mouth with a life of their own. The rage felt uncontrollable. She wanted to strike Zora, but she clenched her fists and commanded her arms still.

"I didn't seduce your husband, Kate," Zora said in a tremulous voice. "I suppose I could have stopped him, stopped *it,* if I'd wanted to, but I didn't and for that I will always be deeply ashamed and so very sorry." Zora stopped to catch her breath and wipe at the tears she knew she didn't deserve to shed in front of Kate. "You and Ollie don't deserve this," she continued. "And I know there's nothing I can do to make it up to you. I've tried to come up with even one single thing, but I can't fix what I've broken." Her voice caught again, and fresh tears spilled down her cheeks, but she didn't bother to wipe them away. "So, like I said, I'm just going to go now."

Kate wasn't satisfied. She wanted Zora to be defiant. She wanted her to beg for mercy, not leave her here with this rage. But what else could she do? If she started a fight, Zora might beat her senseless.

"Good-bye, Kate," Zora said as she quietly walked to the door, but not before placing her key on the table. "I'm sorry," she whispered again, forcing herself to look Kate in the eyes. "I didn't mean for any of this to happen."

"You sure as hell didn't try to stop it, either, did you?" Kate sneered. "Poor little Zora couldn't stop herself from sleeping with my husband! Pardon me if I don't accept your apology, you whore!"

Zora flinched at Kate's words. She wiped at her tears and opened her mouth to say something and then shut it without uttering a word.

"What?" Kate demanded. "What do you want to say to me?"

Zora squared her shoulders, took a deep breath, and spoke. "Kate, I didn't seduce Brad. I didn't make him touch me or look at me or fall in love with me. I don't have those powers. Like I said, I could have stopped him. I could have quit. I could have handled the whole situation with more respect for you and your family. And I apologize a hundred times over for that. But I am not a whore."

Kate was unmoved. "Fuck! You!" she said with icy venom in her voice. "Get out of my house."

Zora turned on her heel and walked out the door.

Before Brad came home, Cindy DiNuptis came over to collect Oliver. Cindy was the only person, not including her family, whom Kate had told. For some reason, she felt like Cindy, more than Fiona, would be able to help her through without condemning her or asking too many questions. Cindy was also one of those instinctively nurturing people.

Sure enough, Cindy rushed right over, sat with Kate, and listened to her rant and rage and cry for almost an hour. Then she told Kate to fix herself up before Brad came home, and she offered to keep Ollie as long as necessary. They both agreed she needed to devote all of her wits to the upcoming confrontation with her husband. "Don't give up without a fight" were Cindy's parting words. "Be strong and make him realize what he's about to lose."

Once Cindy and Ollie left, Kate jumped in the shower and then changed out of her jeans into a pair of tapered khakis and a light blue sleeveless blouse that showed off her toned arms. She didn't know what to do with herself while she waited. Moving around her own house, she felt like an interloper, trespassing in someone else's space. She kept looking for clues, like a stray piece of Zora's hair, a pair of underwear, a toothbrush. Something that would indicate they were carrying on in her home. But she discovered nothing different from the day she'd left. The refrigerator was stocked. The laundry was folded and put away. Everything was neat and clean and in its place. Just the way she liked it.

Brad arrived home at exactly five-fifteen. Kate was sitting in front of the TV with a glass of white wine. She turned off the TV when he walked in the room.

"Hi," he said.

"Hi," she said, and refused to allow herself to cry. Not yet, anyway.

He threw his stuff down in a corner, laid his coat on the back of a chair, and went straight into the kitchen and got a beer. "Where's Ollie?" he asked as he came back into the room.

"He's at my friend Cindy's," Kate answered. "I thought we might need to be alone to talk." She noticed a large white bandage on her husband's left forearm. She pointed to it and asked, "What happened?"

Brad looked a little sheepish and answered, "I got a tattoo."

"You what?" Kate cried. "Have you completely lost your mind?"

"Do you want to know why I got it or not?" Brad asked.

"Yeah, why don't you tell me," Kate said, hoping that he hadn't gotten Zora's name emblazoned on his arm. She wondered when Brad had become this stranger and why she hadn't noticed.

"This is going to sound crazy," he started, "but I needed to hurt myself. I wanted to give myself a small dose of physical pain to match what I did to you. I know it sounds stupid, but it was the only legal way I could think of to pay someone to hurt me."

"You're right," Kate confirmed, "that does sound stupid. Was it Zora's idea?"

Brad clenched his teeth but answered her question in a civil tone. "No, it was mine. I got the word 'forgiveness' written in Sanskrit to help me through this. To help us."

Kate gave her husband a slow round of applause. "Wow, Brad, that was really, really deep. How long did it take you to come up with it? About the same amount of time it took you to ruin my life by sleeping with the help?" Kate knew she was being cruel, but she couldn't help it. She wanted to kill Brad. She wanted to make him cry for days on end, until he felt used up and empty. She wanted to humiliate him and make him question everything he'd ever believed in. And that was just for starters.

"I hate you for what you did," Kate informed her husband, and then she started to cry. This time she didn't try to stop herself. She stood up and faced Brad and allowed him to see what he'd done to her. She wanted him to see her pain. "You ruined my life and our child's life. You are so selfish, you make me sick," she yelled in Brad's face. She was up close to him and could see the tears in his eyes, and she felt momentarily triumphant. Without thinking, she sucker punched him in the gut. He doubled over in pain, and in that instant, Kate understood how she might be capable of committing a crime of passion.

"I know I deserved that," Brad gasped. "But could you warn me next time you're about to throw a punch?"

"Oh, like you warned me you were about to fuck the nanny," Kate taunted as she paced the room.

Brad didn't say anything. He sat on the couch and tried to catch his breath. "I guess I deserved that, too," he finally said.

"I think so," Kate said. "And you know what I deserve? I deserve to know the truth about why you did this to me. Why would you cheat on me with Zora? Have you lowered your standards so much?"

For the first time, anger flickered across her husband's face, but when he opened his mouth, his voice was calm, and he spoke like someone who'd practiced a speech. "Kate, you have no reason to forgive me. You have every reason to hate my guts, and I deserve all of your wrath and none of your goodness. I will say it one more time, but it's not going to make you feel any better."

"What?" Kate tapped her foot impatiently.

"I don't know why I did what I did. It would be easy to say because Zora was here and you weren't, but that would be a lie. Or at least it's not the whole truth. Those were only the circumstances, not the reason all of this happened."

Kate couldn't believe her ears. "So you're saying this is my fault? I left you here alone with the nanny, so you had to sleep with her? You are unbelievable!"

Brad shook his head. "No, that's not what I'm saying."

"What are you saying, then?" Kate pressed. "Because I'd really like to hear your excuse."

"It's not an excuse," Brad started to explain. "I'm just saying I obviously wasn't going out looking to fall in love with someone else. Zora happened to be here in front of me. Every day! In our house! And I don't know why it happened. It just did."

"No! No! No!" Kate shook her head as if she could stop the words from penetrating her brain. She didn't want to hear them. She couldn't believe that she was so easily replaced by this stranger she'd hired to care for her child. She stopped moving and stood right in front of her husband. She had to ask the question. "When did you stop loving me?"

"Oh, Katie," Brad whispered. "I never stopped loving you. I still love you."

Kate sneered at this response, drained the rest of the wine in her glass, and returned to pacing. "Pardon me if I have a hard time believing that, since the last time I checked, you don't *fuck* the nanny when you love your wife!"

Brad stood up and tried to plead his case. "Kate, I am so, so sorry. I do love you. I will always love you, but—"

Kate interrupted. "But what? What are you trying to say?"

Now it was Brad's turn to cry. The tears flowed down his cheeks as he choked out the words. "I just don't think I love you the same anymore."

Kate felt her body and mind go numb. For an instant she wondered if she might faint. Somehow she got herself to the couch and collapsed on it.

"I never meant to hurt you," Brad whispered, sitting gingerly next to her. He tried to take her hand, but she yanked it away instinctively.

"Don't touch me," she hissed through gritted teeth. Her limbs were no longer numb, and the cold she had felt only a moment ago was replaced with rabid heat.

"You are truly unbelievable," Kate declared, standing up from the couch so she could look down on her husband. "I suppose you and your little Black whore are free to run off and . . . and set up house together now. I can imagine it perfectly. You'll be reading comic books while she cooks you dinner. Sounds like a nice life."

Brad clenched his fists and didn't say anything. He seemed resigned to taking any and all of whatever Kate wanted to throw his way. He sat shamefaced on the couch, nodding and agreeing. He wouldn't respond to any of her taunts or insults. And she had plenty.

She called him a cheater, a liar, and even a slut. She told him he was disgusting, cruel, and naive. She punched him a few more times, broke one very expensive lamp and her empty wineglass. And then she cried another lifetime of tears. Kate cried for the second child they would never have together and for the life that was disintegrating before her eyes.

When she was finally spent, Brad broke his silence. "What do you want to do now?" he asked.

CHAPTER 38

Brad

June 30, 2000

Dear Katie,

It feels strange to be writing you a letter when we live in the same city. But it seems like every time we try to talk face-to-face it turns into an argument, so I decided I could explain myself better through a letter. To the point, with no interruptions.

The first thing I need to say, which I know rings hollow considering what I've done to our lives, is I'm sorry. Every single cell in my body is sorry for hurting you and Ollie, for destroying our family and for disrespecting the vows we made to each other on our wedding day. There is nothing I could do or say to express how supremely disappointed in myself I am for causing so much pain.

The second thing I need to say is that whatever you do, however you process our breakup, I don't want you to ever think for a minute that any of this was your fault. Yes, I was irritated that you were working late so often, but that's not why things happened with Zora—because she was there and you weren't. Please promise me you won't spend any time torturing yourself with that thought, that I stopped loving you because you didn't come home on time every night. In fact, when I wasn't moping and feeling sorry for myself, I really was proud of you. I'm sure I didn't tell you that enough.

So here's what I want you to know. Here's what I've realized after this month apart and after talking a lot to my mother, who I think knows me the best. I think, Katie, for a long time I've been living my life doing the right thing instead of the thing that makes me the happiest. I went to business school because I thought it was the right thing to do after working at the bank. I postponed traveling abroad because it wouldn't look right after B-school. I took the Wall Street job because it offered the most money and we wanted to start a family. But with Zora, for the first time in years, I did what I wanted to do, not what I should do. It wasn't the right thing, but I did it anyway. I wanted to follow my heart for once and not my mind. I knew it was wrong, but I did it anyway. And for that I am deeply ashamed because of how I disrespected you in the process.

I'm sure reading this isn't making you feel any better, but I wanted you to understand what was going on in my mind. Because I know you, I know you're probably wondering if I think marrying you was a mistake, something I did because I thought it was the right thing, not because I loved you. To be honest, this question has also been running through my brain. I know for sure that when I walked down the aisle with you, I was a very happy man. I thought you would make a wonderful wife and partner for me. In a way, I think I thought you would help me continue to make the "right" choices in life. And you did. You taught me a lot about planning and being organized and how if I want to make my dreams a reality, that requires a certain amount of dedicated focus and sacrifice. I do not regret a single moment of time we spent together. Not a single second. I owe you so much for what

*you've given. And yes, I loved you, Katie. I still love you,
and I always will, because together we created Oliver, who
is the best thing I've ever done during this lifetime.*

*Love is such a crazy thing. Sometimes you can convince
yourself it's not even real, that it's just this elusive concept,
yet when you fall in love, it can shake your world in ways
you never dreamed possible.*

*As I read this letter over now, I realize it might not
make you any happier, but I hope at the very least it helps
you understand what happened and why.*

*I don't know where we go next, but I pray (by the way,
I found a great Unitarian congregation, and I've started
going to church again) that we can all find some peace in
the very near future.*

Be good to yourself, Katie,
Brad

CHAPTER 39

Zora

I<small>T</small> took a long time for Zora to want to get out of bed. To eat. To feel the sunshine on her face. She knew she didn't deserve it. "It" being physical pleasure. The only thing she knew she deserved was eternal suffering for the pain she had caused. But despite the fact that she knew she'd done wrong, she still couldn't erase the feelings she had for Brad. She still secretly prayed for a happy ending, which made the guilt well up inside her even more.

For the first few weeks after Kate fired her, Zora spent an extraordinary amount of time watching television. She didn't realize how easy it was to pass an entire day without moving. She was able to dull the pain and guilt by focusing on the even more dramatic stories Hollywood packaged and sold as entertainment. In contrast, her own sordid tale didn't seem that bad.

Brad had called only once. They agreed to meet at the coffee shop by her apartment one evening soon after Kate came back from Philadelphia. Brad looked so wounded, Zora had started to cry as soon as she saw him. They sat huddled in the back of the shop for a few moments, holding hands, crying together. When Brad spoke, it was to tell her that he couldn't see her while he was figuring things out with Kate. He had promised Kate that, and he owed her that one request. Zora didn't protest because she agreed. Kate deserved that and more. And after what she'd done, Zora knew she ranked last on Brad's list of obligations, and she forced herself to keep that thought front and center in her mind. Besides, she knew if she pressed him now to tell her how he felt, to ask if he still felt the same way about her, he might say that it had all been a horrible mistake. A lapse in judgment. Or that even if he had felt something at one point, she wasn't worth giving up his life for. Like Alexander, he might quickly realize that she was the kind of girl who was easily discarded.

So she had held his hand and listened and tried to prepare herself for the fact that this might be the last time she was with him. Before he left, he held her tight and whispered in her ear, "This hurts too much." He kissed her hard on the lips and left her standing alone in the doorway of the coffee shop.

That was a month ago.

Angel came by a few times to check on her and say that she was leaving for Italy soon. Even though she was still fifteen hundred dollars short on her travel fund, she decided it was time to go. Apparently, Fiona had heard about Zora and Brad, and she'd gotten frosty with Angel.

"I don't need that kind of attitude from her," Angel had griped. "I take better care of Skye than she does, so she has no right to get snippy with me." Angel had laughed. "And she doesn't even need to worry that I might want to get busy with her scraggly-haired, wrinkly old husband. No, thank you." On the other hand, Angel did threaten to pack Skye in her suitcase, since she'd decided her mother didn't want her anyway.

But now it was time to move on. Zora clicked off the television, looked around her apartment, and wrinkled her nose in distaste. Today she would clean. Tomorrow she would look for a new job. She had enough money to survive for another month, but then she'd be in trouble, and she was in no position to ask her brother for help again. Not when he was just beginning to respect her choices in life. At least Sondra had decided to stay up at Smith for summer school, so Zora wouldn't have to look for a new place to live.

As she started to collect her clothes from the floor, and the empty cartons of yogurt that had sustained her during her period of mourning, she allowed herself to contemplate her future. What kind of job should she look for? What did she want to do with her life? Would Brad be involved? Just thinking about him made her stomach clench in agony. It probably would be easier if he had dropped out of the picture entirely, but he e-mailed her every once in a while, keeping her updated on his life. Nothing romantic or personal, just the dissolution of his former existence. He and Kate were getting divorced. The house was for sale. Ollie was going to day care. The messages came sporadically and were short and to the point. There was never a mention that he wanted to see Zora, and there was no talk of a future, but he continued to send the messages, always signed "Brad." She would write back her own emotionless updates, making sure she never wrote anything that implied she'd like to see him again.

Zora pushed the thoughts of Brad, Kate, and Ollie out of her mind. She would never be able to move forward if she kept thinking about the past. The Carters were out of her life, and the sooner she accepted that, the easier it would be to figure out her next steps. She revived her mantra, "I am a good person," and she attacked the dust on her dresser with renewed energy. She turned on the stereo and forced herself to think positively as the sound of smooth jazz filled the space around her. As she picked up a pile of unopened mail, magazines, and expired MetroCards, she noticed a pink Post-it note with Keith's handwriting. He had written a name—Winsome Clark—a phone number, and a message that read, "Call her about the catering job." Zora vaguely remembered that this was one of Keith's subtle hints for her to find a new profession. She had promised to call this woman but never had, in passive-aggressive protest.

Before she could change her mind or put it off, Zora grabbed her cell phone and dialed the number. Nobody answered, but the voice mail asked her to leave a message, so she did. "Hi, my name is Zora Anderson, and I'm a friend of Keith Davis and I am looking for a job." When she hung up, she kicked herself for not leaving a more eloquent message. Two minutes later, the phone rang.

"Hello, I'm looking for Zora Anderson," a woman said with a strong Jamaican accent.

"This is she," Zora replied hesitantly.

"Oh, hi there," the woman said warmly. "This is Winsome. You just left a message on my phone. You're looking for a job, then?"

"Um, yes," Zora answered as she toyed with one of her locks.

"What kind of job are you looking for?" Winsome asked.

Zora racked her brain, trying to recall the conversation she'd had with Keith about Winsome, what he'd said about her and what type of catering business she ran. Zora wanted to sound informed. But her mind had gone blank.

"Basically, I like to cook," Zora said, offering her only truth. "And I'm a good cook," she added. "I have a degree from the Institute of Culinary Arts in Detroit and have been working for the last ten months as a nanny and personal chef for a family in Brooklyn." She prayed Winsome wouldn't want a reference letter from Kate.

"Thank the Lord." Winsome chuckled. "Remind me to thank Keith next time I see him. My sous chef just up and left to follow his girlfriend to New Mexico. So I'm in a bind. But here you are, calling me out of the blue. You must have heard my prayers."

"Maybe it's fate," Zora said, hoping that the situation might actually work out, but she was careful not to get her hopes too high.

"Can you come in so we can talk some? If you're a friend of Keith's, you must be good people, but we need to see you in the kitchen."

"No problem," Zora said. "When would you like me to come, and where are you located?"

Winsome asked her to come by the next morning and gave

her the directions to their kitchen, which, thankfully, required a single bus ride of only about fifteen minutes.

"I'll see you tomorrow, then?" Winsome finished.

"Perfect," Zora answered, and hung up the phone in triumph. She turned back to her cleaning and for the first time in a long while felt something like hope coursing through her veins. "Zora Anderson is back in the game," she announced to the world.

Later that night, over steaming bowls of pho at their favorite Vietnamese noodle shop, Zora told Angel about her phone conversation with Winsome.

"That sounds promising," Angel said cautiously. "Is that what you want to do?"

"I'm not sure," Zora answered honestly. "But you know what? I'm going to see what happens. If there's one good thing I got out of working for the Carters this past year, it's realizing that I really do love to cook, and I'm good at it, and there's no reason to apologize for that. If the job involves cooking, I don't have to be a personal chef or have some fancy title. I'm just going to"—Zora paused to pay homage to her friend with a pointed stare—"follow my passion for cooking."

"Bravo, Zora, bravo," Angel gushed with a little round of applause. "I told you everybody needs to find their passion. There's no other way to live."

Zora sipped from her glass of French lemonade and considered Angel's words. "You know, I've kind of made a mess out of my life lately, but I've learned a lot, too. I'm not a total screwup."

Angel dismissed Zora's guilt with a wave of her hand. "*Bella,* life is messy. You've been learning and growing and loving. All of that comes with a certain amount of shit."

"I know." Zora sighed, wanting to believe wholeheartedly in

the Tao of Angel. "I just wish the shit didn't have to stink so badly."

Angel laughed. "Hey, your job is to make sure you don't get stuck in the shit. Wipe it off and keep going."

"And how do I do that, exactly?" Zora asked.

"Easy," Angel said, leaning in close to make her point. "Keep following your heart, and don't ever apologize for doing what you love or for who you love."

As soon as Angel said that, Brad flashed in Zora's mind. Angel was the only one she could talk to about him and the only one who knew how she really felt. And Angel was definitely the only person who wouldn't condemn her for falling for a married White man who happened to be the father of the child she'd been paid to watch.

The look on Zora's face clearly prompted Angel to ask about Brad. "Have you heard from him at all?"

Zora told her about the e-mails.

"Look," Angel said, "you have to respect that he's doing the right thing by his wife. That means he's a good person. And if at the end of it all, he still wants you, then he'll be able to come to you free and clear. That's what you'd want, right?"

"Yeah." Zora sighed again. "But it's so hard not knowing how he feels. What if he hates me now that he's lost his whole life?"

"Don't take the blame for something you didn't do. Brad is a grown man, making grown-man decisions. You didn't force him into any of this," Angel said.

Zora shook her head. "But I don't deserve him after what I did to Kate, and he's probably going to wake up and realize that he made a terrible mistake. That I was a mistake."

"First of all," Angel said, her eyes flashing in anger, "you were not anybody's mistake. Brad or any guy would be lucky to have you. You are a wonderful, smart, caring person. Brad saw that in you and fell in love. Y'all just have really bad timing."

Zora bit her lip to keep from tearing up. When she'd swallowed the lump that had risen in her throat, she smiled at Angel.

As soon as she found her voice, she adjusted her face into her best puppy-dog expression to ask, "Do you have to go back to Italy? I don't know how I'll survive without you."

Angel pooh-poohed Zora's worries. "Zora, you'll be fine. And let's be clear about something: I don't *have* to go back to Italy. The only things I *have* to do in this lifetime are stay Black and die. I'm choosing to go back because that's what makes me happiest. It's where I feel the most alive. And it's where I can be me without apology. If I stay here in the United States, I'd dissolve into despair. I'd turn into one of those coulda-woulda-shoulda folks, always lamenting that they didn't follow their bliss."

Zora crossed her arms and sat back in her chair with a fake pout. "How did you get to be so wise, Angel Montgomery?"

Angel threw back her head and laughed. When she was finished, she answered, "Easy. I always listen to my heart, and my mama raised me right."

It was Zora's turn to laugh, but she quickly sobered up. "Thank you, Angel. For everything."

"You're welcome," Angel answered, then quickly changed the subject. "Now, let's get back to my hectic life." She launched into her latest plans to woo back her ex-boyfriend, Valentino, once she hit Italian soil. "Do you think I should stalk him or play hard to get?"

Zora gave Angel her full attention for the rest of dinner and helped her plot her triumphant return. Before they left the restaurant, Angel made Zora promise that she would visit her in Florence in the fall.

"I will," Zora said. "I promise."

"Good." Angel smiled as she turned to go. "*Ci vediamo.* We'll see each other."

Zora thought of Winsome like a Caribbean breath of fresh air. Being around her was both inspiring and invigorating. Winsome loved to cook, and she loved to laugh. She thought all of life's problems could be solved with a good meal and a glass of wine. Everything about her was unexpected. She wore her hair in long unruly dreadlocks, but her eyebrows were always plucked, and her manicure appointments were sacred. She talked about men and sex like a single girl in her twenties, but she'd been married to her high school sweetheart for twenty years. "I'm married, not dead," she liked to say whenever she brought up a hot guy she'd seen on television or at an event.

Winsome's catering company, DeLish, was only two years old but had already built a stellar reputation around Brooklyn for eclectic West Indian fusion cuisine. Their signature dishes included jerk salmon, lobster curry, and coconut crème brûlée with crystallized ginger. They were getting so many jobs, even in Manhattan, that Winsome couldn't keep up with the cooking and managing the business. So Zora's phone call had been a godsend, Winsome claimed, and she hired her on the spot.

Zora didn't make as much money working for Winsome as she had working for Kate, but she loved the work and the atmosphere at DeLish. It wasn't as stressful as working at a restaurant, and she was learning all kinds of culinary tricks. Like how to make homemade ginger beer and the secret to deboning a fish with a single knife stroke. The regular kitchen staff was small, and they worked like a family. Winsome could afford to pay only five people, and just three of them were full-time. The prep cooks and the dishwasher came in for three hours a day, while Zora worked seven hours straight, Tuesday through Saturday. Not to mention the marathon days when they had events. The work was physically demanding and required quite a bit of creative energy. It was the perfect combination to keep her mind off Brad.

She still thought about him a lot, but after time, the hurt wasn't so intense. She was surprised at how much she missed Ollie, too. It pained her to think he probably wouldn't remember her anymore.

After three months, babies forget. Zora figured Ollie wouldn't even recognize her, since she'd whacked her locks off right before starting at DeLish. Like Jezebel, she'd punished herself by lopping off her vanity, her hair. Now her Afro was growing out with thick and springy curls. It had been so long since her hair had been this short, but she liked it. And it was perfect for the summer heat. She felt reborn in a way and was determined to follow Angel's directive and follow her heart's desire. So far it was working. She was happy working for Winsome, living on her own in New York, and she and her brother were repairing their relationship and hanging out pretty regularly. She was this close to getting him to introduce Mimi to their parents. She couldn't help it, but she felt like she owed Brad much of her happiness. He was the one who had encouraged her to be proud of the choices she made. And he'd been the one to force her to call her brother. It was Brad she was thinking of when she dialed her parents' home number.

Her mother answered on the first ring. Zora took a deep breath as she sat on the couch in her apartment, still dressed in her clothes from work. "Hi, Mommy," she said.

"Hello, Zora. To what do I owe this surprise?" her mother said in a guarded tone.

Zora knew her mother was justified in her response, seeing as how she very rarely called home. It wasn't going to be easy, but Zora wasn't going to chicken out this time. While she still felt the glow from a whole day working side by side with Winsome, creating a Jamaican wedding buffet complete with curried goat, rice and peas, and gallons of homemade rum punch, Zora was going to come clean.

"Actually, I just wanted to say hello," she hedged, and then plunged on. "And to tell you that I found a really great job."

"Really? What kind of job?" her mother asked without a hint of expectation.

"It's a cooking job," Zora explained. "I've been working for three months now, but I wanted to make sure it would be a good fit before I told you and Dad."

"So you're working at a restaurant?" her mother queried, doubt in her voice.

"No, it's a catering company here in Brooklyn, not too far from my apartment." She proceeded to tell her mother about DeLish and Winsome and how much she enjoyed the work and how much Winsome liked her and was already giving her lots of responsibility in the kitchen. "She leaves me in charge whenever she has to go out on a job," Zora couldn't help but brag. And then she waited. To see how her mother would react. The silence seemed to drag on endlessly.

Finally, her mother had something to say. "It sounds like the perfect fit for you, Zora."

"It does?" Zora blurted out, having expected a more tepid response.

"Sure," her mother said. "At least you get to use that culinary degree for something."

"I really do love cooking, Mom," Zora admitted. "A lot of people have told me I have real talent." Though she wanted to tell her mother about cooking for Kate and Brad, that would require a confessional session she wasn't up to at the moment. She knew she would tell them eventually. But not now. Instead, she told her mother about some of the fabulous dishes she was learning how to make and some of the more elaborate parties they'd catered, like the one for a New York Knick's twenty-fifth birthday in his penthouse apartment.

It was a pleasant conversation, up until her mother suggested that Zora should learn all she could from Winsome and then maybe open her own catering company.

Zora laughed nervously. "Mom, I just started, okay?"

Her mother sighed. "Sorry."

"It's okay," Zora said. "But I need you to know that I don't have to be in charge of everything, like you do, to feel like I've accomplished something." Her mother didn't say anything, so she tried to clarify her point. "I'm really happy now. I like working for Winsome, and she needs me at DeLish. I like the routine and the people in the kitchen. I make decent money, and Winsome knows I love to travel and says as long as I give her enough notice, I can take time off when I need to. In fact, I'm going to Italy in a few weeks to visit my friend Angel."

"That sounds nice, Zora."

"Care to elaborate, Mom?"

Her mother took a deep breath before responding. "Obviously, you and I have different ideas of success, but as long as you're happy and can support yourself, then I'm learning to be okay with that. It sounds like you've done some real thinking about your life, and I'm working on acceptance of my children's choices. It's a process."

"I appreciate that, and you don't have to worry about me. I know what my life is supposed to be about now."

Her mother didn't jump for joy, but Zora could tell she had hope. "It sounds like you've done some maturing out there in New York," her mother offered.

"I have, but I had a lot of help," Zora said, thinking about Brad again, and Angel, and even Keith.

"Really? From whom?" her mother asked. "Because I cannot imagine it's your brother. He still won't return a phone call in any kind of timely fashion."

"Actually, I got a lot of help from the woman you named me after." Zora smiled. "Zora Neale Hurston reminded me 'To thine own self be true,' and that's exactly what I'm doing."

A few days later, Zora said good-bye to Winsome and the dishwashing crew and headed home. It was a perfect fall evening in

Brooklyn, so she decided to walk instead of catching the bus. At six, the streets were buzzing with the wave of folks coming home from work in Manhattan, and Zora happily blended into the crowd of black, brown, and white faces pouring out of the subways. Even though she'd been living in Brooklyn for only a year, it was beginning to feel like home. She smiled at the Mexican man squatting on the corner selling flowers from his cart, and stopped to buy a banana from the Indian fruit vendor on Lafayette Avenue. "Take four for seventy-five cents," he cajoled.

Zora laughed in spite of herself; he always did this, and she always had to tell him she wanted only one banana for the walk home. It was their routine now.

"Okay," he relented, "but you come back tomorrow."

"I will," Zora promised as she gave the man her quarter and kept walking.

When she passed by Keith's old apartment building, she felt the banana in her stomach threaten to revolt. She knew she owed Keith a call, but she hadn't worked up the nerve to pick up the phone just yet. He'd sent her a postcard a month earlier from Los Angeles with his new phone number and address and told her he'd wait for her to make the first move. Just the thought of telling Keith about Brad gave Zora hives. So rather than dwell on what inevitably would be a painful and awkward conversation, Zora pushed Keith out of her mind, promising to revisit the situation at a later date. Right now she just wanted to maintain her good mood and think about her upcoming trip to Italy. She'd bought her tickets yesterday and would be leaving in two weeks. Winsome said it was the perfect time for her to go because October was generally a slow month at DeLish.

Just thinking about all the delectable food she'd eat in Italy, and hanging out with Angel again, and shopping at all of Florence's famed artisan shops and boutiques, made Zora's thirty-minute walk home fly by.

As she rounded the corner of Myrtle and Clinton, Zora was startled out of her reverie when she noticed a man leaning against her building. It looked like he was waiting for something or someone. It was only six-thirty, but her block was deserted. She squinted to see if she recognized the man, or at least if she could tell whether he seemed like bad news. She considered turning around and waiting in the coffee shop for a few minutes, but then she sneaked another peek, and something looked familiar about the shape of the man's body and the way he was leaning. Zora kept walking, feeling a tingle of something between anticipation and fear rush up her spine. Sure enough, it was Brad Carter.

Zora felt her heart beat faster, and she became achingly aware that she smelled like old cooking grease. She was still wearing her baggy black-and-white-checked chef pants, and her red T-shirt was splattered with food stains. In other words, she looked like a hot mess. She told herself it didn't matter; she didn't know why Brad was standing outside her door. Maybe he wanted to see her in person so he could tell her that she'd ruined his life.

She slowed her steps as she got closer. He must have heard her approach because he turned around. The first thing out of his mouth was, "You cut your hair."

Zora's hand shot up with a will of its own to feel her kinky new do. She forgot sometimes that she looked so different. "You like it?" she asked.

Brad smiled. "Yeah, I do. It looks good on you." He just stood there and drank in the sight of Zora in the flesh. Wearing jeans and a long-sleeved T-shirt, he looked thinner, and his dark hair was longer. Zora couldn't figure out what he was thinking. She didn't know what she should say. She stared right back at him, a challenge in her eyes.

Finally, he broke the silence. "I missed you, Zora," he said, his voice barely above a whisper.

"Really?" Zora said, hope tugging at her heart.

"Really," he answered.

Zora was tempted to grab Brad and kiss him with all her might, to show him how much she'd missed him, too, but she wasn't going to expose herself like that. He had come to her. He obviously had something to say.

"Can we go somewhere and talk?" he asked.

"Let's go to the coffee shop," Zora said, working hard to keep her voice neutral.

They walked the one block in complete silence. Zora felt sweat prickle in her armpits, and her brain frantically played through every scenario of what this visit might mean. Whatever it was, Brad Carter meant complications, no matter what. Was it too late to run the other way?

Brad ordered coffee, and Zora ordered her first hot chocolate of the season. They got their drinks and sat in the back of the café, where it was quietest. For once Zora was relieved Katrina wasn't around to witness whatever was about to happen.

"You look really good," Brad started nervously.

"Thank you. I feel good." Zora smiled, and she told him all about her job. Talking about DeLish and Winsome had a calming effect, and she felt free to tell Brad how much she was enjoying herself at work and how much Winsome seemed to appreciate her. "And I'm going to visit Angel in Italy in two weeks," she added.

Brad was duly impressed. And said as much. But then it was his turn to summarize what was happening in his life. "I guess the place to start is that Kate and I are officially divorced," Brad began. He went on to say that the whole ordeal had been horrible and painful and that he never, ever wanted to go through anything like that ever again.

Zora's first question was about Ollie. "Where is he?"

Brad choked on his answer. "Kate has him right now. She wanted full custody. She's so angry, Z, and I can't blame her. I didn't want the courts deciding the fate of my child, so I didn't fight her. For now."

"What do you mean?" Zora asked frantically.

"I mean she took him away from me because she wanted to punish me. And she said she didn't want you near him."

Zora flinched when he said that. She picked up her mug and kept her eyes focused on the floating marshmallows instead of on Brad as he related the disaster his life had become.

"Kate's struggling," Brad continued. "She has Ollie in day care, but she can't handle her new work schedule and picking him up every day. She got that promotion she wanted so badly, but I've had to pick Ollie up a few times because she couldn't leave the office. So I think when she stops being so angry and hurt, she'll be ready to sit down and talk. We'll work something out."

His last sentence sounded hopeful, but Zora still had to ask. Her voice trembled with emotion when she spoke. "So do you hate me? You've lost your son."

Brad shook his head vehemently. "No, I didn't lose him. I could never lose him. But this really sucks." Zora thought he was going to cry, but he shook it off and took a big gulp of his coffee before he continued. "I understand where Kate's coming from. And I understand why she thinks she has to do this. I just thank God that Ollie won't remember this part of his life."

"Maybe," Zora said distractedly, consumed by her own thoughts of guilt and punishment.

Brad reached for her hand and forced her to look him in the eye. "Zora, this is not your fault. You did not do this. We fell in love, and it hurt a lot of people, and I would never hurt this many people on purpose again, but I won't apologize for loving you."

It took Zora a moment to register what Brad had just said. "You still love me?" she asked incredulously.

Brad raised his eyebrows in feigned surprise. "Yes, Zora Anderson, contrary to what you've just been a part of, when I love, I love really hard and really long."

"Pardon me if I have a hard time believing you on that one," Zora said in all seriousness.

"I guess you're justified in feeling that way," Brad answered. "But would you allow me to prove it to you that I can love for a really long time? Do you think we could start over?"

"Are you sure?" Zora asked, wishing she could see through to his heart. "Because I'm finally in a good place in my life. So if you're not sure, or if you think you owe me something, please don't do me any favors."

Brad leaned across the table, getting as close as possible. "Z, these last three months I've done more soul-searching and questioning than I ever have in my life. I tried to convince myself that what we had wasn't real, that the feelings would fade away, but I couldn't do it. I know the whole world may say we're crazy, that this is wrong, but I don't care. When I'm with you, I like myself the most. I can be myself. And at the end of it all, you're still the one I want to come home to. Will you give me a chance?"

Zora felt momentarily overwhelmed with emotion. After all the pain she had caused, she felt certain the universe could never be so forgiving and generous. She looked into Brad's eyes and tried to find an answer there. What she saw was love reflected back at her. "Okay," she finally answered. "Let's start over." She extended her hand across the table. "My name is Zora Anderson. I was named after the author Zora Neale Hurston, but before you ask, I'm a chef, not a writer."

Brad grinned in response. "It's very nice to meet you, Zora."

CHAPTER 40

Epilogue

Kate

Summer 2001

KATE didn't go to Brooklyn anymore. It reminded her too much of everything that had gone wrong. She couldn't walk down the street in her old neighborhood without seeing a Black woman pushing a White baby in a stroller. Volvos and minivans crowded the streets. All the coffee shops and teahouses overflowed with breast-feeding mommies and sticky-fingered toddlers. Park Slope was where families went to celebrate their familyness, and she didn't have a family anymore.

Kate and Ollie lived in a pleasant two-bedroom apartment on the Upper West Side. Ironically, it was only one block away from the building she and Brad had lived in after they were married. Instead of renting, Kate owned the 750 square feet of space she now called home. She'd taken her half of the money from the sale of their brownstone and plunked it down on this place, thanks to a tip from Fiona. Fiona knew the guy who was selling. It was the easiest New York City real estate transaction ever. Kate had laughed when she told the story to her jealous girlfriends, who were still renting and trying to scrape together enough cash to buy a studio in one of the outer boroughs. Sometimes she was surprised that she could still laugh. But that's how things worked. You got blindsided by life, and then you picked yourself up and moved on.

Fiona claimed she was helping Kate move on, too, by making her celebrate the one-year anniversary of her liberation from Brad. "Why would I want to celebrate the most horrible experience of my life?" Kate had wailed over the phone when Fiona suggested it last week.

"Because that's how you reclaim your life. We have to find the good in what happened and celebrate it so you don't get stuck in the past."

"I'm not stuck in the past," Kate defended herself. "I've set up a nice home for me and my son. I recently got promoted, and I finally found a day-care center that I love. Ollie loves it, too, and they don't penalize me for picking him up two minutes late."

"Two questions," Fiona asked. "Are you seeing anyone, and have you talked to Brad?"

Kate let out an irritated sigh. "No and no."

"Exactly my point. We're going out to celebrate next Friday. Find a babysitter and meet me at Lupe's café on Bleecker Street on Saturday night at seven."

Kate laughed at Fiona's insistence. She expected everyone to do her bidding. And the truth was, Kate would do it. Fiona had been her rock through this whole nightmare, and so far she'd been right about almost everything.

"Fine," Kate agreed. "I'll be there."

Kate walked past Lupe's three times before she noticed the tiny black sign with a gold arrow pointing down a flight of dark, narrow steps. Even though it was seven, it was still warm and light outside, so it took Kate's eyes a moment to adjust to the dimness inside the cozy dining room. She heard Fiona before she saw her. "Kate, over here," she called.

Kate smiled at the hostess and made her way to Fiona's table.

"I love your hair," Fiona squealed as she stood up to kiss Kate on the cheek.

"Thanks," Kate said as her hand slipped up to touch her recently shorn locks. In honor of her "liberation," she'd not only gotten her hair cut in a layered bob, she'd finally allowed Tommy, her stylist, to streak it with copper highlights. She liked it, but it was taking some getting used to.

Kate sat down and picked up her menu. Lupe's was a quirky South American restaurant, famous for tropical mixed drinks and elaborate seafood offerings. She'd checked out the reviews online at work before coming. "Have you ever been here?" she asked Fiona.

"Mmm-mm," Fiona mumbled, studying the drink offerings. "Since this is a celebration," she said, looking up from the hot-pink menu, "let's start with a watermelon martini."

Kate smiled. "Okay, let's do it."

Fiona flagged a waiter and placed the order. She then turned to the real menu. By the time the waiter came back with their pale pink drinks, they'd selected their entrées. Kate chose the mahimahi with green chile sauce; Fiona decided on the coconut shrimp.

"So who'd you get to babysit?" Fiona asked, plucking the wedge of watermelon from the bottom of her glass.

"Brad," Kate said as she took a big gulp from her drink.

"What?" Fiona sputtered.

Kate waited as she let the martini's magic warm her limbs. She wanted to make sure she wasn't going to cry. "You know, I started to think about what you were saying about living in the past. And I realized that holding on to this anger *is* living in the past, and it's not fair to Ollie."

"But I thought you wanted sole custody. I thought you didn't want Brad near Ollie," Fiona reminded her friend.

"I thought so, too, but Ollie deserves a father. And Brad wants to be a father, so I called him."

"Jeez," Fiona said. "I need a moment to process this one." She signaled to the waiter and asked for another martini. "Do you want another one?" she asked Kate.

Kate declined.

"Okay," Fiona said. "This is a good thing, then. Although I have to say, I don't know if I'd be so forgiving."

Kate gave a rueful laugh. "I never said anything about forgiving. I don't know if I'll ever forgive Brad for being such a selfish bastard. But what he did to me doesn't mean Ollie should be punished by not having a father in his life."

Fiona let this sink in. "So I have to ask. Is he still with *her*?"

With all her being, Kate wanted to tell Fiona that she didn't know. That she hadn't asked, but her mind drifted back to her living room earlier that evening.

Seeing Brad standing in her doorway, looking gorgeous in his jeans and rumpled white oxford, made her heart ache. He smelled like Ivory soap with a hint of spicy aftershave. She instantly regretted her decision to be a good mother and allow her son to have his father back. She wanted Brad back, too. But then she noticed his finger. Where he had once worn a gold band signaling their union, there was now an intricate tattooed ring with a very prominent red *Z* in the middle. A rage she didn't know she was still capable of squashed her aching heart. When Ollie came toddling over and then shrank away from the stranger in the doorway, Kate experienced a moment of vengeful satisfaction. It would take work for Brad to win back the affection of his son. They were practically strangers now. Which suited her just fine, since Kate herself hardly recognized the man she used to call her husband. She figured they'd all have to get to know one another again.

Kate watched Brad drop to his knees to talk to Ollie face-to-face. She saw the tears in his eyes, and she felt her own anger recede. A little.

"Hey, big man," Brad said to his son. He pulled out a red wooden car with rubber wheels from his pocket and held it out to Ollie. Kate willed her son to hold fast to his suspicion, but of course he didn't. He loved cars. He walked right over to Brad and took the car from him and said, "Tank you." Brad laughed. He watched Ollie roll the car on the coffee table for a minute, and Kate watched Brad. When he stood, the tears were flowing unchecked down his face. He brushed them away with the back of his hand. "Thank you, Kate," he managed. "I know you didn't have to do this. And I know it's hard for you, but thank you for finally allowing it to happen."

Kate refused to cry. And she refused to feel sorry for Brad. He had done this to himself. "Look," she started, "for Oliver's sake, I want you in his life. And I don't want him to grow up with feuding parents. I still can't look at you and not want to kick you in the balls, but I'm working on that."

"Okay." Brad nodded, steeling himself against her anger.

"So this is what I propose," Kate said. "Since Ollie is happy at his day care up here, I think we should keep him there, and he can stay with me during the week. Then you can come get him on the weekends."

"That's it?" Brad asked, looking heartbroken.

Kate sighed. "Look, Brad, I don't have all the answers right now. But I think we can start there. I mean, do you even have a house, a place where he can sleep? A high chair?"

Brad took a deep breath and let it out before he answered in a measured tone. "Kate, Ollie's room has always been ready in my

home. We have a bed. We have a high chair. We have a stroller . . .
He's my son, too."

All those *we*'s punctured Kate's heart like sharpened needles.
She hesitated, but she had to ask. "So are you and . . ." She could
barely get the name out. ". . . Zora living together?"

Brad looked down at his hands when he answered, but he spoke
clearly. "Yeah, as of last month. We just got a place together in Fort
Greene. It's really close to the park and Ollie's favorite playground."

Kate put up her hand to stop him and closed her eyes. She
had to concentrate to keep the bile from rising into her mouth. "I
don't need to hear the details," she informed him.

"Sorry," Brad apologized.

Composure regained, Kate got back on track. "Look, you have
to respect me on this. You come and get him every Friday night.
If you want to have him some other time, we can do it on a case-
by-case basis. Okay?"

"Fine," Brad said, the resignation clear in his voice.

"And one more thing. If you fight me on it, we can call the
whole thing off."

"What?" Brad asked, looking genuinely concerned.

"I don't want to ever see Zora here with you. I don't want her
picking Ollie up or dropping him off. Maybe that's not fair of me,
but that's how it's going to be. You owe me that tiny bit of respect."

Brad didn't look happy, but he said okay.

"Fine," Kate said, back to business. "Let me show you around."

She gave Brad a quick tour of the apartment, showed him
Ollie's dinner, and made a hasty exit so she didn't have to witness
the father-son bonding that she knew would crush her spirit.

To answer Fiona's question, Kate said, "Yes, they're still together."

"Ouch." Fiona winced. "I thought that was going to be a quickie
jungle-fever thing. I guess you never know."

"Tell me about it," Kate agreed.

"Would you still take him back if he asked?" Fiona wanted to know.

"God," Kate moaned. "Part of me says yes, to get our family back. But it would never be the same. I could never trust him again. And the sad fact of the matter is, he loves her, not me." Just saying those words still hurt so much. Kate wondered if the wound would ever heal. She told Fiona about the tattooed ring and the love nest in Fort Greene.

"Wow, it sounds like he went off the deep end," Fiona said, making a face.

"Not really," Kate clarified. "Brad's always wanted to be different and countercultural. I mean, what can you expect? He was raised by Unitarians and lived in one of the most crunchy-granola, liberal neighborhoods in Philadelphia. I was probably too normal for him."

Fiona laughed at Kate's analysis. "Enough," she pronounced. "This is supposed to be a celebration of your future, not a rehash of what went wrong."

"Right," Kate said, trying to shrug off her melancholy.

"So, in honor of you," Fiona said, reaching into her purse and pulling out what looked like a glossy brochure, "I've booked us into the Montauk Mountain Bliss Spa for two days of pampering and pleasure."

"What!" Kate exclaimed. "For when? Are you crazy?"

"I most certainly am not," Fiona said. "You deserve it. We can get there on the Long Island Rail Road in a couple of hours. Mountain Bliss is one of our new clients, so let's just say I got the friends-and-family rate on a deluxe pampering package."

"When are we going?" Kate asked. "Assuming I do decide to go?"

"Any weekend in the next month," Fiona answered. "It's an open reservation."

"What am I supposed to do with Ollie?" Kate pressed. "Remember, I'm a single mom."

"Um, hello. Didn't you just arrange it so the father is back in the picture?" Fiona reminded Kate. "You're not in this alone anymore."

"You're right," Kate admitted. "I've gotten so used to not making plans that don't involve my son."

"It's time to start thinking about you again," Fiona gently nudged.

"I know," Kate said, trying to get a handle on the merry-go-round of emotions spinning in her mind. Part of her wanted to hold on to the anger and fear and regret because they were familiar, but living like that didn't lead to much. Taking a deep breath that was meant to purge the old feelings, she announced on the exhalation, "I've got to move on."

"Yes, you do." Fiona nodded with an encouraging smile. "And I'll be there pushing you in the right direction."

"Thanks," Kate said, reaching for her glass of water. "You're a good friend, Fiona."

"I know," Fiona joked. "Now, if you'll let me fix you up with a friend of Greg's, you'll see *how* good a friend I can be."

"No, thanks." Kate laughed. "But I appreciate the offer. I'll let you know when I'm ready for the hookup. Right now I think I'm going to concentrate on me, like you said."

"Sounds good," Fiona approved. "And you are going to love Mountain Bliss. It is the best spa on the East Coast."

"I'm sure I will." Kate smiled and was happy to realize that for the first time in a long while, she was looking forward to the future. It was a good feeling.

Acknowledgments

The idea for this book was born in Brooklyn, when I first started to look for child care for my son. Almost every incident, character, and setting comes from my journey as a new mother in Fort Greene and Clinton Hill. So, thank you brownstone Brooklyn for the unending supply of stories.

And although this book was conceived in Brooklyn, the first draft was written in a quiet room in the south of Spain. Thank you Malia-Camacho family for the most beautiful "writer's retreat" a girl could ever dream of.

Of course, my greatest thanks go to my agent, Marie Brown, who read that first draft and told me I was a writer, and then told me to go rewrite the whole thing. I love you for being that kind of agent, Marie. And I love you for believing in me.

Many thanks to the entire team at Atria Books; they continue to support my work with such enthusiasm. To my editor, Malaika Adero, you are my patron saint. And to Yona Deshommes, Todd Hunter, and Sybil Pincus, thank you for all that you do to make me look good. I know it's a heck of a lot.

I have to thank my early readers, Manuel Malia, Danielle Moales, and Stacy Mayes. Your comments and suggestions gave me the courage to make it better.

And to my husband and children, who probably would have appreciated a substitute me while I was writing this book, thank you for your patience, love, and understanding.

About the Author

Lori L. Tharps is the author of *Kinky Gazpacho: Life, Love & Spain,* named by Salon.com as one of their top ten books for 2008, and the coauthor of *Hair Story: Untangling the Roots of Black Hair in America.* She is an assistant professor of journalism at Temple University in Philadelphia, where she makes her home with her husband and family. She does not have a nanny.

Substitute Me

LORI L. THARPS

Readers Club Guide

Questions for Discussion

1. While waiting for the bus on her first day as a nanny, Zora recalls that both of the families she worked for in Paris were White, so "Why was she playing the race card now . . . [she tried] to recall a time when she'd ever been more hyperaware of being Black in a White world" (pages 34–35). Why does Zora feel this way now when she didn't previously? What circumstances have changed?

2. If Zora is so concerned with what her family and friends think about her becoming a nanny, why does she accept the Carters' job offer?

3. "As the words tumbled out of her mouth, Kate wasn't sure where they came from. It was like there was a script in her head and she was just reading the words" (page 44). When she's explaining that she's ready to return to work, are there other examples of Kate saying or doing things she thinks are "right" but are not necessarily how she feels? Can other characters relate?

4. Why does Brad initially maintain a distance from Zora? Why does Zora call Kate by her first name, but Brad "Mr. Carter"?

5. "And that's what she was there for, to help keep his feet firmly planted on the ground. He in turn helped Kate let loose every once in a while. They made a good team, Kate thought" (page 95). Do you agree that Brad and Kate balance each other out nicely? Are they a "good team"?

6. Why does Angel dream so much of her return to Italy? What does Europe represent to both Angel and Zora?

7. Why is Zora so reluctant to enter into a relationship with Keith? How have her past romantic relationships affected her?

8. Why does Brad keep his comic-book project a secret from his wife?

9. How does Kate feel about Zora's relationship with Oliver? Is she at all jealous of how close they are, or does she understand?

10. Why does Kate feel like a "mentor" to Zora (page 188)?

11. Does she feel a sense of superiority, is she just being kind, or both?

12. When does Zora's relationship with Brad begin to change? When she keeps his comic-book project a secret? When he starts showing up at the park? When she starts to cook dinner for him?

13. When arguing about the amount of time she was spending at work, "[Kate] swallowed the comment about what Brad could do with Zora if he was so inclined" (page 212). Was this just a sarcastic thought, or was Kate already aware of a shift in Brad and Zora's relationship?

14. In what order does Kate prioritize her life? Who comes first— Oliver, Brad, or her job? Is it fair to judge her?

15. "'No, it's just her hair and her teeth and . . .' Kate shuddered at the thought of Brad with Zora" (page 289). Why does Kate seem particularly disturbed that Brad's affair might be with Zora? Is race a factor?

16. Why does Brad decide to tell Kate the truth?

17. If they had never invited Zora into their lives, do you think Brad and Kate would have stayed married?

A Conversation with Lori L. Tharps

Almost all the chapters alternate between Zora and Kate. Why did you dedicate two to Brad's perspective, and how did you decide where to place them within the structure of the book?

This book is really about two women, Kate and Zora. I wanted to explore that complex relationship between a working woman and the woman she hires to be her replacement at home. Even though the husband, Brad, plays an important role in the story, his part in this domestic drama is secondary until the end of the book. At that point, I felt he deserved to have his point of view shared. I also thought readers would need to know what he was going through so they wouldn't judge either Kate or Zora too harshly.

Why did you decide to set *Substitute Me* in the years 1999 and 2000?

Basically because New York changed after 9/11, and I wanted to write a story before that change happened. New Yorkers were still living large, and trying to have it all still seemed not only attainable but almost virtuous.

Brooklyn, particularly the Park Slope and Fort Greene sections, is the backdrop for your novel. Have you ever lived there yourself? Why did you choose this neighborhood?

I did live in Fort Greene, Park Slope, and Clinton Hill. And it was there, walking around every day observing the nannies and their charges, that the idea for this story was born.

You frequently write about race. As an author, why are you drawn to this topic?

As a Black woman married to a Spanish man with two brown boys, my life is a melting pot of colors, cultures, languages, and locations. I don't only write about my life, I draw inspiration from my life experiences, so I tend overwhelmingly to write about race and identity. I like to eat, too, so I also like to write about food!

Zora is named after author Zora Neale Hurston. Is she a big inspiration to you?

Yes. I taught a biography class a few years back and we read Valerie Boyd's *Wrapped in Rainbows,* an excellent biography of Hurston. What inspires me the most about Hurston is not so much her literary works but her commitment to write despite the various obstacles—being poor, Black, and female in America—in her way. She didn't wait for permission or praise to write what she wanted to: she wrote because she had to. She wrote because she loved writing.

Like Kate, you have a background in public relations. Why did you decide to change careers?

For me, public relations was that first job out of college. I knew I wanted to be a journalist, but I needed to pay back my student loans first.

Do you share Zora's amazing cooking skills?

I do not. Not at all. Zora's cooking skills were totally stolen from a cousin who trained as a chef. I lived vicariously through her experience and always stand by to sample a new recipe.

The romance of Europe is a big draw for both Angel and Zora. You also spent a year studying in Spain and now spend your summers there. What do you love most about Spanish/European living?

Siesta time. Seriously. I think it's a wonderful thing to be able to eat your big meal of the day at 2:00 P.M. and then be forced to relax because everything is closed for the next two hours. I think we could all benefit from some enforced relaxation time.

Mrs. Rodriguez warns Kate that men "are all faithful to the hand that feeds them" (page 287). Do you agree with her?

Ha! In my husband's case this was true. When we met he lived in a dorm and I lived in an apartment. To convince him to come over, all I had to do was offer to cook for him.

But seriously, I do believe there is some truth to the idea that men respond to women who take care of them. Most of them would most likely never admit that because it makes them sound weak somehow, but culturally men are kind of reared to believe that their wives should feed them, wash their clothes, and tickle their paws at night.

Were you at all apprehensive about how readers might react to the affair between Zora and Brad, two very likable characters? Did you ever consider changing the ending?

I didn't write the book for "readers." I wrote the story of these three characters. As I was writing, I didn't even know how it was going to end, but the ending that I arrived at felt authentic to me. I actually did consider changing the ending to be a bit more ambiguous, but that felt contrived, so I went back to the original version. Real life is complicated and I tried to tell a story that felt real. I'm not saying it did happen, but it could have. And I'm sure some people won't like the ending, but that's okay. I just hope they like the book.

Kate struggles with the balance of work and family. As a working mother yourself, do you think women can "have it all"?

I actually do believe women can have it all, just not all at the same time. I had a career in journalism, then took a break to concentrate on raising my children. Now that my kids are in school, I've returned to full-time work. I can look back at my body of work and see a combination of happy kids and a couple of books and be really happy with my accomplishments.

Enhance Your Book Club

1. Cooking plays a major role in *Substitute Me,* so why not turn your book club meeting into a feast? And like Zora, make sure to use the spiciest, most colorful ingredients possible!

2. Since *Substitute Me* raises important questions about relationships, if you have a significant other, invite that person to read the book and join this book club discussion.

3. To find out more about Lori Tharps and her work, and to read her blog, visit www.loritharps.com.